The Confession

The Confession

SIERRA KINCADE

HEAT | NEW YORK

THE BERKLEY PUBLISHING GROUP
Published by the Penguin Group
Penguin Group (USA) LLC
375 Hudson Street, New York, New York 10014

USA • Canada • UK • Ireland • Australia • New Zealand • India • South Africa • China

penguin.com

A Penguin Random House Company

This book is an original publication of The Berkley Publishing Group.

Library of Congress Cataloging-in-Publication Data

Kincade, Sierra.
The confession / Sierra Kincade.—Heat trade paperback edition.
p. ; cm.— (The body work trilogy ; 3)
ISBN 978-0-425-27801-7
1. Masseurs—Fiction. 2. Billionaires—Fiction. I. Title.
PS3611.I564C66 2015
813'.6—dc23
2014035594

PUBLISHING HISTORY
Heat trade paperback edition / May 2015

PRINTED IN THE UNITED STATES OF AMERICA

10 9 8 7 6 5 4 3 2 1

Cover design by Rita Frangie.
Cover photograph of Young Sensual Lady © Mayer George / Shutterstock.

For Jason

ACKNOWLEDGMENTS

The last year has been wild and crazy and full of excitement. It doesn't seem that long ago that Alec and Anna popped up in my mind, and now their story is (mostly) coming to an end. It's harder than I thought to say good-bye to them. They've given me some of the most memorable moments of my life. I hope somewhere they're living out their happily ever after (in bed . . . against the wall . . . on the kitchen counter).

Thank you to the team at Berkley—you rocked my socks off. Leis, you are fantastic. Jessica, I adore you (you are SO the cat's meow). Thank you to Bethany, and the super-sexy cover model who will forever give me eyebrow envy, and the wonderful marketing team for their awesome taglines and copy. Nailed it, guys.

Thank you to my agents—Joanna, Danielle, Abby, and Molly. You guys deserve Alec massages for everything you've done for me. (I'll send him right over.)

Thank you to my husband for being the kind of man who makes me believe in love, and my son for making me fierce in all the best ways. Thank you to Deanna, Katie, and Courtney for your reads, and for making me laugh every time I tried to do something brilliant, like use the word "lave." (Yes, all references to the laving of things have been removed. No idea what I was thinking.) Thank you to Jaime and Erin for OMG just being the best cheerleaders, and my sassy and cool blogger friends for all your support. You guys. Seriously. You guys.

Huge squeezes to the wonderful Beth Kery for her read, and her mentoring emails, and the awesome quote for the front of *The Masseuse*. Beth, you are made of awesome.

Thank you to Christina Lauren for cheering me on—you were an inspiration long before we ever met. I will never forget the kindness you have shown me.

And thank you, lovely reader, for joining me on this incredible journey. I am so grateful that you gave Anna and Alec a chance.

Much love, Sierra

One

It begins with an offering. I set the mood—dim the lights, start the music, tantalize you with scents that pull you to a different place, a thousand miles away from the office, or the traffic, or your family. I open my door, but you're the one who strips. You're the one who whimpers and begs. You're the one who trusts.

In massage school they teach the technique of *effleurage*, how to increase blood flow to the muscles through a series of gentle touches with your fingertips or the palms of your hands. It's the foreplay of a massage. The tease. The seduction.

It's my specialty.

From there I locate the knots; it's easy enough if you know where to feel. The body tells you just what it wants, guides you to that place of tension. Fights what it needs, until with a sigh or a groan, it accepts the inevitable. Submission.

Petrissage follows, where a deeper pressure is applied to the area. We're not playing around anymore. We're fucking. I'm working you with every trick I've got. I'm pushing you, pushing you, pushing you until you finally give me what *I* want.

Your pain.

Because that's all I have room for now.

My hands made soft, feathering strokes over his trapezius, after-play from the deep-tissue work I'd just finished. I didn't remember what his name was. It didn't matter. He'd gotten what he came for, and I'd given him my best.

Which, admittedly, wasn't stellar. Not that he'd noticed.

For the first time during our fifty-minute session, I took a good look at him. The thick muscles of his shoulders were well-defined and made a gradual slope down his back, beneath the sheet hiding what I guessed was a very nice ass. His arms rested, palms unfurled, at his sides, and his dark brown hair was a little too long. It curled where his collar would have landed. He'd requested a focus on his shoulders, and therefore hadn't turned chest-up during the session.

I think he'd told me he was a baseball player or something. Minor league, maybe? It seemed to me the pros probably had their own team massage therapy staff, and this guy had shown up at the salon on a referral from one of my regulars.

In any case, he looked like he could have been a professional baseball player. And as my gaze lingered on the cut muscles of his upper arms, my mind wandered.

Look how hard I am.

The voice in my head brought a sharp ache in the deepest part of my belly. I shuddered, blinking back the wavering image before my eyes. Placing my flattened hands on each side of the client's spine, I focused on his pale skin. It was smooth and cool, like polished marble. Too pale to trigger the familiar lust heating inside me.

You want me to fuck your mouth.

I withdrew my hands quickly, as if the coolness had burned me. My breath came in one hard rasp. The weight that had settled in my chest for the past two and a half months seemed to liquefy, sliding down through my breasts, making my nipples tighten and tingle.

The man moved. Just a slight adjustment, but it snapped my focus back in place. I returned my oiled hands to his slick back, moving lower, to where his waist tapered. I could feel another man's body now. Feel my nails digging into his back as he growled in my ear.

Push back and fuck yourself on my dick.

Okay, moving back up now. Up and up and up, until I reached his neck. Gently, I stretched his muscles and tipped his head from side to side. His hair brushed against the back of my knuckles.

I closed my eyes.

I could feel him inside of me. The fullness only he could give me. My hands around his neck, fingers spearing through his hair. He was rocking against me, touching places deep inside that felt so good I thought I might die if he stopped. His mouth drifted to my collarbone, his rough stubble scraping my sensitive skin.

I love you so much it fucking hurts.

The man groaned, and I was thrust back into the present—into the massage room at Rave with the scent of cinnamon to sharpen my senses.

I was pulling his hair.

Pulling it, like I did when Alec made me come.

Realizing my mistake, I released him slowly, then gave him another few pulls just to make sure the move looked deliberate. I checked the small clock on the counter by the oils. Thank God it was the end of the session.

"How do you feel?"

I didn't care; I needed to get the hell out.

"Fucking awesome." His voice was muffled through the headrest.

"Take your time getting up. I'll get you some water and meet you outside the door when you're dressed."

He grunted a response. Maybe he said something else, I don't know. I was out of there, door shut behind me, before I could take another breath.

In less than a minute I was in the bathroom. It smelled like the lobby—fresh with the natural products we used in all our services—and had a stack of rolled towels on a wooden tray beside the sink.

I turned to face the wall and pressed my cheek against the cool tile. I was feverish. Sick. I had to be sick. That's why the perspiration had dewed across my forehead, why my whole body felt like it was on fire.

Touch yourself.

No.

I squeezed my eyes shut. My heart pounded against my ribs like a jackhammer. One hand flattened against the tiles, as I fought off the feel of him behind me, shoving me roughly against the wall. Pulling up this flimsy skirt I wore and tearing off my panties. He wouldn't be gentle. Not after all this time.

Feel how deep I am.

The throb between my legs was insistent now. He'd see I didn't need much warming up; I was already hot and slick for him. His fingers would slide right in to the knuckle. I pressed one open hand against my right breast, trying to still the need, but it only served to increase the pressure.

Let go, baby.

"Stop," I said aloud. I pushed off the wall, gulping down air. Facing the mirror, I turned on the cold water and splashed my face. It stung; every inch of my body was burning.

"Stop it, Anna." I stared at my reflection. The wet mascara dripped down my cheeks. Good thing it was the only makeup I'd put on this morning. It had been a while since I'd worn much more than that.

Alec and I were over. I hadn't seen him since I'd said good-bye to him the night Trevor Marshall, aka William MacAfee, had tried to throw me off a bridge. Apart from the time I'd come home to find my things from his apartment on my front stoop, he'd attempted zero contact.

But it wasn't like he'd disappeared. I heard his name on the news reports on the radio. I saw his face on television and in the papers. Alec Flynn. Maxim Stein's body man. Key witness in the biggest white-collar trial since Bernie Madoff.

Alec Flynn. The man that I loved.

Used to love. I didn't love him anymore. I refused to. He'd endangered my life, and the lives of the people I cared about. If Alec and I had never been together, I wouldn't have been kidnapped, carjacked, or nearly tossed off a bridge. My best friend, Amy, never would have been targeted to use against us, and her daughter, Paisley, never would have been in danger.

Alec Flynn was trouble, and I had moved on.

Which is why it really pissed me off to look in the mirror and see a woman on the verge of a nervous breakdown.

I was thinner than I'd ever been. My cheekbones were more severe, and I now wore a size six, something that would have at one time warranted a celebratory parade. I wasn't trying to lose weight—food was bland. My life was bland. I went through the motions from the time I woke up until the time I closed my eyes at night.

And punctuating that blandness were times like these. Times where I could still see him, or hear him saying my name. Times when I imagined us sitting together on my couch eating pizza. When I could almost feel him making love to me.

And times when I wondered what August felt like in Colorado. Or Alaska. Or fucking Greenland, because they surely needed masseuses there just like anywhere else.

I told myself those times would fade.

I was still waiting for that to happen.

Breathe.

I was at work. I had to get my client. Alec was off-limits. I'd promised myself I would be there for Amy and Paisley after learning they'd been abused by Amy's ex, and Alec had compromised that. Not by choice, but they'd been hurt because of us all the same. It would never happen again.

Besides, if he'd really wanted me, he would have fought for me.

I scrubbed the mascara from beneath my eyes, and emerged into the hallway. My client was leaning against the wall outside of the room wearing the black tracksuit he'd arrived in, and as the door closed behind me, his gaze lifted.

His smile was dazzling, I'm sure.

"Your water," I said, touching my forehead. "I'm so sorry. Let me get that for you."

"It's all right," he said, pushing off the wall. He was big enough to block my path. Tall—at least a head above me—and broad. Like a baseball player. Like Alec.

Not like Alec. Not everything in this whole goddamn world circled back to Alec Flynn.

"Well, make sure you keep up the fluids today," I said. "Your body releases a lot of toxins during massage."

He smirked, and my gaze lowered to his mouth. Nice lips. Some freckles on his nose. Friendly eyes. He was younger than me, but cute. All-American cute.

"Anna, right?"

I took a not-so-subtle step back, which he didn't seem to notice.

"That's right."

"What are you doing tonight? We should go get"—he smirked again—"*fluids*."

"Wow." I grinned to offset my tone. "I bet you say that to all the girls."

"Naw." He pulled his phone from his pocket, obviously expecting to get my number. "First time. How'd it go?"

"Really smooth." I tried to angle us toward the exit. "And it's a sweet offer, but I'm busy tonight."

"How about tomorrow? We're on a home stand until Friday."

"I . . ." *should say yes. I should go out with him.* There was nothing holding me back except the huge lump in my throat.

I went for the lie. The truth was too unbelievable. What was I going to say? *Those guns you're packing aren't even close to big enough to carry my baggage.*

"I'm sort of seeing someone right now."

I watched my tip go up in smoke as the hand holding his phone lowered to his side.

"That doesn't sound too serious." He leaned forward, as if we weren't the only ones in the hallway. I breathed in a cologne, something spicy that blended with the cinnamon oil he'd chosen for the massage. "Like I said, I'm gone on Friday."

I laughed. I couldn't help it.

"Now *that*," I said, "was *really* smooth."

He slouched as I led him to the door. He'd actually expected that proposition to work. And maybe it would have, if I wasn't swearing off men for the rest of eternity.

Before he left, I placed my hand on his biceps, but though it was firm and I liked hard muscles, it didn't do a thing for my pulse.

"Thanks for the offer . . ." *Name?* I couldn't remember. "Now's just not a good time."

He opened his mouth as if to say something, but the next moment Amy swept in through the door, wearing a black smock accented at every available location by silver hair clips. Her platinum blond hair was down today, falling in a severe line just below her chin, and her bangs were swept across her forehead. She took one look at the baseball player and waggled her eyebrows at me.

"Hi, there," he said to her, with that same twinkle in his eyes.

I snorted. He didn't waste any time.

After escorting him back to the front desk, I returned to the massage room to clean up. Amy was already there, sniffing the sheets.

"Oh my God, he even smells good," she said.

"So you go out with him," I said. "He's leaving town Friday."
I gave her an exaggerated wink.

We both knew she wouldn't. She was secretly holding out for
Mike, Alec's best friend.

"He actually said that?" She laughed. "At least he's honest."

She helped me strip the table and toss the crumpled sheets
into a pile on the floor.

"You could totally hit that, you know," she said.

"*Hit that*? What are we, sixteen-year-old boys?"

She giggled. "I'm just sayin'. He's hot. You're hot. He's not
looking for serious. You're . . ."

An all-too-familiar silence settled between us.

"Definitely not looking for serious," I finished quietly. "Or
anything, for that matter."

She picked up the pile of sheets while I wiped down the
counter and replaced the bottles of lotion and oils.

"Maybe something casual is just what you need." She didn't
look up.

My jaw clenched, and I forced it to relax. Once, casual was
all I did. No one got too close—romantic or otherwise. Now the
idea seemed incomprehensible. Alec Flynn had made everything
in my life dead serious.

I smiled, because the last thing I wanted was for Amy to feel
guilty over my breakup. Not after everything she'd been through.

"I have everything I need. You and Paisley and my new, favorite roommate."

After Alec and I had broken up, I'd finally told my dad everything that had happened with Trevor and his hit man, Reznik,
on the Sunshine Skyway Bridge. He'd listened quietly, expressing
only minimal concern. I thought I'd dodged a bullet until he
showed up on my doorstep the next morning, complete with his
Great Dane, Mug, and no plans of ever letting me leave his sight
again.

Amy chuckled. "He might as well just get a place here."

"But how would he keep tabs on me twenty-four/seven that way?"

"True." She sighed. "I guess you'll just have to get a bigger house and live out your days as a spinster dog lady."

"There's just one dog."

"So far," she said. "Just you wait."

She followed me as I carried the sheets to the laundry room, just as she would accompany me to the front desk for my next client, and magically appear in the back room when it was time for my lunch break. I sometimes wondered if she thought she was being sneaky. Or if Marcos, the cop who'd been assigned to tail me three months ago, remembered the danger had left with Alec when he randomly sent me text reminders asking me to check in. At least my dad didn't try to hide the fact that he was keeping an eye on me. He had practically reverted to holding my hand before I crossed the street.

"Why don't you guys come over for dinner tonight," she said. "I'll make something glorious from a box. I might even get crazy and throw some corndogs in the microwave."

I knew this wasn't an idle threat. Amy's freezer was always stocked with last-minute meals.

"As appealing as that sounds, Dad has a case he's working on." He'd already informed me he had some PI work tonight— he'd started taking on a few private clients after his recent retirement from the police force in Cincinnati. He'd even managed to snag a couple of cases since coming to Tampa last month.

Amy handed me the detergent after I shoved the sheets into the washing machine.

"Well you should come by yourself then."

The truth was, I'd been looking forward to some time alone. Maintaining the "everything's great" façade was exhausting.

"Actually, I . . ." I hunched over the washer. "You already knew he'd be busy, didn't you?"

She inhaled, cheery as an ad for kids' cereal, and acted as though she hadn't heard me.

"When do you get off? Five?"

"Something tells me you already checked what time I get off."

"You could be over by five thirty. I'll rent a movie if your dad's pulling a late one."

"Amy."

"All right." She rubbed her hands together, avoiding my gaze. "Good talk. See ya at five thirty."

"Amy." I blocked her from leaving the room.

She stayed tense while I sighed.

"Anna, just let us," she said quietly. "Just for a while."

How long? I wanted to ask. They'd been doing it since the night on the bridge. Two and a half months of constant *support.* I'd left Alec so everyone could move on, unafraid, leaving the chaos he'd brought into our lives behind, but instead they'd put everything on hold to watch me like I was a ticking time bomb.

I should have been protecting Amy after everything that had happened, not the other way around.

But as she faced me, green eyes rounding even as her thin lips pursed, I knew there was no turning her down.

"I have a CASA thing at five thirty," I said. "I'll be over before seven."

Two

The Children's Museum ran a special program for foster kids after hours on Wednesday nights. This month they'd brought in local artists to give lessons. It wasn't technically a Court-Appointed Special Advocate event, but it was a good chance for me to check in on Jacob, the first boy I'd been assigned to.

The parking garage was next to the main building, but I took a metered spot on the street. It wasn't that I was afraid of the dark, but I wasn't stupid. Parking garages were prime places for predators to attack, and I didn't exactly have a great track record.

After putting my neon blue sewing machine of a car in park, my fingers grazed absently over the small button hidden beneath the center console. Alec had installed the "kill switch" days after he'd gotten out of prison. It had saved my life once. Now it was one of the few reminders I had left that he'd ever really cared about me.

Grabbing my purse, I left the car. The air was still muggy, the result of an afternoon shower, and immediately made my skin glisten. I had been told this was the hottest August in years, a slow burn in a relentless summer.

The traffic light turned green up ahead, and the cars zipped past, drawing my gaze across the street to the trendy restaurants that lined the block.

My heart thudded to a stop.

Behind the wall of windows making up the front of a tapas bar was a man, seated at one of the tables. He wore a baseball cap, but even from here I could see a hint of dark hair that curled out from beneath it. Though he was turned to the side, it was obvious his shoulders were broad by the thick girth of his upper arms. His legs were too long for the little table he sat at; his knees hit the underside, even with his feet stretched beneath the empty chair opposite him.

He was staring at me.

"Alec."

Saying his name aloud made something in my chest twist even as it made my mouth water.

At the blare of a horn, I jumped back. I hadn't realized I'd stepped into the street, but even as I backed into my car I felt the urge to lean forward again. There was a pull coming from inside that restaurant, like the whole building was magnetized.

When I looked again, Alec was gone.

I didn't think about it. If I had, I would have told myself to go into the museum and say hi to the kids. Instead, I waited for a break in the traffic and raced across the lanes. Even as my hand gripped the door handle, I could feel my blood begin to buzz.

Alec was here. He'd seen me. He was close.

I jogged past the hostess without a word and turned the corner, but the table where Alec had sat was empty.

"Just one, ma'am?" The hostess caught up with me, and as she did, the sounds of the restaurant tumbled past the rushing in my ears. Clanking dishes. Silverware hitting the floor. Laughter and conversation.

My chest went cold.

"N-no, I'm fine," I said. She continued to watch me as I scanned the main seating area. "There was a man sitting there a few minutes ago. Do you know where he went?"

Her brows lifted. "I haven't seated anyone there since lunch."

I looked again at the empty table, feeling the color rise up my neck. Great. I was hallucinating him everywhere now. And even if he *had* been real, what was my plan once I'd gotten here? *Hey Alec, how've you been? Anyone you know been tossed off a bridge lately?* This wasn't a margarine commercial. We weren't running to each other in slow motion across fields of daisies.

"Sorry," I told her. "My mistake."

I'd promised myself I would stay clear of him. For Amy and Paisley. For my own safety. I told myself this like he'd been incorrigible, unable to leave me alone.

That was most definitely *not* the case.

I hadn't changed my number, and he hadn't called once. I lived at the same apartment, worked at the same salon. He knew where to find me, and he hadn't.

There was nothing quite as shitty as realizing you're easy to get over.

It was time I got over Alec Flynn.

I crossed the street, the numbness descending back over my shoulders like the heavy air. I was grateful for it. It was easier to feel nothing than to be constantly aware of the empty pit he'd left inside of me.

The signs were easy enough to follow once I entered the building. The lobby was clean and painted by a rainbow of colors reflected through the stained glass windows. The dinosaur exhibit in the main room had been pushed aside to create more floor area and thirty or so kids sprawled out across plastic tarps, surrounded by stacks of newspapers.

It didn't take long to find Jacob. He was the one with two fingers in his mouth, whistling loud enough to crack someone's eardrums.

Making my way across the floor, I waved at his foster mom, chatting with a few other women on the far side of the room. Squares of newspaper immediately stuck to my shoes, a result of the paste that was being used to papier-mâché balloons.

Jacob's black hair was sticking straight out on one side. He'd probably touched it with his pastey hands. He gave me a lopsided smile and pretended to throw his heavy balloon, smothered with newspaper, straight at me.

"Did you hear me whistle?" he asked.

"I'm pretty sure people in New York heard you whistle," I answered, rubbing my ear. "I have a name, you know. People usually save whistling for dogs."

He knelt back on the ground beside his little sister, six-year-old Sammy, who was making neat stacks of newspaper rather than attending to her balloon. Her kinky hair was in two puff balls on the top of her head, and her eyebrows were furrowed in concentration.

"Stanley showed me how," he said.

Stanley was his foster father at the placement where I'd fought for him to live with his sister. I smiled. Maybe things were crap in my life, but knowing Jacob was happy, and that I'd played a part in that, took some of the weight off my shoulders.

"What are you making?" I asked.

"Hot air balloons," he said. "Mr. Rodriguez is an artist. We're making masks like that one." He pointed to the front of the room, where an elderly man with a long, white beard was showing an intricate tiger mask to a young girl.

"Awesome," I said. "So how's everything going?"

He painted his balloon with enough white paste to drown a horse and then haphazardly stuck pieces of newspaper to it.

"Good," he said. "Lucia and Stanley want to adopt us."

I crouched beside him, finding a clear space that didn't look completely sticky.

"I heard. What do you think about that?" Being adopted was a big deal. Knowing someone wanted you—really wanted you—was both enormously validating, and its own type of betrayal. I'd never felt like I'd let my birth mother down more than the day my dad said he wanted to make me his.

"It's good," he said. "My mom gave up custody."

I knew that, too, but played dumb so he could tell me about it. "Oh yeah?"

"Yeah. Lucia says we don't have to see her again if we don't want to."

"And do you want to?"

Part of me wished I could see my birth mother again, if only for a few minutes. I'd forgiven her for loving the drugs more than me a long time ago, but sometimes I still wanted to ask her why she'd never tried harder to be my mom. Why she'd never fought for me.

Was I not worth fighting for?

"Nope," said Jacob definitively. "She makes me and Sissy feel bad."

I nodded. "Yeah. But I bet there was a time she didn't make you feel bad. And if you're ever thinking about that, and wondering what she's like, you can talk to Lucia about seeing her."

"I won't."

I'd probably said the same thing.

"Okay," I said. "Should we celebrate the adoption?"

Jacob looked up. "Tacos?"

I snorted. "Sure. When it's all done, let's go get tacos." I turned to Jacob's sister. "Hey Sammy, nice stacking."

She smiled at me, and I grinned back. She didn't do that much, and I'd take what I could get. Glancing down, she picked up the newspaper on top and handed it to me.

"You wanna do craps with us?"

"She means crafts," said Jacob.

"I would hope so," I said. But before I could say yes, I looked down at the paper and stalled, because staring back at me was Alec's face.

He was sitting in a courtroom, hands folded on the desk before him. His hair had grown out a little since I'd seen him, but was still kept smoothed back behind his ears. He was wearing a suit and tie, and looked like someone had died.

Key Witness Has Questionable Past said the caption beneath the photo. The rest of the article had been cut away. The date was still at the top, though. It was from four days ago—the first day of the trial.

Resentment at the quote surged through me before I remembered that he wasn't mine to defend.

I'd known when the trial had begun of course. I'd counted down the days until it started, along with half of Tampa. But because of my ties to Alec, to Maxim, to all of it, I'd tried to steer clear as much as possible. I didn't get the newspaper. I'd turned the Internet off on my phone. When I went to restaurants or the gym, I made sure to position myself as far away from the televisions as possible.

And yet Alec still landed right in my lap.

"You coming to the dinner?" Jacob asked. "Lucia says I gotta wear a tie."

"I got a dress," said Sammy. "It's pink."

"Nice," I told her. The dinner Jacob was referring to was a formal CASA fund-raising event this Friday. The program was staffed by volunteers, but training and raising awareness didn't come cheap. This was a chance to reach out to the donors with deep pockets and show them just how important the advocates were to the kids.

" 'Course I'm going to be there," I said.

"You going to bring your *boyfriend*?"

I stiffened. "You don't want to be my date?"

"Ew, gross. You're, like, thirty."

"Not quite," I said. "But thanks."

I'd actually asked Amy to come with me. It would have been nice to dress up for a date. Wear something long and pretty he could have peeled off at the end of the night. But I couldn't picture anyone but Alec in that role, and well, no Alec.

Amy would have fun. She didn't get a lot of chances to go to fancy events.

"Hey, you gotta meet Brendan," said Jacob, pulling me from my thoughts. With that, he was up like a shot and weaving through the kids on the floor. Less than a minute later he was leading over a boy with sun-kissed hair, recently chopped short I'd guess, based on the tan line around his scalp. He took one look at me and his thin mouth fixed into a frown.

"This is Anna," said Jacob. "She can help you out."

"Jacob," I said. "We talked about this."

Since I'd spoken to the judge and helped Jacob get a placement with his sister, he was constantly trying to set me up with other kids who were in need of transfers.

"It's okay," said Jacob. "Brendan's cool. He's got a brother in Sarasota that needs to move here with him, though."

I hummed and made room for the other boy, who sat no less than five feet away from me.

"It doesn't exactly work that way," I said. "A lot goes into a placement. You know that."

"I told you," I heard Brendan mumble. The newspaper made a crumpling sound as I clenched the edges of it. I wanted to find his file and see just what was going on with this brother in Sarasota.

"Do you have a court-appointed advocate?" I asked Brendan. He shook his head without looking up.

I smoothed out Alec's picture, unable to set it aside to be ripped and painted.

"Is your foster mom here?" I asked, but even as I did I wished I hadn't. There was a reason I hadn't taken any more cases on since Jacob. I'd been asked. Not just by kids Jacob had spoken to, but by social workers and other CASA volunteers I'd met.

I was finishing things out with Jacob, and when he and his sister were secure, and Amy and Paisley were back on their feet, I was moving on.

Three

I know I'd said I would go straight to Amy's, but somehow I ended up a few blocks away from the Children's Museum, at a park overlooking the Bay. It was quiet this time of night; only one other car took up a spot at the far end of the lot, but the occasional dog-walker and Rollerblader passed by on the path before me. The sun had burrowed into the clouds on the horizon, throwing splashes of pink and gold across the sky, and the water was flat and calm.

Stupid autopilot had led me here more than I cared to admit. The view was beautiful, but I'd known it would be even before I'd come here the first time. Behind me was Alec's high-rise apartment. This was *his* view. I was just renting it for a little while.

It wasn't like he could see me. Not that he'd be looking anyway.

I aimed all the air-conditioning vents in my direction and removed the square of newspaper with Alec's picture that I'd taken from arts and crafts. I traced my fingertip over his shoulder, remembering too well the feel of the hard muscles beneath this suit jacket. *Questionable Past*, the caption said. Bastards. They didn't even know him.

I turned the picture over, realizing a second later that I'd placed him facedown in my lap. The images came on before I could stop them, burning past the walls of my memory. His head nestled between my thighs. His thick, chocolate brown hair gripped in my fists. The feel of his tongue, gliding over my hidden places.

I love your sweet little cunt.

I snatched the paper, folded it, and tucked it into my wallet.

My phone beeped, and I knew it would be from Amy even before I picked it up. Sure enough, I was right, and shot back a quick response that I'd be there in ten.

Keeping my foot on the brake, I put the car in reverse, but found that I'd been boxed in by a white sedan. The windows were tinted, so I couldn't see who was behind the wheel. Probably some tourist—the car was too clean to be anything but a rental.

"Come on." I tapped my horn lightly, but the car didn't move.

A single drop of fear trickled down the back of my neck. I gripped the Mace on my key chain as my gaze shot around the parking lot. The closest car was half the length of a football field away. I couldn't tell if there was someone inside, but there was enough traffic on the road that ran between the park and Alec's apartment building to catch someone's attention.

I couldn't see through the windows, but I got the distinct impression someone was watching me.

"Five, four, three, two . . ." I laid on the horn. Five seconds was more than enough after all the time I'd given them.

The car jerked forward, as if it were a live thing and I'd just woken it from a deep slumber. Then, before I could get a read on the license plate, it made a tight loop and peeled out into traffic. A car swerved to avoid getting hit, and I could hear the driver's angry yells across the street.

The threat was gone, but a wariness remained in its wake. I didn't know what that was about, but I didn't have a good feeling about it.

*　*　*

Fifteen minutes later I was greeted by Amy, standing outside on her landing while I trudged up the stairs.

"You're late," she called to me.

"I decided to take that client up on his offer," I replied when I reached the second floor.

She tried to hide a laugh as she padded back inside, barefoot. "Either he's really fast, or you're really good."

"I can't believe it's even a question," I said. "What do you think they teach us in massage school?"

She spun back so hard her bangs swung over her eyes. "I knew it. Tell me everything."

"For a price," I offered.

"Hamburger Helper?"

"Sold."

"Hi Anna." Paisley kneeled on a seat at the kitchen table coloring a picture, but as I sat beside her, she met my gaze and smiled. It took a moment for me to respond. Six months ago Amy's little five-year-old would barely acknowledge my presence; now she was making eye contact and initiating conversation. That therapy Amy and she had started a couple of months ago was really paying off.

She twirled a braid around her finger and passed me a purple crayon.

"Hi," I said finally. "How was school today?"

"Fine," she said. "I saw a frog. And then I saw a rabbit. And then I petted them."

"Wow," I said. "Way better than what I did at work."

She smiled and returned to her artwork. She was drawing people, standing outside a purple house. A woman with yellow hair—her mom, I guessed. Two kids, and a man with a huge smile and biceps added onto his stick arms.

"Who's this?" I asked, pointing to one of the kids.

"That's me," Paisley said. "And that's Chloe. And that's her daddy, Mike."

"She's just drawing people she knows," Amy said, without turning around from the microwave. But I'd seen her go still, and knew she was surprised.

"Uh-huh," I said.

Amy had a huge crush on Mike, though from what I understood, neither of them had taken a step forward since the bridge incident two months ago. His mother, Iris, lived upstairs and watched the girls sometimes. Apart from the occasional hello, they rarely spoke.

At least that's what Amy had told me. I had a hard time believing Paisley would draw family pictures of a guy she only knew as her BFF's father.

I set the table while Amy served up something that looked a little like high-sodium dog throw up with noodles, along with some microwaved green beans.

"So," said Amy. "I ran into Alec. How was your CASA thing?"

I dropped my fork.

"You *what*?"

"Here." Paisley had picked up my fork off the floor and stuck it back into my hand.

Amy cleared her throat. "Your foster kid, he's good?"

"When?" I thought of how I'd seen Alec across the street from the Children's Museum. It had been a mistake, the hostess had confirmed it. But it seemed weird that I'd been imagining him when he was actually with my best friend.

"A while ago." Her gaze flicked to Paisley. She reached for a green bean with her fingers and began tearing it into pieces.

"How long's a while ago?"

"A month . . . or . . . or maybe June . . . ish."

This time I carefully set my fork down. I took a deep breath, but my fists were already clenched. "Why didn't you tell me?"

"He, um . . . asked that I not."

I pushed back in my chair, wishing she'd just stab me with her butter knife rather than keep going. She'd seen Alec. He'd told her not to mention it to me.

She'd done as he asked.

I felt the sting of betrayal, but I wasn't nearly as mad at her as I was at him. I'd ended things with him because Amy and Paisley had been dragged, unwillingly, into his world. And now he thought he could contact them? That he could continue to endanger them?

"He shouldn't be talking to you. You need to stay away from him."

"It's okay," said Amy, raising her hands now. I became aware of Paisley's watchful eyes and lowered my voice.

"What did he want?"

"He wanted to know how we were."

We. Not me. Amy and Paisley. I crossed my arms over my chest.

She fidgeted. "He sent someone over to install a security alarm."

I remembered when that had happened. It was just a couple of weeks after the bridge incident. I hadn't even thought to ask Amy whose idea it was to put in the alarm. I'd assumed she was just being more careful on account of what had happened.

"He . . ." She plastered a tight smile on her face. "He offered to pay for our therapy."

"Why?" I asked. "He doesn't have any money." It was a stupid thing to say, but I was grasping at straws. He was trying to take care of my friends, but it wasn't his place. It was *my* place. That's why I'd left him.

She shrugged, looking sheepish.

"I told him I didn't need help."

I closed my eyes and rested my forehead in my hands. "He's the reason all this happened. You wouldn't need a security system if it wasn't for him."

It sounded like I was trying to convince her. I shouldn't have had to; she was the victim, for God's sake, and if anyone knew the signs of an unhealthy relationship it should have been her.

"But we'd still need therapy, you said so yourself. We like it, too, don't we Pais?"

"Yeah," said Paisley, spitting out a green bean in her napkin.

"He was really sorry," Amy said quietly. "He just wanted to make sure we were okay."

There was that *we* again. I wanted to be glad, but the thought of him looking out for them softened me, and that made me feel weak. It made me wonder if he'd asked about me. If he cared how I was doing. If he missed me like I missed him.

"I'm sorry I didn't tell you before." Amy reached for my forearm and gave it a light squeeze. "It's been eating me up. I just saw you with that guy today and thought maybe you needed some closure. Before you, you know, got back out there."

I didn't recall telling her I was dying to get back in the dating game.

"I don't need closure," I said. "It's over. I'm fine."

"I said that, too, once," she said. And it made me feel a hundred times worse because I didn't like her comparing her abusive ex to Alec, no matter how crazy things had gotten.

"Are you still going to marry him?" asked Paisley.

Now it was Amy's turn to drop a fork.

It took a second to figure out why she would ask this, but when she did, I slumped. At the beginning of summer Amy had thrown a picnic. It was the first time she and Mike had formally met, and sometime between tag and cheeseburgers, Alec had told Paisley and Chloe he was going to marry me.

It had been a joke, of course.

"That wasn't for real," I told Paisley. I looked up at Amy. "It was just something he said."

She chewed on her lip, looking worried.

The knock at the door came with perfect timing.

"I'll get it!" Paisley slid off her chair and bounded around the corner.

"Peephole!" Amy reminded her. There was a step stool beside the entryway so that Paisley could see out. Even before Trevor Marshall had kidnapped Amy, she'd been tough on safety, but now she was even more vigilant. She left early every morning now to walk Paisley all the way to her classroom, and had even sprung for a children's cell phone to be added on her account.

Maybe that was Alec's idea, too.

"It's Chloe's daddy!" Paisley squealed.

Amy jolted out of her seat. A second later she combed her fingers through her hair, looking worried.

"You look good," I said.

She flashed her teeth at me.

"All clear."

With a grateful nod, she smoothed down the front of her T-shirt and went to open the door.

"She make it?" I heard Mike ask.

"Yes. Yeah, she's here right now," Amy whispered.

"You aren't talking about me, are you?" I called.

A second later, Mike popped his head around the corner. He grinned broadly, a flash of white teeth against his beautiful dark skin.

"Anna!"

I waved. "And yet you still look surprised to see me sitting here."

He crossed the kitchen and kissed me on the cheek. Amy frowned slightly behind him. She'd never say so, but it bothered her that he was so easygoing with me. He never even gave her a hug to say hello.

I imagined he thought he wouldn't be able to stop if he started things out that way, but of course Amy saw it as a lack of interest.

"How's it going?" he asked.

"All right," I said, and then sighed. "Amy was just telling me she ran into Alec the other day."

I only stumbled a little over his name. Smooth.

"A while ago," Amy corrected. "Several months ago."

I wasn't sure why she needed to make such a clear distinction, but she did.

Mike glanced at her, then back to me. His light brown eyes narrowed with concern.

"Yes," I said. "Contrary to popular belief, I don't turn rabid at the first mention of his name."

"My bad," he said. "I'm not sure he could say the same about you."

"Did you want something to eat?" Amy interrupted.

My gaze had lifted to Mike. "Did he ask about me?" I pretended to laugh. "Jesus, is this high school?"

Mike chewed his top lip, as if thinking of what to say.

"He's always going to care about you."

My breath came out in a huff. "Why does that sound like there should be a *but* . . . attached?" My heart felt like it was strung on a wire, waiting for him to fill me in. Had Alec gotten over me? Moved on? As sick as the thought made me, I couldn't believe it was true. Not after what Mike had said about not being able to mention my name.

Mike turned back to Amy. "He's just got a lot going on."

Right. With the trial. Of course.

Don't ask, don't ask, don't ask.

"So how's the trial going?"

Mike made a sound of disgust. "He hasn't even testified yet and he's taking a beating. Max Stein's attorneys are using every opportunity to tear him up. Making him look like just another thug." He shook his head. "They'll bring out the pitchforks next."

My chest ached. I couldn't help the feeling that I should have been with him through this, standing beside him, offering what little comfort or distraction I could. The only reason he was there in court now was because he'd thought he'd needed to be a better man for me. I'd supported his decision to step into the fire, and then I'd left him there alone to burn.

"Hasn't Stein run out of money yet? Last I heard, all his fancy lawyers were making him broke."

One of his fancy lawyers—the same woman who'd covertly let Alec in on the little secret that he might just take control of the company if Maxim was convicted of fraud—had dropped that information on us.

"Not yet," said Mike. "Alec said that he's been chartering one of his private jets out to old oil company clients for money. It's a plane he gifted his wife years ago, so she's the one getting paid."

"And in turn paying his legal bills."

"Right," said Mike. "She needs him to win so she doesn't get screwed when she divorces him."

Frankly, I was surprised Maxim's wife, whoever she was, hadn't already kicked him to the curb.

"Wish I had some friends who would rent *my* private plane for a little spending money," said Amy.

"Can Chloe come over?" Paisley asked. She'd been quiet until now, and I'd almost forgotten she was here. I looked at her, big round eyes pointed up at Mike, and I remembered why Alec and I were apart.

I would never hurt her. And I would never hurt Amy.

I stood, and turned to my best friend. "Tomorrow night's the fund-raiser. I'll pick you up at six?"

"Tomorrow? No." She shook her head. "Tomorrow's Friday."

"Right." My stomach was starting to pitch. I needed to go outside, get some air.

She looked at Mike. "Tomorrow night's the girls' play at school. Shit. *Shoot*," she corrected. "I thought . . . I honestly thought it was Saturday." She raced to the refrigerator and snatched the invitation I'd given her.

"No," she said. "No, no, no. I have an amazing dress."

"Let's hear about it," said Mike.

She turned bright red from her scalp down.

"It's all right," I said. Air. Anytime now. I went for my purse, leaving my dinner barely touched on the kitchen table.

"Come to the play," said Mike. "Ditch the fund-raiser. Hang out with us. Amy's going to wear an amazing dress."

"Can't," I told him. "I already told my client I'd be there. They're bringing out all the kids the program has helped to give puppy dog eyes to the rich donors."

Mike snorted. "You shouldn't go by yourself."

I snatched my purse, my chest constricting more by the second. "I'll bring my dad. Thanks for dinner, Amy."

"Let me walk you . . ."

"See you tomorrow," I told Amy, cutting Mike off.

With that, I was out the door, swallowing huge gasps of humid night air as I jogged down the steps.

Yeah, I was fine talking about Alec. Totally and completely fine.

Four

I'd already gotten three texts from Amy asking if I was all right by the time I got back to my apartment. I stood in the threshold and texted that I was fine, and good luck with Mike, hoping that she saw my sudden exit as a setup and not a meltdown.

My place was small, and still sparsely decorated. I hadn't bothered to put much up on the walls, and the boxes Alec had sent over from his place were still full, shoved into the corner of my bedroom.

Not much point in unpacking if I was just going to repack in a few weeks anyway. I didn't know where I was going yet, but something would come to me. It always did. The only difference now was that the idea of moving was exhausting, where before it had always calmed me down.

It was probably a sign I'd stayed here too long.

A groaning came from the little couch against the wall, and I stepped into the living room to face my father, lying flat on his back, his socked feet dangling over the couch arm. He had a wet towel over his eyes, and a panting Great Dane under one hand on the floor.

"You all right?" I asked.

"I'm sick as a dog," he said. "No offense, Mug."

Mug lifted his big black head, as if just noticing for the first time that I was there, and then lay back down with a heavy sigh.

"You should have called me," I said. "I thought you were on some big stakeout tonight."

"Taking pictures of men cheating on their wives doesn't exactly qualify as *big stakeout* material."

"So says the hotshot detective." I reached for the washcloth on this face, and, finding it warm, went to rinse it out in the kitchen sink.

"Retired detective," he corrected. Slowly he sat up, and began to cough. I went stone still, hating the sound of it. My dad was quite literally my hero—he'd saved me after my birth mother had overdosed—and ever since my *real* mom had died of cancer, I'd become more and more aware of his mortality.

He was a thorn in my side sometimes, but he was steady, and I didn't know what I'd do without him.

I filled up a glass of water, and brought both that and the washcloth back to him. Then I kneeled on the floor and began to unroll the air mattress he meticulously put away each morning to leave some walking space in this closet-sized living room.

"I've been thinking about getting a place here," he said, after blowing his nose and throwing the tissue into a very full trash can beside him. "Maybe close by. Give you a little bit of space."

I pictured him renting an apartment right next door to mine. I was sure that's what he had in mind.

"Who says I'm staying here?" I asked, without looking up. He grunted a response. "You can stay in my living room as long as you like."

"How's Amy?" he asked.

"How do you know I wasn't out on a date?"

He smirked. "Hotshot detective, remember?"

"Retired, I thought."

Another storm of coughing took him, and I winced.

"Dying," he said. "This is what a dying man looks like, Anna." He sniffled, and then groaned.

"Want to go to urgent care?"

He scoffed at this. "Men don't go to the doctor for colds. Men beat their chests and whine for their daughters to make them chicken noodle soup."

I plugged in the mattress, and once it started filling, rose to fill his request.

"Men are such babies when they're sick," I said, hoping I didn't sound worried. He rarely got colds. He was the strong one in our family. I sometimes wondered if he'd even tell me if he ever did get really sick. He'd probably just ride off into the sunset like in the old cowboy movies. He'd probably saddle up Mug. The dog was big enough.

"Your mom used to say that," he said. I stared at the pantry, missing the chicken soup that was right in front of my face for a good thirty seconds.

"She told me it was a good thing she'd gotten the cancer. If it had been me, everyone would have abandoned me on the road-side because they'd get so sick of my bellyaching."

"She had a point," I said.

"Your mom was the tough one," he said. "She was always strong. Even in the end."

I blinked back the tears that had sprung up. I hated that she was gone. I missed her—how gentle she'd been, how she'd never once tried to pretend she was my birth mother, but proved she was my *real* mother by being a million times better in every way. But mostly I hated that she'd left my dad. He got on fine without her, but a piece of him was missing. He'd never be the same.

He'd never *want* to be the same.

Maybe it was shallow since Alec and I had had such limited time together, but I understood that now.

My dad's cell phone rang, and I picked it up. The caller ID said UNAVAILABLE.

"Want me to answer?" I asked.

"No, I got it." He motioned for the phone, and I tossed it to him.

"This is Ben," he said, voice nasally. "Yep. She's here. She's . . ." I stuck my head around the corner. Was he talking to Amy? Mike? Unbelievable. Was my text not good enough?

Just let us, Amy had said. I pulled out a soup pot, not bothering to keep quiet as I banged it against the stove. A friend in therapy after an abduction, a kid who witnessed her father abusing her mother, a dad out sick on my couch, and who were they all worried about? Me.

"She's doing well," I heard my dad say.

"Who is that?" I tried not to sound snappy but wasn't very effective.

Terry, he mouthed.

Oh. Terry Benitez. His friend on the Tampa Police Force. I'd been being paranoid. Stupid. Not everything was about me.

When my dad was settled, I retreated to my bedroom and kicked off my shoes. Still dressed, I lay down and stared up at the ceiling.

Mike's voice echoed in my head. *He's taking a beating. Max Stein's attorneys are tearing him up.*

Maybe I'd been going about this wrong. Alec had been in touch with Amy, so it wasn't like I was betraying her if I just checked in and offered my support.

I just wanted to tell him not to give up. He was doing the right thing.

Before I could think it through, I snatched my phone out of my bag and flipped to his number, still programmed as my first speed dial. It went straight to voice mail. It wasn't even his voice, just a recorded message. I turned off my phone, and with shaking hands flung it across the bed.

Weak.

Talking about my mom, hearing that Alec was hurting, even hearing that he'd tried to help Amy, it had all screwed with my head. I'd made a decision, now I had to live with it.

I slept in one-hour bursts, woken by the usual nightmares and my dad's coughing in the other room, and when the sun finally rose I was already dressed and ready for the day. Work went by uneventfully, apart from Amy asking me forty-seven times who I was bringing to the CASA fund-raiser, and five o'clock found me in her chair, getting my hair flatironed into a soft wave that kept swinging in front of my eyes every time I turned my head. It was annoying, but Amy called it mysterious, which of course was a perfect look for an event that supported foster care.

I'd started dreading the evening. It might have been all right with Amy, but without her dressing up, going out, smiling, and *pretending* . . . it all seemed like an excruciating amount of work. If I hadn't told Jacob I'd be there, I would have ditched.

Amy finally ducked out to go to the girls' play. I promised I'd follow her out, and was just about to get my stuff when I heard male voices in the break room.

I stuck my head inside the small kitchenette, lined on one wall with lockers, and grinned at the two men sitting at the metal table.

"Your hair's really long," said Marcos, crossing his arms over his white V-neck T-shirt disapprovingly. He'd let his dark hair grow out a little himself in the last couple of months. No more military buzz. No more polo shirts either. I couldn't help but think the second man at the table had something to do with that.

"She looks hot." Derrick, Rave's owner, was wearing a yellow tank top with black leather pants today. With his thick eyeliner and pouty lips, he looked like a runway model.

I pushed the smooth strands of hair back over my shoulder. "It just looks longer because it's straight." My hair was naturally wavy. Flat-ironing it had given it another three inches in length.

Marcos looked unconvinced. "You work at a barber's. You could get it cut, you know."

Derrick's eyes narrowed to slits. "A *barber*? *Excuse me?*"

"Whoops," I said. Marcos's comment didn't bother me. He'd practically been my big brother from the day he'd been assigned as my bodyguard. Saving my ass at the bridge had only served to solidify the role.

While Derrick educated Marcos on the difference between a barbershop and a salon, I grabbed my stuff.

"So, who's the lucky guy?" asked Derrick.

"What guy?" said Marcos.

Derrick laughed, and patted his cheek, which immediately had him blushing all the way to the tips of his ears.

"You're cute," said Derrick. "A girl doesn't get her hair done *that* nice unless she wants a man to mess it up."

"Wait . . ." Marcos was frowning. "You didn't tell me you were seeing someone."

"I'm *not*," I said, exasperated. "Not that I feel the need to run every little thing by you."

"Then where are you going?" pressed Marcos. He did look handsome in his wrinkle-free white shirt, even with his serious mouth and thick eyebrows. They were sort of his trademark.

"A fund-raiser," I said. "For CASA. Hey, what are you guys doing tonight?"

"Believe it or not, I own a business," said Derrick. "Which I probably should be getting back to."

I looked at Marcos. "Want to come to a fancy schmancy fund-raiser? It's formal." I might as well have told him they'd be serving rotten fish.

He glanced at Derrick, who smirked back at him. Wow. They were already to the silent-ask-for-permission phase.

"I'm not dancing," said Marcos.

"I wouldn't let you even if you wanted to," I told him.

"Then yes," he said. "What time? I'll pick you up."

"Pick me up in an hour," I said. We were all standing now, and though Derrick had already announced his exit, he had yet to leave.

Marcos glanced between us, and then shifted his weight to the other foot.

"Are you waiting to kiss good-bye until I leave?" I asked. "That's adorable."

Marcos cleared his throat. "We weren't . . ."

"Yes, we were." With that, Derrick grabbed his boyfriend's face between his well-manicured hands, and kissed him right on the lips. Marcos, still uncomfortable with the whole *out* thing, made a sound like he was dying.

And then started to melt.

I turned, just as his eyes drifted closed and his hands came beneath Derrick's elbows. It was too intimate to watch, and even if I was a little jealous he had someone to sweep him off his feet, I was genuinely happy for him.

"An hour," I called, as I cruised to the door.

Five

"There's a handsome cop at the door to see you." My dad stuck his head into the bathroom where I was just finishing my makeup. His nose was red from the cold, and he'd succumbed to wearing his giant glasses rather than his contacts. "You can see how I'd find this surprising, given our lengthy discussions about dating cops."

I blinked, checking my mascara for lumps. My dad had two rules when it came to dating: one, Don't date, and two, Don't date cops.

"We discussed it when I was seventeen, Dad. Anyway, that's Marcos. He's the one Terry assigned to my protective detail before . . ." Everything fell apart. "I thought you'd met him."

He made an unconvinced noise. "I would have remembered."

"He's just a friend," I said. "He's dating a friend of mine."

"Oh." Dad's face lifted. "Well, that's good news."

I followed him out to the living room where Marcos was waiting, looking somehow more comfortable in his formal police blues than in jeans and a T-shirt. A cop, through and through. It occurred to me I should have told him he could have just worn a suit, but I doubted he had one.

"You look nice," I said.

He was staring at me with a scowl on his face. "Don't you need a sweater or something?"

The dress I'd chosen wasn't as sexy as you might have believed based on the concern in both men's eyes. It was black satin, with ruching along one side of the waist, and a hemline just below my ankles. Though my shoulders were bare, the neckline was modest, and the back was only open over my shoulders.

The material was thin enough that I couldn't wear panties, but I wasn't about to tell them that.

My dad slapped Marcos on the shoulder. "I'm liking you more by the second, kid." Marcos managed a smile, just before my dad followed with, "I think it goes without saying that if you touch her, I'll kill you."

"Don't worry," Marcos mumbled.

"*Dad.*" I reached for my clutch, and kissed him on the cheek.

If I'd known how the night would end, I would have told him I loved him, too.

The fund-raiser was held at the Savoy Hotel downtown. Marcos had brought his cop car, which wasn't exactly easy to squeeze into wearing a fancy dress. The monitors and radio stuck out over the passenger seat, leaving me pressed against the door with a side view of the customary pump shotgun above my head.

"My dad used to drop me off at the mall in his patrol car when I was in high school," I told him while we parked.

"Bet your friends thought it was cool," he said.

I groaned. "Amy called it the *birth-control mobile.*"

Marcos smirked. It occurred to me that he had brought this car for the same reason.

When we got to the second floor where the event was being held, I gave the doorman our tickets, and we stepped into a bustling ballroom lined with enormous, half-draped windows overlooking the Bay. Men in suits and women in dresses that put mine to shame loitered in groups, taking appetizers from the waiters that passed by with trays. Along the walls on either side of the entrance were bulletin boards with blown-up quotes and testimonials from children and families who'd benefitted from the program.

"Wow," said Marcos. "How much do they pay you again?"

I slapped him on the arm. He knew the day-to-day dealings of CASA were far less glamorous.

A woman I recognized from the courthouse smiled at me, and unconsciously I fiddled with the straps of my dress. Her white chiffon gown could have easily made a red carpet appearance at the Oscars.

Marcos glanced at me. "Stop it," he said. "You look fine."

"Fine," I repeated. I never felt just fine when I was with Alec. I felt hot. Scorching. I felt like the most beautiful woman who had ever walked the face of the earth.

Marcos stilled my hand and gave it a squeeze. I looked up at him, seeing a sad sort of kindness in his eyes.

"You look really pretty."

"Thanks," I said quietly. I don't know why it hit me right then, but I nearly told him I was going to be leaving soon. I hadn't told Amy, or work, or even my dad really, but something about the moment made me feel like I ought to confess that secret, just so he'd know not to invest too much in our friendship.

I think he thought I was regretting my decision to come, because he said, "Can we eat first, or do we need to find your kid?"

I focused on Jacob. That was why I was here. To support Jacob. To support this important program. I would talk to Marcos later about things. When I had a plan.

"Let's meander," I said.

It was actually kind of fun cruising around with Marcos. We tried strange, fancy hors d'oeuvres and champagne. We made fun of the donors who were clearly afraid of the children that ran between them. We listened to the welcome speech by the president of the local CASA chapter, and clapped for the kids who had graduated from the program. Jacob found me after a little while. He'd already lost his tie, and his shirt was untucked. He gave me a card he'd made with his foster mom. It made me cry.

While we were talking, Marcos had gone to say hello to some cop friends he recognized, and when Jacob bounded off to play with his friends, I found myself alone.

My champagne glass was empty, but I clung to it anyway, needing something to hold in my hands as I stared absently at the posted testimonials. The old familiar feeling was creeping back over me again. I was an advocate, a welcomed guest at this event, and yet the sense of belonging was somehow overwhelmingly uncomfortable. Jacob was okay now. He didn't need me. If I stuck around too much longer I would become a burden to Marcos.

Amy and Paisley . . . well . . . I think we could all safely say that their lives would be a lot less *exciting* without me in it.

I didn't like thinking this way. I hated it. It made me feel small. The way my birth mother had made me feel—like I wasn't important, even with the proof otherwise all around me.

A new place would change my perspective. Open up new opportunities. I just needed a fresh outlook on life. Somewhere with a lot less drama. Somewhere with a lot less Alec.

"Anna."

I fumbled with the glass as it slipped from my fingers. When I'd caught it, I held it so tightly I thought it might break.

He was right there in front of me as if he'd never been gone. Dark, wavy hair that curled at his collar. A small scar over the bridge of his nose. That piercing blue gaze that reached straight into my soul and ripped it to pieces.

He was wearing a black suit with a baby blue silk tie, and my eyes locked on the knot because it was the same one we'd used in the bedroom one night when he'd bound us together.

My heart was pounding so hard I could barely breathe. He was gorgeous and he was perfect and he was tired—I could see the stress weighing him down like a physical thing. I wanted to hold him. I wanted him to hold me. I wanted to kiss him and fan my fingers over his broad chest and scream, *What took you so long?*

The memories shook through me, one after another. The first time he'd kissed me. His hand between my thighs in his Jeep. The tight feel of his grip on my waist when he pulled me down over him. The look on his face the night we'd said good-bye.

"Alec," I whispered.

As his gaze lowered down my face to my mouth, I became aware of how dry my lips were and licked them. His jaw flexed and his eyes roamed again. My throat. My bare shoulders. My fingers, white with their grip on the empty glass. Every part of me came alive under his stare. My blood felt like fire coursing through my veins. My skin, so sensitive I could feel the air from the vents brush across it and raise goose bumps. I felt so alive in that moment I wondered if I'd been dead before, because nothing felt as real as I did when I was with him.

Clapping came from around the stage behind us, reminding me of our surroundings—reminding me that this was a fund-raiser dinner for court-appointed advocates and that Alec shouldn't have been here. I blinked, trying to decipher if he was real, or if I'd just imagined him again. I hadn't had a lot to drink lately; maybe the champagne had pushed me right over the edge into psychosis.

I couldn't decide if I was more relieved or disappointed at the prospect of him being a hallucination.

Test: "What are you doing here?"

His gaze shot back up to mine, giving my pulse a jolt. It was too intense, too exposing, and I looked down at my glass. My hair swung over the side of my face, and in those seconds I was grateful for Amy's flatiron work, because I was in serious need of a curtain to hide behind.

But then he had to go and touch me.

I was unable to move as I watched his hand move toward my face. His warm fingertips brushed my cheek, eliciting the tiniest of gasps that made him pause. Slowly, the back of his hand slid down the edge of my hair before tucking it over my shoulder.

As if he'd done something wrong, he scowled, and shoved his hands into his pockets.

"How are you?" That voice. Low and smooth, falling over my whole body like this satin dress.

"I . . ." I'd asked him something first, hadn't I? I couldn't remember what. "I'm great." Could he hear the lie? I couldn't tell. "What about you? How's your chest?"

I placed my hand on my own side, in the place where he'd been stabbed. But the flashes that returned from that night weren't of a man with a knife. They were of a lap dance. Red lingerie. My hips grinding against his.

"What? Oh." He shook his head. "Fine."

My thoughts shifted to his back, and the scar that would forever serve as a reminder of when he'd been jumped in prison. How many times had Alec's life been endangered because of Maxim Stein?

"And everything else? Work? Parole?" *Smooth, Anna.*

One of his brows lifted. "I had to stop work. With the trial it got . . . complicated. And parole's done. I finished last month."

I smiled. "I don't know why I said that. Nervous, I guess."

I closed my eyes tightly. He chuckled, and the velvety sound loosened every one of my muscles.

"Alec, there you are." A woman came up from behind him holding a champagne flute in one hand. She looked stunning in her short red dress with her auburn hair swept up in a twist on the back of her head, and it took me a moment to place her.

"Anna Rossi," she said, as if we hadn't seen each other in years. "I was wondering if you'd be here."

Something in her voice told me she wasn't thrilled.

"Janelle," I said, tensing. "I'm still a volunteer. Is everything all right?" I glanced back to Alec. "I didn't know you were planning on coming."

She wiped at the lipstick on her glass with her thumb. I tried to remember her in one of her suits with a gun in her holster, but couldn't. All I saw was full makeup, dangly earrings, and the way Alec stiffened as her shoulder brushed against his arm.

"Before the FBI I worked for the state police busting child abusers," she said. "CASA's always been an important program to me."

"You're a donor," I realized.

"You make it sound like I'm giving a kidney or something." She laughed. Sipped her drink. "I just write a check."

"Well." Something was wrong here. Very, very wrong. "Thank you."

Alec was scowling. I wanted to reach up and rub the lines between his brows away with my thumbs. Once, I would have done so without thinking, but things were different now.

"You look good," I said to Alec. Wow. Nice move. I turned quickly to Janelle. "I mean, you both do. Like . . . movie stars. Or something."

What the living fuck.

"Aww," said Janelle. "That's sweet. I wasn't sure how this would go, but Alec insisted it would be all right. I should have trusted him."

"This?" I asked, right as she slipped her arm into the crook of Alec's elbow.

My lips parted, but I immediately shut them. I was an idiot. I was the world's biggest fool. What did I think he was doing here? What had I thought when I'd seen them together? That he was just a friend, like Marcos was to me?

I felt ill. My head was starting to pound, right at the base of my skull.

"That was fast," I muttered.

I straightened and looked him in the eye, wishing I could see past the wall he'd thrown up.

"It was nice seeing you," I said. "Excuse me."

My ankles wobbled on my high heels as I turned and walked faster and faster through the crowd of people toward the nearest door. I'd hoped for the exit, hell even a bathroom, but I found myself in the kitchen.

"Can I help you?" a woman in a black tuxedo asked me as I rushed past. I didn't stop, I kept moving until I'd reached a quiet corner, surrounded by metal racks, and sunk down against the cold metal wall of the refrigerator.

Alec and Janelle were dating. They were here as a couple. She'd always had a soft spot for him—even at the safe house when she was angry with him, I could see it. I wondered how long they'd been together. If he kissed her the same way he kissed me. If she fell to pieces in his arms when they fucked.

I wondered if he loved her.

I pushed down on my stomach, trying to stop it from twisting.

Two and a half months ago he'd been mine. *Mine.* And I'd let him go. Of course he had moved on. He needed someone who understood the pressures of the trial, who wasn't afraid of his dark side. He was too gorgeous and too sexy to be alone. I wondered how long after I'd left it had been before Janelle had swept in. Maybe she'd been there to comfort him after we'd broken up. Hell, he'd been working with her while he was still in prison. Maybe he'd wanted her the whole time.

It wasn't until now that I realized I'd been holding out hope that we might someday find each other again.

I pushed myself back up the wall. Fuck Janelle. And fuck Alec. And fuck me for throwing such a pity party. I was Anna goddamn Rossi. I'd lived through a kidnapping and attempted murder. I'd survived the drugs that had killed my first mom, and the cancer that had taken my second. I would survive Alec Flynn.

I turned around the corner, prepared to find Marcos and get completely wasted on free champagne, and ran straight into Alec's hard chest.

"Jesus Christ!" I stumbled back, and he caught my arm as I teetered on my heels. Warmth from his touch shot up through my shoulder, through my whole chest, and I jerked back.

His hand fell away slowly, but not before I saw the thin white scar tissue that surrounded his wrist. That night on the bridge Reznik had cuffed us both. I remembered now how he'd struggled against the restraints. His wrists had been bloody and bruised when they were finally removed.

"You all right?" he asked.

I was trapped between the cold door of the freezer and Alec's hot body. His scent floated around me, that dark, spicy musk that conjured images of naked bodies sliding against each other in the night.

"Back up," I said. And when he hesitated, I added, "Please."

He took a step back. The world, which had gone fuzzy with him so close, slid back into focus, but the tension remained. It sizzled through the air, had me rocking back onto my toes to get closer.

"What do you want?" I asked, my eyes finding that stupid tie around his neck again. Why was he wearing it anyway? He probably didn't even remember what we'd done with it.

He leaned back against a clean, metal table, gripping the edge behind him until his knuckles turned white. His broad shoulders hunched, and in response, mine did, too.

"You took off pretty quick back there. I wanted to make sure you were okay."

He's always going to care about you, Mike had said. I thought of Amy's sudden interest in my love life after all these months. It all made sense now. They wanted me to move on because Alec already had.

It occurred to me Amy may have known Alec was dating Janelle when she'd seen him, months ago.

I would deal with that later.

I straightened, lifted my chin. He had a world of secrets tucked away. I could see them, right behind his eyes, and yet here he was trying to get *me* to bare *my* soul.

"I'm fine." I glanced around. The waitstaff was all busy on the other side of the kitchen, preparing more hors d'oeuvres for the guests. "Just hungry. Kitchen seemed like the appropriate place."

He gave a small smile. "I saw you called last night. I was . . . on the other line."

"Oh." I waved my hand, overjoyed that there was no apparent end to tonight's humiliation. "It was an accident."

He nodded. "I called you back. Your phone was off."

"You did?" I clenched my fists, irritated at how eager I sounded.

He pushed off the table, came a step closer. I bit the inside of my cheek. His fingers were twitching against his thigh. I wanted them on my waist, sliding around to my back and then lowering. His jaw flexed, as if he was in physical pain.

Silence.

I tucked my hair behind my ear, wishing I had a rubber band, or even a chopstick, so that I could knot it out of my face. I had to show him I wasn't some poor sad puppy.

He leaned closer.

"You look . . ." He laughed dryly. "Christ. You know."

I closed my eyes. Why did he have to say that stuff? He shouldn't have been. He was here with someone else.

"Janelle, huh?"

He cleared his throat. Looked at the floor. "It's complicated."

No, *we* were complicated. I refused to believe they'd been through anything like what we had.

"Do you love her?" I asked.

I could hear him breathing.

"Don't ask me that," he said. "You know the answer already."

It felt like I'd run full force into a brick wall. Every part of me hurt.

"I called to tell you you're doing the right thing with the trial." I forced myself to look up at him, at his perfect mouth that I used to kiss whenever I wanted. "Don't give up."

Before I could say more, I skirted past him, and made for the door. I didn't hear if he followed.

It didn't take long to find Marcos, and he didn't ask questions when I told him I wasn't feeling well. He told me in the car he'd seen Janelle, but even if he knew she'd brought a date, he didn't mention it.

Twice, he tried to convince me to stay out with him. We could go get drunk. We could rent bad horror movies and go back to his place. I told him I was tired.

He walked me to the door, and waited until I was inside to leave. Luckily, my dad was already asleep, so I didn't have to face the questions about what had happened or what I was about to do. As soon as I saw Marcos's lights disappear down the street, I grabbed my keys and headed back downstairs.

It was pain that guided me to that bar. Pain that had me freshening up my lipstick in the rearview mirror when I got there. I had a picture message from Amy of Paisley and Chloe dressed like farmers. She'd asked for a selfie of me in my dress, but I didn't respond.

Alec and I were over. Whatever was left inside of me that still clung to him needed to be severed. Tonight.

I barely looked as I crossed the parking lot. A white car nearly hit me, and though I waved a halfhearted apology, I couldn't see the driver through the tinted windows. A couple standing outside asked if I was all right, and I smiled and said something about needing a drink. I went straight to the bar and sat down, and when the bartender asked what he could get me, I said a Long Island iced tea.

I swiveled on the bar seat, staring blankly at the fancy bottles on the mirrored shelf straight ahead of me. It was the first time I didn't feel uncomfortable sitting alone.

I didn't feel anything.

It wasn't long before a man took the seat next to me. He was a little younger, and had a tattoo peeking out from the collar of his starched white shirt. A star, or a spiderweb or something. No ring on his finger, no tan line there either. He had intense green eyes and a nice body, and when he placed his hand on my thigh I realized I couldn't do this.

"I need to go," I said.

He raised his hands in surrender. "My bad," he said. "Sometimes I can come on too strong. Let me buy you a drink to make up for it."

I should have gone. I should have stood up right then and walked out.

Just one drink, I told myself.

That was the last thing I remembered.

Six

"Ma'am."

My head felt like someone had hit it with a hammer. No, more like it *was* a hammer, and I'd been pounding it against a wall for the last twenty to thirty years. My body didn't feel much better. Every part of me ached. I felt like I had the flu. I must have caught what my dad had.

"Ma'am." The male voice broke through the ringing in my ears, more insistent this time.

I blinked. Too much light. God. I either had the flu or the worst hangover in the history of the world. How much had I had to drink? I couldn't even remember.

"What should I do?" he asked.

He could leave me alone for starters.

"Ma'am, can you hear me?" This time it was a woman speaking.

My hip hurt. And I was freezing. I blinked again. I was so drowsy I could barely keep my eyes open. My fingers spread over the ground, rising up and down the rough bumps in the asphalt.

Something wasn't right.

I was so tired I almost didn't care.

"Go away," I muttered.

"She's homeless," said the guy. What the hell was he talking about? Who was homeless?

"She doesn't look like it," said the woman.

Finally, I succeeded in opening my eyes. The sky was white, painted with thinly stretched clouds, and floating between it and me were two faces. A teenage boy with acne, and a heavyset woman with streaks of red in her hair. They were wearing uniforms. Beige button-up shirts and black pants.

I shivered, and clutched my arms. My skin was damp and cold. I was only wearing this slinky dress—the same one I'd been in last night at the fund-raiser, only it was open in the back. The zipper must have fallen down.

The wave of self-consciousness came with nausea, and I slapped a hand over my mouth as the bile clawed up my throat. Sweat broke out over my scalp as I choked it down. Something stank, and as I turned my head, I realized I was propped up against a Dumpster.

My black dress was dirty and torn open in a slit that went from my knee down. My shoes were gone. I couldn't find my purse.

"What's going on?" I asked, my voice low. "Where am I?"

The panic was swelling inside of me, making my head pound harder, my skin too hot.

"What's your name, honey?" the woman asked.

"A-Anna." I tried to stand but the nausea hit me again. I leaned over my knees and pressed my thumbs into my temples, trying to stop my brain from sloshing around like water.

"Anna, we called your friend."

What friend? Marcos brought me home. I remembered that. But then I went out. I couldn't even remember where.

"How . . . Who are you?" I asked.

"Better call the cops, too," the woman said quietly to the guy, who ran inside the restaurant behind them. My eyes followed him, until they found the play place, separated from the outside by a wall of glass.

What was I doing here?

The fear hit me like a slap to the face, and I scrambled up.

"Who are you?" My voice trembled.

The woman held out her hands. "I'm Rose," she said. "I work at the restaurant. One of the customers just came in and said they saw you lying here . . ."

My head was spinning now.

"What do you want?" I asked.

"I just want to help."

She was lying. I told her as much. She was a liar. Something was seriously wrong here.

"Where are my keys?" I asked. "Where's my . . ." *Car*. I just needed to get in my car and go home. I looked up across the parking lot, but my electric blue Fiesta was nowhere to be seen.

She touched my arm. I told her not to touch me. I was naked beneath this dress. I wasn't even wearing a bra. I crossed my hands over my chest.

"I need to go," I told her. "Let me go."

Then I stumbled back against the cold metal Dumpster and everything went black.

The next hours were a blur. A cop came. And then an ambulance. The EMT gave me a blanket to put over my shoulders. He asked me my name, and what the day was, and who was president. I didn't give him anything. I didn't know him. I didn't know who had sent him. If he thought a blanket was enough to earn my trust he had another think coming.

My head was killing me.

They threw around words like *shock* and *drugs* and told me I was going to the hospital. I said that wasn't going to happen. I'd answered their questions, I wanted to leave. They couldn't hold me. I was the daughter of a cop; I knew my rights. Each one of them looked suspicious, and when they grabbed my arms and made me sit down on the gurney, I struggled.

"Anna!" I honed in on the voice. It cracked something open in me and I began to cry. Big, hot, salty tears rolled down my face.

"Anna?" Alec stopped in front of me. In a wrinkled T-shirt and jeans, he looked like he'd been the one to wake up beside a Dumpster. His hair was a mess, and his eyes were wild.

They grew stone cold as they dropped to the rip in my dress.

"Do you know this woman, sir?" asked one of the EMTs.

He came close, blocking out the people behind him. One of his hands cradled my face, and I clung to it, and filled it with my tears. Alec was here. He was the one thing that made sense.

"Yes," said Alec. "I know her."

He never took his eyes off mine.

"What are you doing here?" I asked.

His jaw twitched. "The kid that found you called me. He said you gave him my number."

I didn't remember doing that. Then again, I couldn't quite picture the kid who'd found me either.

"She didn't give a last name," said the EMT.

"She's in shock," said Alec. He looked angry. "She's been missing for three days."

I pulled back.

"No," I said. "I saw you last night."

He didn't argue.

"Alec, what's going on?"

He sat beside me on the gurney. "We have to go to the hospital, all right?"

I shook my head. The last time I'd gone to a hospital, they'd taken Alec away from me. He was here now, and I needed him to stay.

"It'll be okay, sweetheart," he said.

I believed him.

He lifted me in his arms and carried me up the steps into the back of the ambulance. He whispered the whole time. *It's okay. It's okay. I'm here. I'm not leaving.* Tucked in his embrace, I felt warm and safe, and for the first time since I'd woken, I was calm. I wanted to ask him what he'd meant by three days, but the world was going dim again.

I closed my eyes.

I woke in a small room with peach walls and furniture that looked like it had been covered by plastic picnic tablecloths. A steady, high-pitched beep came from a monitor to my right. The bed I laid on had metal railings and made crinkling sounds when I moved. There was an IV sticking out of my right arm, and I was wearing a thin hospital gown and scratchy underwear.

My head ached, but not like before. My body was sore, but not unmovable. I pushed the blanket back and stared at my bare legs. Apart from a couple of bruises, they looked all right. My arms felt fine. My body was all accounted for.

But something had happened to me. I knew something had, I just didn't know what.

The door creaked open, and a man stepped through the threshold. Against the bright lights of the hallway, I could only see his silhouette, but I knew immediately who it was. Those broad shoulders and tall build. The mess of wavy hair. That familiar clench in my belly that happened every time he was close.

"Hey, you're awake." He came beside the bed, the wariness now evident in his dark eyes. His hand reached for mine, but he pulled back at the last moment, like he was afraid I might break. Dread whipped across my rib cage.

I covered my legs.

"How do you feel?" he asked.

I rubbed the back of my neck, remembering how safe I'd felt in his arms when he'd taken me in the ambulance. Now the strain from the fund-raiser was back between us, only multiplied by a thousand.

"Considerably less crazy," I said. "Did I get in an accident or something? Everything's . . . cloudy." I wondered if I should be embarrassed. Maybe I'd done something stupid.

"You look cold. Are you cold? I'll get a blanket."

"I'm okay."

"You're hungry though," he said. "Let me go find you some food."

He turned to go.

"Wait," I said. "Tell me what's going on first."

His posture was curtain-rod straight. "I don't know yet."

My stomach had started to churn again.

"You said . . ." I squeezed my eyes shut, trying to focus on his words drifting across my mind. "You said I'd been gone for three days."

When I opened my eyes again he was staring at the wall.

"Look at me," I murmured.

Slowly, he turned, and when his gaze found mine, I nearly broke down. There was so much grief there, I didn't know how it hadn't knocked him to his knees.

"Anna, it's Monday," he said.

Monday. The fund-raiser was Friday. I'd lost track of a full weekend? That didn't make sense.

"That's not possible," I said.

He gripped the bed railing, staring at it as if he might bend it just with the strength of his hands.

"I didn't drink *that* much," I said. But I couldn't say for certain if that was true. My frown deepened.

I was suddenly struck by the thought that something was wrong with me. Really wrong, like the cancer that had taken my mom. When she was nearing the end, she lost time, too, although that was mostly due to the pain medication. Maybe there was something messed up in my brain. A tumor, or . . .

"Hey," said Alec softly. He still didn't touch me. What I would have given for him just to hold my hand.

He belonged to someone else, though. Or maybe they were just friends with benefits. It was *complicated*. That much I could remember.

"I talked to your dad and Amy after we got here. They're on their way."

"I'm sure my dad's called in the cavalry," I said, voice shaking, trying to smile. "I'm surprised he isn't already here."

Alec got that look on his face again.

"We're outside Orlando," he said. "I was already out looking for you when the kid at the fast-food place called. It's going to take everyone else a little while to get here."

"Orlando?" I shook my head. This sure didn't feel like the happiest place on earth. "What the hell happened?"

"You're going to be okay," he said, avoiding the question. "You were dehydrated. You need to eat something. Everything else . . ." He released the bed and took a step back. "What's the last thing you remember?"

He looked desperate, and that scared me half to death.

I closed my eyes, concentrated. "The fund-raiser. We talked in the kitchen. I remember Marcos taking me home. I . . . I went out after that." I laughed dryly. "I don't even remember where. That place on Himes, I think."

"Anna?" Amy burst through the door, followed by a nurse. She was still dressed in her work attire, even with the black, hip-length smock lined by silver hair clips.

"Ma'am, you need to sign in!"

"Jesus jumped-up Christ, where have you been?" She didn't wait for an answer. She grabbed me by the shoulders and pulled me into her arms like I was a rag doll. "I thought you were dead, you know that?"

"I'm not dead," I said lamely.

The nurse, an older woman with kind blue eyes, looked at me for approval of Amy's presence, and I nodded.

Amy pulled back and looked at my face. "You don't remember anything? Alec said on the phone that you have amnesia or something."

"Amy." Alec motioned for her to step away while the nurse began checking my blood pressure with cold hands and asking me questions about my pain level. I tried to listen to what Alec was telling Amy, but he was speaking too quietly. It didn't matter; their body language was enough to tell me it was bad news. Amy sagged, and turned away, and Alec stared at the floor.

When Amy turned back, she was all smiles and red, tear-filled eyes.

"All right," she said. "Let's eat something, huh?"

"Actually, if it's all right, now might be a good time for us to talk," said the nurse. She sat on the bed beside me and patted my hand. "Why don't your friends give us a minute?"

"No." My voice cracked. Maybe she was nice, maybe she was freaking Mother Theresa, but I didn't want to be alone with anyone I didn't know.

The nurse stroked my forearm. "Okay. That works." The bed's plastic sheets crackled as I sat up. She gave me a Time to Be Brave smile, which of course made me feel exactly the opposite.

I willed her to talk fast. Bad news always was better swallowed fast, and she was taking her sweet time about sharing.

"While you were resting we did some blood work. You've tested positive for Rohypnol, do you know what that is?"

The world seemed to slow, then ease to a stop.

My first thought: Thank God I don't have a brain tumor.

My second thought: Oh shit.

Rohypnol. It had been a long time since I'd heard of the drug, but it wasn't foreign to me. My dad had included it as part of his birds and bees talk when I turned thirteen.

Cops could go a little overboard sometimes.

Amy came around to my other side and grabbed my other hand. She was trying not to cry—her lip was quivering. *If you cry, I'm going to kill you,* I wanted to tell her. One of us needed to keep it together.

The nurse went on to explain. It felt like she was speaking to me from the end of a long tunnel.

Rohypnol. Roofies. The date rape drug.

Rape.

I jerked up in my bed. No. That wasn't possible. I felt fine. I hadn't been raped.

Amy turned to Alec, who was staring at me from where he'd frozen in place against the wall.

"Alec, why don't you go find Ben? He's probably just getting here."

My dad was here.

"Don't tell him anything," I demanded. I couldn't look at Alec. I couldn't look at any of them. "Nothing happened. I don't want him panicking for no reason."

Alec left silently.

The nurse said she needed to do some more tests. I knew what a rape kit was. I'd been introduced to them in my days as a social worker. Like an annual exam, but they were looking for signs of forced entry. They would give me a shot for possible exposure to hepatitis. They would see if I had HIV. There was a discussion of the morning after pill.

She could have the doctor do it right then. I wouldn't even have to be inconvenienced by going to another room.

"I haven't been raped." I looked at Amy. "I know you think I'm crazy, but I would know."

"Let's just get this over with then, okay?" Her voice shook.

"I'm serious," I said. "That isn't what happened."

"All right." She squeezed my hand, and damn her all to hell, she started to cry.

Seven

sank down to the floor of the narrow tile shower, gripping my knees to my chest. The IV line twisted around my wrist, a constant reminder that I was tethered here, unable to leave. That my body was too weak to work on its own.

That someone had done this to me.

I'd agreed to the test just to prove them wrong. I took the shot, and did a blood test and mouth swab for HIV. I lay back in my bed while a female doctor came in and gave me her best pity smile. Amy held my hand the whole time, but I felt like I was the one holding her hand, because she was the one who was scared.

I hadn't been scared.

I'd been humiliated.

Alec had known this would happen before I'd woken up. He'd known the drugs were in my system. That's why he wouldn't touch me. He probably thought I would fall apart. Or maybe he thought I was damaged. The idea of either made me sick.

The doctor had frowned when she was finished, and asked me

for the second time if I remembered anything from the last couple of days.

"*You may,*" she'd said when I told her no. "*They might just be images, like how you remember a dream. I'd encourage you to call the police if that happens.*"

I closed my eyes as tightly as I could. I let the shudders work through me, wishing I had something to hold me down besides this IV line.

I willed myself to remember. I tried to focus on anything after the fund-raiser, but it was like those days didn't even exist.

What had happened to me?

"*There's no sign that you've been assaulted. I'd say you may have gotten really lucky here, Ms. Rossi.*"

Lucky. I sure as hell didn't feel lucky.

I hugged my knees so hard my arms started to shake.

I hadn't been hurt. That was all that mattered.

"*Whoever gave you this drug may have gotten scared, or changed his mind. That might be why he left you so far away from where you started.*" Her frown had irritated me. It was like she'd wanted to tell me bad news. I told myself it was just because the situation confused her.

Welcome to the club.

"*When can I leave?*" I'd asked.

A couple of days. She wanted to keep me for observation. My fluids were low, and there were still traces of the drug left in my system.

She wanted me to talk to a psychiatrist.

"*You've been through quite an ordeal, Ms. Rossi. You may have questions you want to talk to someone about.*"

Oh, I had questions. Questions like who the hell had drugged me and why.

My mind turned to Alec and the trial, and I couldn't help wondering if this was all related to Maxim Stein. It wouldn't be the first time someone had threatened us to keep me quiet.

Those were questions for later. For now, I could only focus on the present.

I was okay.

I hadn't been hurt.

The relief seeped through me, but it felt like poison. I crawled to my knees, leaned over the toilet, and threw up.

The knock came less than two minutes later.

"I got you some soup," Amy said. "And orange Jell-O. Yum, right?"

The door didn't lock. When I was silent, she pushed in, and without a word, helped me up and into the bed. I felt weak now, no longer driven by anger or pride. I was hollowed out, too tired even to hold my head up.

She crawled onto the foot of the hospital bed and sat cross-legged, the tray of food between us.

"I'm sorry I didn't go to the fund-raiser," she said. She looked up and blinked rapidly, eyes watery. Amy wasn't much of a crier; I hated seeing her so torn up.

"It's not your fault." My voice was raw.

She scoffed pitifully, as if this was a joke. What happened wasn't her fault, and I needed the subject changed ASAP.

"Did you know Alec and Janelle were . . . a thing?" Dating? Together? I didn't know.

She peeled back the cover on the broth, refusing to look up.

"I didn't know how to tell you," she said. "It was different with him. I knew it wouldn't be as easy as us eating brownies and throwing a pity party. It was going to wreck you, and I . . ."

She covered her mouth with her hands. "That's why you went to that bar, isn't it? Alec said the bartender saw you there drinking alone before you hooked up with someone."

"I didn't hook up with anyone," I said, wondering if this bartender had seen who had taken me. "I don't even remember going."

Amy handed me the spoon. The idea of eating made me even more ill, but my growling stomach disagreed.

"It was in the news," she said. "The woman he's seeing was the FBI agent working his case. She got demoted or something when their affair went public a month or so ago."

I couldn't help but feel a little validation at that, but it still felt like a betrayal. If Alec had to date someone, I wished it was someone that one, I didn't know, and two, wasn't such a ball-busting bitch.

I leaned forward, and Amy propped a pillow behind my back. "Is it too late to try brownie therapy?"

"Never." She picked at her fingernails.

"I have so many questions."

"I'm sure."

"Does anyone have any idea who did this?" I tapped the tray with my spoon, not totally sure I was ready to try eating yet.

Amy shook her head.

"You're dad's been raising hell with the local PD trying to figure it out, and Alec's using his resources at the FBI."

"You mean Janelle, his girlfriend."

She nudged the tray in my direction. So they were together.

"Whoever thought orange Jell-O was a good idea?" she said. "It tastes like cough syrup. Twenty bucks for an Advil, but they can't spring an extra fourteen cents for strawberry or cherry."

I looked across the bed at my best friend, sitting there like she had ten years ago when our biggest concerns involved boys and parties. I hoped in ten years she was still sitting there. I hoped in fifty years I could still count on her to be the one holding my hand and crying the tears I couldn't cry.

I leaned over the tray and hugged her. "I love you, Amy."

She sighed and squeezed me as tightly as she could. The soup sloshed up against my knees, probably soaking the sheets.

"I know," she said. "I love you, too."

"Can you do me a favor?"

She sat back. "Anything you want." Her eyes darted from side to side. "Want me to take a hit out on the girlfriend?"

I smirked. "She carries a gun."

"Well, I carry sharp scissors, so she can kiss my skinny ass."

I laughed, and it felt like ice chipping away inside of me. I tried a sip of the broth. The second it touched my tongue, my stomach started grumbling for more.

"Can you hold off my dad for a while?" The momentary lightness was doused in shame. "I know he's probably freaking out but I just . . ." I bit down on my lower lip, trying to keep my voice from trembling. "I can't see him right now."

I was sure by now he knew that they'd found roofies in my system. Alec had probably told him they'd done an exam to see if I'd been raped, as well.

I was his little girl, and I wasn't ready to see the way he looked at me now.

My mind shifted to Alec, and where he was. He probably didn't know that I was okay. I wanted him to know, for some reason, but the thought of facing him, too, seemed overwhelming.

Amy gave a sober nod. "Sure. I'll tell him visiting hours are over."

"Okay."

She took a deep breath. "Which probably means I should go, too, otherwise he'll never believe me."

"Yeah."

I didn't want her to leave, but I was getting sleepy again. I didn't understand why. I'd slept for three days. I should have been more awake. Must have been the drugs in my system.

"I'll be back tomorrow with real food," she said.

"Corndogs and Hamburger Helper?" My eyelids were getting heavy.

"Watch it," she said, pointing a finger at me.

One more hug, and I was alone.

For the first time in three days, I dreamed.

I was lying in the back of a car, my cheek pressed against the smooth, cool leather of the seat. Fuzzy images, just flashes, nothing I could hold on to. Nothing that should have been terrifying.

I woke up screaming.

My arm was tangled in wires. From behind my head came the beep of the heart rate monitor. I gasped for air.

"Anna, it's all right." I blinked, but the room was dark, and I could barely focus.

"It's all right, I'm here."

Alec. His voice wrapped around me like a soft blanket. His hands found my shoulders and slid down my arms. The touch was soothing, and I gripped his forearm with both hands, using him as an anchor.

"Anna?" A nurse in pink scrubs raced into the room. She moved directly to the side table and flipped on a light. I turned away, blinking, while my eyes adjusted, and found my forehead pressed against Alec's hard stomach.

I didn't move.

"Tell me what's wrong," said the nurse. "Are you in pain?" She sounded younger than the one from earlier. There must have been a shift change.

I focused on the warm feel of Alec's chest against my cheek, and the place right below his elbow where my hands gripped his forearm. His skin turned white around the indentation of my thumb, but I couldn't seem to let him go.

"B-bad dream," I said. "I'm fine."

The beeping of the heart rate monitor gradually began to slow. The IV was gone—I remembered the other nurse had taken it out before she'd left.

"Let me give you something to help you sleep," she said. "A mild sedative."

"No!" I didn't mean to shout. The beeping accelerated. "No drugs."

"We're okay." One of Alec's hands moved to my hair, smoothing it down my back. I closed my eyes, savoring the feel of that simple caress.

We're okay, he'd said. Not *she's okay.* Right then I would have given anything for that to be true.

A moment later the light went out, and the nurse's shoes squeaked away.

As soon as the door closed, I became aware that Alec and I were alone. The last time we'd been alone together had been at the safe house, when we'd made love half the night. I didn't know why I was thinking of that now.

I meant to ask what he was doing here, but I didn't want to draw attention to the fact that he could have been somewhere else. I could have asked if he knew more about what had happened to me, too, but I knew it would just make him go cold. Maybe it was pathetic of me, but I wanted him close, just for a few more seconds. Reality could wait.

"I can't let go of your arm," I said.

"I don't mind," he said. But he stopped stroking my hair, and gradually began to ease back.

"Not yet," I whispered.

He stilled.

I nuzzled closer against his chest, listening as his heart sped up to match the monitor. Just a thin layer of fabric between my cheek and his skin, not enough to hide the heat of his body, but enough of a barrier to remind me he wasn't mine. He barely moved; I was fairly sure he wasn't even breathing.

Even in this sterile place he felt like home.

"Do you ever miss me?" I asked. The question came out before I thought about it. Some things were easier to say in the dark.

I could feel him swallow.

"It's the worst at nighttime," I confessed. "I can barely sleep."

He stepped back, and the weight of my words crushed me down into the thin, crinkly mattress. Finally my grip on his arm slid away, though my hands stayed half-closed, unable to forget the shape of him.

"Thank you for looking for me," I said.

He made a sound like a sob. Or a choke. Or both.

I heard the slide of the heavy, tablecloth-covered chair as he pulled it closer to the bed, then the click of a button. The beeping silenced, and he felt his way to my wrist to remove the monitor. I glanced up at him, but he was cloaked in darkness.

Then one strong arm slid behind my shoulders, and the other slipped beneath my knees. I felt his breath move my hair as he leaned down, spreading warmth like a wildfire across my body despite the chasteness of his touch. As if I weighed nothing, he lifted me, and lowered into the chair, cradling me in his lap with my head against his shoulder. His hold on me was tight, like he knew I needed it, and I pretended he needed it, too.

"You don't have to be afraid tonight," he murmured.

"I'm not afraid."

"No one's going to hurt you."

"I know."

He moved the blanket over my body, and though it kept me warm, I wished I could feel more of his skin. I became aware of the places we did touch: my forehead against his neck, my bare feet tucked between the arm of the chair and his outer thigh. It would have been easy to tilt my head back and kiss him. But his arms tightened, and all the pieces of me that were stretched too thin began to rip apart.

The tears tumbled down, dampening his shirt.

"Please don't go," I whispered.

"I'm right here," he said. "I've got you."

Eight

I woke back in the hospital bed, to the sound of a muffled cough. When I opened my eyes, light was peeking through the mini blinds over the window on the far wall, and my dad was sitting in the chair where Alec and I had slept.

At least, I thought that was what happened. Now that it was light the whole thing seemed too much like a dream to be true. Alec had a life that didn't involve me. He had the trial. He had a girlfriend.

A cold sensation settled right between my ribs.

"Hey, pretty girl." My dad was wearing an old flannel shirt over jeans. The buttons were misaligned, and his eyes were red and watery. "Good morning."

I groaned in response.

"You want something to eat?"

I shook my head.

He tried to hide his worry, but wasn't very effective. He kept clasping and unclasping his hands, an odd nervous habit for a man who always kept his cool.

"You gave us quite a scare," he said.

I offered a half smile, but it didn't come easily. What had happened wasn't my fault—I knew that—but I still somehow felt responsible for frightening him.

"I'm okay. The doctor said . . ."

"I know," he finished, so I wouldn't have to. He turned his head into the crook of his elbow and started to cough. I guess at least one thing hadn't changed since I'd been missing.

"Hey," I said. "This is a germ-free zone. Try not to get the patients sick."

He smirked. It made me feel a little better.

"Local PD is going to swing by this morning and ask some questions if you're up for it," he said.

I nodded. "Any idea who did this?"

He looked grim. "Working on it. We'll know soon enough. You remember anything?"

I thought of the dream I'd had—the smooth leather seat of a car against my cheek. It was hard to tell if that had been real, or a figment of my imagination.

"Not really."

"It's all right," he said. "If it's going to come, it'll come. You just need to focus on getting some food in that skinny body."

I sucked in my cheeks.

"What are you talking about? This is all part of my new diet plan."

"Not funny," he said.

So much for lightening the mood.

"Dad, did you by any chance see Alec?"

A frown immediately pulled down the corners of my father's mouth. "I caught him on the way out around five a.m. Strange, considering I was told visiting hours were over last night at eight."

He'd left early. I wondered if he'd slept at all.

I worked on peeling the edge of my fingernail. "He's a real rule-breaker."

"Yeah. That seems to be the case."

"Did he say if he'd be back?"

My dad's face warped to pity. I was getting pretty tired of seeing that look on people's faces.

"I didn't ask." He reached for my hand and gave it a squeeze. "His schedule wasn't exactly my top priority."

No, I imagined that was true. Still, as I looked down at the chair where I'd spent much of the night, I couldn't help but feel that things weren't over between Alec and me. So what if he'd ducked out early. He'd known I was missing and looked for me. He'd come when I'd called. And he'd held me when I needed it. Those weren't things you did for someone you didn't deeply care for.

My day was slammed with visitors. Amy came back first, with a brown bag of "real food" and a ragged-looking Mike. Their kids were with Mike's mom, Iris, who was staying at Mike's house as a safety precaution.

"They're our baby girls," Mike had said. "Maybe this thing is linked to Max Stein, maybe not, but I'm not taking any chances. Until this trial's over, anyone Alec has looked at twice is staying close."

When I looked guilty, he sat on the side of my bed. "So when you get out, you want to come have a slumber party at my place?"

I half-laughed, glancing to Amy, whose eyes darted to the floor. Mike saw the move and grinned. "Amy already said yes."

"Oh *really*," I said.

"The girls are going to be there," my best friend said quickly. As much as I regretted her growing humiliation, I was happy to transfer the focus off of me for a while.

"Does that mean we have to be on good behavior?" Mike teased.

"Just until their bedtime," she shot back. With all the squirming, it wasn't a great demonstration of her quick wit, but it was enough to make Mike's brows rise.

He pretended to check his watch. "Good to see you, Anna. We've got to go."

They didn't, of course, but I could tell both of them were already running through what might happen later that night in their minds.

Amy was going to get lucky. Maybe not tonight, but things definitely looked like they were heading in that direction. I wondered how long it had been since she'd been with someone. For as much interest as she showed in my love life, we barely ever discussed hers.

By lunchtime I was sick of being cooped up in my room, and changed into a T-shirt and pajama pants combo that Amy had brought. An officer from the local police department met me in a quiet corner of the cafeteria to take my statement. After I'd written everything I could, I leaned back to answer his questions, but my eyes were drawn to the news report on the television behind him. They'd been talking about a new sinkhole that had opened up in the central part of the state, but switched to an update from the Maxim Stein trail.

"Bad news for the prosecution, whose key witness, Alec Flynn, came down with food poisoning just after the trial began last week, throwing a wrench in the prosecution's apparent plan to hit the defense hard with evidence of Stein's participation in white-collar crimes." The reporter, a Hispanic woman with glossy black hair, folded her hands across the desk.

Alec's face popped up on the corner of the screen. It was the same shot I'd seen in the paper: him in a suit, looking both beautiful and miserable. My fingers began drumming against the table.

Alec didn't have food poisoning. He'd been looking for me, and then stayed with me here, in the hospital. That must have been what he'd told his lawyer, or at least what his lawyer had conveyed to the judge. I wasn't sure if I should feel more guilty or grateful.

"Rumors were already flying that Flynn, Stein's body man of

fourteen years, was getting cold feet when he failed to show for a briefing Saturday morning. Not entirely surprising to our confidential sources in the investigation, who have maintained Flynn's own questionable ethics and shaky past."

"Is there anyone you think might want you harmed, Ms. Rossi?" asked the officer before me. He scratched a hand over the deep dimple in his chin, eyes on the pathetic single paragraph I'd written.

"Shh." I pointed to the screen.

He gave an annoyed grunt.

"But was Alec Flynn actually ill?"

Uh-oh.

Behind the woman, film began rolling of Alec leaving a quaint pink stucco building wearing a baseball cap and sunglasses. Beside him was a woman in a loose, teal summer dress. When the reporters caught up with them, Alec hunched, and pulled the woman under his arm.

Janelle.

As she turned her head into Alec's chest to hide from the barrage of reporters, I could see her profile more clearly. He lifted a hand to block the flash of the cameras.

"Just after nine o'clock this morning, Flynn was spotted exiting a small bed-and-breakfast outside Orlando with his girlfriend, Janelle Jamison. Ms. Jamison, as many of you may recall, was the FBI's lead investigator in this case until she was asked to step down due to inappropriate conduct."

His head bowed down to whisper something in her ear. I could see his lips moving as the camera lens zoomed in. My toes curled in my slippers. My fingernails dug into the table.

He'd left me at five, and hopped straight into bed with her. I didn't even have room to be mad. He'd been gentle, comforting. At the most a good friend. Which was why watching him with his arm around Janelle made my heart feel like it was breaking all over again.

"Was Alec Flynn really sick? It doesn't appear so. Which

leads us to wonder if this was a deliberate stall by the prosecution, or a notable example of their star witness's inconsistent behavior. All will be revealed in the coming weeks as the trial continues . . . that is, if Flynn and his girlfriend don't suddenly disappear for a weekend cruise." The reporter grinned at the camera, probably thinking she was funny. "*And now for what's new with the Rays, I'll hand it over to Jimmy . . .*"

I stared at my lap for a full ten seconds, before I looked back up at the cop.

"Who did this to me?" I asked sharply.

He looked down at my statement. "We're still working on that."

"You don't have any leads?"

He inhaled slowly. "We can't exactly pull fingerprints off your skin. With your examination results clean . . ."

I groaned internally. "Someone drugged me, then dumped me in Orlando. There was a reason this happened."

"I know it feels like there should be," he said. "There isn't always. There are a lot of bastards out there who get off on a power trip . . ."

"No," I said, feeling a strange, vicious anger build inside of me. I could still feel Alec's arms around me. I could still feel a blank space in the center of my brain. Questions needed answering, and I was tired of sitting in the dark.

"There have to be fingerprints on the glasses at the bar. Or security cameras. Or witnesses—a bartender, or someone else I sat near. Someone had to see me leave." My dad was upstairs in my room. I hadn't wanted him to be a part of this, even though he already knew what would be said, but I couldn't help but want him here with me now. He wouldn't have stood for this lackadaisical detective work.

The officer snorted.

"The bar you were seen at doesn't have a security camera."

"I've been targeted in the past," I said. "Or did you even do your homework before you showed up?"

It was rude, but I was past caring. Maybe the drugs were finally out of my system, because things were now crystal clear and sharp as a knife.

"Your affiliation with Alec Flynn is off the table."

"Off the table," I repeated.

His mouth tightened. "The FBI has made it clear we can't run an investigation with anything related to him or Stein's trial."

"Well what good is that?" I threw my hands up. "Why am I even talking to you?"

The cop gave an exasperated shrug. "You sure there isn't anyone else who might have wanted to teach you a lesson? An ex-boyfriend, maybe?"

"What are you insinuating?" I asked, shoving back. "That I need to be *taught a lesson*?"

"Good lord," said the officer. "I'm not the one who did it, lady."

"Her dad's a cop." A voice from behind me drew my attention, and I turned to see Marcos, back in his blue Tampa PD uniform, holding the purse I'd taken to the fund-raiser.

"That explains the interrogation," grumbled the officer.

Marcos sat beside me, unwilling to look in my direction. He tossed my purse onto the table.

"You two know each other?" I asked.

"We spoke earlier," said Marcos. "When I gave my statement. You know, about Friday night after the CASA dinner, when I walked you to the door of your apartment because you told me you were sick and going to bed."

My temper diffused a little.

His brows stayed flat, but a muscle in his neck was jumping.

"You found my purse."

"Bartender called when your dad reported you missing."

I opened it, checked my cell phone. The battery was dead. "Any prints on any of this?"

"Just the bartender's," said Marcos. "And yes, he made you a Long Island ice tea and saw you with a guy about twenty-five, dark hair, nondescript features. Unless you've got some idea, I'm going to call him John Doe."

"Did he kidnap me?"

"The bartender doesn't remember seeing you leave, but he doesn't recall anyone being carried out kicking and screaming."

I scowled, trying to remember. "The last thing I remember is getting in my car after you dropped me off."

I couldn't remember putting my keys in the ignition. I couldn't remember driving to the bar. I didn't even remember if I'd ordered something.

"Well, I guess I've got everything I need," said the Orlando officer. "We'll be in touch if anything comes up."

He sounded doubtful.

"You've got my number," said Marcos.

I withered in my slick wooden chair. Marcos sat beside me, staring straight ahead at the television, now showing a local car commercial. I shouldn't have been so hard on that cop. This wasn't his fault. I didn't know what came over me.

"I'm sorry." My voice was barely a whisper.

Marcos shook his head. He pulled something out of his pocket—a small piece of folded paper—and placed it onto the table. Tentatively, I reached for it, and opened the picture of Alec I'd taken from craft night at the Children's Museum.

"He's the one who called to tell me you were gone," said Marcos. "Your dad and Detective Benitez had been trying to get me. I was . . . off duty."

Otherwise known as *with my boyfriend.*

"Okay," I said.

"He thought you and me were a thing."

"Oh." I tried to shrug off the image of Janelle and Alec on the news report. "Who cares what he thinks?"

Marcos turned to face me. "You, for starters."

I refolded Alec's newspaper picture.

"It's the second time he's called me. The first was just after the bridge, when he asked me to look out for you."

I looked down.

"I told him I would, but not for him."

Marcos lowered his head, until he caught my gaze. "Derrick says I shouldn't yell at you because you've been through enough."

"Do you yell?" I asked. "I'd like to see that."

And it was true. I wanted him to yell at me. I wanted him to tell me it was stupid going out when I was upset. That I should have told someone where I was going. I wanted someone to, so I didn't have to.

He shook his head, then grabbed me and pulled me into a hug.

"You're like a goddamn cat," he muttered. "What life is this? Four? Five?"

I laughed into his shoulder, squeezing him hard.

"Don't push it, all right? One of these days that luck is going to run out."

Nine

Alec didn't come back that day. The psychiatrist came, and the doctor, and the nurses. My dad stayed in my room, taking the occasional call related to his PI work. I asked to be released. They all said no. Tomorrow.

Relax, my dad said. *Eat.*

I told him my muscles were going to atrophy if I stayed in this bed much longer. I refused to turn on the television, afraid of seeing anything that might pertain to the trial.

It made for a very boring, frustrating day.

That night I barely slept. It seemed the rest had caught up with me, and now we had switched gears back to insomnia. With my dad at home to check on Mug, I spent the night staring at the ceiling, trying not to think of Alec.

It was basically about as effective as trying not to think of donuts while dieting. The worst part was, I kept wondering what he was doing now, and the conclusion was always the same.

He was in bed with another woman.

I sat up and flipped on the light. My phone was finally charged, and I flipped through the messages. About four thousand texts and missed calls from my dad and Amy. A few voice mails from Mike. Marcos's blunt text: CALL ME ASAP.

A message from Alec.

I scrolled down the list and pressed the Play button.

"Anna it's me." Hesitation. *"It's Alec. Look, if you get this, can you call me? No one's seen you for a while and I just want to . . ."* Pause. *"Just call me, all right? Or call Amy or Mike or your dad. Just call someone. Soon."*

My chest began to ache. He sounded seriously worried. I imagined him driving around town, trying to figure out where I'd been.

And then going back to Janelle at the bed-and-breakfast.

Searching for me was what any friend would do. Just because he didn't love me like I loved him, didn't mean he didn't love me at all.

I bit down hard on my top lip. I bet Canada was nice this time of year. Mountains. Skiing. People who ended sentences with "eh?" I'd known a woman in Baltimore who'd spent a year in Canada on a work visa. I wondered how long it took to apply for those.

I opened the Internet on my phone. But instead of researching Canada, I searched for the bar I'd ended up at after the fundraiser. Marcos had given me the name—Barrow's. I could imagine the sign out front, but couldn't tell if that was from a recent memory, or something older.

It was just after two. I doubted they were still open.

A man picked up on the third ring. "Barrow's. We're closed, so if you left your shit here, you'll have to wait until tomorrow to get it."

"Hello?" I said. "Are you the bartender?"

He waited a beat. "I may or may not be. Depends on who's asking."

His voice was familiar, and brought a cold sweat to my brow.

"My name's Anna," I said. "I think I was in the other night. Friday night, to be exact."

"Yeah," he said. "Anna Wright or something?"

"Rossi."

"Yeah," he said again. I tried to picture his face, but couldn't. "People are looking for you. A few cops. Your boyfriend came by like seven times."

"My boyfriend?"

"Tall guy, looks like he could wrestle a bear and come out on top."

Alec. Just being a good friend, I reminded myself.

"Right," I said. "They found me. I was just wondering if you saw anything that night. Who I was with, anything."

I heard a screech, like a stool being dragged across the floor. "Look, like I told the cops, we have a lot of people in and out of this place. A lot of girls looking for dates. I don't judge, everyone's got their reasons."

My fists clenched. I willed them to relax.

"Do you remember what time I was there?"

"Had to be early. Ten or so. You looked sad as hell. I remember thinking you could use a fucking hug. A guy I'd never seen before picked you up before you finished your first drink. I didn't see you leave, but it was before the band started at eleven. Hey, the cops mentioned he might have dropped something in your drink. Is that true? If it gets out people are dropping roofies in my bar . . ."

"I can say for a fact that people are dropping roofies in your bar."

"Shit." The implication of this hit a moment later. "*Shit.* You all right?"

I pressed the make-believe Pass button.

"Did I look uncomfortable?" I asked. "Or frightened?" I felt like an idiot asking questions about myself like this.

"No," he said. "Just sad, like I said."

"Anything specific you can remember about the guy?" I asked. "What he was wearing? Any scars or glasses or missing teeth." *Anything.*

"I'm sorry," said the bartender. "Honestly. I barely looked twice at him. Friday nights are jammed here. I can't remember if I even got him a beer."

"But you remember he bought me a drink," I huffed.

"You're a little prettier than he was."

I frowned. "You don't have security footage?"

"Naw. I've got a camera out front, but just to scare people straight. I don't keep it on. I . . . yeah. Sorry about that. Anyway, it'd hardly matter. Some kids fucked it up after the band anyway."

"They stole it?"

"No. They busted it. I bet I know who it was, too. Crazy-ass college kids. When I left that night it was in pieces behind a bush."

This didn't sit right. "You're sure it was college kids?"

"Could've been anyone, I guess."

It could have been the guy who met me, thinking that he didn't want to get caught. He wouldn't have known it wasn't connected to a live feed.

"All right," I said. "If you think of anything else, can you call me?"

"Sure." He took my number. "Sorry about all this. If you find that asshole, send me his mug shot and I'll make sure he never steps foot in another bar in the state."

"Thanks," I said, and hung up.

I grabbed a pad of paper and pen from the nightstand and wrote down everything he'd told me. I read it again and again, trying to remember the things he'd said, until dawn's orange light began sneaking through the window and I finally fell asleep.

The next morning, the nurse told me I would be discharged after the doctor made her rounds. When I asked how much this would cost, she told me not to worry, they'd already worked it out in billing. I suspected that meant I'd receive a nice fat itemized list in the next few weeks.

I packed up my few belongings and checked my complexion in the mirror. Not exactly beauty queen material, but not terrible either, considering I'd been found at a Dumpster a few days ago.

When the knock came, I'd assumed it was the doctor.

"Come in," I called. My dad, who'd been reading in the chair, put down his book.

It wasn't the doctor. It was Janelle Take-Your-Man Jamison.

I planted the heels of my rubber flip-flops into the floor. Not usually the jealous type, a surge of anger rose so quickly within me, I'd have sworn my eyes turned green.

She was wearing a pants suit today, with her auburn hair pulled back in a tight ponytail. It was like the first time I'd seen her in the hospital. All business, no room for softness.

I was even jealous of her mascara.

"Anna, you look well."

"I'm fantastic," I said tentatively. "Never better. You?"

She avoided my question.

"Special Agent Jamison with the FBI," she announced to my father. Her head turned back to me. "Can we speak privately?"

"Of course," said my dad. "I'll be downstairs in the cafeteria. I hear they've got powdered eggs on the menu today."

He squeezed my forearm on the way out.

When the door shut behind him, Janelle moved to the side of the bed, heels tapping on the hard linoleum. I prepared myself for the inevitable *Jerry Springer* showdown and grabbed the edge of the lunch tray.

"You've been through some terrible things lately," she said. It sounded nice, but I didn't want her kindness.

I released the tray and crossed my arms over my chest.

"What do you want, Janelle?"

She looked up at me, green eyes flashing with a hurt that made my stomach clench.

"I want you to know I didn't mean for this to happen," she said.

She was genuinely sorry for hurting me. I could see it on her face. Feel it in the heavy air around us.

"He's . . ." She took a breath. "Well. You know how he is."

Yes. I knew. I could already feel my tough front stripping away. I didn't want her to talk to me about Alec. I didn't want her to care about him, and I certainly didn't want him to care about her.

"I make him happy, if that matters to you."

It did matter, though I couldn't admit it to her.

"Is that all you came to say?" I asked.

"I wanted to tell you I'm looking into who took you. If it's linked to the Stein trial, I'll find out."

"I thought you were demoted," I said, the cattiness gone from my voice. "Inappropriate conduct or something."

She gave me a dry grin. "I was. But they still find some uses for me, I guess. Agent Tenner's heading the case now."

"He's all right." It was a relief. The last time I'd seen him, he'd been knocked unconscious by a tire iron before Alec and I had been taken to the bridge.

Janelle nodded. "Matt's his second. And I'm . . ."

"Watching Alec's back." I didn't like it, but I wanted him to be as safe as possible.

"Of course," she said.

Her phone rang. She pulled it from her hip and checked the number, then turned to me. "Sorry, I have to take this."

She stepped in the hall, leaving me staring after her. I wasn't sure I felt better with her in charge of my case, but at least I believed she would look into it. If she cared for Alec at all, she'd want to make sure she didn't let Maxim Stein get away with anything, even something to do with me.

Outside in the hallway, I heard her answer the phone.

"What's up, Tenner?"

Curiosity had me tiptoeing toward the crack in the door. The last time I'd seen Janelle and Agent Tenner together, it was quite obvious who had been in charge.

"I'm with her now."

I heard Janelle's shoes clack as she went a little farther down the hall. I stood in the gap of the door, listening.

"She doesn't know."

Doesn't know what? I held my breath, trying to silence the background noise to hear her better.

"No," she said, lowering her voice. "Flynn's in court. Matt took him. Why?"

Her shoes stopped.

"Are you sure it's him?" The emotion in her voice caught me off guard. "Where is he? Is he okay?"

A pause.

"Is there only one Residence Inn in Lakeland?"

Another pause.

"No, of course I'm not going to tell her. She'll find out soon enough."

I was trying to make sense of her scattered responses. Alec was supposed to be in court, but it sounded like Tenner had found him somewhere else. The concern in Janelle's voice turned my paranoia to fear. Was Alec in danger? Was he hurt?

I nearly pounced on Janelle as she came back through the door seconds later.

"What was that?"

Surprise crossed her face for only a moment before she wiped it clear. "Nothing you need to worry about."

"You were talking about Alec. And me."

"You're nosy, you know that?"

I stepped closer. "Is he all right?"

"He's fine. He's in court."

"Don't lie to me, Janelle."

She placed her hands on her hips, beneath her tailored suit jacket, and sized me up.

"I can't talk about this now. I need to leave."

"I'm coming with you."

She laughed. "No, I don't think so."

I grabbed my bag and the purse Marcos had brought. "Just because he's not mine anymore, doesn't mean I don't love him."

Later I'd regret saying that, I was sure. Right now, I just cared about getting to Alec.

"Calm down," she said, her voice becoming more clipped with urgency. "Really. You've just been through something traumatic. You need to take things slow. Find your father. Talk to your doctor. Let me do my job."

"You don't understand."

"I do," she said. "I know how you must be feeling. I'd feel the same in your position. But right now, you need to trust me."

She gave me a firm look, and I rocked back on my heels. She was an FBI agent, she could do things I couldn't. I looked down at my pajama pants and pink flip-flops, clashing with the black sequined clutch in my hand. I was wasting precious time distracting her when she could be helping the man I loved.

"Will you call me when you find him?" I asked.

She nodded, and strode quickly from the room.

I waited five seconds, and then I grabbed a pen from the nightstand and scribbled a note to my father.

FBI needs my help. I have my cell, will call you soon. Love, Anna.

"That ought to piss him right off," I muttered. Then I grabbed my stuff, and headed for the stairs.

Ten

I made it to the lobby without a hitch, and searched frantically for Janelle. A minute ticked by. Then another. My heart rate climbed. Outside, two black taxicabs waited, and I looked past them to the walkway that led to the parking garage. I spotted her there, jogging across the street to the concrete building adjacent to the hospital.

Both cabdrivers were leaning against the sides of their cars and chatting. The first was younger, and hoping this meant he was a faster driver, I waved him down.

"Where to?" he asked.

"Residence Inn in Lakeland," I said.

"All right." He was pleased. The small residential town between Orlando and Tampa was a good fifty miles away, meaning a hell of a fare. "Do you have an address?"

"I don't."

"That's all right, that's all right," he said, all smiles. "I have GPS."

The meter was already ticking.

"I'm in sort of a hurry," I said.

"No problem."

It may not have been a problem, but it still took a long time. Heading out of the city, we hit traffic. I didn't know if Janelle was stuck, too, but either way it was a while before we could pick up speed.

The cabdriver tried to chat with me, but I gave him only monosyllabic answers, and soon he gave up and turned on the radio.

My phone beeped with a text message.

Dad: It strikes me as odd that the FBI couldn't wait until you were discharged.

I winced, and typed a quick response: The world bends to their schedule.

Dad: You ok?

Me: I'm good. Love you.

Dad: Love you.

I tucked my phone away and stared out the window, trying not to imagine what trouble Alec might be in right now. Maxim Stein was confined to house arrest. Reznik was dead. Trevor Marshall and Bobby Calloway were in prison.

But that didn't mean that he was safe.

We pulled into the parking lot of Residence Inn an hour and twelve minutes after I'd gotten into the cab. I prayed this was the right place as I stepped outside into the blazing August sun. Within seconds, my skin dewed with sweat.

Like many of the motels in Florida, the doors to the rooms all exited to the outside of the building, but no one was coming or going. The only movement was behind me at a bus stop, where two women sat on a weather-warped bench, a few feet apart. The sign on the overhang above them advertised a straight shot to Tampa, which made it a fairly appealing option after my hundred and sixty dollar cab fare.

I scanned the parking lot, wishing I'd followed Janelle to see what her car looked like. There were plenty of black, silver, and white rentals; any of them could have easily been a government car. Subtly, I started looking for any clues on the license plates, but realized I looked more than a little sketchy scoping out vehicles in my current attire.

I decided to try the lobby, and asked the desk clerk if anyone matching Alec's description had checked in. Luckily, she seemed not to have heard of him from the trial coverage, and offered me some complimentary hot chocolate in apology.

Perhaps she didn't notice that it was five thousand degrees outside.

At least she verified that there were no other Residence Inns in the area.

Worried that I'd heard Janelle wrong, I tried Alec's cell, but just like when I'd been in the taxi, it cut straight to voice mail.

"Where are you, Alec?" I wondered if this is what he'd felt when he'd been searching for me. Probably worse. I'd been gone for three days.

I walked around the lobby for a few minutes, purse in my small duffle. I smoothed out my hair and tried not to look like a bag lady. Ten different scenarios flashed in front of my mind. Alec handcuffed. Locked in a room. Beaten. I told myself I wasn't crazy—these things had all happened before.

I returned to the woman behind the counter, and maybe I wasn't as polite this time when I asked about Alec, because she told me to leave.

I returned to the parking lot. Twenty minutes passed. I considered knocking on doors.

I was just about to call him again, when a door on the first floor thirty yards away opened, and Janelle stepped outside.

Her hair was down and messy, and her blouse was unbuttoned at the top. She held her rumpled suit jacket over one arm, and dabbed at her lipstick with one finger.

"Don't make me chase you down," came a muffled male voice from inside.

It took a full five seconds to realize what was happening, but when I did, it hit me with the force of a Mack truck.

Alec wasn't in danger. Alec was perfectly fine. He and Janelle had just met up for a quickie in this small-town motel. My head still wasn't right. Maybe the drugs were still in my system. Maybe they'd done permanent damage.

I wanted to disappear.

Which was sort of impossible when wearing candy-cane striped pajama pants.

I thought about ducking behind a car. I considered just turning and running into traffic.

"I have to go," said Janelle. She giggled. I didn't know she was capable of such a sound.

I couldn't turn away.

A man stepped outside wearing nothing but a towel around his waist. His pale back was dripping with water. He was thin, tall. A little lanky, actually.

This was wrong. Alec's skin was darker, his back more muscled. His broad shoulders gave way to a slim waist that cut into his sexy hip bones. I'd memorized his shape; I'd studied it on more than one occasion.

"Seriously, go inside." She laughed. "Someone's going to see you!"

He lunged to smack her on the ass, and when she turned, I got my first good look at his face.

He had dark facial hair and glasses. Any doubt left was erased. That was *definitely* not Alec.

I sagged in relief. But a moment later it was replaced by a white-hot anger. Anger not for me, but on Alec's behalf.

"Oh God," Janelle said. She'd seen me. She was staring straight at me, her face white as a ghost. "Anna."

I was walking toward her. I hadn't meant to. I'd meant to turn around and leave. Find another cab, or catch the bus, *something*. Instead I found myself getting closer and closer, my fists so tight my nails dug into my palms.

"Stop," Janelle told the man. "Go inside. Now."

"Who is that?" he asked, concerned.

"Go inside," she snapped.

He took a step to the side, and then retreated into the motel. He left the door open. I could hear him rustling around.

"What are you doing?" My voice shook. She made Alec happy, that's what she'd told me. And Alec had all but said he loved her the night of the fund-raiser. It didn't matter what I felt for him. Alec had a shot at something good, and Janelle couldn't ruin it.

"Anna, you shouldn't be here."

"*You* shouldn't be here!" My vision compressed. The bag over my shoulder hit the ground with a dull *thunk*.

"I thought he was hurt," I said. "I heard what you said on the phone." I'd been wrong; she hadn't been talking about Alec. He was still at the trial. She'd been talking about someone else. The emotion in her voice had been for him.

"This isn't what you think," she said, raising her arms as if to make sure I couldn't come closer.

I wanted to punch her. How could she be so stupid? She was in the FBI. She was supposed to be intelligent, and trustworthy, and at the very least covert.

She was hurting someone I loved.

"You bitch," I said, between my teeth. "You don't cheat on Alec Flynn. You hold on to him and you never let him go."

Her eyes flickered with regret.

"You weren't supposed to see this," she said.

I scoffed, snatched my bag off the ground, and turned away before I did something really bad. On the road, a bus had just pulled into the station, and the women on the bench were gathering their things.

"Anna, wait," said Janelle. "Let me take you back to the hospital."

The man was outside now; I could hear them arguing behind me.

I kept walking, without looking back. I walked straight onto the bus and paid my fare by credit card. It was heading to Tampa, but at that point I really didn't care if it was heading to Fair-banks, Alaska. I wanted to get as far away from Janelle Jamison as possible.

I sat in a carpet-covered seat in an empty row and stared out the window, my mind churning with what I'd just seen. I felt like I'd been tossed into a washing machine and put on the spin cycle. An hour ago, I'd feared Alec was in danger. I'd thought Janelle had honestly cared for him. And maybe she did, maybe that's why she was so worried that I'd caught her. She thought I was going to tell.

I should have told him.

But the thought of breaking his heart again pressed me back into the Lysol-scented bus seat. He deserved better than her. Better than me, though I never would have betrayed him that way. When we'd been together we'd loved each other fiercely, fought like cats and dogs, and clung to each other when things got tough.

Right up until Amy had been taken.

Amy was okay now, as was Paisley. They were probably with Mike and Chloe. I thought of the picture Paisley had drawn. Their little family.

I wanted that.

I wanted Alec.

I wanted him so badly I could barely breathe. A piece of my-self was missing without him. I wasn't whole.

I barely registered how far we'd come until we pulled into the station in Tampa. I got out with the other riders, who immedi-ately ran to catch their connections, or headed deeper into the city. I followed them, my feet carrying me faster and faster. It felt good to walk after so many days in the hospital, and maybe it was a bad idea to be out here alone, but I needed the fresh air.

I cut across the business district to the Bay, and walked along the path past the cruise ports and the aquarium at Channelside. I kept going when I reached the shops, staying in crowded areas. The sky turned a rosy hue as the sun began its descent below the horizon. My feet began to ache, while my head echoed with the same question.

Amy's safety, or Alec's love.

I needed both.

But I couldn't have both.

Just before dark I ended up outside Alec's apartment building. I didn't know what I was doing here, or if he was even here at all. I didn't know if I could tell him about Janelle, or half the things that were running through my mind. *I love you. I made a mistake. Pick me.* I still hadn't decided if being with him was the right decision after everything that happened. I considered that I'd lost my mind and wondered if people who were certifiably insane still thought they were behaving normally.

Showing up at my old apartment dressed in pajamas and worn-out pink flip-flops after leaving the hospital before a formal discharge and stalking my ex's girlfriend was definitely crazy. It was impulsive, and stupid, and would probably warrant at least two restraining orders.

When it came down to it, I didn't care. I just needed to see him. I needed to say good-bye.

Eleven

entered the familiar lobby of the building where I'd once lived. Everything looked the same—the marble floor, the broad-leafed potted plants, the tinted glass windows. Even the handsome African American man in the beige uniform sitting behind the security desk.

"Anna?" Mike shot up, his face warped in a look somewhere between confusion and shock.

"Hi, Mike." I continued in the direction of the elevators. I pulled my key chain from my purse inside the duffle bag. The shiny silver key to Alec's apartment was still on its own special ring. I hadn't been able to throw it away.

Mike was out from behind the desk like a shot. His hand found my shoulder and forced me to stop.

"What are you doing here?" He lowered his voice as a woman stepped off the elevator. "I thought you were in the hospital."

"They let me go," I said. I looked into his worried gaze and stepped closer. "I'm okay. I just want to see him."

"Don't take this the wrong way," he said. "But you don't look so okay."

I followed his gaze down to my pajama pants.

"It's been a long day," I said, feeling my conviction waver. I planted my feet and held strong, but the truth was my muscles were fatigued and my throat was so dry it was scratchy.

"Let me call someone to cover my shift," he said. "I'll drive you home. Does anyone know you're here?"

"Excuse me." A man trying to herd two toddlers waved at Mike. He looked, if possible, more frazzled than I did. "We're here to see Marie Browning. Do we check in with you?"

Mike's lips pulled thin. "Hold on, okay? Don't go anywhere."

He had to know that wasn't going to work. The second he turned around, I walked to the elevator, still on the bottom floor, and pressed the button for the thirty-fourth floor.

My anxiety rose with each number that flipped by on the screen over the doors. Mike was right. I should have just let him call Amy or my dad to pick me up. Alec might not even be here, and even if he was, he might be here with Janelle. Surely she could have made the trip back to Tampa faster in a car than I could have by bus. The thought of facing both of them together made my stomach turn.

I ran through things I could say to him if he opened the door. *"Hi, I was just in the neighborhood and thought I'd drop by,"* or *"Maybe I forgot to mention this at the hospital, but I'm moving to Kalamazoo,"* or *"Your girlfriend's a cheating bitch and it would be a huge help if you asked her not to file charges against me."*

I was still trying to think of a good reason to be here when the elevator dinged, and I stepped out into the hallway and walked to his door.

For a moment I stood on the threshold. I straightened, and tied my hair back, and took a deep breath. It calmed me, and gave me a chance to harness every last bit of strength I had left. I couldn't control what had happened to me after the fund-raiser, but I could control this. I could move on with my life and start fresh, and then hopefully someday my heart would finally heal.

I knocked.

No one answered.

"Come on," I said quietly. Could absolutely nothing in my life go as planned?

I knocked again, and when there was no sound from inside, I fitted the key into the lock and opened the door. He wasn't home, and since he wasn't answering his phone, I could leave a note. I needed to know that I'd tried to close things up with us, even if he had already moved on.

I added trespassing on private property to my gold star day.

The door hinges squeaked a little as I pushed them open, and I was hit by a wall of warm air. The AC must have been off for a while.

"Hello? Alec?"

No answer.

I stepped inside, looking at the blank walls where I'd once hung up pictures. I cut into the kitchen, and was surprised to find two empty liquor bottles in the sink. There was one on the counter as well, turned over on its side with barely a drop left inside.

It brought back memories of the time I'd cleaned all the booze out of Alec's father's apartment, and that worried me. I hoped Alec hadn't drunk all of this himself.

My fingers trailed over the counter, and my body heated in the way it had the last time he was inside of me. I remembered a time we'd made love here, and against that wall, and on the dining room table. I remembered the way his mouth had lowered over every inch of me, finding that place between my legs that made me forget about everything but the wicked dance of his tongue.

It felt like we'd been happy here just yesterday.

My eyes were drawn to the nook between the dining room and the kitchen, where a shattered frame leaned against the floor. The pieces of glass had been kicked to the side, but not cleaned up, and as I squatted, I saw that it was Alec's college degree. The one I had framed and put up for his homecoming from prison.

What had happened here?

I glanced around the corner into the dining room, worried that I would see the rest of the place vandalized, but there was no other damage. It looked bare though, with only the essentials, as it had the first time I'd spent the night.

I walked to the couch, felt my way over the smooth armrest.

"Anna?"

Alec came crashing through the kitchen, wearing a black suit and that same sky blue tie, slung loosely around his neck. The glass from the broken frame crackled beneath his shoes. Crackled, like the sudden electricity that filled the air. Even now, even as I was preparing to say good-bye, I couldn't deny the pull I felt toward him.

He stopped. His gaze flew over me, as if surprised I was still in one piece. His Adam's apple bobbed as he swallowed. His soft, full lips parted. I could hear the smallest sounds—the rustle of his shirtsleeve against his side, the unevenness in his breath.

I tore my gaze away.

"I'm sorry, I . . ." I still had the keys in my hand and held them up. "I shouldn't have come in. I didn't hear you inside and thought I'd leave a note."

I would have paid my life's savings for some kind of magic wand that would have taken me back to the point just before I stuck my key in the lock.

"What happened? Are you okay?" The concern in his voice made my heart lurch.

He touched my arm. He shouldn't have touched me, because it did more than warm my skin. It warmed the deepest places of me. The places that responded to him even when I was lost, and scared, and wandering. That centered me.

I jerked back.

He leaned closer.

I breathed, and was made dizzy by the dark, rich scent of his skin.

"I'm great," I lied.

"What are you doing here?" he asked quietly. His gaze was too probing; he saw too much of what I wanted to keep hidden. I focused on his collarbone, on the tiny V at the base of his neck. His hands touched the tops of my shoulders and traveled down my arms. I trembled.

I came to tell you good-bye, I wanted to say. I *willed* myself to say. But I couldn't.

Just one tiny kiss. One last kiss.

I leaned forward and pressed my lips against the small inverted triangle on his collarbone. Gently. Softly. Silently.

"Anna." His voice was a broken plea. To stop or continue, I didn't know.

His hands had stopped their descent near my forearms, and I turned my head to the side and kissed his biceps, still covered by the jacket. Briefly, I thought of Janelle, but I refused to let her come between us. Not after catching her with another man.

We were close now, though I was unsure how that had happened, and when he turned his face toward me, the rough stubble on his jaw scraped against my cheek, making the heat rise to my skin. My hands roamed over the tensing muscles of shoulders, up his neck, to bury in his hair. It was silkier than I remembered, and as my hands fisted he gave a soft groan.

The sound tumbled through me, heating all the cold places, fighting back the darkness. Making me want more. His arms drew me tight against him, and as I shifted, and pushed him back against the couch, his breath released in one hard rush. He fell into the seat, and I climbed over him, straddling his hips.

I could feel him then. His hardness beneath my thighs. Too much clothing separated our most intimate places, and in a hurry, I reached between us for his belt to change that.

Just one more time.

"Wait," he said. "You're not . . ."

"I'm not afraid." It was a lie. All the pain and the fear and the need thrashed together inside of me, making my voice quake.

"Maybe I am," he said. And then as I pulled his belt open and unbuttoned his fly, his lips parted and his eyes squeezed shut. His breaths were coming in harsh waves, and I placed one hand on his heart, just to feel it race. He looked up at me, and when I saw the uncertainty in his gaze, I was the one who said *it's okay.*

My fingers brushed against the head of his cock, and he jerked. He grabbed my wrist, but didn't hold tight enough to stop me from reaching deeper. When my hand surrounded him, he grimaced, head falling forward. His open hands circled my back, rising up my spine beneath my shirt and then fanning out over my ribs. I freed him from his slacks, and he gripped the sides of my pants and started to tug them down.

When I helped him, he released the fabric, but held fast to my waist.

"This is wrong," he muttered. His forehead pressed to mine. I could feel his breath on my lips and longed for a kiss he still hadn't given.

I closed my eyes. If he turned me away, if he made this thing that had always been perfect between us ugly, I would rip into a million pieces and there would be nothing left.

"Just one more time," I said, and any argument died in his throat when I rocked against him.

His body tightened. He scooted to the edge of the couch. His arms surrounded me, and his hands moved down my back to my bottom to pull me closer. There was a rush of fabric, and a frenzy of hasty touches. A groan as my fingernails dug into his shoulder. The driving voice in my head: *take him, take him, take him.*

"You want this?" he asked. "We're doing this?"

"Yes," I said.

There were sighs and gasps as he readied me with his fingers, and then my muffled cry against his neck as he lifted me, and worked me down onto him.

It was rushed and desperate. Our rough breaths and the wetness of our skin were the only sounds. I was too weak to ride him so he took control. With his fist in my hair, he held my face against his shoulder and guided my hips with his other hand. We never separated more than absolutely necessary. He stayed inside me. Rocking deeper. Stretching me, and burning me, until every shattered piece unified for one singular goal and we shuddered to a finish in each other's arms.

Less than a minute passed before he pulled out. I gave a weak sound of protest as he slid from my body and tucked himself back in his pants.

"Jesus," he said, pushing back my hair. "Anna, God. I . . . Are you . . ." He pulled me close again, arms trembling. He still hadn't kissed me.

"I'm sorry." His voice trembled. "Christ. Fuck. I'm so sorry. I'm so fucking sorry."

I hated that he was sorry. I didn't think I could ever forgive him for saying those words right then.

"It's over," I said, and I felt the weight of it now, punishing me for what we'd just done.

Twelve

On weak legs, I stood, and pulled down the front of my T-shirt to hide myself as I snagged my pants off the floor. He looked away quickly, either giving me privacy or because he was ashamed, and I made my escape to the easiest place I could: his bedroom.

I locked the door behind me and went straight to the master bathroom, unable to even look at myself in the mirror.

What was that? What had come over me? I hadn't come here for a pity fuck, but that's what he'd given me. He'd told me it was wrong, and then he'd said he was sorry.

That was *not* how I'd wanted him to remember me, nor was it how I wanted to remember him. I felt out of control, more so than when I'd yelled at Janelle, more than when I'd searched for Alec at that hotel, or ridden a bus all the way to Tampa. I was losing it, and it scared the hell out of me.

I splashed water over my face, refusing to let myself remember that this counter once held my makeup, and hair products, and blow-dryer. Quickly, I cleaned up, making myself as presentable as possible, and went back to his bedroom.

Facing him was not going to be my favorite thing in the world.

It was time for a quick retreat; I could gather the broken pieces of my pride later. But because apparently I was the biggest masochist in the known world, I walked to the bed, and touched the comforter.

As my fingers walked over the soft fabric, I remembered the first night I'd slept here. I'd had a nightmare and Alec had held me, and I'd known our time together would inevitably end because I loved him, and he would break my heart.

I moved to the dresser. The top drawer was where I used to keep my things, and I opened it now not to find a collection of tank tops and naughty lingerie, but a large manila envelope.

I don't know why I reached for it. Maybe I thought it was mine, something he'd missed when he'd cleared out this drawer, though I couldn't be certain.

I should have put it back.

I should have walked out of the bedroom, said my final farewell, and gotten the hell out.

The first picture I pulled out caught me by surprise. It was an eight-by-ten of an older man with styled silver hair, embracing a woman in a long black dress on a balcony. The woman's back was to the camera, and you could see a hint of her shoulders beneath the tendrils of wavy black hair. Her head was resting on his shoulder.

The man was Maxim Stein.

The dress was mine.

"Anna?" Alec knocked on the door. There was an urgency in his voice as he rattled the handle. I barely registered it.

A cold dread snaked in my belly as I pulled out the next picture. They were lying on a chaise lounge. Max leaned over the woman. His hand had hiked up the hem of the dress and was gripping her thigh.

"Anna!" *Bang, bang, bang.* "Let me in, okay? Please? We need to talk."

By the third picture I was shaking.

The woman wasn't wearing a dress anymore. She was wearing only a black strapless bra, and she was splayed across Max's naked chest. His mouth was slightly open, his eyes closed. Her long black hair spread over his shoulder, and her leg was hooked over his thigh.

Her profile was clear.

My profile.

My face. My dress. My body.

"Open the door. Please, Anna."

I couldn't let go of the pictures. They warped as I squeezed them in my grasp. This was a terrible trick. I'd never been with Maxim. I'd never touched him and I never would. He was a cold-hearted, manipulative bastard. This was obviously Photoshopped. They'd found a girl with a body like mine, found my same dress, and then transposed my face over hers.

She's been missing for three days.

I was going to throw up.

The roofies. The black spots in my memory.

I could deny it all I wanted, but a grim voice whispered in my ear that this nightmare was real. That I'd been taken from that bar for just this reason. My breath was coming faster now, too fast. My vision was starting to waver, but I couldn't look away from the prints.

The door caved inward with a crash, the feeble lock broken. Alec stood in the threshold, chest rising and falling. He took a quick step toward me, then stopped as I jerked the pictures behind my back. I didn't want him to see them. They needed to be burned immediately. Burned and forgotten.

But this was his apartment. These pictures were here. He'd already seen them.

He held up his hands, palms open.

"Anna," he whispered. "I'm so sorry."

He was sorry. Just like when he'd fucked me.

I blinked. He started to sway. Or maybe I was swaying.

"It isn't me," I said. Was I crying? My face was wet and my throat was thick.

Alec stepped forward, and I crumbled the pictures in my fists.

"Anna. You need to sit down. Please sit down."

I wished he would stop saying my name. Every single time he said it, it was like a hammer to my heart.

"I didn't do this." I needed him to understand this. "The doctor did a test at the hospital. She said nothing had happened to me."

She'd said I'd gotten lucky.

Yeah. This felt *real* lucky.

"I know," he said. But I couldn't tell if he was referring to the test, or my innocence.

"They're fake," I said, even though we both knew it wasn't true. "They're fixed. This is part of some stupid scheme Maxim is playing. He's trying to . . . scare us . . . or screw up the trial . . ." I took a harsh breath. The hot air scraped my throat.

"Slow down." He tried to step closer, but I jolted back, hitting my hip against the dresser. The drawers rattled.

"How long have you known?"

"Anna . . ."

"How long?"

His head tilted forward. "The photos were in my car the morning I left the hospital."

That didn't make sense. I'd seen him on the news.

"But you and Janelle . . ." I shook my head. "I saw you on TV leaving a bed-and-breakfast."

His face was pale.

He'd seen these pictures, and still gone to her bed. He must have gone for her help, that's why he'd done it. That had to be it. But believing this meant the pictures really were real.

Every possibility of truth hurt.

"Does she know?"

His eyes turned to steel. "Nobody knows."

I should have been relieved, but for some reason this scared me more. Why wouldn't he trust Janelle, his FBI agent girlfriend?

Maybe he already knew she was a scumbag.

"Have I been drugged again?" I almost hoped I had been, and this was all some fucked-up trip that would end as soon as the buzz wore off.

"We need to leave," he said. His voice wasn't gentle.

"*We?*" I asked. "You live here."

"I'm staying with a friend. Mike called me when you showed up."

A friend. Right. Janelle. They were probably shacking up together.

"I shouldn't have come."

"You need to come with me," he said, more gently this time. "It's not safe here."

I laughed, a cold, wretched sound that I cut off with a hand over my mouth. *Not safe*, he'd said. Was it safe five minutes ago when we were clinging to each other on the couch? These photos pretty much confirmed that safety in any form was about as plausible as Bigfoot.

"Why didn't you tell me?" I pulled the pictures out in front of me now, but couldn't unfurl my fist. They were crumbled and starting to tear from the pressure. "You say this happened two days ago. These were here, the whole time, while we . . . you and me were . . ."

"Anna, please." Alec took a step closer. His jaw was working back and forth, his eyes desperate. There were beads of sweat on his hairline. His cell phone started buzzing.

I guess that meant it was on now.

He reached for my arm.

"Don't touch me." I gasped for breath, gripping the table. I knew I was hyperventilating. I could feel the oxygen shutting off to my brain. Bright white spots began to flicker in front of my vision.

"Shit," Alec muttered.

A second later I was in his arms, pressed against his chest. My legs were too weak to stand and I gave in to his strength. He hoisted me higher, and his lips pressed against my jaw.

"Breathe," he whispered. "We're going to figure this out later. Right now, I need you to trust me."

I focused on his heartbeat, strong and steady, and I swallowed a rasping breath. My fingers grasped his shirt, and I turned my head to press it against his chest.

Just like Janelle had when they'd left the bed-and-breakfast.

Just like I had with Maxim in the photo.

"No," I tried to push back, but ended up gripping his shirt to stay upright.

With a sharp curse, Alec lifted me in his arms. He carried me to the bed, where I'd first known for certain that I loved him. Where I now curled up in a tight ball on the comforter. I could hear him moving behind me. Not more than thirty seconds later he was back, my duffle bag slung across his chest. I could see the corner of the pictures sticking out of the open zipper.

He lifted me in his strong arms and carried me quickly out the door, down the hall, and to the elevator. My head was spinning as we reached the bottom floor, only when we got out, I didn't recognize the lobby. We were on a different level, one with offices, and a heavy metal door that Alec backed out of into a stairwell. He jogged down the steps, barely jostling me.

"Mike?" Alec called. Out of the corner of my vision I saw a man running toward us. I jerked in Alec's arms, but his grip was solid.

"Alec Flynn! Who is that with you? Is that Anna Rossi? Is she sick?"

"Close your eyes," said Alec through gritted teeth.

"Hey!" I recognized Mike's voice. "Back off! I've already called the police."

I closed my eyes as tightly as I could, feeling the last of my pride strip away, and buried my face in Alec's suit jacket.

"Over here!" shouted a woman. "Mr. Flynn, was your absence from the trial really due to illness?"

Alec kept moving. I could see the bright camera flashes even through my closed eyelids.

"Mr. Flynn! Is it true that you've been paying for Ms. Rossi's drug rehab?"

Drug rehab?

"This is private property," growled Mike.

I'm not sure what he did, but a few moments later a man yelled, "Hey! That was worth more than your life, asshole!"

"Go, *go!*" shouted Mike.

"Thanks," muttered Alec.

Within seconds, I was shoved into the passenger side of a car. I kept my head down when Alec slammed the door. Soon, he was inside. The engine growled to life. His hand on my shoulders pulled me down across his lap, and I rested my cheek on his thigh, gripping his knee as he tore out of the parking garage.

Thirteen

"We're here," Alec said. I wasn't sure how much time had passed. An hour. Maybe a little more. In this unfamiliar SUV, he'd taken turn after turn after we'd left the parking garage, so many my stomach had started to churn with a new sickness. Then he'd gotten on a freeway and I'd heard nothing but the acceleration of the engine.

I never sat up. The camera flashes were still bright in my mind. The words of the reporters—I assumed that was who had cornered us in the garage—kept echoing through my head. *Was your absence from the trial really due to illness? Are you paying for Ms. Rossi's drug rehab?*

Did they know about the pictures?

Did they know I'd been in the hospital?

If they did, soon everyone would know. My father would see the pictures. Jacob and the people I'd met through the CASA program would know I'd been missing. My clients at the salon would surely ask questions, and any grace I had left with Derrick would finally run its course.

The humiliation would never end.

As Alec pulled onto a gravel driveway I finally pushed myself back into my own seat. Echoes of the panic I'd felt in Alec's apartment returned as we drew apart. My throat burned from thirst, my fists ached from squeezing Alec's pant leg. Despite the whirlwind of thoughts in my mind, I'd felt protected with my cheek on his warm thigh and his hand on my shoulder. Now I couldn't even look at him. He'd known about the pictures and hadn't told me.

Alec's phone was buzzing again, and he reached into his pocket.

"It's your dad," he said.

I turned my face the opposite direction. It was dark now, and a few neon lights shone through the foliage, blocking a turn in the road. My head had finally cleared enough to wonder where we were. It looked like we were heading toward a bar of some kind.

I really hoped he knew better than to bring me to a bar right now.

"Ben, hey," said Alec, voice weighed down by fatigue. With everything else that had happened, it didn't even seem odd that my dad was calling Alec, or that Alec had answered like it was a regular thing. Why would it? Nothing else made sense.

"She's with me. Yeah. Yeah, she's . . ." He cleared his throat. "I'm going to keep her with me awhile, all right? She'll be safe."

In the pause, I thought about finding the nearest hole and spending the next twenty or so years there. I should have left town weeks ago. Why had I waited so long? I kept telling myself it was for Jacob, and to make sure Amy and Paisley were all right. Well, Jacob had been with a steady foster family for months now, and was about to be adopted. And Amy and Paisley were doing fine.

I was the one who couldn't move on.

Alec's shoulders rose.

"Fucking vultures," said Alec. "Ignore them. They'll take off once they realize there's no story there."

The reporters must have figured out where I lived. I tried to picture my dad dealing with them, but if they were talking about his little girl, I doubted he could reach a resolution that didn't involve a shotgun.

"She's not feeling great." I felt Alec glance over at me. "I'll have her call you as soon as she can."

He hung up.

"So," I said, as he pulled to a stop against the side of a two-story barnlike building. "You and my dad are pals now, huh?"

Alec shut off the car. In the absence of the engine's rumbling, I could hear piped music coming through speakers nearby. The neon lights were brighter now, but still hidden behind the brush, and to my right was the flat black surface of the Bay.

For a while we sat in the car, listening to the honky-tonk guitar wail, staring straight ahead at nothing. The pictures were in my duffle bag in the backseat, but though I could feel their presence taunting me, I didn't need to look at them again. The images had been seared into my mind.

"Where are we?" I finally asked.

"Mac's restaurant," he said. I remembered the place—a dive where Alec had taken me for burgers on our first date. We must have come at it from a different angle, because I couldn't see the parking lot or the front of the building from here.

"I'm not really hungry," I said.

His thumb tapped against the steering wheel, then relaxed. "He's been letting me stay in the apartment above the kitchen. It's not much, but you'll be safe here."

I'm staying with a friend, he'd said.

Not Janelle. Mac. It shocked me that this simple truth actually made me feel a little better. It seemed impossible that something so trivial could break through the wall of chaos that had surrounded me.

But at the same time my head screamed that this was a really bad idea. Just sharing the car with him was enough to make my heart hurt. Being this close to him, even for a short while, would be torture.

"You don't have to do all this, you know," I said.

His eyes flashed my way, a shock of blue in the reflection of the glowing lights in the dashboard.

"Yes I do," he said.

I sat straighter. There were things I wanted to be to him, but none of them included being a burden.

"I'm not your . . ." I struggled for the word. Problem? Responsibility? I looked away. "Girlfriend."

He tilted his head. Slowly, his hand rose, but his fingertips never reached my cheek. They lingered an inch away, close enough that I could feel the warmth of his hand and start to lean toward his touch.

Yes, staying here was a *very* bad idea.

"That was your decision, not mine," he said, not unkindly. Just as a fact.

I pulled back, and his hand dropped back into his lap. My decision? Maybe breaking up had been, but I hadn't had a choice. Dating him had too much collateral damage. Besides, staying away from me, never even trying to make things work, *dating Janelle*, those things were all on him.

"How did Maxim take those photos?" I asked, focusing on the real problem. "I thought he was on house arrest."

"I don't know."

"Did he give them to anyone else?"

Alec's voice lowered, and took on a dark edge.

"I doubt it." He hesitated. "We don't have to talk about this now."

"You didn't take them to the cops? The FBI?"

I didn't want to have this conversation, but I still needed to know the answers to the questions.

"No."

"Why?"

"He's trying to blackmail me," explained Alec. "He's looking for leverage. If I drop my testimony, he won't leak the photos. He knows I'll do whatever I have to in order to protect you."

The dedication in his voice was solid, as if we were still a couple. Maxim certainly thought we were, if he was trying to use me to hurt Alec. I turned toward him, feeling my brows pull together.

"You're sure that's what's happening?"

"I'm sure."

"Why me?" I asked. "Why not—"

He interrupted me before I could say Janelle's name.

"You know why."

There could have been a dozen reasons, I realized. Because maybe Maxim thought I'd convinced Alec to go to the FBI, or because Maxim wanted to punish Alec and didn't know we'd separated. But the way Alec said it made me wonder if Maxim's information hadn't been wrong at all. That he had hit Alec exactly where it would hurt him the most.

"But . . ." I teetered toward the edge of panic again. "But you went to court today."

Maxim must have realized the threat didn't work. He was going to leak the pictures.

I buried my face in my hands.

He touched my shoulder, gently, then pulled away.

"I just met with the judge," he said. "My lawyer's restructuring things so that I can finish my testimony later. The judge and the prosecutor wanted to . . . make sure I was still on board."

I looked up at him, trying to imagine what that meeting must have been like. They clearly thought he was backing out—either getting cold feet, or lying about what he'd seen.

"And are you still on board?" I asked.

His answer was a one-shouldered shrug.

"You're doing this for me. To protect my privacy."

He breathed in slowly. "Max and I shouldn't be in the same room right now."

The threat was obvious. I pictured Alec's hands around his old boss's throat. The darkest part of me felt a sick sense of satisfaction imagining Alec beating the shit out of him.

"What do we do?" I asked.

He rubbed his hands on his thighs. "Let me worry about that part."

I wasn't sure what that was supposed to mean.

"Someone had to have helped Maxim." He couldn't have done this alone. My mind flashed to a car seat cushion, the image from my dream. Again I tried to focus on the night I'd been taken, but I couldn't remember anything after leaving my apartment.

"I wish I knew what his plan was," I said. "That way we could be ready."

"He's going to . . ." Alec paused, jaw flexing. "My guess is he's going to try to say those pictures were taken before I went to the FBI."

"What? Why?" It didn't make sense for him to admit that we'd been together while I'd been on record as a missing person, and then in the hospital with roofies in my system, but I didn't understand why he'd want to claim we were involved beforehand.

"I'm not sure exactly," said Alec. "It could go a lot of ways. He could be threatening to implicate you as part of the case, or saying that I only turned him in because I'd found out you two were together."

A rage, just under the surface, broke free.

"That's bullshit." My voice cracked. "This is all fucking crazy. You went to the FBI out of spite? Because you were *jealous*? He stole three days of my life and . . ." I couldn't even find the words that described the violation I'd endured. "He did all this to make you look like a vindictive boyfriend?"

The internal lights of the car shut off, hiding Alec's expression.

"Wait," I said, shocked that he wasn't as furious as I was. "You don't believe that, right? You know the pictures are new. I *never* would have slept with him. You know that."

My words faded off at the end. Talking about this felt too intimate. I could feel my skin grow thin as glass, like even in this
darkness he could see all my roiling emotions just beneath the
surface.

"You don't have to explain," said Alec.

I faced him fully, turning in my seat. I grabbed the arm of his
suit jacket. This was deeper than Alec simply thinking I'd been a
bad girlfriend. If he thought I would have touched Maxim Stein,
he didn't know me at all.

"You have to say it," I said. "You have to say you know I
didn't do this willingly."

His teeth clenched, a flash of white in the darkness.

"Alec, please." In that moment, I needed this acknowledgment.
I needed him to believe me. This one thing, I needed to be solid.

"I know it," he snapped, and though his tone had me releasing his arm, I was glad for it. I wanted him to be pissed. "I
fucking know, Anna. Don't ask me to say it out loud. It's taking
everything I've got to stop myself from driving to his house and
ripping his fucking head off."

His fury was so sudden and consuming it filled the entire car.
With a muttered curse, he shoved out the door and slammed it
behind him.

I sat there for another moment, staring out the driver's side window to where he stood outside, silently trying to regain his composure. As ugly as this was, the first breath of relief rolled through
me. Everyone's pity isolated me. But Alec's anger made me feel less
alone.

After a moment, he rounded the hood of the SUV and opened
my door. When I stepped out, a car, nestled against the back of
the windy drive, flashed its lights. The reporters' ambush at the
apartment still fresh in my mind, I turned, and found myself back
against Alec's chest.

"It's all right," he said gruffly. "It's just Matt. The FBI has
him tailing me."

I recalled the freckle-faced man I'd met during my short stay in the safe house, months ago. I turned toward the now dark car, straining my eyes to try to make out his shape. I couldn't, but when Alec offered a short wave, I followed suit. I'd really warmed up to the whole protective detail thing.

I followed him up the dark wooden staircase on the exterior of the building, to a weathered door with a new security box. Alec typed in a code, and I followed him inside, wondering what the hell I was getting myself into.

He leaned down to turn on a small lamp on a wooden end table, and the narrow room was bathed in soft yellow light. On one side was a sliding door that led to a narrow deck overlooking the bar's outdoor seating area. On the other was a small kitchen, with a refrigerator, a microwave, and a stove. The countertop was cluttered with papers and plates. Against one wall were a threadbare couch and a garage-sale metal coffee table with a duct-taped leg, and both were cluttered with papers and half-empty mugs.

"Interesting décor," I said, motioning to the punching bag that hung from one of the exposed wooden support beams near the glass door.

Alec rubbed the back of his neck, grimacing. "It's kind of a mess."

"Kind of," I said.

He gave a short, dry chuckle. "Come on."

He led me to the kitchen, grabbing a handful of plates and dumping them into the sink on his way. On one side was a door that led to a bathroom. The shower seemed newer than the rest of the place, with a glass door and beige tile.

"This place used to be storage for the restaurant. Then it was Mac's booze bunker. He turned it into an apartment a while back after he got sober," said Alec. "All the rooms have been added-on."

That accounted for the strange layout.

Across the kitchen was a small bedroom with a queen bed. The denim comforter, the lack of pillows, and the huge poster of an openmouthed bass hanging over the headboard made me think Mac probably hadn't built this place with a woman in mind.

"Is this all right?" he asked. I turned my head to look at him, hearing the concern in his voice.

"It's very nice. Thanks." I swallowed. "Where will you sleep?"

He turned toward a wicker chair in the corner, where some of his clothes were strewn over the arms. It was odd seeing things so messy—he'd never been that way before. His apartment before I'd lived there had been Spartan, at best. He gathered a couple of shirts and shoved them into a dresser drawer.

"On the couch. Don't worry about me."

I always worry about you, I wanted to say. I thought about the liquor bottles at his apartment. Combined with the mess here, it didn't look like he'd been doing that well. You'd never tell from looking at him, though. His suit was neat, his face showing just a hint of dark stubble. His chocolate brown hair was shoved back in that careless, sexy way. But there was a strain in his eyes, something he was trying to hide by avoiding my gaze.

"Are you okay?" I asked quietly.

He stopped what he was doing, and bowed, just slightly, as if I'd punched him in the gut. I took a step closer. His jaw flexed.

I put my hand on his, feeling the heat of his skin. Feeling the way he was trembling, as if he might combust at any moment.

"Jesus, Anna," he whispered.

The tension coming off of him was blinding, as if I'd flung open the door and was staring straight at the sun. I gave a small gasp, feeling his pain, feeling his fear, feeling an anger so powerful it could destroy us both.

And just like that, he slammed that door shut. He backed up, his hand sliding away from mine. I was speechless.

"The washer's downstairs behind the kitchen," he said. "I'll go get you some towels."

He retreated outside, closing the door behind him. I stepped back into the living room, taking a look around at the mess. No, something was definitely not right here. I thought about what Mike had said about the trial, all the shit they were putting Alec through. The reporters on the news that I'd seen while I was at the hospital, talking about his *questionable past*. A new fury rose up inside of me. I wished they would all leave him the hell alone.

I'd wandered to the couch, and glanced down at the papers that covered one cushion and the coffee table. There were calendar pages, marked with dates of appointments over the last few years. Documents from different aviation companies. Copies of forms with Alec's signatures from the apartment complex, and a restaurant, and another bar Maxim owned.

My eyes were drawn to a piece of scratch paper that said *CASA fund-raiser* in Alec's handwriting. It was circled, with the date just below it. I picked up the paper, chewing my bottom lip. Beneath it were other notes, things that took a moment to figure out.

My work schedule at Rave. Amy and my dad's phone numbers. The name and address of Barrow's, the bar on Himes where I'd been taken. Some of this was from after my abduction, but not all of it. There was a copy of my work schedule from July, almost six weeks ago.

The door opened, and Alec stepped inside, three towels under his arm. He took in the scene before him in stages. First surprise, then concern, then irritation.

"What is all this?" I asked, the papers still in my hands.

He moved closer and set the towels on the arm of the couch. One more step, and I could feel the energy crackling off of him. I felt my weight draw forward, so that I was standing on the balls of my feet.

He took the papers from my hand, and gathered them with the rest of the pile on the coffee table. I watched his throat as he swallowed. He was still wearing that damn blue tie, slung in a loose knot below his open collar.

"Why were you looking for me?" he asked quietly. "Why did you come to the apartment tonight?"

He was standing too close; even through his jacket I could feel the warmth of his body. My eyes focused on his perfect lips, and for a flash I could almost feel them soften against mine.

"I . . ."

His eyes searched mine for truth. I couldn't lie to him.

"I was going to tell you good-bye," I said. "It's time for me to move on."

Fourteen

Unlike the rest of the apartment, the shower was clean, and I drained the hot water tank soaking for a good long while. Nothing in my life made sense. I couldn't reconcile my missing memories to those pictures. If an experience that insane had happened to me, you'd think I would remember *something*. I fantasized about ten different ways to torture Maxim Stein, and then became so frightened by the fact that he'd taken me, *used* me, without me even knowing, that I had to press myself into the corner of the shower stall and remind myself to breathe.

Alec didn't make any sense either. Why did he gather all that information on me? Was it simply because he'd been trying to figure out the details of my abduction? It seemed odd that he would need old work schedules. Or Amy's phone number. Or my father's. I remembered his phone call with my dad in the car. It was as if they'd spoken regularly; Alec had known the number the second it had popped up on his screen, and yet my dad had mentioned nothing about talking to Alec.

I couldn't get a read on his relationship with Janelle. It didn't feel right that they were together, but I'd seen it, and Amy had verified it. Hell, the news was reporting on it, not that that meant anything. I couldn't figure out what was going on with us either. He should have told me about the pictures. He'd known they were in his apartment and still had sex with me, and even though I understood the intensity of our attraction, that didn't sit well.

Making a move on him when I knew he'd been with someone, even if their relationship wasn't exclusive, wasn't my finest move either. Not that I was even capable of regretting it. It seemed I could regret nothing when it came to him.

As the water began to cool, I stepped out into the steam and dried off with a towel Alec had brought from downstairs. I wiped off the mirror and examined my naked body. It looked the same as it had a week ago. There was no sign I'd been manhandled, no sign I'd been hurt.

My body was still my own.

And it was feeling things it shouldn't have been.

I'd been through something traumatic. I should have been recovering. I should have been wearing ten layers of clothes and swearing off intimacy for the rest of my life.

But Alec was behind this door, and somehow, despite everything, he felt safe.

I wrapped the towel around my body and leaned my forehead against the door. He was just beyond in the kitchen; I could hear the clatter of plates in the sink and the groan of the pipes as he turned on the water. He was mad at me, even if I couldn't see him, I could feel it. That was another thing I didn't understand— how he could possibly be angry at me for wanting to leave town after everything that had happened.

I thought of the way his eyes had narrowed when I'd told him I'd come to his apartment to say good-bye. How the papers had crinkled in his grasp. Maybe it was wrong, but I was glad he didn't want me to go.

Taking a deep breath, I opened the door. He turned when he saw me, standing before him with only a thin green towel around my body. I became aware of the droplets of moisture on my skin, and my long, wet hair stretching down my back. I remembered that he'd always liked my hair wet.

His mouth opened, then closed. His gaze got stuck somewhere around my belly, lighting a fire right beneath my skin. He'd taken off his coat, dress shirt, and tie, and was just wearing a white undershirt, untucked from his slacks. Through the thin fabric I could make out the shape of his chest and the hard contours of muscle.

The desire was sharp and demanding, tightening in the base of my stomach and making my breasts so sensitive, I had to wrap one arm over them. But I felt my shoulders hunch, and my brows pull together, because I shouldn't have wanted him, not now, not after this day. I could still see my body draped over Maxim Stein's, and yet it did nothing to dampen the yearning I had for the man before me.

Something was seriously wrong with me.

"You . . ." He shook his head and blinked. "I'm sure you're hungry. There's not much. I can run out if you want . . ."

"I'm not hungry."

His jaw twitched.

"You have to eat," he said. "You're too goddamn skinny."

I forced my chin up. Though I knew he was worried, it still felt like an insult. The space between us seemed suddenly too tight. The energy had changed, layering the tension with something darker.

"I just want some water."

"You need more than water."

My shoulders rose. I stepped forward. "You're right. I could always try a wholesale-sized bottle of whiskey. That seems to work out for you."

His eyes flashed with anger before he turned away.

"Well you're out of luck. I'm all out."

"What a shame. I've been on such a lucky streak, too."

His hands gripped the counter. For the first time I looked around the kitchen. The counters had all been cleared, the dishes washed. The papers on the coffee table and couch were all gone now as well.

His posture sagged, and his hands ran down his stubbled jaw. The anger dissipated, leaving only defeat.

Nothing broke me down faster than Alec's vulnerability.

"I know I can't fix what happened," he said quietly. "And I know you don't have any reason to trust me. But I'm asking you to stay just a little while. I promise I'm going to nail Max to the fucking wall for what he did to you, and I need to know you're safe until I do."

The dedication in his words gave me a small blossom of hope.

"My schedules, and the phone numbers. That's all part of it?"

He nodded. I pictured him poring over those papers. Trying to decide what to do about the photos. Going over my every move trying to figure out what had happened to me when I went missing.

Alec Flynn was a good man.

"I want to be there when you confront him."

He looked at me, gaze reaching straight into my soul.

"I never stopped trusting you," I murmured.

He watched me walk past him, out of the kitchen and into the bedroom, where I closed the door quietly behind me.

Exhausted from the day, I'd fallen asleep quickly, but woke around two a.m. with nightmares of my cheek pressed against the soft leather seat of a car, and a sky filled with black stars. I shoved off the crisp sheets, pulling the hem of one of Alec's T-shirts down my thighs. I'd found it in one of his drawers before going to bed, and hoped he wouldn't mind.

It smelled like him. That was what had relaxed me enough to fall asleep in the first place.

I glanced at my duffle bag, sitting on the wicker chair in the corner. When I'd gotten back to my room the pictures Alec had stuffed inside at his apartment were gone. I didn't know what he'd done with them, and I didn't care. I was just glad I didn't have to look at them again.

A shuffling sound in the other room drew my attention, and I got out of bed and walked to the door, where a dim light peeked out beneath the bottom. I thought about trying to find some pants, but mine were dirty, and the shirt was long, and anyway, it wasn't like he hadn't seen me in a lot less.

It wasn't like his cheating girlfriend/fuckbuddy/*complication* could say anything about it, either.

I cracked open the door, finding Alec in the sexiest pair of worn gray sweatpants I'd ever seen and a thin, blue T-shirt. He sat on the couch, a pen between his teeth, flipping through a spiral notebook, but his gaze shot up when I stepped out of the room.

My hair was probably a wild mess after falling asleep with it wet, and I didn't have a bit of makeup on. Why did he always look so perfect when I looked so average?

He blew out a breath. "Wow."

"Yeah?"

A small smile pulled at his lips, mirroring my own. "Am I making too much noise?"

I shook my head, and crossed my arms. Maybe it was decent enough to show off my legs from the thighs down, but the lack of bra was definitely noticeable.

He set down the notepad and stood, the smile disappearing. "Is everything all right?"

The strain from our last conversation was gone. I approached him, and sat on the opposite side of the couch, trying to stay out of the Alec Flynn brain-scrambling force field. I pulled my knees up beneath the shirt, so that only my toes stuck out.

"Can't sleep."

He sat again. He didn't ask if I wanted to talk about it, but the way he leaned back, arm draped over the back of the couch, like he had all the time in the world, told me to go ahead.

"I've been having this dream since I was taken . . . since Maxim took me . . . where I'm lying in the back of a car." I kept my eyes on my toes. I was in serious need of a pedicure. "It's probably nothing."

He leaned forward, elbows on his knees. "Maybe it's a memory."

I loved him for not pushing me.

"The seat's cool and leather—my cheek is resting on it. I'm not scared when I'm lying there, not until I wake up."

"Are you scared right now?" He didn't move any closer, but his voice was so gentle, I leaned back against the cushion and relaxed.

"No," I said. "This time in the dream I looked up and saw black stars. Weird, right?"

He shrugged. "Any idea what it means?"

"That I've lost my ever loving mind?" I tried to smile.

"Well that's nothing new."

I snorted, and could feel him grin at me, even though I wasn't looking.

"So you have more this time than last time. It might keep building. Give us a little more."

"Us," I repeated. It felt like I had just told him a deep, dark secret, and he was cradling it in the palm of his hand, taking more care of it than I ever could.

"Yeah," he said. "Us."

His gaze lifted to mine and held, making it hard to breathe. I wondered if he could still feel that connection between us, because his eyes lowered to my mouth, and he swallowed.

"I'm starving," he said.

He rose, and walked to the kitchen, where he took a pan from the stove. How long had it been since I'd eaten? Yesterday I'd had lunch at the hospital. Nothing after that. Not that I had much of an appetite.

While he removed a pan from the cabinet, I glanced down at the notebook he'd been looking through. It was a directory filled with black-and-white pictures.

"What's this?" I asked.

"Some stuff for the prosecutor," he answered, opening the refrigerator. "Max sent me to bribe one of the dealmakers in that fuel company. I never knew the name. I'm hoping her face looks familiar. It's been a while. Six years, maybe."

I glanced over the pictures of the smiling men and women, all in suits, all sitting in the exact same position for the company directory. How many of these people had been affected by Maxim Stein's corruption?

"How did you know who to meet?" I asked.

He gave a dry chuckle. "Jessica Rowe set up the appointment. I thought I was paying off one of Max's girlfriends so she wouldn't tell his wife. I didn't realize it was something else until I got there."

I thought of Maxim Stein's secretary, the smooth, cool woman who ran his house, while Alec started mixing something in a bowl.

"Still no word from her?"

Alec scowled. "Nothing."

"Surely someone knows where she went." Even if she was dead, it seemed impossible that no one had found her. "Doesn't she have family? Anyone?"

"Not that she talked about," he said. "Max mentioned she had a kid once, years ago, but there's nothing on paper."

How could a person have no connections? Even I had connections, and I had a pretty convoluted childhood.

"Maybe she had a getaway plan in case things went south," I said. "A hidden shack in the woods or something." Yeah right, I couldn't picture a woman who only wore designer brands strutting through the mud in her five-inch heels.

"More like a villa on the French Riviera," said Alec. "She made three times my salary. Plus bonuses. Always in cash."

My mouth dropped open. "You're kidding. What's a secretary doing making six figures?" Or maybe *who was she doing* was the better question.

"Keeping her mouth shut," Alec surmised. "Jessica worked for him a long time. More than two decades. If she testified against Max, this whole thing would be over."

I couldn't imagine all the things Jessica Rowe had seen in her time with Force. Information like that made you a liability, and with a man like Maxim Stein backed into a corner, there was no telling what he might do.

"Do you think she's still out there?" I asked.

"I've got a guy looking into it," Alec said grimly. "The FBI's reined in their search to focus on the trial."

That seemed like a pretty stupid idea, considering Jessica's testimony could probably give the prosecution a slam dunk.

"A *guy*," I repeated. "We've got a guy, while Maxim's renting out his private jet to fund his defense. That seems more than a little unfair."

Alec's brow rose.

"Mike told me," I explained.

"You should write down a list of things you need," Alec said, changing the subject. "Any food you want, or clothes. Pants, maybe."

I glanced over at him, just in time to see him looking away from my legs, now exposed from beneath my shirt. A wave of self-consciousness had me pulling the hem down over my thighs.

"Sorry," I mumbled. "I should've—"

"I don't mind." He hesitated. "I don't mind a little too much."

I smirked down at my bare thighs and stood. This time when he looked, his gaze stopped at my breasts. I felt the world slow, just as my heartbeat climbed.

I wanted him to look at me. When Alec stared at me like this, I felt powerful. Beautiful. Not like I'd been used as a prop in some fucked-up photo shoot.

Behind him rose a narrow tendril of smoke.

"Something's burning," I said.

He glanced back and swore. The pan clattered as he lifted it off the stove.

My nose scrunched as the smell reached me. I joined him in the kitchen, smirking as he scraped a blackened pancake off the pan into the sink.

"Nice job," I teased.

He shot a glare my way. "I was distracted."

"It's a good thing this shirt isn't any smaller then. You might have burned the whole house down."

"If that shirt was any smaller, you wouldn't have made it halfway out of the bedroom."

He stiffened suddenly, and then bit down on his top lip.

"Forget I said that." He went back to scraping the pan.

I liked flirting with Alec. It made everything feel less serious. So when he took that away, the weight on the center of my chest grew heavy again. I rubbed my knuckles just below my collarbone to ease the pressure.

He put the pan back on the stove, turning his back to me. Part of me wondered if I should return to the bedroom. The other part wanted to wrap my arms around his waist and rest my head between his shoulder blades.

"I missed something," he said.

The statement took me off guard, and it wasn't until a moment later when he looked down at the pan and the bowl filled with batter, that I realized he was talking about the food.

The way he was looking at me made me wonder if he hadn't intended it to mean more, though.

"Cooking spray," I said. "Or butter. That way the batter won't stick."

He nodded, and went to the fridge for a stick of butter. I leaned against the counter while he made pancakes, my stomach rumbling as the smells began to fill the small apartment.

He didn't pull out two plates, just one. But he did put an extra fork on the counter. As he poured syrup over the stack, my mouth watered.

"Ladies first," he offered.

We stood side by side, too far apart to accidentally touch, but too close not to be aware of each other's movements, and ate pancakes at two in the morning. Maybe he thought I wouldn't notice that he only took one bite for every three of mine. Maybe I thought he wouldn't notice the way I stiffened when he reached across for the syrup.

The whole Feed Anna plan had been sneaky, and I was too hungry to object.

When we were done, he left the dishes in the sink, and turned off the lamp on the side table in the living room. Darkness swallowed us, and only the light of the moon outside the sliding glass door lit his silhouette as he moved toward me.

My heart was pounding as he took my hand, and led me into the bedroom.

Fifteen

I was following Alec Flynn into a room with a bed.

The pull was undeniable. I wanted him, and from the looks of it, he wanted me. But things weren't that simple. My feet began to slow, but though my grip on his hand loosened, he didn't let go. He turned to face me.

"Alec, I . . ." I needed a moment to think. I was in a strange place right now. It wasn't just that I'd been through the wringer this past week—he and I had a history. I'd ended our relationship; we'd spent time apart. He might have found someone new, but it didn't look like he was thinking about her now. Had he brought me here thinking this is what would happen? That fucking at his apartment would begin some kind of affair? Why hadn't I considered that when he'd parked the car outside?

Because I trusted him.

"I can almost see the smoke coming out of your ears," he said.

I gave a short laugh, which caught in my throat as his thumb slid along the side of my hand. Warmth blossomed there, and traveled up my arm, making my whole body tingle.

"It's all right," he said quietly. "I'm not going to try anything."

I exhaled slowly, feeling a piece of my anxiety chip away. I wished I could tell him how confused I was by everything I was feeling, but I didn't know where to start.

He moved again, and I followed.

I'd drawn the curtains over the window, but he opened them now, revealing the black night sky. It was different out here, on the opposite side of the Bay. Without the lights from the city, the sky was darker, the moon brighter.

"All white stars," he said.

Another worry slipped away.

He pulled back the blankets. In silence, I climbed in, but he didn't follow. He pulled the covers over me.

Then he lay down on the side of the bed, and rested his head on the pillow, so that he was staring at the ceiling. For a long time I listened to him breathing, aware of every rise and fall of my own chest, and the thickness of the blankets between us.

"I wish I could face him," I said. "Maxim, I mean."

I hadn't meant to bring him up now, but couldn't help but feel his presence, or at least his actions, as much a barrier between Alec and I as the covers on the bed.

"I took flying lessons once," Alec said. "I thought it would help me get over my . . . thing."

Thing. Otherwise known as fear of flying. Apparently men didn't admit to things like that out loud.

"It didn't work," he said. "It only helped me hate it more."

I tried to picture Alec in the cockpit of a plane, and nearly laughed. It was like trying to imagine a fish driving a car.

For a long time we were quiet.

"You can sleep," he said finally. "No one's going to hurt you."

His words made me feel safe, though they weren't necessary. I hadn't been afraid since I'd stepped into this apartment.

The warmth of his presence descended over me. It made my

eyelids heavy and my body relax. The darkness made me brave, and it was in that drowsy place between sleeping and awake that I reached for his hand and pulled it over my body. His chest pressed against my back, and his fingers wove between mine. He adjusted his position to move closer. He nuzzled back my hair with his chin.

I thought he might have kissed my cheek, but maybe I dreamt it.

We slept halfway through the morning, until the beep of Alec's cell in the other room woke me. It was the longest I'd slept in months, and when I rolled onto my back, Alec's arm tightened around my waist.

I smiled. He was still exactly where he'd been when I'd fallen asleep, stretched behind me, with the blankets layered between us. I turned so that I was facing him, my face just inches from his. His eyes were still closed, his hair messy. His perfect lips slightly parted.

There was a certain kind of safety in Alec's arms now, in knowing that I could look at him without him looking back. It felt like a secret in the making; a one-sided confession. With him lost in dreams there would be no expectations.

I couldn't help myself; I traced his bottom lip with my finger.

"Anna," he murmured, and the sound of his voice, husky with sleep, moved me. I inched closer, very much awake now. His hand, now around my back, lowered, and I sighed as his warm skin found the place where the fabric had ridden up.

I swallowed, and froze as he closed the space between us and gently pressed his lips to mine. His fingers spread on my lower back, and his eyelids blinked open.

He sat up fast enough to leave me dizzy.

"Sorry." He rubbed his face. "I didn't mean to fall asleep."

I pulled up to my elbows. It was too late now to pretend I'd been dreaming.

He was facing away, and his hands disappeared in front of him as he adjusted himself. His body wanted me, even if his brain was saying no.

I knew the feeling.

"How'd you sleep?" he asked, still looking away.

"Well," I said. "Really well, actually."

"No dreams?"

I slumped. "No."

"How do you feel?"

"Can you look at me at least?"

After a moment he half turned, and looked over his shoulder.

"I'm fine." I sat up, and pulled my knees to my chest. "You don't have to worry. You didn't do anything wrong."

"Sweetheart, I've done enough wrong things to last a lifetime."

I looked down, hating how coarse his voice had become. "You've done a lot of right things, too."

"But you're not here because of any of them."

He sat up, and strode out before I could answer. I hated that he'd woken with storm clouds over his head when minutes ago I'd felt a peace I hadn't experienced in a long time. Now the force of the previous day shoved me back down against the pillow. Maxim Stein had touched my nearly naked body. He'd shown Alec and I he could do whatever he wanted, and he'd driven the wedge between us even deeper.

I had a sudden urge to see the pictures again, to find something on them that proved they were taken over the last weekend. When I did, I was taking them to the police and the trial wouldn't even matter, because Maxim Stein was going to jail for the rest of his life.

Alec returned to the door of the bedroom a few minutes later, cell phone in hand.

"I have to go out for a while. Are you okay here? I'll ask Matt to stay."

Great. A babysitter.

"Where are you going?"

He gave me a tight smile. "Just some things to do in town. I'll pick up some clothes for you."

"I'll come," I said, sliding out of bed. It would be good to get out for a while.

"That's not a good idea." The way he said it made me pause. When I looked at him, he looked at the ground.

I stood. "You're not going to see Maxim are you? Because if so, you said I . . ."

"I have to meet Janelle."

The air grew brittle. "Oh. Right."

I pictured her standing outside the hotel room, the half-naked man slapping her on the ass. Maybe he was going to end things with her. Or maybe Janelle wanted to meet him so that she could confess.

Or maybe they were doing actual important FBI trial work and not everything was about me.

He went to retrieve some clothes from the drawer.

"You should stay inside. Keep the doors locked. The cable doesn't work, but there's a DVD player and movies. And no phone. There's a prepaid cell in the drawer next to the kitchen sink if you have an emergency."

"Alec . . . I saw Janelle yesterday." It felt sort of snitchy, but I hated the idea of him not knowing what he was walking into.

"I know," he said bluntly. "She told me everything."

"She did?"

"Yes." He waited a moment for me to continue, but I wasn't sure what to say. Alec already knew she was a cheater, unless she'd lied and tried to cover it up.

"Did you tell *her* everything?"

A muscle in his jaw jumped. "I told her enough."

He didn't tell her about the pictures, that had to be what he meant. But whether or not he'd told her about our night in his apartment, I didn't know. Either way, I had the sudden sense that it was time for me to step out of his business.

"Do you want me to stay?" he asked. I couldn't tell if he wanted me to say yes, or give him permission to go.

I wasn't going to beg him to hang out with me. I wasn't that desperate.

I pulled my hair back and wound it into a knot. "I'm fine here. Go do what you need to do."

I think he knew I was lying, but that didn't stop him from getting dressed, or leaving, with only a promise he would be back soon.

I changed into a pair of his boxer shorts and another T-shirt and wandered around the apartment. Any remaining calm had left with Alec, and now that I was alone, I was getting antsy.

The view of the Bay outside the sliding glass door was beautiful. The restaurant was right on the beach, and the water stretched out until it met the shores of Tampa, ten miles away. I could see the high-rises in the distance that marked downtown— Alec's apartment, the courthouse. I could even imagine the roads to Davis Island, where Maxim lived.

Okay, the view wasn't *that* great.

My mind turned back to the pictures. Alec wouldn't have taken them in the car unless he planned on showing Janelle, and he'd made it clear yesterday that he wouldn't chance jeopardizing my privacy. They had to be somewhere around here.

He'd cleaned up the clutter, and the stack of papers on the coffee table were all related to his court case. I looked in the entertainment center, and in the bookshelf near the worn punching bag that hung from the rafters. Nothing.

I returned to the kitchen and opened the cabinets and drawers. No pictures—none of the papers I'd found yesterday that pertained to me either. He'd hidden them.

I didn't like that.

I did find the prepaid cell phone, though. It was in a drawer, right next to a black handgun and a box of ammunition. Apparently Alec wasn't messing around with security anymore.

I turned over the bathroom, but only found a box of cleaning supplies. Completely agitated, I considered calling Alec to ask where they were. But I didn't want to interrupt him and Janelle.

When I first came to live with my mom and my dad, I'd accidentally broken a plate one night clearing the table. I'd gotten a pretty good read on my dad, but I wasn't sure what my new mom would do. Those ten seconds waiting for her to react had been torture, but she'd just smiled, and handed me a broom, and said, "Things break. The good news is you can always clean them up."

There wasn't enough bleach in the world to fix my life right now, but I thought I'd give it a try anyway.

I grabbed the cleaning supplies, and I started scrubbing. I did the floors, and the sinks, and the shower. I dusted every inch. I fluffed the goddamn couch pillows. I cleaned the holy hell out of that apartment.

Time passed, and my brain gradually slowed down. That was when I found the folder, hidden in a cardboard document box beneath the couch. When I opened it, I found the familiar envelope, the edges now bent from when Alec had shoved it in my duffle bag. Beneath it was a stack of folded papers. The schedules and notes I'd seen yesterday were absent; he must have found a really good hiding place for those, or thrown them away.

I focused on the papers. The creases were starting to wear through in some places, and as I opened the first, I recognized my handwriting.

These were the letters I'd written Alec when he'd been in prison.

I wasn't sure why he'd kept them, but as I read over them, the same longing I'd felt during those months he'd been away returned to me. God, I'd missed him. I *still* missed him.

I didn't understand the man who brought me into his home,

who vowed to protect me and kept pieces of our time together, and who left to meet another woman.

Putting the letters down, I opened the folder and reexamined the pictures. I tried to use a critical eye, and think about the kinds of clues my father would have searched for. The pictures were slightly grainy, so it was hard to see any markings on my skin that might indicate a struggle. My face was never shown until the final shot, and even then my eyes were closed.

Maxim looked no different than the last time I'd seen him. His hair was the same length, his figure still trim. The balcony we were on was unfamiliar. It belonged to a hotel of some sort, and was obviously a penthouse or suite based on the size of the landing. The railing was straight iron, a glass barrier blocked the edge, and the wall was made of smooth white stone. A palm tree leaned in from the side. The photo was close enough not to show any of the surrounding area.

It looked like half of the hotels in Florida.

Maxim had done a good job. There was nothing to indicate the date apart from the dress I'd worn earlier to the fund-raiser, but I'd bought that dress on a sale rack years ago. I couldn't prove I'd never worn it before that night.

"Remember," I told myself. I closed my eyes, and focused on the dream. My cheek against the car seat. Black stars.

That was all there was.

A knock came at the door.

I shoved the pictures back in the envelope and jumped up.

Before I walked to the door I put everything back in the box, and shoved it beneath the couch. "Who is it?"

"Matt. I've got a special delivery."

Slowly, I cracked the door, and when I recognized the FBI agent from the safe house, I stepped back to let him in. He was wearing cargo shorts and a polo shirt, and his strawberry blond hair was a little scruffy around the neck. He lingered on the stoop, and handed me the paper bag in his hand.

"Hi," he said. "Smells bleachy in here."

I smiled. He was always the nicest of the agents. "I've sort of been on a tear."

"Got you a burger from downstairs."

I'd lost track of the time, but when I looked at the clock on the stove I saw that it was almost four. Alec had left hours ago.

"Thanks. You can come in if you want." A little company sounded good.

"Hard to watch for bad guys from in there," he said.

I faked another smile. "Thanks for keeping an eye out, and thanks for the burger."

I locked the door behind him, and found myself back in the kitchen. I grabbed the phone, and while I picked at the food, called my dad.

"This is Ben Rossi."

"This is Anna Rossi," I replied.

"There she is," he said. "The one who gives me gray hair."

I smiled sadly. "I'm on Alec's prepaid phone. I just have a couple minutes."

"Sure," he said. "Alec filled me in."

"Did he?"

He hummed thoughtfully. "Good to keep you out of this media circus for a while. You need to rest anyway."

Not exactly the answer I was expecting. Even if he didn't know about the pictures—which I didn't think he did—he was taking this all a little too well. The last time we'd had a real conversation about Alec, my dad hadn't been crazy about his status as a walking tornado.

"It's hard work being such a celebrity." I pulled at the ends of my hair. "Are you really okay with me staying here with Alec?"

He thought about this a moment. "I'm more okay than if you were staying with a serial killer, but less okay than if you were sitting here in the car with me right now."

I thought about how hard all of this must have been for him.

Somehow he and Alec had formed some kind of trust when it came to my safety. I didn't understand it, but it was a relief all the same to know they were getting along.

"That's a pretty wide range," I said.

"Should I not be okay with you staying with Alec?" he asked, his voice thinning.

There was the Ben Rossi I knew and loved.

"No, Dad," I said. "He's been a perfect gentleman." Almost too perfect.

"If he's not . . ."

"He is, Dad. I promise."

He gave a stubborn *humph*.

"You need to stay out of sight, all right? Promise me you'll stay inside. No taking off."

My dad had never made me promise this, even right after I'd come to live with him, when he knew that I had a history of running. He'd always told me I could tell him if I felt like it, and to always remember his phone number, but never that I couldn't escape.

"All right," I said quietly. "I promise."

"Are you okay?" he asked.

The question hung between us. He didn't know about the pictures; if he had, he wouldn't have been so calm. I was glad Alec hadn't told him that.

"I'm fine. What are you doing?"

"Some very important investigating. I'm on a stakeout right now, in fact."

I imagined him in an unmarked rental car, binoculars raised to his eyes as he waited outside some seedy motel.

"Exciting," I said. "Where at?"

I could hear the grunt of a dog in the background. He'd taken Mug. Of course he had.

"The Keys. Your mom and I came here once before we got you. It was *very* romantic."

"Geeze," I muttered. "Spare me the details."

He chuckled, and I couldn't help but feel a little surprised that he'd left town so soon after I'd been in the hospital.

"How's the head?" he asked. "Any clearer?"

"Not really." My frustration was returning. The cleaning hadn't helped.

"Well, I'm checking in regularly with the boys in Tampa and Orlando. I'll let you know if they find anything. Any word from the FBI?"

I'd forgotten my last communication with him had been when I'd left the hospital early to track Janelle to Lakeland.

"Nothing useful." I checked the time, unsure how many minutes were left on the phone. "I should go."

"Call me soon," he said. "And tell Alec if he even looks at you the wrong way, I'll shoot him."

"Got it." I set down the burger. "Love you."

"Love you, too."

I hung up.

I'd thought talking to my dad might help me feel better, but it had just turned the spotlight on all the pieces of my life that weren't working. Alec was with Janelle. My dad was gone. And I had a black spot in my memory that blocked me from sending the biggest asshole in the world to prison.

I went back to the couch and pulled out the box. A break had done nothing, I still couldn't remember what had happened, or figure out where we were. If I knew what hotel it was, then at least I could see if they'd recognized me during check-in. Then I could pin him for the time, and line it up with my abduction.

I hated Maxim Stein. I hated him for what he'd done to Alec, and I despised him for what he'd done to me.

Before I knew it, I was at the punching bag. The first hit made my knuckles crack, and a bright shock of pain shot straight up my wrist into my shoulder. I shook my hand and hit it again. Harder this time, so that the bag swung a little. I tried my left hand, huffing out a breath as the impact bolted through my arm. The chains holding the leather creaked. I hit the bag harder.

The pain felt good. It centered me.

I hit that bag again and again. I kicked it. I pictured Maxim's face in front of my hands. I pictured a night of black stars. I pictured myself, lying in a torn dress outside a Dumpster, weak and confused, and Alec's silhouette in the dark, telling me he was sorry he'd fucked me.

I tore off my shirt when I got too hot, and kept going. Soon the blood pounding through my ears was all I could hear.

A hand came down on my shoulder, and I spun fast, and lifted my hands to block my face. Alec was standing before me, arms raised in surrender, and when the punching bag swung back it bumped me flush against his body.

He didn't move. Didn't back away. He didn't even lower his hands. I could feel his chest moving with each breath, fast, but not nearly fast enough to catch up with mine. Sweat dripped down my hairline and between my breasts, and my bra felt suddenly too constricting as my nipples hardened against the soft fabric.

I watched his eyes darken, saw the surprise change to something more primal.

Need. We both felt it. Too much thinking got in the way, and I was sick and tired of thinking when nothing but this made sense.

My body acted of its own will. I rose on my tiptoes, and reached for his hair, burying my fingers in the silky strands. I pulled him down to me, and kissed him hard. I bit his bottom lip and he growled, and soon his mouth opened and his tongue rasped against mine. He tasted like night itself; frightening but familiar in all the best ways. The kiss deepened, made my blood pump faster. Brought every memory of what that mouth could do to the present. I wanted to feel him everywhere. I wanted him to make me forget.

To hell with the consequences.

Sixteen

I t didn't take long to realize he wasn't touching me. His hands were still out to his sides, though they seemed to be working under different orders, because his body curved down to meet mine, and I could feel his hard length rub against my stomach as he moved.

I reached for his fingers, trying to pull them to my waist, but he broke our kiss, and with a harsh breath, lowered his forehead against mine.

"Slow down, Anna," he said, voice husky. "Think about this."

"No more thinking," I said. "I'm tired of thinking. I just want to feel good."

The desperation was making me tremble. I could feel the last of my control cracking apart. But the pictures were flashing in the back of my mind, images of my body doing things I wasn't aware of. Things against my will. I pushed them aside.

I *had* to push them aside. Maxim had taken three days. I refused to give him any more.

"Close your eyes," Alec said, taking a step back.

His rejection felt like a punch to the gut.

"Goddammit." I tried to turn away, but he caught me by the wrists.

"Close your eyes," he said again.

I did as he asked, with the humiliation just beyond my reach, threatening to swallow me whole.

His fingertips ran up my bare arm, sending goose bumps across my body. I shivered.

"Does that feel good?" he whispered.

I gave a reluctant nod.

His other hand flattened over my bare stomach, and his thumb circled my belly button. His knuckles lowered to the waistline of the boxer shorts I'd taken from his drawer, and then rose to the bottom of my ribs. My body was electric, and each touch shot through me like lightning.

"Does that feel good?"

My gasp was answer enough.

His jaw skimmed mine, and the tip of his nose brushed against my ear. I shuddered, and tilted my head to expose more of my neck. His lips touched my throat, just as his fingers trailed down the slope of my waist.

I tried to wiggle closer. He held me in place with his hands on my hips.

"Slow down," he whispered.

My body was caught in a tug-of-war. Too hot to back away, too cold from his slow pace. I hated his control in the face of my lust. He didn't need this like I did, otherwise we could have already been done by now.

"It's just sex," I said, wishing it was true.

His hands tightened around my hips, then pulled away.

"It was never just sex," he said. "Not even the first time."

Though my eyes stayed closed, I could feel his gaze, heavy and intense, holding me in place.

"I'm making a choice," I said. "You're not taking advantage of me while I'm vulnerable or something like that."

"Like Max did?"

My eyes opened. My jaw locked down. Any success I'd had at pushing the images aside failed, and they came tumbling back.

"Don't do that." I tried to steady my voice, and failed. "This isn't like that. You're nothing like him."

"I know that," he said. "Do you?"

The rage, still so close to the surface, broke through again.

"I wouldn't be here if I didn't." I wouldn't be hiding in this tiny apartment from my friends, and my job, and that monster Maxim Stein.

"Your knuckles tell a different story." I looked down at my hands, now cracked and bleeding. They would hurt like a bitch tomorrow, but for now, they were mostly numb.

Alec tilted his head, so that I was forced to meet his eyes. His navy shirt was wrinkled, untucked from his jeans, and as he rolled his shoulders back I watched the way the buttons across his chest strained.

"If we hadn't stopped, what would happen tomorrow?"

I searched for my top to cover up. Stupid, impulsive move kissing him. Too hotheaded.

"Would you stay in my bed?"

I'd been confused, that was all. Alec and I were finished.

"Would you tell Amy?"

I halted. My weight shifted from one leg to the other. Amy. Paisley. I'd stayed away from Alec because they'd been hurt. What was I doing?

"That's what I thought." Alec's voice was low. "I won't be your mistake, Anna. Not anymore."

I snatched the shirt off the coffee table and jerked it over my head. My body was warm in all the wrong ways now. Embarrassment and shame lit me up like a stoplight.

"Quit acting like I'm throwing myself at you like some kind of whore."

He moved fast, boxing me in against the punching bag. Though he was still an arm's length away, his big body blocked out the light, making me realize how small I was beside him.

"I never said that. I would *never* say that." The anger made his words sharp. His close proximity was making it hard to breathe again.

"No." I shoved him back, the words spilling out before I caught them. "You'd tell me wanting you was wrong. And then apologize for fucking me."

A strangled noise came from his throat.

"For not being a better man. That's what I apologized for." He looked at the ceiling, raked back his hair. "You have no idea how hard it is not to act on every fucking urge that rises up every time I look at you."

His words tripped me up.

"Maybe you should tell Janelle that."

Confusion drew his brows together. His chin lifted.

"Janelle's married."

Well. That was unexpected.

"I thought she told you that when you saw her at the hotel," he said. "She's been married seven years. The long assignments keep her and her husband apart a lot. That's why he came. No one was supposed to see them together."

I could still see her with that stupid smile on her face and her messy hair. She was in love. With her husband.

"You knew she was married?" I asked weakly.

"Of course," he said. Then he laughed. "Jesus. Anna. We were never together. I'm not *that* big of an asshole."

I crossed my arms over my chest, and his grin melted. Part of me had known this all along. Part of me was pissed he hadn't come out with it sooner.

"It was a diversion," he said. "After you and Amy were hurt at the bridge, Janelle stepped in to draw the focus away from the people I care about. Only a handful of people knew about it. Mike nearly kicked my ass when I told him I was seeing someone new."

I'd been targeted by Trevor Marshall because it would hurt Alec. He was trying to avoid a repeat performance. I thought of how Mike and Amy had subtly encouraged me to move on. They'd legitimately thought Alec was dating someone else.

"Your plan didn't work," I said.

Now it was his turn to look away.

"No. It didn't work."

"Then why did you meet with her today?" I asked.

"We're maintaining the front," he said. "We had lunch at a hotel. The press showed up. They're not talking about you if they're talking about Janelle."

It was becoming increasingly more difficult to dislike her the longer he talked.

I pulled my sweat-dampened hair back, trying to make sense of this. Alec had lied to me about Janelle for my protection. They'd never been together. Janelle was still on the case.

One question rose above the rest.

"Why didn't you fight for me?"

A shadow crossed over his face. "What?"

"Why didn't you try to change my mind after that night on the bridge?"

He shoved his hands in the pockets of his jeans and sighed.

"For the same reason you ended it in the first place. Because I'm the worst thing that's ever happened to you."

We stood across from each other, soaking up these truths. The words were out now, the curtains all pushed aside. All that remained was the question of where that left us now.

Neither of us asked it, probably because neither of us knew the answer.

His head fell forward. His shoulders rose as he inhaled, and then, as if he'd made some decision, his gaze lifted, and he shoved back his dark, wavy hair with one hand.

"You want to get out of here?"

"Yes." I didn't care where we went, I just needed some air.

He strode back to the kitchen, where two new bags had been set on the counter. He must have brought them in when I'd been on my kickboxing streak. He rifled through them quickly, and pulled out a smaller paper bag.

"What's that?" I asked.

"A surprise."

Now that my blood had cooled, I could feel the fatigue in my muscles. My shoulders would be sore, not to mention my torn-up hands. I walked tentatively toward him, pausing when he retrieved the gun out of the drawer and tucked it into the back of his waistband beneath his shirt.

"Are we going to stick up a mini-mart?" I asked. "Because if so, I forgot my ski mask at home."

He smirked. "Just a precaution."

I looked down at my outfit—boxer shorts and an undershirt tank top, mostly see-through thanks to the sweat on my skin. My hair was a mess. I would have killed for some lip gloss or even some tinted ChapStick.

"I should change."

"Not for where we're going. Come on."

Where we were going turned out to be the waterfront. Mac's restaurant was doing good business tonight, but we walked the opposite direction from the deck, down to a private beach, where the path was clear, and the music was just a whisper over the waves.

Night had come, and the moon was hidden by wispy gray clouds that stretched across the black sky. The air was tinged with the smell of salt, and a light breeze played with the tips of my hair, cooling off the thick, warm August air.

Matt stayed fifty yards behind us, but after a while disappeared. I think he was still there, but was giving us our privacy.

Alec and I sat on the shore, and slipped off our shoes. He passed the bag to me, and I almost cried when I saw the familiar pink box and plastic fork.

"You got me a cupcake?" The shop was down the street from Alec's apartment. I'd gone there way too much when he'd been in prison.

He smiled. "I got three. I wasn't sure what kind."

"Is there chocolate?"

"They're all chocolate," he said. "Different types of chocolate."

"I have fantasies less satisfying than this moment," I admitted.

He chuckled. "I'm not sure how I feel about that."

He leaned back on his arms, long legs kicked out before him, and I mirrored his position, burying my toes in the sand. The first bite was the perfect mix of German chocolate cupcake and coconut frosting. I moaned, and flopped onto my back, savoring the taste.

When I passed him the bag, he waved it off.

I narrowed my eyes at him, trying not to stare too long at the way the glow of the stars off the water softened the lines of his face, or made his eyes shine even brighter.

"Is this part of the Feed a Starving Anna plan?"

"No." He stared out at the water. "It's part of the Make an Anna Smile plan."

I sat up, touched by his words, and this utterly satisfying gesture.

"It's working."

He glanced over, as if to check, right as I was licking some frosting off my finger. For one long beat he stared at my mouth, before looking away.

I set down the uneaten half of the cupcake on the box before I did something embarrassing, like shove the whole thing in my face.

"Just to be clear on something," I said. "Janelle won't be filing any charges against me for going to that hotel, right?"

He threw back his head and laughed, and I giggled, too, because the sound of it was so contagious.

"No, you're in the clear."

"That's a relief."

After a while he fell quiet. "What made you follow her?"

I clasped my hands, glad that the darkness hid my blush.

"I heard her talking on the phone. I guess I was still messed up from everything. I might still be." I waved my empty hand. "I thought you might be in trouble."

I remembered the fear I'd felt sitting in that cab, willing the traffic to clear so we could get to him faster. It hadn't been a question that I would go to him. I hadn't thought twice about it.

"So you came to rescue me?"

The water was close. I might be able to drown myself before he caught up.

"It was pretty stupid in hindsight," I muttered.

The humor in his voice was gone when he spoke again.

"No one's ever taken up for me like you."

A wave reached our feet, but neither of us moved. The water was only slightly cooler than the outside temperature. Our hands were close, and I hooked my pinky around his. It was the only place we touched, but it felt like a lifeline.

"When all this is over, where will you go?" he asked quietly.

The hollow feeling returned, reminding me how empty I could feel inside. A week ago I'd felt it when I thought about staying. Now it returned at the prospect of saying good-bye.

I stood up, and walked toward the water. A soft wave hit my feet and pulled me down, the wet sand squishing between my toes. The darkness protected me, and the starlight made my skin glow, and with the breeze moving my hair and tickling the back of my neck, I knew what I needed to do.

I waded deeper.

The sand compressed behind me as Alec rose.

Deeper.

I could hear him coming toward me.

The water hit my knees. My thighs. It wet the bottoms of the boxer shorts, and brought a sharp intake of breath as it rose between my legs. I took off my shirt and threw it back behind me.

I dove, just as Alec called my name. The saltwater washed over me, dragging through my hair, making me clean. I stayed down until my lungs burned, and Alec's slippery hands gripped my bare ankle.

And then I rose, and wrapped my arms around him, soaking any part of him that wasn't already wet. I held on as we rocked side to side in the waves, as he gripped me hard against his chest and buried his face in my neck.

I was his anchor, and he was mine.

Seventeen

His cock filled me with one, slow, deep stroke. My legs wrapped around his hips as he began to work me, harder and faster, the pressure rubbing all the right places as he lifted my hips and pumped downward. His eyes stayed on mine, even as the dark strands of his hair fell forward.

The throbbing between my legs stole my focus, tore my thoughts away from everything but the slick, heavy feel of him inside of me. Heat raced through my body. Coils of lust twisted tighter and tighter, until I thought I would burst. I was close. So close.

I groaned his name, begging for the release only he could give me. And woke.

The breath raked my throat. My body was damp, trembling, flushed with need. I ran my hands over the sheets, wishing that this wasn't real, that he was still inside of me. I could still feel him there, thrusting in and out. My thighs were wet with what he had done to me.

The bed was empty. *I* was empty.

My tongue rubbed against the roof of my mouth, remembering the taste of him from earlier. Spicy and dark. Demanding. I hungered for it now. I wanted more than that. I wanted to lick the head of his cock and draw him deep into my mouth. I wanted him to fist my hair and lose control.

I was so hot I was going to explode.

My hand slid down my stomach, over the thin fabric of the tank top Alec had picked up at the store on his way home. Where was he? I'd fallen asleep in his arms but now he was gone.

I couldn't wait. I kicked off the sheets, and reached lower, beneath my panties, to where I was hot and swollen and *needing*.

I gasped as my fingers found my clit. I didn't waste time; I needed to get off. My fingers circled and pressed, following the exact motions I knew would give me what I needed. It wasn't as good as Alec's touch, but even so he was there in my mind. Saying my name. Saying how good I felt around his dick. Grabbing my hips to thrust harder.

Telling me he loved me. Only me.

"Alec," I moaned into the pillow.

The wicker chair in the corner creaked.

I bolted upright, heart in my throat. Digging in with my heels, I shoved my body back into the bedframe and jerked the covers up to my neck.

Alec stood, his shape barely discernible in the dark room, and in three steps he was standing beside the bed.

"Keep going." A barely controlled demand.

Slowly, I lowered the blankets. I slid down again so I was lying on my back, looking up at him. His eyes glinted in the reflection of the moon through the open window, but the rest of his expression was hidden by shadows.

I was falling, gaining momentum with each second that passed. We weren't even touching, both fighting for a control that was slipping through our fingers.

"Show me what you need," he said. "I won't get in the way."

Nerves made my moves jerky, but any shame or disappointment was burned away by the recognition of what was happening. He wanted to watch me come.

I wasn't the weak party favor Maxim Stein had tried to make me. I wasn't scared, or hurt, or embarrassed. I was on fire. I was sexy as hell. And this gorgeous, protective man wanted me.

My fingers slipped beneath my panties again, but before I could go further, he gave a throaty growl.

"Take them off."

I hooked my thumbs in the sides, lifted my ass, and shimmied out of them. He breathed in sharply.

"Fuck," he muttered. "Look at you."

A silent competition was building. Who would break first. Who would give in and finish what we'd started in the apartment. He denied me his touch, and I defied him with temptation, laying myself out before him like a feast. Challenging him to keep his hands to himself.

There was a muffled sound of moving clothing, and then the bedframe creaked as he gripped it.

"Touch yourself," he said, voice strained.

I wanted to be graceful and seductive, but there was too much desire surging through me. My knees parted, and my hand slipped lower.

"Tell me what it feels like," he said.

I closed my eyes. I wished he would feel for himself, but there was something incredible erotic about knowing he got off on watching me give myself pleasure.

"Slippery," I said. "Hot. I'm so wet."

"Spread your legs wider."

I opened my knees as far as I could. I doubted he could see much, but he could surely hear the rhythmic movement of my hand against my slick skin. My breath came faster.

"Do you like that?" I asked. I wanted his dirty words.

"It kills me," he whispered. "It fucking *destroys* me."

A brushing sound reached my ears. His hand was sliding over his cock, still trapped within his pants. I had him now. I was winning. Victory mingled with desire, and made the strokes of my hand heavier.

But as much as I wanted him to give in, I found myself afraid of taking the next step. What had happened at his apartment had been desperate, but this was something else. Loving Alec Flynn was dangerous, and if he touched me now there would be no turning back.

"You're close," he said. "I can hear it. *Fuck*. Pinch your nipples."

I reached beneath the thin fabric of my tank top, and found the peaks already hard and hypersensitive. A breathy shudder raked through me as the surge of pleasure slammed into my cunt. He knew what I needed even without touching me.

"Was I fucking you?" he whispered.

I could feel his breath on my bare hip. The knowledge that his mouth was so close to my center catapulted me to a new level of desire. If I moved my leg, I would straddle his face.

If he wanted that, he would have to take it himself.

"It wasn't gentle, was it? Not the way you were moaning in your sleep."

I didn't want to come yet, but I couldn't slow down.

"Do you remember how it feels when I'm inside you?"

"Alec," I whimpered. "Alec, please."

He groaned. The bedframe creaked. My back arched as every muscle in my body pulled taut. He moved again, and I readied myself for him to touch me, or kiss me, or fill me with his huge cock. But my body couldn't wait for him to catch up. My mind was spinning, barely registering the groan of the wooden door in the background. Then the pleasure spilled over, in a shock of bright colors that made me cry out in relief.

I came down too fast, not the way I would have if he'd been inside me. My own hand was efficient, but couldn't give me the kind of touch that left me reeling.

It only took a few seconds to realize I was alone.

I sat up, looking around the small room, hoping that this was a mistake. It was dark, maybe the shadows had played tricks on me. He wasn't beside me though, and he wasn't in the wicker chair.

The door was closed. He'd seen me vulnerable, *made* me vulnerable, and then left.

I pulled my knees into my chest, trying to listen for him over the thundering of my heart. The door creaked again, as if something pushed against it. The wooden floor creaked beneath his bare feet.

And then I heard the muffled thud of his fist striking the punching bag.

I lay back in bed, listening to him hit it again and again, the sound reviving the hurt in my own knuckles.

He didn't stop for a long time, and even when he finally did, he didn't come back to my bed.

After a fitful night of sleep, I woke to a silent apartment. Wrapping a blanket around my shoulders, I wandered out to the main room to find Alec standing outside the sliding glass door on the balcony. In just his jeans, he was leaning over the railing, staring out into the water. The curve of his naked back rose with slow breaths, and my gaze paused on the scar on the bottom of his ribs, a light pink line against his tan skin. My heart gave a little lurch. He'd gotten that in prison—the attack that would lead him to spend his remaining months in solitary.

My eyes lowered to the band of his jeans, and his perfect ass. Down his long legs to the frayed hems that met his bare heels. He could have been a model in some travel ad. Or a movie star, shooting the satisfied, peaceful scene just after an incredible night of passion with his lover.

But the reality was he was probably thinking about what a huge mistake he'd made, and how he was going to break the news to me.

I wrapped the blanket tighter around my shoulders, my grip reminding me of my now bruised knuckles. After he'd left me, I'd been embarrassed. I'd exposed too much—not just my body, but my soul. Gradually, my shame had warped into irritation, and by the time I'd crawled out of bed, I was pissed. He'd been flirting with me, I hadn't made that up. And he wasn't doing me any favors by reeling things in every time someone turned up the heat.

I'd considered that he was trying to be a gentleman. But every time I asked myself why I came back to the same point. He thought I was damaged, and either he was afraid of breaking me more, or it had changed his ability to see me as the sexy woman he'd once loved.

And that *really* pissed me off.

As if he'd heard my thoughts, he turned and met my eyes across the room. There was longing in them, unmistakable desire, and I turned away before he could pull me under his spell.

I went to the kitchen to make some coffee. He'd stocked up on that, at least.

A few moments later he approached behind me.

"Anna, listen . . ."

I gave him the cold shoulder. "Coffee?"

"No." He hesitated. "Thanks."

Awkwardness prickled between us.

He leaned back against the counter. I could see him in the corner of my eye, his strong chest tipping forward. His perfect abs rippling like a flipping Bowflex commercial.

"If I hadn't left then, I wouldn't have stopped."

Even if I had had my reservations about going further, I hadn't voiced them. The fact that sex with me was something he wanted to avoid for any reason felt like a kick to the gut.

"Well, it's a good thing you did then," I said.

The coffeemaker hissed, then started to bubble.

"I slipped up last night," he said. "I'm trying . . . I need to go slow."

"For me or for you?" I asked quietly.

His jaw flexed. His thumb began tapping on his thigh. There were things he wanted to say, that much was obvious, but nothing came out.

"I need that, too," I said, feeling exposed again, just like last night. A long moment passed.

"I've arranged for someone to come by later. I have to meet Janelle today. I won't be back for a while." He cleared his throat. "Not until tomorrow actually."

That same anger that had been just under the surface since I'd woken in Orlando punched through again, and I laughed coldly. "Slumber party. Sounds fun."

He grabbed my arm, forcing me to look up at him. "It's not real. You know that."

I shook free, the blanket falling off my shoulders and pooling around my feet. The thin red tank top and striped pink panties were all I had on, but I didn't care, even when his gaze lowered and his eyes narrowed.

"It wouldn't matter if it was," I said, pushing him back. "I've got no claim on you. You're not mine. Anyway, as we both saw last night, I can take care of myself."

His eyes flashed, lighting on the open sea. I hated that I was raging at him, but I was just so sick of being mad and needed a place to put it all. I spun away, searching for a mug to busy my hands with. I opened the cabinet above the coffeemaker, but they were on the top shelf. Another interior-decorations-by-man move.

I stretched up to my tiptoes and reached, but fell just short of grabbing the nearest ceramic handle. He drew closer, my pulse beating faster with every step. Soon he was behind me, his hard body pressing against mine. His hand rose up my side, bringing a hitch to my breath as he skimmed the side of my breast. Immediately my nipples hardened, just the slightest tease pulling everything within me taut. I jerked into the counter, feeling the ledge against my stomach, just as his hard body pressed against me from behind.

"You don't need me," he said.

I shook my head.

His other hand started on my bare hip and rose. His thumb slid under the side of my panties and twisted the fabric around his finger, pulling it tight against my center. Another twist, and the discomfort bordered on pain, but still made me squirm for more.

"You don't need anyone," he said.

He dipped lower, and his hips rocked against my ass. The pressure of his hard cock had me leaning forward, which gave him the opportunity to do it again. I bit my lip when a hoarse moan snuck out, and grabbed the counter, because my legs had gone weak.

"You can take care of yourself," he murmured.

I barely nodded, too focused on the shock of his knee parting my thighs.

"Well that's a goddamn shame for me," he said.

I blinked, trying to clear my head. He was turning the tables on me again. It was like a game to him. I was always right where he wanted.

"You're right," I said, and slipped to the side. The blanket was still on the kitchen floor, and I bent to pick it up, giving him a full view of my pink-pantied ass. If he thought he was the only one with the power, he had another thing coming.

I rose slowly, feeling his scalding gaze on my back, then turned to meet his gaze.

"I'm stronger than you give me credit for," I told him.

He looked at me for one long beat, watching as I hid my body beneath the blanket.

"No," he said. "You're stronger than you give yourself credit for. I've never doubted you."

He walked to the living room and grabbed a shirt off the arm of the couch. He shrugged into it, a scowl on his face, and then stalked back toward me, growing bigger somehow, as if his energy had broken free from his body and was filling the room. I held my ground, even as his fingers trailed down my arms to my wrists, and then pulled my hands to his chest. His skin was hot, smooth, like satin over iron.

He lifted one of my hands to his mouth and kissed my bruised knuckles, never taking his eyes off mine. His tongue raked slowly across the ridges, and then he blew lightly on the swollen skin. I gasped. It was then that I saw the matching bruises on his hands. Small scabs had already risen there. He'd hurt himself when he'd attacked the bag last night.

"Tell yourself whatever you need to," he said. "That you don't need me. That I'm not yours. But I told you that you'd be safe here, and I meant it. I'm not going to hurt you again."

With that, he left, leaving me leaning against the refrigerator with my heart thudding in my chest.

Eighteen

Just after noon there was a knock at the door. I'd forgotten Alec had said someone would be coming by. I figured it was Matt, bringing by lunch again, but when I opened the door I was surprised to find he wasn't alone.

"Special delivery," he said, stepping aside to reveal a platinum blond pixie in suspenders and black skinny jeans.

"Amy!" I didn't even have time to step out before Amy collided into me, arms so tight around my ribs I actually coughed.

"Alec put her on your approved visitors list," Matt said. "Sorry I didn't check with you earlier."

"No, it's fine," I wheezed, finally dislodging Amy, who went back outside to grab her rolling suitcase. She jerked it over the doorframe and into the apartment.

"Thanks," I told Matt as he descended down the stairs. I locked the door behind him, and beamed at my best friend. "How did you . . ."

"Alec," she answered. "He called a couple days ago and said you needed a pick-me-up."

"He did?" I chewed on my thumbnail. She looked me over, head to toe, touching my arms, patting my hair, as if to make sure I wasn't about to fall apart. When she'd finished her inspection she hugged me again.

"I would have come earlier, but I had to get a background check," she said. "The FBI fingerprinted me and everything. And then Alec made me leave my car at the port authority when he picked me up."

"Alec met you this morning?" I asked, as she pulled away. I checked the clock. He'd left over two hours ago.

"He brought me here," she said. "After a scenic detour to make sure we weren't followed. I'd call him paranoid, but I think that only applies if someone hasn't already tried to kill you."

"You and Alec were alone in a car." They'd been together at the hospital, but those circumstances had been different. I couldn't imagine them being friendly after everything that had gone down three months ago on the bridge.

"He said you needed me." It was that black-and-white for her, and I loved her for it.

She lifted her bag with her deceivingly slim arms and dropped it on the couch. "He said he had to run, otherwise he would have come in and said hi."

I felt my lips purse. He did have to run. He and Janelle had a supposedly fake sleepover.

"Which," she added, "makes me think you guys are fighting. Which makes me think that's the reason why he called in the reinforcements."

One brow was quirked up beneath her bangs when she looked over.

"We're not exactly fighting," I mumbled. Was that why Alec had called her? To pawn me off on someone else?

I motioned to her bag. "Are you spending the night?"

"Sadly, no." she said with a pout. "That's just my day bag.

Paisley's at Hot Mike's with Chloe and Iris, and I said I'd be back before bedtime."

I'd forgotten that Amy and Paisley had been staying with Mike and his mom since my disappearance.

"Ah," I said. "How's *that* going?"

She flopped onto the couch beside her bag. "If you mean, have we had hot sweaty sex yet, the answer is no."

"How about a hot sweaty kiss?"

She bit her thumbnail. "He may or may not have kissed me."

I squealed, and a moment later she squealed, and then melted onto the wooden floor dramatically. I bent over her, fists on my hips while she stared wistfully at the ceiling.

"Spill it," I said. "Now. Details. All of them."

She sat up. "Okay, but after you have to fill me in on everything— why all the secrecy, and why you're staying here, and why Mike said you showed up at Alec's wearing your pj's and then got mobbed by reporters. I'm sure that's all super important and every-thing, but honestly, it's probably not as mind-blowing as the fact that Mike grabbed my boob."

"*What?*" I sat on the floor beside her as she wriggled even more. Her joy made me feel light. I hadn't seen her this giddy in years.

"He played it off like it was an accident, but you know he was trying to cop a feel."

"Amy!" I covered my eyes. "Start from the beginning."

She sat up, sitting cross-legged just like me. "So we were doing dishes after the girls went to sleep, and I was drying a bowl and he reached for the soap and was like, 'Oops.' Totally elbowed me in the boob."

"That doesn't count."

"It absolutely counts," she argued. "I'm not Triple D Anna Rossi. I've barely got mosquito bites. You have to go out of your way to get to them." She stuck out her chest to make a point.

"Mine are Cs, thank you very much," I said. "And a boob grab only qualifies as a boob grab if he doesn't say 'oops' afterward."

She scrunched her lips to one side. "Point taken. But he did kiss me."

"When?"

"After we left the hospital. That night. We'd put the girls down and he was showing me my room, which was actually *his* room because Iris is sleeping in the guest room in his cute little house. Anyway, I was arguing with him that it was fine that I sleep on the sofa and he was arguing that it wasn't going to happen, and then I said something about not wanting to impose and he called me stubborn and then *bam*. Kissed me."

She'd been motioning with her hands, but when she stopped, they fell on her stomach, and she got that faraway look again.

"Was it good?" I asked.

"Anna." She put her hand on my arm. "I would give up ice cream if it meant he would do it again."

"Wow," I said. "What happened after that?"

She winced. "After that I told him I thought I heard the girls in the hallway and sort of made a mad dash into the closet. I thought it was the bedroom door. I was a little disoriented."

I clapped a hand over my mouth. "Oh. That's not good."

"I'm well aware," she said, with a frown. "He hasn't tried anything since."

I put my hand on hers. "I'm sure he's still interested."

She shrugged. "It's all right if he isn't. That kiss was worth it. I wouldn't know what to do next anyway."

God, she made me so sad sometimes. She honestly believed she wouldn't get a happily ever after.

"Based on the fact that you have a child, I'm pretty sure you have some idea of what comes next."

She kicked out her legs. "It's been a while since I've gone there. Like, an embarrassing amount of time."

"How long is embarrassing?"

"A few months," she said with a cough. "Or a year. Or two."

My eyes widened. "Not since Danny?"

She crossed herself, as she always did when her ex's name was mentioned.

"It's not like I haven't been busy," she said defensively. "I've got a kid."

She was still lying on her back, and I lay down beside her, staring at the exposed beams in the ceiling. Doing the math wasn't hard. Her divorce had gone through around the time I'd moved to Tampa, less than a year ago. Which meant that she and Danny had still been married awhile without any intimacy. I wondered just how long things had been bad between them, or if they'd ever actually been good.

"Maybe Mike's trying to go slow."

Alec's voice filled my mind. *We need to take this slow.*

If that was what Mike was doing, I hoped Amy's experience was half as frustrating as mine.

Amy laughed dryly. "Did you know before he left, my ex told me part of the reason he didn't love me anymore was because I wasn't as attractive as I used to be. What a dick, right?"

I hated that guy.

"Total dick," I agreed.

"Right." She hesitated. "So is it true?"

I sat back up. "Are you kidding?"

"Scratch that." She kicked off her silver ballet slippers. "I came here to take care of you and instead I'm turning it into the Amy Show. Sorry."

"It's most definitely *not* true," I said. "It's nowhere near true. I've known you since we were thirteen, and you've never been hotter."

"Honestly?"

"I swear."

She frowned. "Then why hasn't he carried me off to bed, caveman style, and fucked my brains out? Is it the mom thing? Do you think he's freaked out by stretch marks? Because mine are almost all faded. Well, except this one on my—"

"No," I said. "*No*. You don't see the way he looks at you. He's probably waiting for you to make the next move."

She considered this.

"So what am I supposed to do?"

I felt my shoulders hunch.

"I'm probably the wrong person to ask right now."

She sat up and scooted back against the couch.

"Is it hard being here with him?" she asked, her voice softer now. "On the way over he was pretty tight-lipped about it. Where was he going anyway?"

I focused my gaze on my feet.

"Overnight with Janelle."

"God," she sputtered. "He's got the nerve to shove that in your face? I thought *my* ex was bad."

Amy still thought Janelle and he were dating. Mike did, too, according to Alec. I looked at my friend, seeing the rage flash up in her green eyes, and wanted to tell her everything. About Janelle, and the pictures, and how it was breaking my heart that Alec didn't need my touch as much as I needed his.

But I couldn't tell her everything yet. The more she knew, the more potential danger we were all in. I couldn't risk her life again. It was bad enough that she was here with me at all.

"It's complicated," I said. "But he's not a bad guy."

She sighed. "Yeah. I know he's not." She squeezed my hand. "If it's any consolation, he's still in love with you."

The butterflies in my stomach woke up in a hurry to flutter their wings.

"What makes you say that?"

"Well, for starters how nice he's been to us. The security system at the apartment, offering to pay for therapy. And then, okay, this may be totally unrelated . . ." She leaned forward. "I

got a check in the mail while you were . . . missing. From my ex.
For *child support*."

This came as a shock. Danny hadn't paid her a cent since he'd
signed the divorce papers and skipped town. I didn't even think
she knew where he lived.

"Really?" I asked.

"Back pay included," she said. "It's enough for the down payment on a house. Not a huge house, but still."

I knew Amy had wanted a house. Somewhere that had a yard
where she could put up a swing set for Paisley. I beamed at her,
but my smile faded.

"You think Alec has something to do with it?" I asked.

"I don't know," she said. "I probably don't want to know. Either way, I couldn't bring myself to ask him about it today. Felt
like I would jinx it or something."

I remembered the picnic at the beginning of summer when it
had been revealed that Amy's ex-husband had hit her. Alec has
casually asked for his name, and though I hadn't given it, he'd
seemed convinced he could find it anyway.

I felt a surge of affection for him, feeling, like Amy did, that
Alec's good will and the timing of this check were oddly coinci-
dental.

"He's a good man," I said. "That doesn't mean he still loves me."

She stood and walked to the punching bag, giving it a firm
enough push that the chain creaked as it swung in a slow pen-
dulum.

"When you were missing he refused to rest until you were
found," she said. "He and your dad practically headed the Find
Anna Task Force. Mike said he took the breakup hard, too. Drinking a lot, refusing to see anybody. Well, anybody until Janelle."

She glanced over her shoulder at me, as if searching for some
response, and I tore my thoughts away from the empty bottles
I'd seen in his apartment. When I said nothing, she continued.

"Plus, Mike told me he's been getting death threats. He kept telling the FBI to keep an eye on you, but they didn't have proof you'd be involved. I guess he thought they'd use you to hurt him."

Hence Janelle becoming his fake public girlfriend. There was a tightness growing in my chest, but I didn't want her to stop. Alec was receiving death threats? From Maxim? I wanted to pull him right out of his Davis Island fortress and kick his ass. Just like I wanted to kick Alec's ass, and Amy's, too, for not telling me.

"Alec thinks your disappearance is connected to the trial. When the FBI wouldn't put you back in protective custody, he asked us to look out for you."

I remembered the papers that had been sitting out on the coffee table when I'd first arrived here. My work schedule. Amy's and my father's phone numbers. Even Marcos had said Alec had called him and asked that he look out for me. I thought of all the dinner invitations from Mike and Amy, and my dad staying on my couch, and how I'd barely had a second alone up until the night of the fund-raiser.

"He asked you to babysit me?" Everything was becoming clear now. Alec had been there the whole time, watching me from a distance.

"Well, it wasn't like he had to twist our arms," she said. "Your dad and I would have done it anyway."

"My dad was in on this."

My mind shifted to the phone calls he'd gotten from Terry Benitez. Had they actually been from Alec? My father should have been trying to convince me to head for the hills, but instead he'd left me in the care of the one man he'd once held completely responsible for the danger I'd been put in.

Amy nodded. "He asked your dad to look into the death threats in case there was a connection to you. Something separate from the FBI."

His PI work. Was he in the Keys now looking into something for Alec?

Annoyance had me rising to my feet. "Why didn't you guys tell me?"

"Alec didn't . . ." She scrunched her tiny nose. "Alec wanted to respect your decision. He was trying to give you space, I think."

"While asking everyone else to smother me?"

"Hey," said Amy firmly. "We smother you because we want to smother you." She paused. "Look, I'm not trying to say Alec's a prince or anything. You know I have my reservations."

"Uh-huh."

"But he blames himself for everything. If it comes back that this happened to you because of him, he's never going to forgive himself. Which maybe he shouldn't. I haven't quite made up my mind about that yet." Her brows pulled inward.

It had come back that this was linked to him. The pictures were proof. Maxim Stein was blackmailing Alec, and using me to do it.

And Alec hated himself because of it.

"I never thought you'd be the one standing up for him," I said.

She flipped open the suitcase. "Well. You love him. And I love you. And he loves you. And I probably love his best friend. So it's all just one big love cluster fuck, and I figure if I don't get on board now I'll miss out on the best and worst thing that's ever happened to any of us."

After I untangled *that*, I laughed, and sniffled, and hugged her again.

"Loving him hurt you," I said. "Loving him hurt me."

"Loving you hurt him, too," she said. "But I doubt he'd say you weren't worth it."

I wouldn't say he wasn't worth it either.

She patted my arm.

"Now," she said. "Don't take this the wrong way, but you look like crap."

She flipped back the lid of her suitcase, revealing the case that held her scissors from the salon, a blow-dryer, nail polish, clothes, and a fishing tackle box filled with makeup.

"Let's fix you up, okay?"

Nineteen

Sunset found me sitting on the edge of the bed, clutching the burner phone in one hand and a business card in the other. It had been hard waving good-bye to Amy as she got in Matt's car, but not as hard as making this call.

Therapy. Something I hadn't done since I'd first come to live with my dad and mom. I believed in it, of course, and I supported Amy and Paisley going, but the idea of talking about what had happened to me made me a little sick.

I didn't want to feel sick. I looked hot. Amy had trimmed my hair, and given me a pedicure, and put me back in clothes that maybe weren't the most practical for a safe house, but made me feel stronger and prettier all the same.

That was probably why I'd agreed to make this call.

"Remember when you ambushed me with Mike's self-defense class?" Amy had said. *"I want you to set up an appointment with my therapist. Don't be mad. She's really nice and can do everything over the phone."*

"Screw it," I said. Alec wouldn't be back until tomorrow. Matt had lectured me about leaving the premises while he took Amy back to town. My dad was in the Keys, and I was effectively shut off from the rest of the world. It wasn't like I had anything better to do. Might as well rip open some healing wounds.

I dialed the number, expecting just to leave a voice mail, but a woman answered on the third ring.

"Carolyn Singer," answered a chipper voice.

Perfect. She sounded like she was fourteen. I nearly hung up—not to discredit Amy's situation, but what would this girl be able to offer me? I was staying in a safe house for God's sake. I had issues.

But I'd promised Amy I would do this.

"Hi, my name is Anna. You see my friend Amy and her daughter, Pais—"

"Anna, I'm so glad you called," said Carolyn. "I've got some time right now, want to chat?"

Shit. "Um. Sure."

"Great. Well let me start by saying everything you tell me is confidential, with two exceptions."

"If I have an imminent plan to harm myself or someone else," I said.

"That's right. Therapist?"

"Social worker," I said. "In the past."

"So you know how this works." She was more direct than I'd thought she'd be, but her voice was still kind. I tried to picture what she might look like. Young. Cute. Blond. With a name like Carolyn she had to be blond.

"Uh-oh," she said. "You're trying to analyze my voice, aren't you?"

My lips tilted up.

"I can always tell," she said. "I don't blame you. I do the same thing when I'm put on hold with the credit card company. Who is this person I'm talking to? What do they know about me? Do they look more like Cher or Dennis Rodman?"

"Or Britney Spears," I admitted.

"Ooh," she said. "Good one. So what do you want to talk about, Anna?"

I pulled on a string from the cutoff shorts Amy had brought for me.

"I guess Amy probably told you about my . . . situation . . ."

"Why don't *you* tell me?" She paused. "Actually, why don't you tell me what's on your mind right now? We can unravel from there."

Okay, this girl was all right. And maybe it was because she was on the phone and I didn't have to look her in the eye, or because everything I was feeling was so confusing and contradictory, but I decided to tell her. I took a deep breath and jumped in.

"Do you think it's weird to still want someone after being kidnapped, and drugged, and knowing that you were . . . violated, even if you weren't raped?"

I clutched my stomach, feeling it turn just to say the words out loud.

"I don't know," she said, not missing a beat. "Do you think it's weird?"

"No," I said. "I still feel like me."

"Then what makes you wonder?"

"I think he might think it's strange."

"Ah," she said. "There's a *he*."

"There is." Maybe it was confidential, but I wasn't going to say his name. "We kind of have a wild history, but he's the one who found me and took me to the hospital. I'm staying with him now."

"And you want him."

"Yes." I breathed the word. Admitting this felt like letting go. Like relief.

"Are you two intimate?"

I crossed my legs. Uncrossed them.

"Yes. No. We get close, and then he backs off."

"How do you feel about that?"

"Not great," I mumbled. "Sometimes it feels like things are normal again. Other times it's like he can barely look at me."

"And that hurts," she inferred. "What do you mean when you say 'normal again'?"

I gave a short laugh. "I guess we don't really have a baseline. But in the past I've never had to wonder if he wanted me."

"And now you do."

I wasn't sure how to answer that. He did want me, I could see it in his eyes and feel it in his body, but something was different. We were different. Maxim had made sure of that.

I guess when I'd told him good-bye, I had made sure of that, too.

"Okay," she said. "Let's say he walked in right now and things started to heat up. What do you think you'd be feeling?"

I felt the blush creep up my neck.

"Excitement," I said. I could feel his hands on my body, sliding beneath my thighs to pull me closer. "Need. Safety. He had this way of making me feel like I was the only woman in the world."

"That's good," she said, and I could hear a shuffle sound in the background as she moved. "When I was a kid I used to ride horses. I competed in equestrian events—hunter/jumper, things like that."

"Okay," I said slowly, unsure where this was going.

"Then I fell off. *Lost my seat*, as it's called. So pretentious." She chuckled. "Anyway, it was nasty. My horse rolled on me and broke my leg. She was skittish after that, and even when I was better, I never got back on. Not, at least, until about six months ago. Back in that saddle . . . Anna, it's better than I remember. Like flying. But it also scares the hell out of me because I still remember exactly what it feels like to fall."

Her meaning struck home with a pang to my heart.

"So things start to heat up between you two," she said again. "What are you feeling?"

"Scared," I said. "Scared that it's not the same. That he doesn't feel the same, and that it's short-lived just like before and he'll be gone again." I tilted forward, until my elbows were on my knees. "Scared that I won't be able to push aside the things that happened to me and they'll be right there between us."

My breath came out in a whoosh. I could hardly admit those things to myself. I couldn't believe I was telling her now.

"Sure," she said. "It makes sense to have those fears. Those are normal for any couple, but they're probably magnified with you, given all that you've been through."

"I keep telling myself that things will be the same."

But things couldn't be the same.

"Maybe it's a good thing that they're not," she said. "Same scenario. Things are getting hot. What do you think he'd be feeling?"

You have no idea how hard it is not to act on every fucking urge that rises up every time I look at you.

"Torn," I said, scowling. "I think he'd feel torn."

"In what way?"

"I think . . . I think he wants me, but is scared to act on it."

"Why?"

I closed my eyes.

If it comes back that this happened to you because of him, he's never going to forgive himself.

"Because he blames himself for what happened to me."

Carolyn was silent while I gathered my thoughts.

"It's not his fault," I said. I had to have told him that before. He had to know that.

"In my experience, it doesn't matter if it is or it isn't," she said. "If he believes it is, that's his truth, and it will continue to be until he learns differently."

I stared at the wall before me, feeling boxed in. Wondering if he felt boxed in, like he couldn't do the right thing, couldn't get away from Maxim Stein, no matter what he tried.

"Can I call you again sometime?" I asked.

"Sure." I could hear the smile in her voice. "I'd love that."

I'd promised Matt that I'd stay inside, but after talking to Carolyn I'd wandered around the apartment like a hamster in a cage, and finally decided to go for a walk. I held on to the burner phone just in case and crept quietly down the stairs to the beach just beyond the driveway. There, I kicked off my sandals and walked toward the water, to the place where Alec and I had been before.

Again, the beach was empty, but it was darker tonight on account of the cloud cover over the moon. The wet sand crunched beneath every step, and the air felt heavy and electric, like a storm was coming. My skin was misted by the time I reached the water.

Everything Amy had told me about Alec mashed together with Carolyn's words and my own experiences. He'd arranged for my safety, even while giving me space. He'd stayed away because he thought he was the worst thing that had ever happened to me. He'd made everyone, including myself, believe he was seeing another woman, just to draw the danger away from me.

Everything he did came back to me.

And yet he thought he was undeserving. That was his truth.

If the circumstances had been different, I didn't know if Alec and I would be together, but I knew we wouldn't have met. Maybe this path was one we were destined for, our histories had made us both strong enough to take it. And maybe it had stretched us thin because in the end, we were supposed to rely on each other to get through.

Or maybe we were always going to crash and burn.

It didn't surprise me when I heard his voice; I'd been hearing it all day. What surprised me was when he appeared from out of the shadows, like my own thoughts had conjured him.

He was wearing the same clothes he'd left in this morning—a casual T-shirt that somehow managed to fit him perfectly, and jeans that only hinted at the slender muscles of his long legs— and as he jogged toward me I could see the urgency in his stride.

"Anna!" he said. "What are you doing out here by yourself?"

I tensed, ready for bad news, and moved quickly to meet him.

"Just walking," I said. "Is everything okay? You're back early."

We stopped a foot apart, and even in the dark I could see the glisten of his skin from the humidity, and the shape of his lips. The pull was immediate and undeniable. Just being close to him sent a sharp ache echoing through my body.

He shoved his hair back with one impatient rake of his hand.

"You shouldn't be out here. Matt thought you were still in the apartment. I sent him home to get some sleep before I even came upstairs. You left all your things . . . I thought maybe . . ."

I gave him a small smirk. "Are you worried about me, Alec?"

"You're damn right I'm worried."

I reached to touch his chest, feeling him stiffen beneath my hand.

"I'm all right," I said. "What happened? Where's Janelle?"

He looked down at me, eyes growing wary. I hated the way his brows drew together. The way he seemed to question himself when I reached for him.

It was time to change that.

"She's . . ." He stared at my mouth.

I stepped closer, so that my toes were touching his sandy shoes. His chest moved faster.

"Alec?"

His tongue darted out to wet his lips. Something was shifting between us again. Another change that would shake our very foundation. I didn't know what would happen, but I could feel it coming. In the distance, thunder rumbled.

"I had to see you," he said quietly.

"Why?"

A gentle wave reached my feet, making me sink an inch in the wet sand. He didn't seem to notice the water, even as it lapped over the side of his shoe. He reached for my hair, running his fingers through the length to my waist, where his knuckle rubbed up the side of my white tank top. Heat spread from that spot, tingling through my core.

"You look beautiful," he said.

Amy had done fine work. Plus, included in her "day bag" were a dozen outfits from my closet, including bras and panties. I felt a lot more normal back in real clothes.

"Thank you," I said.

A raindrop landed on my shoulder, cool against my heating skin. Another landed in his hair, gleaming like a diamond in the dark strands.

"We should go inside," he said.

He didn't move

"Why did you come back?" I whispered.

He shook his head, as if to clear it, and I could feel him back away, even before he rocked onto his heels. The rain pattered against the palm trees and long grass that lined the shore, more insistent than before.

"I'm scared, too," I said, more loudly now. "What happened to me scares me, and losing control scares me, and you, *you* scare me more than anything." My fist closed in his shirt. "But mostly I'm scared that if we keep pushing each other away, we'll forget how to do anything else."

His eyes filled with regret. His hands moved to my hips, touching me too lightly, as if I might break.

"I forgive you," I said. "For whatever part you played, and whatever part you think you played. I forgive you."

"Anna, don't."

"I forgive you."

"Anna . . ."

"I forgive you."

His breath came out in a shudder. He looked up, and it wasn't the rain that dampened his face, but his own tears. His throat tightened as he tried to swallow, and he gripped my hips so hard I could feel his hands shaking. I slid my open palms up his chest to his neck, but before I could pull him down to kiss me, he'd lifted me against his body, and crushed his lips to mine.

The passion in that kiss touched me like none before it had. It shook me to my very soul. As his arms surrounded me, his mouth claimed mine with a force he'd kept pent up far too long. His tongue pushed past my teeth, stroking me in a way that lit my blood on fire. Exploring, but yet demanding. Slow, but fierce. I gripped the back of his neck and held on, losing my equilibrium as my eyes drifted closed.

I couldn't breathe. I couldn't think. His hair sifted through my fingers as the need in my belly twisted tighter. He broke away and I gasped for breath, but that breath turned to a moan as his teeth scraped down the length of my neck. I fisted his hair, and kissed his jaw and the corners of his eyes, tasting the tears on his skin. I held on to his shoulders as he slid me down his body. My breasts rubbed against his chest, my stomach over his hard length. His hands spread over my back, then reached lower, over my bottom, to where my cutoff shorts ended. He slipped beneath the denim, kneading the sensitive places so close to where I needed his touch.

And then we were falling, only not. I wound my arms around his neck as he took us to the ground, and the cool sand beneath my back crunched as I wriggled my knees open. He settled between them, pulling back for a moment to look down at me.

"Anna," he whispered.

A wave crept up and splashed over my hip, drenching my side. The raindrops were growing heavier. I barely felt them.

One hand moved down my body to my thigh, and pulled my leg higher up his side. His hand hooked beneath my bare knee, tickling the skin just beneath. Then he was kissing me again, and there wasn't room for fear, or insecurity. Only him. Only Alec.

Water from the sky dampened his hair, and his shirt, while water from the Bay soaked my clothes. He rocked his hips against mine, and I answered with a breathless gasp. His fingers intertwined with mine. A rhythm began, a slow but intense dance that hastened with each pull of the waves. This night belonged to us. The sky and the sand and the water were all ours.

The tension was all drawing to my center, into that place he rubbed with each flex of his hips. My pulse raced. My eyes fluttered closed. His tongue licked mine. Our clothes began to twist and pull the wetter they became, but the strain of the fabric only pushed us higher.

My breath hitched.

"Alec," I said, realizing suddenly what was happening. I had my clothes on. I wanted to feel his skin when I came. I wanted to feel him inside me.

"Alec, I . . ."

He kept moving. He knew.

Then his hand was between us, over my shorts, rubbing, circling, pressing. His hips kept up their movements, faster now, and I wrapped my arms around his back, nails digging through the thin, wet fabric.

"Not yet," I begged. "I need . . ."

The words were lost. I cried out into the night as the tension spiraled outward, claiming my body. I bit his shoulder through the T-shirt, just as another burst of heat shattered my thoughts. My body stretched tight, heels digging into the denim over his calves. Then there was nothing but lightness, and warmth, and Alec's harsh breaths in my ear.

"Thank you," he said.

I buried my face in his neck, a little embarrassed that I'd come on a beach with my clothes on. But he didn't seem to care. He kissed my forehead, and my cheek, and my collar. His hands roamed over my legs and my ankles, even as the rain clattered against the water and thunder boomed overhead.

Finally, he drew back, and pulled me to a stand. Lightning cracked over the sky, but though I looked, he continued to stare at me, eyes flashing with desire.

He took my hand, and we ran for the shelter of the apartment.

Twenty

He didn't release my hand until we were inside with the door safely locked behind us. As he reached down to turn on the small end table lamp, I flattened my hands over my belly, trying to calm the nerves that were multiplying by the second. We were soaked to the bone, dripping from our clothes and every angle of our bodies. Puddles formed beneath our feet on the wood floor, but I couldn't move, not even to get a towel to dry my hair.

It was pouring outside now. The rain had washed away the sand and saltwater, but not the words that I'd said, or the intensity of what had happened between us. Those things were all around us now, layering on top of our desire, and our pain, and that single force that forbid me from letting him go.

I loved Alec Flynn.

And nothing about that felt wrong.

There was no guilt about Amy finding out—she already knew where this was going. There was no fear about Maxim Stein and the pictures. That was all left outside. No one could hurt us worse than we could hurt ourselves, and we were done with that.

I swallowed. "Were there other women?"

I didn't want to know, but it was important regardless. Thinking of him seeking out someone else to ease his loneliness made my stomach hurt.

"I told you," he said quietly. "You're it for me. There's been no one since you."

He stood, watching me with questions in his eyes. But those faded as I lifted the hem of my tank top and pulled it over my head. It stuck to every inch of my skin on the way off, heavy with moisture. I dropped it on the floor beside me.

"You aren't going to ask me?" I said.

His hand twitched.

"It doesn't matter."

"You don't care?"

"I didn't say that."

He was just out of reach, but his gaze touched me all the same. My skin warmed, and my nipples, already straining against the wet silk of my white bra, ached almost painfully. He stripped off his T-shirt, dropping it beside mine. Then toed off his shoes and removed his socks.

It seemed impossible that he was so perfect. His chest was smooth, but for the dark groomed hair across his pecs. His shoulders, like his abs, were defined by muscle; swells and slopes that ran with tiny rivulets of rainwater. There was a knotted pink scar on his ribs from where he'd taken a knife in my protection, and I knew a matching one on his back from prison. His hair fell in dark points, dripping down his hard jaw and neck. I wanted to lick those places, taste the sky and the salt on his skin.

"I dreamed about you," I said. "I could *feel* you. It would have been impossible to let another man touch me."

I undid the button on my shorts, then lowered the zipper slowly, one click at a time. The denim stuck, but I peeled it away slowly, feeling his hunger grow as the matching white silk thong was revealed. It had been made see-through by the water, and clung to my bare lips. A small groan tore from his throat as I kicked the shorts aside.

He huffed out a breath. "You're so damn beautiful." He shook his head. "The words aren't right. I can't think."

I smiled. "They're good enough."

"Nothing's good enough," he said. "Not for you. Anna, I would give you anything. I would do *anything.*"

And he had. He had given me everything he could, including time apart. As he opened his hands before me, I felt humbled. Even giving him my soul didn't feel like enough.

"I want you," I said.

He took a tentative step forward. "Are you sure?"

I nodded. "I've never been more sure of anything."

His hands lifted to cup my face. The kiss was gentle, sweet, and made my knees weak. I slid my hands over his chest, stopping on the scar to trace it with my fingers.

I pulled back, then lowered to kiss him there, first gently, then trailing my tongue over the puckered skin. His breathing grew ragged, even as his fingertips were soft over my hair and down my back.

I kissed my way up, and when my tongue lanced over his nipple his grip tightened around my arms. He pulled me up to kiss me again, his hands staying on my biceps, as if to make certain he wouldn't go too fast.

I reached for his fly and undid the button. He helped me then, never breaking our kiss. As he bent to pull his legs free, I melted into his chest, and when his legs were bare, he held me tightly, our wet bodies sliding over each other. He was still wearing his boxer briefs, and as I reached for the waistband, he lifted me. I wrapped my legs around his hips and my arms around his shoulders, unable to stifle the sounds that slipped out of my mouth when his strong fingers kneaded my buttocks and pressed me against his cock.

He hurried to the bedroom, tensing as I took his ear between my teeth. I expected him to throw me on the bed and lose control—I wanted him to—but he set me down gently, and then slowly climbed over me.

"If you want to stop, just tell me," he said.

He edged down one bra strap and kissed my shoulder.

I told him not to stop.

He reached behind me and unclasped my bra in one easy move. My breasts felt suddenly too heavy without the support, but he didn't yet remove the fabric that covered me.

He pulled the other strap down my shoulder. I squirmed beneath him. He was still on his knees, not yet resting his weight on me. I could feel the doubt in him, see it flash in his eyes.

He cleared his throat. "If I do something wrong, or . . ."

His hesitance was breaking my heart. I hoped my touch would heal him.

"Alec." I pulled his chin up so that he was forced to look at me. "Make me feel good."

His eyes went dark, and he gave one curt nod.

I slipped out of the bra, exposing my breasts. They felt swollen, tender, like that hot, wet place between my legs. For one long second he looked at me, awe and lust and something deeper in his eyes.

Then he touched me.

It started gentle. He eased his weight between my legs. His knuckles glided over the swell of my left breast. His fingertip circled the hard point. He watched my nipple tighten further, then brushed his thumb over it, then gave it a light pinch.

I arched off the bed, my chest colliding with his.

"Alec . . ."

His kiss stole my breath. His arms surrounded me, then pulled me farther up the bed. Fire followed his lips as they trailed down my neck to my shoulder. It lashed through my veins as his wicked mouth moved lower. He kissed my breast, swirled his tongue around the nipple, and then sucked it into his mouth with one tantalizing scrape of his teeth.

"God," he murmured. I could feel him losing the battle for control. His lids had grown heavy, his voice raspy. He moved to my other breast, working it until I was writhing beneath him. More. I needed more. And it had to be now.

I reached between us, trying to pull off his boxer briefs, but he grabbed my wrists and stretched them over my head. His tongue made a slow line from the inside of my elbow toward my body as I quivered and wrapped my legs around him. He stopped me with one hard thrust of his hips.

"Yes," I said. "Alec, please."

Still holding my arms with one hand, he shifted onto his side, and rolled me toward him. His other hand slipped between us, doing what he wouldn't let me do. He cupped me over my panties, the fabric still soaked from the rain and the beach and now slick with my desire.

I started panting. He was delaying. It was killing me.

"Let me touch you," I said.

"Not yet."

He looked into my eyes while his fingers slipped beneath the fabric. He kept watching as he traced the curves of my body. I could feel how slippery I was when he pushed just the tip of one finger inside and pressed against my clit with the heel of his hand.

I bit my lip hard, but the cry came anyway.

"Is this okay?"

He couldn't be serious. It was beyond okay. It was better than my memories and fantasies combined.

I nodded, my wet hair sticking to my cheeks.

His finger slipped lower, deeper, and circled my entrance.

I clapped my knees together, trapping his hand. I could feel my hungry body clenching, longing to be filled. I was too sensitive; every movement of his hand sent electric bolts surging through my body.

"Come on my hand," he said.

I shook my head. I wanted to come on his cock.

But he destroyed me anyway. His thumb reached up to my clit just as one finger probed within. The pressure increased, inside and out, and I gave a hoarse yell as the wave built, and built, and then dragged me under. He didn't stop massaging both places, even as I arched and strained against him. Even as that soft velvet whip pelted me again and again.

As I succumbed to trembles and gasps he held me, one hand still cupping my wet center.

"Fucking beautiful," he muttered. "I'm here. Hold on to me."

I did. But the orgasm had left me longing for something deeper. It was as if he'd just scratched the surface; the ache was growing harsher. The power of it almost frightening.

He left me for just long enough to ease my panties off. Then he was back, kissing his way down my body, between my breasts, over my ribs.

I kept trembling. I couldn't stop shaking.

"You okay?" He kissed my belly button.

I nodded, but I wasn't sure what was happening to me. I should have felt pliant, relaxed, ready for him. But my body was so starved for his cock I could barely hold still. I fisted the bed-sheets, jumping when he pulled my thighs wider.

"Do you want me to stop?" he asked.

A sudden fear ripped through me that he would stop. That he would back away like he had the other night when he'd watched me. It wasn't rational, I knew that. Things were different now, but still I couldn't help it.

"Anna?"

I rose to my elbows, and pulled him up.

"You don't have to do that," I said.

He pushed off the bed, and my sex gave one hard throb as his weight shifted off my thighs. He reached for my cheek.

"It's all right," he said. "We don't . . ."

"You have to make love to me," I said hurriedly, trying to pull his body over mine. "You have to. Right now."

"I . . ." He tilted my chin up. "I don't understand."

"I don't either," I nearly yelled. All I knew was the ache was so intense it was threatening to swallow me whole.

I pulled at the band of his boxer briefs. "I'm ready. I don't want to be apart anymore."

He stopped my hands. "Just because I'm not inside of you doesn't mean we aren't making love."

I looked at him, the certainty in his tone dousing my sudden panic.

He rolled onto his back, and peeled off the last bit of clothing separating us. Then he returned to me. But he didn't thrust inside. Not even as I laid back and hooked my knees around his hips.

His gaze captured me, held me. The world slowed.

"Every time I touch you, it shakes me. Every touch, even when it seems meaningless."

His hand trailed down my side, leaving warm shivers in its wake.

"And when we're here, so close to the edge . . ."

He shifted his weight. Lowered.

"Anna," he said. "I love you."

My eyes filled with tears. My heart was swelling.

I felt him there, pressing against my entrance, and my body stilled. I closed my eyes, focusing on that hard, smooth feel of him. Feeling my anticipation grow with each second.

"I love you so much," he murmured. "So fucking much."

With his weight on his elbows, he pushed into me so slowly I could feel my muscles grip the head, and then stretch to accommodate his girth.

I finally wept, and held on to his shoulders as the muscles beneath flexed. He was back. Finally. Mine again. My heart had been broken, but he was fusing it back together with the searing heat of this long, slow thrust.

It became apparent now that he was shaky, too. Either with the magnitude of the emotions rolling through us, or from his own imposed restraint, I couldn't tell, but I held his face in my hands and kissed him. On the lips. On the sexy scar that ran along the bridge of his nose. Between his eyebrows, in the place that always revealed the concerns he couldn't voice. This was different than it had been in his apartment. This felt like the way it should have been. Like the way it always had been but better.

"I love you, Alec," I said. "I love you. I love you."

His control slipped, and he drove his cock in to the hilt. The breath huffed from my lungs. His eyes shot to mine, searching for a sign that I was all right, and as my body stretched to fit to him, I gave him a small smile.

For a moment we stayed like that. Getting used to each other's bodies. Feeling the pounding of each other's hearts. Trembling like virgins.

He rotated his hips and my breath caught. Like an experiment gone right, he moved the same way again. My nails dug into the back of his shoulders and he hissed.

"Sorry," I muttered, releasing him.

"No," he said. "It's all right."

He withdrew halfway, and then pushed into me again. I gripped him tightly, from my nails to my heels.

"Oh," I said. His cock rubbed that place even the memories couldn't touch. I adjusted my hips so I could pull him deeper, even when it felt like he was as deep as he could go. I'd taken him all the way to the base.

He continued these slow, measured thrusts until his brow dampened again with perspiration and a grimace took over his look of bliss. His pace had pushed me just beneath the threshold of insanity. It felt so good I could have come if he'd just given me a little more, but he held back, keeping the need blinding but my relief just out of reach.

"Faster," I urged.

"I won't be gentle." He rested his forehead on my shoulder. "I'm trying, but Christ, you're burning me alive."

His good intentions touched me, but I needed him to let them go now. I was about to lose my mind, and I couldn't fall apart alone.

I clenched my pelvic muscles, squeezing his cock. He groaned, and lifted his head to give me a warning look. I kissed him, and bit his bottom lip hard. My nails scraped up his back.

He must have been barely hanging onto control, because that broke him. Before I could take another breath, he was fucking me. With one hand tangled in my hair, and the other pinning my hips down, he pumped into me, throwing me over the edge without warning.

"Stay with me," he growled. "Please, God, Anna. Say this is right."

"Yes," I said. "Yes, yes, yes."

I shouted his name then, blinded by the explosion of colors and sensations that assaulted my senses. Then my words were gone, swallowed by the storm. I lost awareness of my limbs, of the parts of us that strained against each other, just as they fought to pull closer. There was only the sweet, shocking pulse that started in my center and radiated throughout my body.

Broken words flew from his perfect lips. *Take it . . . take all of me . . . feel how deep . . . so fucking good . . . good girl . . .*

I arched back and tried to straighten my legs, but he rose up, grabbed my hips, and yanked me against his body. His perfect abdominals flexed with each thrust. The sound of our sex rose above the rain pelting the outside of the building. Above the rush in my own ears.

In a burst, I pulled my knees toward my chest and kicked out, shoving him back. His cock came free from my body, and I groaned at the lack of pressure. The orgasm was still resonating through my core, but I wanted more. I could focus on nothing else.

With a look of surprise on his face I shoved him back and clambered over him. Straddling his thighs, I took him all the way, striking the root with a flash of pain so sweet it had me instantly craving more.

"*Fuck,*" he muttered, grabbing my hips. "Look at you."

Lightning flashed across the room, followed by the shattering crack of thunder. I arched my back and rode him hard, never pulling too far out. I used his cock to rub the deepest places of my ragged soul. The passion made me wild, and I scratched his chest and tossed my head back.

His thumb found my clit and one rough rub made me come again. I shouted out as the first wave hit, then I was at his mercy, locked against his chest as he filled my clenching body. A sudden rush of power overrode my pleasure and I forced myself to move over his slippery cock. This time it was him that jerked under me. His fingers that bit into my sides.

"So good," I moaned.

"*Anna.*"

"I can feel it. I can feel it." He was still coming. His body giving me everything—all his pleasure, all his pain. I took it all. I rode him straight through the fire without looking back. It ravaged us both. Made our bodies slick with sweat. Made our hearts pound as one.

"Love you," he said, his voice breaking.

One final jerk and he forced me to be still. Then he eased me onto my side. He kissed me, the rasp of his tongue soothing my raw emotions.

Still semihard inside of me, he flexed his hips. He pulled my knee over his thigh. It had been a long time since we'd been together like this, and I could already feel the whispers of soreness, but he was gentle now, riding out the last of my shudders, until a new warmth built again.

My breasts slid up and down his damp chest. My body rubbed against his. I broke our kiss with a shudder as my last jagged edges were softened by the overwhelming force of his love.

He came a second time, strong arms wrapped around my body. And in the aftermath we surrendered to soft touches and shy smiles, while the wind outside pelted rain against the windows.

"Don't ever let me go again," I whispered.

"Never," he promised.

Twenty-one

Some time later, my fingers were walking down Alec's bare back, skimming over his muscles. He groaned as I found a place between his shoulder blades and pressed lightly.

"Sore?" I asked.

He scoffed, the sound half muffled by a pillow. Outside the rain had turned to a consistent patter, the storm having moved past.

"I'm a man," he said. "What kind of question is that?"

"Oh, sorry. I forgot men don't feel pain." I dug my fingers a little deeper, and he flinched and gave a wince. I smiled, and inched closer to whisper in his ear.

"I can fix that, you know. I'm a trained professional."

"You're off the clock right now."

He pulled my hand from around his back to his mouth and slowly kissed my knuckles. They were still bruised from when I'd attacked the punching bag, but the softness of his touch made me forget all about that.

"Alec," I murmured. "I'm going to rub your back, and you're going to like it. Flip over."

He narrowed his eyes, but did as I said, and I straddled his lower back, trying to swallow the sudden jolt of sensation that came when my bare, swollen center touched his skin.

He gave a grunt and stiffened, and I ignored the self-consciousness that rose up inside me. One of his arms reached back, and his hand gripped my ankle, assuring I couldn't go too far.

I leaned over him, my breasts coming flush against his winged shoulders. I warmed him like that, using my body the way I would have used a blanket with my other clients.

"Relax," I whispered, and nipped the side of his neck.

"You're naked," he said, by way of an answer.

Grinning, I pushed up, intent to show him just how much I adored his body. I started at his neck, gently running my fingers down the muscles. Then I moved to his shoulder blades and stopped short when he flinched.

I fanned my hands over his skin, then moved lower.

"Alec." I closed my eyes, heart heavy. There were so many knots in his muscles, I could feel them with the lightest touch. I'd worked on car accident victims with less damage. The pain must have been tremendous.

He turned his head to face the other way.

I placed my flat hands on his back and let him grow used to this different kind of touch. A warmth, without the rush of heat. Part of me wanted him to share what was bothering him, but I knew Alec, knew that he would throw up his defenses if I addressed his problems directly. In time he would trust me again, but until then, I needed to come at them from the side.

"You have the sexiest back I've ever seen," I said.

He gave a small grunt.

"I love this part right here." I leaned down and pressed my lips against the place where the swell of his deltoids implanted in his shoulder. While he exhaled, I began kneading the opposite side, gently working my thumbs into the knotted rope that continued down between my open thighs.

He tensed. Then gradually relaxed.

"And this part, here." I made my way lower, keeping my body pressed to his. A calmness came over him. His hand loosened around my ankle. His body told me things he couldn't. About our time apart. About the trial. Not the details of what had transpired, but how difficult they'd been for him. Some people talked about their problems. Alec carried them right under his skin.

I changed positions, so that I was off to one side. He tensed again as soon as our bodies were apart, so I lay on one side, draped my leg over his, and continued to massage my way down his lats. Slowly, he became putty in my hands.

My fingers found the scar from where he'd been stabbed in prison, and ran down the two-inch length of raised skin.

"How much do you think about this?"

He turned to look at me, face half hidden in the crook of his arm. I continued to rub him, never straying too far from his body. He needed that connection now, I could feel it.

"Sometimes not at all." He closed his eyes. "Sometimes more."

"You never told me what happened." I moved his arm so that I could open up his shoulder blade and rub beneath. He groaned in pleasure. I hoped I was healing the wounds I reopened.

"I was in the cafeteria. There was a fight in the line for food. When I turned to look, I got a shank in the back."

I'd paused, but as soon as he finished, I started again. I didn't want him to feel alone when he was thinking about something so terrible.

"I hope the guy who did it got his balls chopped off."

He smirked. "I'm not sure the state would have approved that."

"*I* would have approved it," I muttered. I rose to my knees and began working the far side of his back.

"You should be a prison warden if this whole massage thing

doesn't work out," he said. "The guy who did it walked away with a week in the hole."

"What?" I bent down to meet his gaze, just to be sure he wasn't kidding.

"The security cameras were all on different rotations. His prints weren't on the knife. Later it went down as an accident with a broken fork or something. Max has a long reach."

I breathed out slowly, pushing back the hold he'd had on me.

"Fucking ridiculous," I said, trying to keep my voice calm. "You're sure it was Maxim and not Charlotte MacAfee's brother?"

"I'm sure. MacAfee doesn't have that kind of pull. I checked."

I felt myself frown. "You went to see Trevor . . . I mean, William?" Trevor Marshall, aka William MacAfee, was still in prison as far as I knew. He'd been transferred there after he'd recovered from the gunshot wound he'd sustained on the Sunshine Skyway Bridge three months ago.

Alec didn't answer right away.

"We needed to clear some things up," he finally said.

"Such as?"

He turned on his side, effectively ending the back rub, and pulled me close.

"Such as I never meant for his sister to die," he said. "Such as he'll have no reason to contact you if he ever makes it out of prison."

I tried to swallow down the lump in my throat. No. I had no desire to see Trevor again.

"You've been looking out for me," I said.

He brushed my still-damp hair back.

"I know you put in Amy's alarm system and offered to pay for her therapy, too."

He glanced away now. "Your friend's got a big mouth."

"Yes," I agreed. "But I wish she'd told me sooner. I wish you had, too."

I kissed him softly on the lips.

"She got a child support check recently," I continued, gauging his reaction. "I don't suppose that comes as a surprise to you."

He inhaled. I kissed him again.

"Do I want to know what happened with that?"

He smirked.

"That was all Mike," he said. "I was just providing . . . moral support."

"Uh-huh," I said, secretly delighted that Mike had taken up for Amy. I wondered what she would do if she found *that* out. "You're a good man, Alec."

Before he could disagree, I was kissing him again. It felt right to kiss him. Like a missing part of me was finally settling back into place. His arms tightened around me. Never having completely lost his erection, I could feel him growing hard again against my belly, and wiggled closer. His hand lowered down my spine and gripped my ass, fitting me against him.

Just like that, my heart was pounding again. I gasped as his cock settled between my legs. I was ready for him. Always ready. Nothing that had happened had changed that, a fact that relieved me greatly.

He broke our kiss suddenly, and cleared his throat.

"We should eat."

"We should?"

"Yes," he said. His eyes were on my mouth, and he leaned in again. Before he could kiss me, he pushed himself up, sitting with his knees bent while he ran his hands down the sides of his face.

His sudden distance worried me. I sat up on the other side of the bed and tucked the sheet around my chest.

"Sure," I said slowly. "I could eat."

"Good."

He didn't get up. My throat grew tight. He was probably overwhelmed by everything that was happening between us.

If that was the case, he could go ahead and get over it. We were in this together now. The time for secrets was past.

"Did I do something wrong?" I asked.

He looked over his shoulder, brows pinched together. "What? No. *No*." His gaze lowered to the sheet I'd used to cover myself.

"I just got you back," he said after a moment. "Don't want to push my luck."

"By over-sexing me?" I couldn't help but grin.

He snorted, but looked away again.

I thought of how he'd been trying to take things slow. How he'd brought me chocolate cupcakes and made me pancakes, and even when we'd finally made love, he'd been so concerned with my comfort.

"I love you," I said.

He wasn't facing me, and I watched his shoulders lower the smallest bit when I said the words. What I would have given to ease his tortured soul.

"Well, I need to clean off," I said. "Go eat if you want. But I'll be in the shower. Naked. Rubbing soap over my body."

I rose, letting the sheet drop onto the ground, and walked to the door. I didn't have on a stich of clothing, and every bit of me, every curve and imperfection, was out on display. I didn't feel self-conscious, though. I felt epic. Like a model posing for one of the great Greek sculptors. That's what Alec's love did to me.

When I reached the threshold, I looked back and saw the tight grimace on his face, and one hand on his hard, swollen cock.

"It would be a shame if no one was there to wash my back," I said. And then stepped out of the bedroom.

I was going to give him ten seconds to follow. He only took three.

He made me come four times in the shower. Twice with his hands, and twice on his cock. He held me when I could no longer stand,

and then washed me gently, and dried me off with a towel. Over and over he told me I was beautiful, and that I felt good, but even when he came I felt him holding something back.

I reminded myself we needed time to work out the kinks. Though we had history, this relationship was still new. And like I'd told Carolyn the therapist, he was probably feeling torn. He loved me, I could feel that in every touch, see it in his eyes, but he was still frightened for what that love might cost us.

I didn't blame him. It frightened me, too.

A few minutes after he'd left the bathroom, I followed. He'd dressed, in worn jeans and a black V-neck T-shirt that accented the shape of his chest, and was reading over some papers on the kitchen counter. Though he looked sexy, it didn't seem like the most comfortable ensemble for lounging around at eleven p.m., and in response, I felt myself wrap the towel a little tighter around my chest.

"Going somewhere?" I asked, trying to sound casual.

"No, I . . ." He cleared his throat and looked up. There were shadows under his eyes, but relief relaxed him when his gaze moved over my face.

"You're feeling all right?"

I nodded.

He tapped his knuckles on the counter.

"No memories coming back, anything like that?"

The question came from kindness, but it still made me think of the pictures, and Maxim's hands on my body.

"Nothing new," I said, straightening.

"The doctor at the hospital said that might happen." He exhaled. "Intimacy might trigger some memories."

I could tell this conversation was something he wasn't entirely looking forward to, but when he reached for me, his grip was strong. It made me wonder if the clothes weren't some kind of shield. A separation from what had just happened in the shower.

Even if that was the case, he pulled me close and held me tightly against his chest.

"If it does, we'll get through it, okay?" His words may have been quiet, but they were fierce. "You can tell me."

I closed my eyes and breathed him in, letting the darkness slide away. After a moment he kissed the top of my head.

"I did something you may not like."

I pulled back, wishing I had a harder boundary between us. Nothing good started with words like that.

"And just when things were going so well," I said.

He didn't let go of my arms. "I told Janelle about the pictures."

When I flinched, his brows drew together.

"She's promised to keep it under wraps for now."

"*For now*," I said slowly. How long was that? Until she decided she needed it as leverage in the case against Maxim Stein?

"Max won't find out until we can make sure of the date they were taken," he explained.

I backed away, hugging my arms against my chest. "Sounds like you guys really bonded. I guess I should be grateful you were talking about me."

"I didn't mean to hurt you."

"You should have told me you were going to do that."

"I know." He stood, clasping his hands behind his neck. "I know, but we need her help. She has resources." He sighed. "She's invested in putting Max away."

"And I'm not?" I asked. "*You're* not?"

On one hand I understood; Janelle was in the FBI. She had been working the case against Maxim Stein since Alec had delivered the copies of the stolen Green Fusion patent to her months ago. But the other side of me was humiliated all over again. I almost wished we could forget they were ever taken, that I could go back to not knowing what had happened to me.

"Of course I am." He reached for me, palms open. "You're what's most important here. If assuring your safety meant getting hit by a damn semitruck, I'd do it, all right? I don't like this. I didn't want to tell anyone what happened. But I had to."

I couldn't help but soften. His pride was wounded, and for a man like Alec, that was a pill not easily swallowed.

"So she knows," I said, wishing I had a shirt on. Or a parka. I felt entirely too exposed. "What can she tell us?"

He gave a quick nod, then reached for my hand.

"I need you to look at this. Tell me if it means anything to you."

I swallowed.

"You found something?"

"Maybe."

He turned back to the counter and opened a folder he'd been looking at when I walked in. I tensed as I saw the color pictures, but these were different from the ones I'd stumbled upon before. Nobody was highlighted in these. Instead, they were shots of what looked to be the interior of a hotel.

"I took these earlier and had them printed before I came back. Does anything look familiar?"

I scanned through a photo of a pristine lobby. Plush white couches lined the walls, crystal chandeliers hung from the ceiling. There were half a dozen glass tables shoved against a front desk that looked like it was made of solid black marble. A sign on the other side of the room hung on an easel: PARDON OUR DUST. UNDER RENOVATIONS.

There was nothing familiar here.

I turned to the next picture. The inside of a room, centered around a huge, antique four-poster bed. The white comforter on the mattress was topped with a mountain of fancy pillows. A sliding glass door gave way to the veranda.

It looked like something from a dream. Something I'd seen in a movie. My eyebrows drew together. Alec's arm tightened around my waist. I felt him watching me closely.

The next picture was a hallway. Just a hallway. Just like any other hallway, with doors lining the walls. But there were candle-holders attached to the walls, coiled silver snakes, whose mouths opened to narrow glass sconces.

I dropped the picture on the floor and took a quick step back.

"Anna?" Alec grabbed my elbows. "What is it?"

Silver snakes.

Black stars.

My dress, ripping, as I fell forward.

"*I'll carry her.*" A voice I couldn't quite pin.

"Let go," I said.

Alec released my arms.

"No." I shook my head, trying to bring back the shard of memory that had been so clear just moments before. "No, that's what I said. 'Let go.' "

I closed my eyes and saw a white sky with black stars.

"Shit," I muttered.

Alec led me to the bar stool, watching me worriedly.

"Take your time," he said.

"Black stars." I forced my breath to steady. "I don't know why I keep seeing that."

"It's all right."

"I remember the candleholders," I told him. "At least, I think . . . It's hard to tell. It's like I saw them on television or something. Silver snake candleholders. I was so tired. I could barely walk. I kept fall-ing. He said he would carry me."

"Who's he?" Alec's voice had hardened.

"I don't know."

"Max?"

"No." I would have recognized Maxim's voice. It was someone else. I tried to focus on it. "Someone younger, maybe."

"Okay," he said. "Okay, that's good. Take a deep breath."

I wasn't sure who needed it more, him or I, but I did as he said anyway. One breath, then two. Again, until the memory faded. I stared at Alec the whole time, letting his dark eyes center me. Letting his hands on my shoulders keep me grounded.

"Where is this?" I asked.

"Miami," he said.

Twenty-two

"*Miami?*" I asked.

"Yeah." He sat on the stool across from me. "That's where I went yesterday. I've been trying to find a match for the shots Max had taken with you on the balcony. Flight records show his jet was already overseas that week, and he couldn't have gotten you on a commercial plane without an ID, so I figured wherever it was had to be within a drivable distance. I ran a search of all his properties within a thousand miles and dug up any of his old friends or rentals he's used before. This is a place he invested in years ago. I didn't recognize it right away because I'd never been there—Bobby covered it."

I was still trying to wrap my mind around the fact that I'd been taken all the way to Miami. That was almost a five-hour car ride.

"Janelle and I flew down in the afternoon and checked into a hotel down the street. She tipped off the media." He rolled his shoulders back. "Reporters were already waiting at the hotel when we arrived."

I tried to shake off the sudden rise of jealousy that rose up.

Alec had been there for me, but it still stung a little to think of
the media adding more fuel to their supposed love affair. Even if
it was a fake relationship, I didn't want the world thinking he
was with another woman.

"You got on a plane?" For as much as Alec loved planes, he
hated flying. The only way he'd gotten through our last flight together was my well-timed blow job.

He scowled. "I did. And there was turbulence."

How this man had ever thought pilot lessons were a good
idea was beyond me.

I laced my fingers in his. "I wish I'd been there to distract you."

His hand gave a sudden squeeze, and his dark eyes shot to
mine. I smirked, unable to help myself.

He coughed.

"If Max saw you on the news, he'll know you figured out
where he took me," I said.

"Exactly," said Alec, recovering quickly. "I hope it scares the
shit out of him."

Victory surged over the dread. Alec was sending his old boss
a message. I didn't know what he'd do with it, but I couldn't
think of that yet.

Alec shuffled aside the papers to reveal the last photo. It was
the veranda with the iron railing. Palm trees leaned in the background. There was an empty chaise recliner on the tiles.

"It's nothing personal."

Maxim Stein's voice whispered in my ear. *Nothing personal.*
Fucking bastard. My nails dug into my palms.

"Did he rent a room there?"

"No," said Alec, expression grim. "The hotel is temporarily
closed for renovations."

Which meant limited staff, if any. Still, there had to be construction crews on-site. Somebody had to have seen something.

"I need to go there," I said. "See if anyone recognizes me, or
if I recognize anyone. There should still be security footage from

the elevators . . . something . . . We have the location where it happened, we just need to pin him to *when* it happened." Then we could show that he'd violated his parole, and if it came down to it, we could offer proof from the hospital that I'd been drugged as well.

Alec shook his head. "All the cameras are down while they're remodeling. From the shape of the balcony in the pictures, I think he took you to one of the six suites on the east side. I searched all of them, but the place has been cleaned. Really cleaned. I couldn't even pick up a print. Whoever helped him knew what they were doing."

"But the pictures," I said. "They were taken from a distance. Maybe someone saw the photographer."

I was grasping at straws. Miami was packed with tourists snapping pictures.

"I thought of that," said Alec. "There's a hotel next door that's open. Janelle checked the guest list for those nights, but there was no one that matched the profile of the bastard that took you from the bar. No one remembers seeing Max either."

I stood, unable to sit any longer. "Son of a bitch."

"Right."

"How did Max even get there? I thought he was on house arrest."

"I don't know." Alec's mouth turned down. "I'm still working on that."

I paced the length of the narrow kitchen. "So what? The trail just goes cold now?"

"Not yet," he said. "Max is smart, but he's arrogant, and that makes him lazy. That's why he kept me around—so I could deal with the details. I guarantee he missed a step somewhere, and when I find out what it is, we're going to string him up for it."

I felt his confidence spark in the center of my chest.

"Janelle is still there asking some questions. We'll know something as soon as she does."

"Damn," I said. "She really does make it hard to hate her."

He smirked. "She's not that bad."

I narrowed my eyes. "Let's not get crazy. She did still steal my boyfriend."

He chuckled. "She didn't steal anything. You left me."

"Technicalities." I waved him off.

"That technicality nearly broke me."

The mood had turned serious fast. He hung his head, rubbing the back of his neck. He seemed unsure what to say next.

I melted onto the stool.

"You never came," I said quietly. "I thought you were done with us. You'd moved on."

He reached for my hand, slowly flattening it against his large palm. His fingers stroked the inside of my wrist, sending shivers up my arm.

"There is no moving on," he said. "There's just surviving."

"Alec." I leaned closer. He so rarely voiced his feelings, especially outside the bedroom. The impact was not lost on me.

He scowled. "When I was gone before, I could still hope you were waiting. But when you ended it, God, Anna. There was nothing left. I told myself it was better that way, but nothing made sense without you. Mike told me you were doing well, which fucked me up even more. He said this cop—the one who'd been at the bridge that night—kept showing up at the salon to see you. I drove there one day and saw you two leave together. You were laughing. You looked so fucking happy. I swore I'd keep my distance if it meant somewhere you were laughing like that."

He blurred as the tears filled my eyes. I let them fall, unwilling to let go of his hands.

"And now you're back, and you keep crying." He laughed dryly.

I giggled, and wiped my cheek on my shoulder. I shifted onto his lap, and he wrapped his arms around me.

"Marcos is just a friend," I said. "Anyway, he wasn't coming to the salon to see me, he was coming to see Derrick."

Alec contemplated this a moment. His brows rose.

"Huh. That's good news."

I snuggled closer, my hair over his shoulder.

"What happens now?" he murmured against my neck. His fingers had found the end of the towel and slowly inched it up my thigh.

The weight of those words hung over us, heavy and illusive. What *did* happen now? Were we together? Not according to the rest of the world, who was convinced he was with Janelle. Even a secret relationship seemed strange at this point when Maxim had pounded such a wedge between us.

Each second brought more unease. What did I expect to happen here? What did he want? We couldn't be seen in public together, much less date. And what about our future? He didn't have steady work, and mine was in limbo. Massage wasn't a career for me anyway, it was a job. I had things I wanted to do—continue with CASA, maybe even get my social work license renewed. I couldn't do those things if I was stuck in a safe house.

I should have told him all this. Laid it all out on the table. But I took the coward's path.

"I don't know," I said. "I'm sort of living day by day right now."

He gave one slow nod, and if he didn't believe me, he didn't call me on it.

"I'll take whatever you can to give me," he said.

I turned my face to kiss him on the jaw. "What if what I can give you is baked ziti?" I asked. "With lots of cheese. And a spinach salad with strawberries. And some grilled asparagus. And maybe a piece of cheesecake."

His brows rose. "That's very specific."

"Would you be agreeable?"

"Very." This time when he laughed, I laughed with him.

"I want to cook," I said. "I have had many orgasms and one icky flashback. I demand a feast."

He smiled, genuinely, and it warmed away my insecurities.

"Let's find a supermarket, and then I'll make you the best midnight snack you've ever had," I said.

He considered this a moment, and I watched as he checked the clock.

"Matt's taking a break until morning, but it's late enough. There shouldn't be too many people out."

I batted my eyelashes at him.

"All right," he said. "You okay with just me?"

I grinned. "Always."

We took the rented SUV. My seat had been covered with a stack of unopened mail, junk mostly, which Alec told me was from the PO box he'd taken out when he'd moved above the restaurant. I tucked it into the side compartment on the door as we made our way back out into the rain.

The water made the streets glisten, and fogged up our windows so fast even the defrost couldn't keep up. Somehow, Alec managed to find a supermarket in St. Pete that was still open, and parked in the back of a lot.

He turned off the car, but the rain was still pelting so we waited before getting out. My hand was on the console, and he took it, weaving our fingers together. I reveled in the contrast—he was large where I was small, rough where I was smooth. Our bodies fit together in every way possible.

"This all right?" he asked, glancing down at where we touched. The rain whipped against the windshield.

"Yes," I said. "You don't have to keep asking if I'm okay."

He pulled my knuckles to his mouth and planted a gentle kiss there. The stubble on his jaw rubbed against the back of my hand, and I had the sudden desire to feel it scrape against my tender breasts, and the insides of my thighs.

The windshield was completely steamed, the sound of the rain the only evidence that a world outside the windows existed.

"Can I ask you something?" he said.

"Yes." I don't know why his question made me nervous, but it did.

"Why didn't you let me put my mouth on you?"

The nerves increased by two hundred percent. When I tried to withdraw my hand, he held tight and sucked one of my fingers in his mouth. Shocked, I gave a small whimper and sank in my seat.

"Focus." He smirked as his teeth scraped the pad of my finger. A sharp throb ricocheted through my body, making my stomach contract and my thighs squeeze together. Demanding Alec had been absent in our lovemaking since we'd come back together. His return made my nipples instantly harden.

"Did he touch you there?"

Max, he meant. But I couldn't wonder what *had* happened to me. Not while Alec was turning the heat up in my veins.

"No . . ."

"Then why?"

"I . . . I didn't want you to stop."

He moved to my thumb, biting the flesh at the base hard enough to make me jump.

"Why would I stop?"

I couldn't take my eyes off his mouth. The perfect shape of his full lips, opening, his wet tongue sliding up my palm.

"I needed . . . inside." I could form sentences. Really.

"I would have given you what you needed."

His mouth found the sensitive place on the inside of my wrist. My pulse began to flutter.

"You kept backing off," I managed. "I needed your . . ." His tongue made a slow, wet circle on my skin. I closed my eyes.

"My what?" His voice darkened. The rain slapped against the car, heightening the sensation.

"Your . . ." *Words, Anna.* "Possession."

He sighed tightly, the sound ending with a soft growl.

"There's more than one way for me to possess you," he said, his words a dark threat wrapped in velvet.

Keeping one hand in mine, he reached across the console with the other and touched my knee. Very slowly, his fingers trailed up the bare skin of my inner thigh, stopping when he reached the hem of my shorts. His eyes flashed with raw desire, and my breath hitched in my throat. I leaned toward him, unable to fight the pull, and he leaned in, too, meeting me halfway.

"We good?" he asked.

When I nodded, his fingers dipped beneath the frayed fabric, glancing off the edge of my panties as they rounded the swell of my thigh. His thumb found a ticklish spot on my hip and pressed down, making me slide farther into the leather seat.

"How about now?" With agonizing precision, he made his way back toward my center, and adjusted his wrist, so that he could feather his fingers over my satin panties.

"You want it?" It took everything I had to taunt him. Already I was spreading my legs to give him more access.

"You know I want it," he said, voice sharp enough to bring my gaze back to his. His finger slipped under the panties to my wet center and probed deeper.

"Oh," I managed. "Oh God."

"I miss the taste of you," he said. "How soft you are. How every movement makes you react." He pressed inside, and I threw my head back, biting down hard.

"You get off on it," I said between my teeth.

"Hell yes, I do," he said, adding a second finger and twisting. "You want to hear a secret? Making you come . . . It's a power trip, and I fucking love it."

"And just when I was starting to think you were a nice guy." I yelped as his thumb found my clit.

He laughed, the low sound rolling through my body.

"Don't fool yourself," he said. "I've got nothing but bad intentions right now."

"Is this the part where you get bossy?"

He'd leaned closer, his voice a low rasp in my ear.

"This is the part where I fuck you with my tongue, Anna. Right here in this car."

I swallowed. Or tried to, at least.

"Get in the backseat," he ordered. "Take off your shorts and spread your legs."

His hand withdrew suddenly, leaving my head spinning. He left the car, and for a few seconds I stared after him in shock, wondering what he was doing. Then the back hatch opened, and he reached into the trunk, eyes blazing.

"The backseat." The words were a crisp demand.

I shimmied over the center console onto the soft leather of the backseats. I didn't know how he was planning on doing this; he was much too big for both of us to lie in the right positions. But before I could consider it too long, my seat reclined to an almost flat position. He did the same with the other side, making a make-shift bed that connected to the trunk.

"Your shorts," he reminded me.

I shivered in anticipation as the trunk closed.

Quickly, I pulled them down, leaving my pink satin panties. I wanted him to see them, not that he could get much of a view in the car. The back was sheer, with a small bow that landed at the base of my spine. I thought he might like that.

The door opened and he returned inside, hair wet and messed and dripping down his jaw. His button-up shirt stuck to his chest, outlining every muscle. The butterflies exploded in my belly as he tilted his chin toward the back of the vehicle.

Wordlessly, I scooted back, keeping my eyes on his. I was already trembling, and a thin sheen of perspiration covered my skin. It had been a long time since we'd done this. How many times had I fantasized about it? How many times had I touched myself these last few months, only to reach a disappointing climax?

The interior light in the car flickered off.

He crawled toward me, muscles rolling like a jungle cat. I pulled at the bottom of my tank top, feeling the fabric stretch. It seemed suddenly too tight. This compartment was too small. I could hear Alec's measured breaths, feel his presence taking up every inch of space.

"Open," he said.

My trembling knees spread, my bare heels still planted in the seat cushion. There was barely enough light to see; I wished I could read his expression, but all I could make out was his shape.

The seat creaked under his weight. His hands rested on my knees, then slid down the outside of my thighs to the thin straps on my panties. One hand curved beneath my bottom, feeling the fabric and then manipulating the bow. His breath warmed my shin.

"Very nice," he said.

The compliment made me shine. It had been a long time since I'd wanted to dress sexy and be noticed.

Slowly, he grabbed the sides, and inched the thin fabric down my legs.

He wasn't going to kiss me, not on the mouth at least. There was no urgency in his movements, even as I began to tremble. It was like he had all night.

"You're shaking," he said.

"You're killing me."

He chuckled. "No, I think the opposite is true."

When my panties were finally off my legs, he lifted one ankle and kissed the top of my foot.

"If you need to stop, it's okay," he said, breaking from commanding Alec to give my heart a hard lurch. "Just being with you, like this. It's enough."

But it wasn't. Not for me.

I shook my head. "I don't want to stop."

He placed himself between my knees.

"Spread your legs," he said. "Wide. I want to see you."

I lay back, biting my lower lip hard as I opened my legs. "Wider."

I stretched them open as far as I could, until I could feel my damp lips exposed, and the cool air on my center. My hands were fisted in the bottom of my shirt, and I stared at the ceiling of the car, praying that he liked what he saw.

A finger gently circled my opening. Then skimmed up one side to my clit, and down the other. The back of the knuckles of his opposite hand rubbed the bottom of my buttocks. I tried to hold still. I tried, but it was impossible. I was already squirming.

"So sensitive," he murmured.

He blew over my pussy, and I arched back. He wasn't even touching me now, and I was close to coming. I could feel that desperate, familiar flush already creeping up my spine.

"You're so beautiful," he muttered. "Everywhere."

I loved hearing that edge in his voice. He wasn't as in control as he was letting on.

The heat of his breath touched me an instant before his lips. It was a slow, dark, sensual kiss that moved from the top of my slit lower, and lower, until his tongue slipped inside.

I ripped apart that fast. The heat tore down my limbs, then raced back up, exploding in my core. I threw one arm over my mouth to stifle the yell, but it barely helped. The noises I made were wild. My toes fanned out, my feet flexed. I tried to push away from him, but his arms had wrapped around my thighs.

While I was still reeling, he bit the inside of my thigh, drawing my attention to a different kind of sensation.

"Yes," he hissed. "I'm so hard. God, Anna. Those sounds you make."

It was as he had said. A conquering. He got off on the knowledge that he, only he, could give me a pleasure this intoxicating.

He nibbled his way back toward my center.

"Wait . . ." I pushed up to my elbows. It was too soon, I was still too sensitive.

He didn't care.

He buried his face between my legs. My soft, swollen lips against his. His tongue dipping inside of me, deeper, until his teeth scraped me. His hands spreading me wide, palms on my inner thighs while his tongue lashed at my clit.

The tension built and built and the orgasm hit me so hard the frames of my vision turned white. I grabbed his hair, all thoughts vanquished, and held him against me while he licked and sucked and kissed. His fingers joined his mouth. One pumped inside of me, then two. Then his thumb pressed against my ass. He reached up with his other, beneath my shirt, beneath the cup of my bra, to pinch my nipple. A band formed between the places he touched—my ass, my cunt, my breast. It tightened, and tightened, and then snapped. I shouted his name. I thrashed and fought and ultimately surrendered.

His pace slowed. I lost time. I may have blacked out. I was covered in sweat, slick with what he'd done to me. He lapped at me slowly, using the back of his tongue, the rough part, all over. He said I was soft, so soft, the softest thing he'd ever touched. He said I tasted like the ocean. He said he wanted me like he'd never wanted anything in his entire life. He said my sweet cunt belonged to him, and my pleasure belonged to him, and that I was his.

He said he loved me. He said my name: *My Anna. Sweet Anna. My dirty girl.*

And after I broke that final time, he rose, the evidence of what he'd done gleaming his mouth, and gathered me against his chest while the rain outside continued its assault.

Twenty-three

I was still having trouble making my legs work right by the time we finally entered the twenty-four-hour supermarket. I tried to pawn my clumsiness off on my slippery, wet flip-flops, but Alec only smiled smugly and kept an arm around my shoulder for support.

As we got a cart and passed the checkout counters, one of the employees, a guy in his early twenties with a killer tan and a T-shirt with Greek letters peeking out from above his apron, did a double take. For a moment I thought he'd recognized us, even in the baseball caps Alec had pulled from the back of the car. But then I realized my white tank top was now see-through from the rain, and doing little to hide the pink bra beneath. Lucky for me, the fabric was thin enough to showcase just how well the store's high-powered air-conditioning worked.

The checker grinned, then pulled a phone out of his pocket and began texting. Now closer, I could see that his shirt boasted a university emblem. He was probably going to college at one of the local schools. Fucking frat boys. I pulled the second skin off my stomach and turned Alec's attention toward the produce section before he caught on.

As soon as he was out of sight, he was out of mind. Alec and I were the only ones around, and I was thrilled about some time away from the apartment. We picked up things we needed, discussed the phallic nature of butternut squash, and made out surrounded by pretzels. He tickled my ribs, I escaped. He caught me, I ground my ass against his semihard cock. He made threats. I made promises.

In the cereal aisle he stopped and stared at the rows of cartoon characters promising their contents were made of whole wheat.

"You really think I'm bossy?" he asked. I'd forgotten I'd told him that in the car.

"You really think I'm pretty?"

He smirked, picking up a box of Crunch Berries. Fixing his gaze on the nutrition facts as if there might be some redeeming quality in a cereal that was both blue and pink.

"Too bossy?" he asked.

"Too pretty?"

He barked out a laugh. "Yes."

I slipped my hands in his back pockets and rested my cheek between his shoulder blades.

"I like it," I said. "Besides. Boss me around all you like. We both know who's in charge."

I was kidding. But he wasn't when he said, "Yeah. I know."

It was so like a date, I forgot we were in a supermarket, in the middle of the night. We walked up and down the aisles, talking, telling stories, laughing. Remembering.

What it was like when we were together.

What it was like when we were apart.

What it felt like to matter, mean something, be *everything*, to someone.

Frat Boy ruined it.

He was in the bread aisle, pretending to organize when we came around the bend. Instantly, Alec and I pulled apart, realizing the weight of what it would mean if someone caught us together in public. His cover with Janelle would be blown. The media would have a heyday.

Who knew what Maxim Stein would do.

Frat Boy didn't even look at us until we passed. But the second we did, I heard it—the click of a picture being taken. Alec and I both turned, too quickly for Frat Boy to hide his smart phone. He tried to stuff it in his apron.

Alec strode straight up to him, and I hastily followed, feeling his intentions in the fury sparking off of him.

"Give me the phone," he said, holding out his hand.

Frat Boy scowled and stepped back, straight into the soft cushion of the bread aisle. His cheeks turned a blotchy red.

"I don't know what . . ."

"The fucking phone," Alec annunciated.

"Screw you," said Frat Boy. "Get your own fucking phone."

Before Alec could act, I jumped between them, my back to the checker, my hands on Alec's hard chest. He didn't look at me—his gaze stayed over me, pinned on Frat Boy.

"Where'd you send the pictures?" Alec asked.

My stomach felt like I'd missed a step going down stairs.

"Nowhere. You're crazy."

"I'm going to ask you one more time, then I'm going kick your ass, you understand?"

"Alec," I whispered. "Come on. Let's just go."

His pecs flexed beneath my hands. A buzzing filled my ears. This guy had taken pictures. Pictures were bad. I immediately saw an image of myself sprawled out over Maxim's bare chest. Bad, bad, bad.

Frat Boy said nothing. Then I heard a rustle of his hand in his apron.

"There's this local celebrity site. I just posted a couple."

I turned around.

"We're not celebrities."

He laughed, like I'd said something funny, but the sound died in his throat when Alec took another step closer.

"He's on the news," said Frat Boy, nodding at Alec. "There was a skit about the whole thing on *Saturday Night Live* last weekend. And you're his mistr— like, girlfriend, right?"

Alec's hand shot out and grabbed Frat Boy's T-shirt around the collar. This time I didn't stop him.

"Let me see what you posted," I said, my voice like syrup.

He swallowed, looking around for backup. "You've already gotten like eighty hits. No one gets that kind of play unless you can see tits or ass. It's a compliment, if you ask me."

He wilted under Alec's glare. After a moment, he handed the phone over. Alec released him and flipped through the pictures. There were a dozen, at least. Me in my see-through shirt, arms hooked around Alec's neck. Us kissing. His hand in my back pocket while we walked. Us laughing.

"Shit," I said.

"It's nothing personal," Frat Boy said.

It's nothing personal. Maxim's words. My breath came in one harsh pull, loud enough that both men turned to stare at me.

"It's our lives." My voice shook. "It's *my* goddamn life." I stepped closer. This time it was Alec's hand on my shoulder. He stopped me, but I could feel the rage just beneath the surface.

He stuffed the phone in his pocket, and lifted a cold gaze to the other man.

"You've got three seconds to get out of my sight."

Frat Boy scrammed, tripping over his own shoes before he hit the turn. Alec grabbed my hand. We left the cart. He pulled me toward the exit, but it was too late. There was a car outside, another pulling into the parking lot. The door opened. A flash blinded me.

"Mr. Flynn! Does Ms. Jamison know of your affair?"

"Is it true, Ms. Rossi, that you worked for Maxim Stein as his personal masseuse? What else did you do for Mr. Stein?"

"Ms. Rossi, how does your relationship with Mr. Flynn affect the trial?"

The questions rolled out as a third car pulled in. A woman in an orange rain slicker jumped from the passenger seat with a video camera.

"Jesus," Alec muttered. "Keep your head down."

We ran toward the SUV, the place that had less than an hour ago been our safe haven. We shouldn't have ever left the apartment. What would have happened if they'd caught us in the car together? What if *those* pictures had surfaced?

I never wanted to see myself in another photograph again.

In the front seat of the car I doubled over, face in my hands as Alec sped from the parking lot. He went the opposite direction, making turn after turn I didn't recognize. The apartment at Mac's restaurant had only been five minutes from the store, but we were still driving twenty minutes later.

I finally looked back, no one was following.

Alec fished his cell phone out of his pocket and dialed a number.

"Matt, hey. We have a problem." He paused. "More pictures. Some jackass in the supermarket caught me and Anna." Another pause, and this time I could hear his teeth click together. "She won't leave again. Look, can you do your thing? The guy said people were already commenting on them. I'll meet you at the apartment with his phone."

"*More* pictures?" I asked weakly. "The other photos . . ." Me. Maxim. My nearly naked body. I grabbed the door as he swung around another curve.

"Not those photos," he said. "Pictures of me."

I waited a beat. "This has happened to you before?"

He nodded, thumb tapping the wheel.

"This kind of thing happens to you often," I said.

His gaze shot in my direction. "I thought it was late enough, you'd be all right. I didn't think this would happen." He shook his head. "Fuck. I didn't think."

He beat himself up in silence while I considered what he'd said. Frat Boy wasn't kidding. Alec *was* a celebrity now. I knew he'd been in the newspaper and on the news broadcasts, but I'd deliberately turned off my Internet since he started popping up because it hurt too much to see him. Strangers were taking pictures of him. *Saturday Night Live* had done something.

I looked across the cabin at him, horrified. He wasn't a public person. He didn't like the spotlight. He'd flown under the radar his whole life—first with his alcoholic father, and then with a criminal megalomaniac boss. He was way out of his league here.

My poor Alec.

I searched for something to break the tension. Something told me he wouldn't have believed *It's not your fault.*

"At least you don't have to pretend with Janelle anymore," I said. It made me feel a little better, at least.

The wheels whirred over the wet pavement.

"You have to stay at the apartment until this clears," he said. "If I could be sure you'd have protection, I'd send you as far away from me as possible."

I stiffened.

"Because that worked so well before."

"Max will know you're with me," he said sharply. "If he wants to find you, all he has to do is follow me."

"Then let him," I said. "Let him find me. I've got a few things I want to say to him."

He scoffed. "You don't know what you're talking about."

I turned to face him, blood simmering. "I don't? It was *me* he took, Alec. *Me* he drugged. My naked body he used for his porno pictures."

"Stop!" Alec slammed his hand down on the steering wheel.

"I won't stop!" I shouted. "I get to face him. You know what he told me? He said it *wasn't personal.* He fucked up my life, and it wasn't personal."

Alec slammed on the brakes, and I braced myself against the dashboard. I looked up. We were back at the apartment. Another set of headlights was pulling in behind us, and I ducked behind the seat before I recognized Matt's car.

"It wasn't just you he took," Alec said quietly. "I bled the whole time you were missing. I still do, every single day. I've thought of twenty different ways to kill him, Anna, and every minute that passes that I don't makes me less worthy to be your man."

My rage hit a brick wall.

"I'm sorry for what happened tonight," he said. "It won't happen again."

With that, he left the car, walked me to the door, and left me inside while he went to talk to Matt.

I paced around the apartment for ten minutes. Then twenty. I peeked out the curtains for Matt, but though he was in his car, with the lights on, Alec was nowhere to be seen.

I moved to the veranda, and searched through the darkness. The rain had stopped its tantrum for the time being, and the sand on the beach was glowing a pale silver. After a moment I saw him walk around the edge of the darkened restaurant. He stopped as a motion-activated light flipped on, then pulled a chair from the deck beneath it. I watched as he climbed up to adjust the positioning.

He checked all the lights, making sure we were safe. Then he disappeared again within the restaurant.

I thought of what he'd said. How he'd bled for me when I was gone. I had no doubt that was true—Alec internalized his pain like no one I'd ever met. I could feel it when I'd tried to massage his shoulders and seen it in the shadows beneath his eyes. I thought of Frat Boy, and how Alec had been made into some sort of celebrity. Part of me wanted to find my cell phone and turn on the Internet feature, just to look up what people were saying, but I stopped myself. If there was anything that could make me homicidal, it was someone hurting him.

I bled for him, too.

The door creaked and made a suction noise as he entered. He looked tired now—it was close to two in the morning. He barely glanced at me as he put a plate on the counter.

"I got some stuff for a sandwich from the restaurant," he said. "I know it's not what you had in mind, but . . ."

"Alec."

He rolled back his shoulders, and slowly lifted his eyes to mine, as if this took some feat of strength.

I moved closer. Closer, until the wariness in his deep blue eyes turned to curiosity. I reached for his belt, and unhooked it.

"I don't want us to hurt anymore," I said.

I lowered to my knees.

"Anna." He reached for my hair, combing it back with his fingers.

I unhooked the button, slowly unzipped his fly.

"Leave everything else outside," I said. "All that matters is inside. You and me, right?"

He whispered my name, a broken sound that made my heart lurch. I didn't know what the future would bring, but I knew us. I knew he needed to regain some of the control he'd lost. I knew I needed him to take it.

"Right?" I asked again, looking up at him as I tugged his still-damp jeans down his legs.

"Right," he said.

He stepped out of his pants, and I pulled my tank top over my head. He leaned back to look at me.

"Do you like the way I look?" I asked.

"Yes."

I bit my bottom lip, liking the immediacy of his answer. My eyes lowered. Directly before me was his cock, covered by the thin cotton of his black boxer briefs. It looked huge, jutting up at an angle, the head barely still trapped beneath the elastic waistband.

My mouth began to water. I'd done this occasionally before Alec, but I'd never enjoyed it. It was just a step in the dance, a means to the end. But with Alec, everything was different. I longed to touch him. I wanted to taste him. His body pleased me in so many ways.

"Do you like seeing me on my knees?" My voice had changed to a soft rasp. It wasn't deliberate. Something primal was taking me over. I could feel it transforming me, changing the way I moved, making my breasts tender and my skin more sensitive.

He gave a throaty groan that I took as an agreement. The long, lean muscles of his thigh flexed as I placed my flat palms on them. My hands slid higher, moved to the front over his hard length. I stroked him like that for a moment. He tipped his head back. His breath came out in a huff.

I crawled closer. "You think you're the only one who likes this power?"

Gripping the waistband, I began to pull his underwear down his thighs.

"Take your shirt off," I said.

He reached over his shoulders, like men do, pulling it over his head from the back. It was tossed somewhere on the floor beside us.

He stood naked before me. I hadn't looked at him like this in months, and instantly I felt the arousal heat my veins. His body screamed sex. His wavy chocolate hair was a mess, like he'd just got out of bed. His perfect mouth made my nipples hard, made my center ache with memories of what it could do. His thick arms were made to lift my body, his fingers to tease me, his muscular chest to slide over mine. And his cock . . .

I felt a little dizzy staring at it.

Thick and long, like steel encased in velvet, his cock was meant to fuck.

That wild creature rousing inside of me tore free. There was no gentle teasing as I had intended. No slow seduction. A crazed need to touch shut off the power to my brain. I grabbed the base of his cock in my hands and licked his engorged head. I tasted salt and night and *him*, all of him, and I drew him deeper, wanting more.

"Christ," he sputtered. "What are you . . ." He groaned.

I pumped my fist, reaching around his hips to his lower back. I dug my nails in a line down his spine, making him arch toward me. I took his cock as deeply as I could, until I gagged, and then I took more.

His hands gripped my hair, and soon he was fucking my mouth. I could hear his grunts of pleasure. Hear the suction of my wet lips. I scraped my teeth down his length, and his hand tightened, searing my scalp with a brilliant flash of pain that bolted down my body like lightning.

Frantically, I reached behind me to remove my bra. Shaking with need, my fingers fumbled, and the clasp only partially unhooked. With a cry of frustration, I jerked the cups down, letting my heavy breasts spill free. I rose higher on my knees, hating the emptiness in my mouth but giving into the sudden need to feel his dick on my chest.

Still holding him in my fist, I rubbed him over my aching nipples, moaning with the bursts of pleasure that smooth, wet touch brought. Alec spread his legs a little wider so that he could get lower, and I tucked him between my breasts, shoved together by my impatient hands. I bounced on my knees, giving him that friction he craved, while I licked the head of his cock each time it poked through.

"You like that?" I taunted. I knew he liked it. His cock had turned a deep shade of red, and his abs were flexing. His eyes were dilated, his jaw locked tightly.

He swore. He muttered something about my beautiful tits. He said I needed a good fucking.

"So give it to me," I said, throwing out the challenge.

With a roar he grabbed me under the arms and hoisted me toward the couch. My hip hit the lamp, and it cracked against the wall. My feet seemed unable to keep up. It hardly mattered; he jerked my shorts down over my hips and bent me over the arm of the sofa. I wasn't wearing panties—I'd left them off after our escapade in the car, and now I was bare and ready for him.

"You tease," he ground out. "You naughty little tease."

He slapped my ass. I yelped. My skin felt the sting for one second before he lowered and kissed me there. Kissed me, like he'd kissed between my thighs earlier. With his wet tongue lapping me up. He rose, and slapped again. The wet sound punctuated our heavy breaths. The strike made my pussy vibrate. He licked me again. Slap, lick. Slap, lick.

He spread my buttocks. And I tensed for what was to come, a second before he spanked me.

I jolted straight. Every nerve came alive. Every part of me quaked with the hard ripple of need.

He pushed me back down, spread me open.

And then kissed me.

He massaged my buttocks. Squeezed my damp inner thighs. His thumb made a pressured arc around my entry and then forged within while his clever fingers gave my clit a series of hard pats.

He kissed his way up my spine.

"She's quiet now," he mocked. And then he positioned himself at the entrance of my pussy, and thrust inside.

Twenty-four

I don't know when I started coming. There was no beginning to it, no breath before the fall. There was only the fire, consuming me, while he pumped into my body.

"Is this what you want?" His voice was rough.

I could hear us fitting together. Wet sounds. *Slap, slap, slap.* Like his hand on my ass. Like his fingers on my clit.

"You need this," he said, half in awe. "You're grabbing my dick like a fist."

My muscles clenched around him, held him, even as he withdrew and entered again. All my senses focused on that place we connected. I didn't know what I clung to, or even where we were. There was only his punishing cock, forcing me higher, making me his.

He turned my head, swiping my hair back from my face. His chest came flush against my back as he watched my face.

"Harder," I demanded.

His pace slowed a little, but he slammed back into me. The noise I made was something between a shout and a sob.

"Yes. Yes, Alec. *More.*"

His fingers dug into my hips. I arched my back. He was striking that place inside me that made my blood turn to fire. Each thrust felt like another orgasm.

"Fuck!" I screamed. "*That*. Don't stop. Don't stop."

He went wild. Faster. Harder than ever before. The space between us was disappearing. The time we'd been apart was disappearing. We had always been this way. Nothing had ever come between us.

Nothing ever would.

He lifted my knee and pulled it onto the arm of the couch, situating himself even deeper. My shaking arms collapsed, my damp cheek fell to a pillow. I ground my clit against the leather, unashamed, riding the tidal wave of pleasure that seemed like it would never end.

"Closer," he said. "Can't get close enough. Fuck. *Fuck*."

He reached around my body, clutched my breast. He pulled me to him so that we were back to chest, skin to skin. He swore. I reached over my head and gripped his sweat-dampened hair. I yanked it as he bit my shoulder.

He came so hard I felt it like another hot thrust. His hoarse shout filled the room as he rode it out.

Then he collapsed over me, and we both crashed sideways onto the floor.

"Ow," I managed when I had regained the power of speech. He'd taken the brunt of our weight in the fall, and had yet to move off his side. I was still tucked against his body, and his heavy arm was slung across my waist.

A low chuckle rumbled in his chest.

I started to giggle.

Soon we were both laughing.

"What just happened?" I turned slowly, aware of every muscle in my body. It felt like I had just run a marathon. He rolled onto his back, running his hands down his face.

"You," he said. "You happened."

I crawled onto his chest, looking down at him.

"Is that such a bad thing?"

"The worst." He smirked. I wanted to swat at him, but ended up just rolling my wrist limply over his pec. I nuzzled my cheek into his neck and slid my knee up his thigh.

"Sorry about your bra," he said.

I vaguely remembered the rending of fabric as he'd pulled the last clasp free. I glanced behind me, finding it a tattered mess amidst our scattered clothes.

"I guess this gives me an excuse to buy something new."

He hummed his approval.

"Are you all right?" he asked. "That was kind of rough."

"Kind of?" I said. "Tomorrow I'll be walking like I just spent the last eighteen hours riding a horse."

He began drawing slow circles on my back with his fingertips.

"It wasn't quite eighteen hours."

This time I did swat him. But I laughed, too, and could feel his smile even though I couldn't see his face.

"I'm okay," I said, when it became apparent he was still waiting for an answer. "I liked it."

"I got that."

"You're awfully gloaty," I said. "You seemed to be enjoying yourself, too."

He became still, and in that stretch of quiet, I grew vulnerable.

"This is the best moment of my life," he said.

"Oh, come on." He was grinning again. Maybe he'd never stopped.

"What's the best moment of your life?" he asked.

He was serious, and as we lay in the dark, my fingers began their own exploration of his chest.

"Like, ever?"

"Yeah."

The first time you told me you loved me. The day you took me to the beach. Just now, when you finally let go.

There were dozens more, but they all seemed too intimate, even after what had just happened. I didn't want to scare him.

It already scared me enough as it was.

A memory came to me from years ago.

"The day my dad told me what had happened to my birth mother." It was two weeks after he'd been called to that fast-food restaurant where I waited for her to return. I'd been put in a temporary foster home, but he'd come to visit every day. We were sitting on the front porch swing when he said she wasn't coming back this time.

"Why?"

"Because she died, Anna," he'd told me gently.

There wasn't sadness, but anger. I hated her so much in that moment.

"How?"

He'd looked at me, and pushed the big glasses he'd worn up the bridge of his nose. *"Drugs."*

"You're sure?" I'd asked. *"Sometimes it's hard to tell. Sometimes she just goes missing, too."*

He'd told me he was sure. That it was a heroin overdose. He'd asked if I knew what that was, and I'd told him yes. We didn't say anything more about it that day, but it wasn't the last time we'd discussed it.

Alec pulled me closer. "Why?"

I rested my chin on his chest, surprised that I hadn't been overwhelmed by the memory.

"He was the first person who didn't try to bullshit me." I winced. "God. That was heavy. Sorry."

His brows pinched together, and I wondered if he was thinking about the times he'd lied to me.

"If that's your best, what's your worst?" he asked, undeterred.

I thought about this. There had been bad times, many of them since I'd met Alec, but he had a way of healing them.

"That was my worst, too."

His hand came to rest on my lower back.

"Your turn," I said. "What's your best moment? For real this time."

"I wasn't kidding. Right now."

I smirked. "That's cheating."

He wasn't smiling. He stared up at the ceiling, and wove our fingers together.

"Sweet talker," I said. "You know you've already got me naked, right?"

"Oh, I know," he said.

I rose up on my forearms, needing to see his face. He looked peaceful. No worry in his eyes. No tension in his jaw.

"You mean it," I murmured.

His mouth quirked up on one side. He brought my hand to his lips and kissed my knuckles.

"Right now," he repeated. "The day I got out and you were waiting in my clothes. The night I watched you touch yourself against the window in your old apartment. The first time I talked to you in your car outside the house." He paused. "When you told me you'd never come with another man inside you."

I swallowed, swamped with emotions.

He lifted our hands to my face. "Every single time you've given yourself to me. Every time you say my name. And when you bite your lip and scowl like you're doing now."

I promptly stopped biting.

"What's your worst?" I asked breathlessly.

"All the times I lost you."

"Alec . . ."

His gaze returned to the ceiling. "If I wasn't around, what would you be doing right now?"

His questions kept throwing me off. I could hardly keep my balance.

"I can't . . ." I touched his lips with my index finger. "I can't see you not around."

He studied me while the impact of this truth settled on us both. I'd tried living without him, but nothing worked. It wasn't that I couldn't do it, but that everything suffered without his presence. Life was less colorful, less important, and certainly less exciting.

"I talked to a therapist," I said. "Amy's therapist. I called her." Sometimes I was so smooth.

"Yeah?"

I nodded.

"That's great." The genuine pride made me feel stronger.

"Yeah." I sat up, keeping my toes tucked under his thigh as I hugged my knees to my chest. "I want to help people like that again."

"Kids?"

I nodded. "Maybe women, too." Not that I was exactly in a position to act objectively right now. But maybe someday.

The idea took hold in my mind. Helping kids like Alec and I had been. Helping women who'd been victimized. If nothing else, at least I could empathize.

He sat up. "Am I stopping you from doing that?"

I shook my head. "Actually, you've been pushing me that direction without even knowing it." I'd started volunteering for CASA because of the stories Alec had told me about his youth.

I waved my hand. "I mean the whole safe house, can't-be-seen-in-public thing sort of works against the idea of steady employment, but you know."

"And massage?"

"Maybe I'll just keep a few of my special clients."

"A few." His eyes narrowed.

"Just the really sexy ones." I rested my head on his shoulder,

grinning. "What about you? No trial. No asshole billionaire trying to kill us. Where would you be, Alec Flynn?"

He shrugged.

"Come on." I pushed his shoulder. "I told you."

He rocked back, as if I'd shoved him hard, and when he came
back he looked me right in the eye.

"I'd be working on planes. Preferably when they're on the
ground," he said. "And I'd be trying to convince you to marry me."

Twenty-five

slept. I'm not sure how, after Alec had dropped the *M* word, but I did. After we'd talked, we cleaned up and went to bed. We didn't mention what he'd said—we hardly had spoken at all. He hadn't seemed upset by my silence. To the contrary, he seemed pleased to have made me nervous.

If he only knew.

I told myself we'd been playing the hypothetical game, that's why he'd said what he had. But I'd be kidding myself if I said I thought he wasn't telling the truth.

He'd fallen asleep first, looking as peaceful as he had when he'd told me all his favorite moments were spent with me. Watching him, I made up lists in my mind of all the reasons why he and I wouldn't work out. "One of us might die" being somewhere near the top. Then that we hadn't collectively spent that much time together. A dozen more followed, including that he was out of my league. I even made up scenarios where women passed him their numbers and cornered him in restaurants.

And then I fantasized about kicking their asses and punishing him with the best blow job he'd ever had.

As hard as I tried, I couldn't imagine letting him go again. Ever. And that was the most frightening revelation of all.

Finally, his breaths became hypnotic. I'd fallen asleep in his arms, waking in the late morning with such a feeling of rightness it couldn't be anything but wrong.

I'd slipped out of his arms and gone to the living room, where I promptly started cleaning again.

Marriage. Fucking Alec and his fucking pillow talk.

I was scrubbing the sinks when I heard him call my name. Something in his tone had me dropping the sponge and racing around the corner into the bedroom, yellow rubber gloves still sudsy.

He was rising from bed, naked, semierect. His hair was a just-been-fucked mess, and his body was entirely too lickable. But there was panic in his eyes.

"Alec?" I kept my hands up so as not to drip on the floor. "What's wrong?"

He blinked at me, and my throat went dry as his gaze shot over the tank top and panties I wore. Then he sat, beckoning me closer.

"Nothing," he said gruffly. "I didn't know where you were. Are you cleaning again?"

I turned my hands. "Caught."

Our knees touched. He opened his legs and pulled me between his thighs. "Do you always wear these gloves?"

"Sometimes."

He tugged up the hem of my shirt, showing off my belly button. His thumb started there, and drew a slow line to the waistband of my panties. All my concerns from last night went up in smoke.

"Maybe we should take this off and you can show me how you scrub the floor."

I smirked. "Dirty boy."

He pulled one glove free, taking his time to reveal my forearm bit by bit.

"Very dirty," he said, throwing the yellow rubber on the floor and moving to the other side. "Feel free to take the necessary action."

I laughed. "There's no point at all in wearing clothes around you."

"Nice to hear you're catching on."

But as his fingers slipped within the side of my panties, he paused.

He turned me, and I followed his gaze to the bruises on my hip. Looking at them brought a tender ache between my legs, an echo of last night's activities.

He kissed that spot slowly. My breath hitched at the rasp of his stubbled jaw on my side, but his lips were feather soft.

He eased my shirt higher. Examining my ribs, my other side. He gathered the fabric and moved it over the swell of my breasts. Hard peaks formed under his gaze, but he frowned at another bruise on the left side of my chest.

That, too, he kissed.

"Are you very sore?" he asked.

I was a little, but even this touch was enough to make my body blush and my heart stutter. The need for him was unquenchable. Sore or not, I would take him again, and again.

"I'm all right," I murmured as his mouth lowered to my nipple. His eyes drifted closed as he drew me deeper, and I gave a small gasp at the gentle way he touched me. His arms circled my back, petting me softly, never too tight.

After a moment he stood, taking me with him, and turned to lay me on the bed. He kissed every inch of me. My neck, the inside of my wrist, each one of my ribs. He kissed my toes and the backs of my knees and the insides of my thighs. And finally, he kissed that place between my legs.

The soreness evaporated. My heart felt like it might burst. He was so careful, so attentive. He worshipped my body—I could feel his intent in every slow stroke of his tongue and press of his lips.

There was no struggle, no staggering flash of heat. There was a softness to this pleasure, and as the warmth shivered through me, I sighed.

He held me after, and when I palmed him, and stroked him to his release, he barely met my gaze.

He left not long after to meet with his lawyer downtown. I tried to keep myself busy in his absence, but I could only clean so much. There was a television, but though I stuck an old DVD in the player, I couldn't sit still long enough to watch it.

I tried to think about Miami, but nothing new came up. I needed to go there, see if anything jogged my memory. There had to be something that showed I was there that night with Maxim Stein, I just had to find it.

Somehow that didn't seem satisfying enough.

Hiding from him wasn't exactly satisfying either, but it was keeping me alive. I wasn't exactly dying for a replay of the whole kidnapping routine.

I called Carolyn again, and after filling her in on my relationship status, she asked if I was having buyer's remorse.

"Buyer's remorse," she said. "You know, you've lusted over those Louboutin pumps for months, but after you buy them you can't even enjoy them because all you can think is, *Did I really just drop a thousand dollars on shoes?*" She laughed. "Too much self-disclosure?"

I grinned.

"No remorse," I said. "I love being with him. It's the times in between that are hard."

"How come?"

I was sitting on the floor in the living room, my back against the couch where we'd gone crazy on each other last night. For some reason, it was hard to look at it now.

"I guess I keep waiting for the other shoe to drop," I said.

"Well, let's hope it isn't a Louboutin pump." She chuckled to herself. "Is this waiting for the other shoe thing new?"

My initial reaction was to say yes, but if I was being honest that wasn't entirely true. The day my birth mother had taken me swimming—one of our best days, really—I'd known it had been our last. Then there were the countless nights lying in a new bed, wondering when my new dad and mom were going to send me back to foster care. In high school I'd questioned if Amy was really my friend or if she just pitied Orphan Anna, and when I'd first fallen for Alec it seemed all I could do was wait for him to leave. Even Frat Boy's pictures last night had felt more like an inevitability than a true shock.

"I guess I've been thinking that way awhile now," I said.

"Would you call yourself an expert?"

"In pessimism?"

"Sure," she said. "Whatever you want to call it."

I frowned. Therapy wasn't exactly making me feel better about myself today.

"Maybe."

"No judgment from me," Carolyn specified. "You seem like an intelligent woman, Anna. Smart people learn from their experiences so they can anticipate what to expect in the future."

"But I keep coming back to him, even when I know this is going to hurt me."

"Has he hurt you?" she asked.

Alec had never directly hurt me. His lies and omissions had been wounding, but he'd made up for them. It was all the chaos that surrounded him that was dangerous.

"No," I said.

"So you keep expecting heartache, and he proves you wrong," she said. "Sometimes it's hard to be vulnerable when you've spent a lifetime protecting yourself."

"I don't like being vulnerable," I said, thinking of Maxim Stein and the pictures.

"Not many people do." She adjusted the phone, making a soft whooshing sound. "Being vulnerable isn't the same as being a victim."

"I'm not a victim," I said quickly.

"I didn't say you were," she said. "But how's thinking like one working out for you?"

Okay, therapy was definitely not making me feel better today.

"So what am I supposed to do, think happy thoughts?"

"You've practiced assuming the worst will happen, what would happen if you tried changing things up?"

"Bad things," I said, exasperated. "The last time I tried *changing things up* someone took me, and drugged me, and took pictures of me, and I woke up by a Dumpster without a clue where I'd been for *three days*."

In her silence I pressed my forehead to my raised knees. My wounds, that had only started to heal, were exposed. She'd ripped the Band-Aid right off.

I wished Alec were here.

"Take a deep breath," she said after a moment. "And when you're ready, let's talk about that."

By the time Alec came back, I was emotionally drained. Carolyn and I had talked for over an hour, and even though she'd patched me back up before we'd ended, I still felt weaker than before.

Not weaker, she had said. Just exhausted. She'd told me avoiding the things that had happened to me would make them fester. It was a defense mechanism. It was what I'd done for years with my birth mother, which was probably why I still carried around her baggage.

I didn't want her to haunt me anymore.

I didn't want Maxim Stein to haunt me either.

I just wanted Alec.

From the veranda, I watched him drive up, park, and sit in

the cab of the SUV for two full minutes before exiting the car. I
didn't know what he was doing, but when he stepped outside he
looked as heavy as I felt.

He walked to Matt's car, and after a short exchange, they
shook hands through the driver's side window, and Matt drove
away. It seemed odd—Matt usually stayed through the night.
But maybe Alec had offered him some time to crash again.

I met Alec at the door, and before either of us could talk, I
rose on my tiptoes and wrapped my arms around his neck. He
settled into me one breath at a time, until his muscles relaxed,
and his hands fanned over my back.

"I missed you," I whispered.

"I missed you, too."

"What happened today?"

He didn't let go or back away. He nuzzled his chin into the
crook of my neck.

"Can we just sit awhile? Watch a movie or something? I can
get Mac to make us something."

"That sounds perfect."

And it did, but I worried about what had happened to him
today. As if reading my mind, he added, "I'll tell you everything
later. I just need to be with you now."

Later didn't end up being that night. We'd sat on the couch
and cuddled, my head on his thigh, his fingers threaded with
mine, both of us in our own separate worlds. We barely talked,
and when it was time for bed, his hands never roamed.

I dreamed of black stars again that night, and when I woke in
the morning, Alec was gone.

For two days it continued that way. He became increasingly more
distracted, and distracted *me* every time I asked why. He touched
me at every chance, and held me a little too tightly, and when we
made love he was careful, and gentle, without the dirty words and

hard passion I'd come to love. There was a sadness in him I couldn't touch, and it worried a hole right through the middle of my chest.

He left to meet his lawyer during the day, and while he was gone he made me keep the prepaid phone in my pocket. He'd text friendly reminders every so often.

Lock the doors.

Did you lock the doors?

Check the doors.

I didn't mess with him too much. Even though he seemed concerned, I was comforted by a police patrol car that I caught passing by, and even once turning around in the gravel drive in front of the apartment.

On the second night he told me that Matt had done what he could to remove the pictures posted on the Internet, but he couldn't do anything if people had copied them to their social media sites. Our FBI tail still hadn't come back to watch the apartment, and when I asked Alec about this, he said Matt was taking an extended break. Then he told me that Janelle was coming back from Miami, and that she'd found nothing but a surveillance video of a white sedan pulling through the gate early Saturday morning. She texted Alec an image of it, and when he showed me it did look vaguely familiar.

"You recognize this car?" he asked.

I pulled at my hair lightly, trying to trigger the memory.

"A few days before I went to that bar, there was this CASA thing—an art class."

"At the Children's Museum," said Alec.

"Right," I said, glancing up at him. He'd been to see his lawyer again, but wasn't dressed for court. He was wearing a T-shirt and the blue ball cap that I now realized he wore when he was trying to avoid being recognized. The ends of his hair stuck out the back in unruly waves, and my fingers itched to throw that hat to the ground and grip it in my fists.

"I thought I saw you that night," I said.

"In the café across the street." He glanced down, a small smile on his face. "That definitely was not me."

I shoved him lightly, but it made me feel all glowy inside that he'd been there that day, like some kind of guardian angel.

"Creeper."

He shrugged. "The car."

I refocused on the issue at hand.

"I'd gone to the park on the Bay walk, the one by your apartment."

"Who's the creeper?" he asked.

I glared at him. "I was just looking out over the water, and this car stopped behind me. A white car."

"This car?"

He showed me the image on his cell phone again. It was grainy and at an angle, hard to make out clearly.

"I don't know." I frowned. "Maybe. I had a bad feeling about it. I rode the horn for ten seconds before he moved."

"Did you see anyone through the windows?"

"Tinted," I remembered. "Too dark to see through." I paused. An image filled my mind: a flash of lights as I hurried across a parking lot. A couple asking if I was all right.

"What?"

"The night. At the bar. I . . . I think this car was there."

Alec was sitting straighter now.

"I think . . ." I closed my eyes. The memory was unclear and slippery. The harder I focused on it, the more it slid away. "I was wearing heels. I couldn't move very fast. I'd parked, and was trying to go in, and this white car almost hit me. A couple outside asked if I was okay."

"Why were you rushing?" he asked. "Was someone after you?"

I shook my head. "No, I don't think so. I was upset. About the whole you and Janelle thing."

He leaned away, the scowl so deep on his face it looked permanent.

"That's why you went to that bar."

I realized we'd talked around this, but never actually about it.

I picked at my fingernails. Needed a manicure. Yes. Definitely needed a manicure.

"Anna."

"I didn't want to think about you anymore. It hurt too much." I rose. "Please don't apologize or go away. I don't want to do that anymore."

"All right," he said after a while. He still wasn't looking at me. I shouldn't have said that. He hadn't needed to know. I could have made up something else. I could have just told him I needed a break from Amy and my dad's babysitting.

He finally looked at me.

"Will you have dinner with me tomorrow night?" he asked.

His telltale thumb was tapping on his side. Was he actually nervous?

"Yes," I said. "Of course."

He smiled, but his eyes stayed distant.

"I'll pick you up at six."

"Are we going somewhere?" That seemed like a bad idea.

"It'll be safe," he assured. He stuck a thumb over his shoulder in the direction of the door. "I need to check some things out and call Janelle about the car. See if they can find a plate number."

"Okay."

He left, and was gone a long time. So long I fell asleep on the couch, and woke only briefly, to the feel of his safe arms carrying me to bed.

Twenty-six

By five thirty the next night I was dressed and ready. Between replaying moments from my therapy conversation, answering Alec's hourly check-ins via text, and trying to remember more about the white car and its driver, I'd been preparing all day. Amy, likely having known Alec and I would head this direction, had packed some of my cuter things when she'd come over, including a knee-length, halter-top summer dress with a lacy white hemline. It was clearly romantic without being over-the-top sexy.

I'd pinned my hair up in a twist, leaving a few loose tendrils to frame my face. My makeup was perfect. I'd even repainted my toenails pink with polish from the supplies she'd left. I didn't know where we were going, but even if we just stayed in the car, I wanted to look good for him.

At five thirty-seven I checked the clock again.

"So much for making him wait," I muttered to myself.

As if by magic, a knock came at the door. Alec had a key, so I suspected it might be Matt, returning from his extended break, but I was wrong.

Alec stood on the mat outside. In a white dress shirt with the sleeves rolled up to the elbows, black slacks, and his baby blue silk tie, he'd never looked sexier. His face had been cleanly shaved, but his hair was still shoved back carelessly. His eyes glimmered like the ocean under a clear, blue sky. And in one hand was a fragrant bundle of greenery with small white flowers—not the normal vase bouquet, but perfect nonetheless.

"I was going to wait," he started. Then blinked. "I couldn't."

"I'm glad."

His breath came out in a rush. He rubbed one hand down his throat. I smiled down at my feet, feeling the blush warm my whole body.

"I look nice," I prompted.

"Yeah." He cleared his throat. "I'm getting there."

I laughed. He laughed.

"God," he said. "You really are the most beautiful woman I've ever seen."

I moved closer and breathed in the soft, clean smell of the flowers.

"Are those for me?"

"Yeah."

Yeah. He really was off his game. I smiled.

"I love jasmine."

"I know." He let me take them, set them on the counter. "You said that once. At Max's place. You said if you ever got a house here, you would let it take over your whole yard, that way you could smell it all night."

He had a good memory; I barely recalled that conversation. But then again, when Alec was near it was sometimes difficult to focus. I looked for a vase, but of course there wasn't one. I settled for a bowl, and filled it with water, feeling his eyes on me the whole time.

"Thank you," I said.

He'd followed me into the kitchen, and when I turned, I was

the one thrown off my game. Real men didn't get to be this sweet when they looked so hot. I could only process one sensory over-load at a time. As if beyond my control, I reached for his tie and slowly wrapped it around my fist.

"You're killing me with this thing." I gave his tie a light tug. "Every time you wear it, I remember—"

"Being blindfolded on my bed?" He smirked. His hands found my waist, big and warm. "Why do you think I kept it?"

I stepped closer, so that our bodies came together.

"Maybe later you'll let me wear it again," I said.

His smile melted. I became increasingly aware of my mouth as his gaze lowered to my lips. They felt dry—even with my lipstick—and I licked them. His nostrils flared, and his grip tightened on my waist.

Maybe *later* would be right now.

He hissed slowly, and then pressed his lips to my forehead. "Are you ready to go?"

"I guess that depends on where we're going." I couldn't help but feel a little disappointed in his inability to be distracted.

"This great burger place," he said. "It's close."

I grinned. "Close as in downstairs?"

"You've been there before?" He took my hand and led me to the door.

"This hot guy took me there once," I said.

He closed the door behind us and activated the security system. "Hot, huh?"

"Smokin' hot," I said. "Total perv, though. Always trying to get his filthy paws on my panties."

We walked down the steps, admiring the pink sky and the setting sun.

"Hope you learned your lesson," he said.

"Oh, I did." I leaned close as we rounded the deck. "Now when I see him coming, I don't wear panties at all."

He stopped, and made a noise that sounded like a dying animal. My eyes had fixed on the sign on the door, though. CLOSED, it said, in big black letters.

"Um?"

"Go inside," he ordered. "Before I see if you're telling the truth."

I gave him a wicked, teasing smile, and pushed through the swinging door. It was open, despite the sign, and at the sight of the people gathered on the far side of the room, I automatically jerked back. My back came flush with Alec's chest, and he steadied me with a hand on my shoulder.

Just a few days away from the real world, and already I was gun-shy. It was more than a little pathetic.

"It's all right," Alec whispered. Then he stepped back and let me go.

Everyone had turned to face us when the door had opened, and it took one long moment for my brain to catch up. I knew them. All of them.

"Dad?" Emotion squeezed my throat.

"There's my girl."

My father was the first to break from the pack and approach. In jeans and a polo shirt, he looked no different than he had the last time I'd seen him, but for some reason it felt like years since we'd last been together. I raced toward him and threw my arms around his neck.

"What are you doing here?" I looked over his shoulder to see Amy's smiling face. Mike was beside her. Alec's father, Thomas, was here as well. He was sitting at one of the tables beside a man with a big gut in a U.S. Veteran ball cap—Mac. Even Marcos had come, in full uniform.

"What are you *all* doing here?" I amended.

"We missed you." My dad gave me an extra squeeze. "You look really pretty, honey."

"I missed you," I said, glancing back at Alec, who had gone to shake Mike's hand. "Are you all . . . this is . . . for me?"

"You're cute, but kind of dense," said Amy.

I laughed as she jumped in on our hug, arms around us both. "Who did this?" I asked.

"Who do you think?" she whispered.

Alec. Of course he had. My eyes were getting damp again.

"It's all safe," said Dad, mistaking my quivering lip for worry. "We met at the department, and came in different cars."

"On loan from impound," said Marcos. He stood with his thumbs hooked in his utility belt. It was amazing how much more confident he was in his cop attire.

I hugged him, too, and kissed him on the cheek.

"Come on," he groaned. "Don't get all mushy on me."

It couldn't have been easy arranging all this. I felt another swell of tears and blinked them back.

"Are you on duty?" I asked, smearing the lipstick down his cheek with my thumb.

"Who do you think's been running your security detail these past couple days?"

My brows lifted as I remembered the cop car I'd seen make a turn around the gravel lot outside. I guess that meant Matt's break really was extended. I hoped he was all right.

The next hour was a blur. I found myself in one embrace after another, and when I'd hugged everyone we started again. Thomas told me I looked ravishing, and after I'd reminded him he was blind, he told me there were some things he could still see—and also that there were laws against harassing the less fortunate. According to Mac he'd been sober for nine weeks, and I agreed he was much more pleasant when he wasn't throwing bottles.

Marcos didn't say much about Derrick with the others around, but when I asked him how things were going, his cheeks turned red, and he grinned and told me to mind my own business.

Amy and Mike were an interesting study. They moved around each other with a new comfort, leading each other into conversation, talking about their girls. But every time they got too close, they would immediately take a step away.

"What's with you two?" I asked Amy, when we had a second alone.

"Nothing, why?" she asked. "Did he say something? He keeps talking to Alec and looking over here. Do you think they're talking about me?"

I guessed that meant they had yet to move past the post-kiss escape into the closet.

Mac announced that he was just putting the finishing touches on dinner—a chicken with mojo sauce and mixed vegetables— and Alec went to help while Marcos chatted with Amy and Thomas joked with Mike. It was then that I noticed my father had stepped outside on the back deck to take a call. He was just finishing when I followed him.

"What are you doing out here?" he asked when he hung up the phone. "Your party's inside."

"My party's right here," I said, sliding under his arm. It was such an easy thing now, but there were years where even being near each other had been hard for me.

We leaned against the rickety wooden railing beneath the Christmas lights that Mac had left off on account of the restaurant technically being closed.

"How are you?" he asked. "Mug's been worried. He's been making sure nobody takes your bed in your absence."

"Great," I said, imagining all the dog hair I'd be coming home to.

Home. I hadn't thought about that apartment being home since I'd left. Now the thought of leaving my little refuge with Alec seemed incomprehensible.

"I'm good, Dad. I've been resting and eating and talking to a therapist and singing in the church choir and doing all sorts of healthy mind/healthy spirit activities."

He smirked. "I hope some of that's true, smart-ass."

"Some of it is." I rested my head on his shoulder. "How were the Keys?"

"Hot and boring," he said. "But I had some good Key lime pie."

I smiled. My dad was a sucker for sweets, an addiction he claimed came from my mother's baking habits. "What were you doing there?"

He squeezed me a little tighter. "Missing woman. Picked up a couple leads, but the trail went cold."

"That sounds less like PI work and more like actual detective work," I said.

"Believe it or not, I am an *actual* detective."

"Retired."

"On paper."

I sighed. I was used to him not sharing much about his cases, and didn't press him further.

"Tell me how things are going upstairs," he said.

I stiffened, and immediately felt a Dad Filter slide over my more X-rated thoughts.

"Fine." I felt my nose scrunch, thinking about what Carolyn had said about waiting for something bad to happen. "Things are sort of complex right now."

"I can't imagine why." He snorted when I elbowed him.

The sky was growing purple, the water silver. It stretched on for miles, until it connected to the silver high-rises and beige hotels on the opposite side of the Bay.

"He loves you," my dad said after a while.

It was a statement of fact, but it still felt a little uncomfortable. Like loving another man was somehow pushing him away.

"I know," I said. "Does that bother you?"

His opinion mattered, whether I chose to be with Alec or not.

"It did," he admitted. "He's been working hard to change my mind."

How many times had they talked these last few months about my safety? My world hadn't crumbled when bad things had happened because I had the strongest net in the world to fall back on. I was fortunate in ways most people would never know, and that awareness humbled me just as it filled me with joy.

So much for thinking like a victim.

"You love him?" my dad asked.

I nodded.

He brushed my hair back. "Then one day all this mess won't matter."

"You say that with such confidence."

He waited a beat. "Your mom and I didn't have it easy in the beginning either."

I pictured her sitting on his lap at Christmas while I opened my first presents. Snapping him with a dishrag when he ate the cookie dough before she could bake it. Holding hands when they came back from date night.

They'd always made it look easy, even when they were fighting.

I remember he'd mentioned this once, that they had their own story.

"I thought you guys met at the holiday ball," I said. It was a fund-raiser my dad's precinct put on each year for homeless families.

"We did."

"And it was love at first sight."

"It was."

"So?"

He inhaled. "She was there with her husband."

"She *what*?" I withdrew from beneath his arm so I could look at him face on.

He smashed his lips to the side, scratched at his jaw.

"She was wearing this purple dress and these terrible shoes with these big white bows on them. The music started, and she couldn't dance in them, so she threw them into the corner and danced in her bare feet. I looked right at Terry Benitez and said, 'I'm going to marry that woman.'"

I'd heard this story before, but there hadn't been a husband, and he'd said these words to his partner.

"Wait," I said. "Terry was your partner? I never knew that."

"I told you we went way back." He hunched. "I didn't know she was married when I said that."

"When did you find out?"

"Oh, about five minutes later when I asked her to dance with me, and her husband punched me in the jaw."

"Did you know him?"

"I did." My dad was nodding. "Nice guy, too, apart from his right hook. He and I had gone through the academy together."

"So what happened?"

"I couldn't stop thinking about her. I ran into her about a month later at a coffee shop. Then we ran into each other again. And again. After a while it was pretty obvious what was going on." He gave a heavy sigh. "I told her I was going to get a new assignment in a different precinct. Cops have rules, Anna. We don't throw each other under the bus, and we certainly don't mess around with each other's wives."

I stared at him, surprised, unable to find the words.

"You know your mother. She had quite a bit to say about that. Long story short, she blamed me for screwing everything up, and said I was a coward if I didn't figure out a way to make it work." He smiled now. "We told her husband together. I got wrung up on some BS charge after that and was demoted. I rode a desk for three years for that woman. But Anna, she was worth every minute of it."

I turned back to the bay. "Wow."

"I know complex, honey," he said. "And I know good men can make mistakes. What matters is how they fix them. I just hoped that you'd skip all that heartache and go straight to the good stuff."

Alec had caused me a lot of heartache, but as I slid beneath my father's arm again, and heard the laughter coming from inside the restaurant, I couldn't help but wonder if this *was* the good stuff.

"Ahem."

I turned to see Amy, leaning through the door, grinning.

"Some of us are starving in here."

Looking up at my dad one more time, I thought of everything he'd been through to get my mom, and then me. Yes, he knew complex, but he also knew which battles were worth fighting.

We sat around a big wooden table, Alec on my right, Amy on the other, the savory smell of chicken filling the air. Thomas argued with Mike and Marcos, and my dad talked to Mac about Vietnam. We laughed and ate and told stories, and as the moments passed, I could feel the years pass, too. I could see us all growing older, see a ring on Amy's finger, see Paisley, her nose in a book at the end of the table, and Chloe arguing with her dad about going to see her boyfriend. I could see my dad's hair thin, and a few more wrinkles on Thomas's face, and Marcos bringing Derrick without a second thought. I could see Christmases, and Thanksgivings, and birthdays. One after another after another.

And I could see Alec, right by my side through all of it.

"You okay?" he whispered in my ear.

I blinked back the image to find the whole table staring at me. But I wasn't embarrassed that I'd been daydreaming, or of the tears that rolled down my cheeks. It was so warm, I couldn't even remember a time I'd ever been cold.

I turned to Alec, grabbed his face in my hands, and kissed him.

He was tense at first, but soon kissed me back, a smile on his lips. His hands found my bare shoulders and pulled me closer.

"Have I mentioned I have a concealed weapon?" I heard my dad ask.

Alec and I kept kissing.

"Complicated is right," muttered Amy.

"Is something happening?" asked Thomas.

"Love, my friend," said Mac. "Love is happening."

Twenty-seven

They all left too soon, and though I was sad to see them go, my heart pounded in anticipation of what the night would bring. As Alec and I walked up the steps to his apartment, a weighted silence hung between us.

Before we went inside, I stopped.

"Thank you for tonight," I said. "It just topped my all-time-favorite moments list."

He smiled. It killed me, every time.

"So I'm on the list now?" he teased.

"You *are* the list."

He was tilting forward, his free hand running over my ribs. The tip of his nose touched my cheek as he pressed his lips to my jaw.

"Alec?"

"Mm hmm?"

"When we go inside, I want you to touch me."

He pulled back. His eyes flashed, drawing my need to the surface.

"I want you to do whatever you want to me," I said.

"Whatever I want," he murmured.

I nodded. "What do you want, Alec?"

He moved closer, until my back came flush against the door. His jaw skimmed mine. His teeth found my ear.

"I want this never to end."

There was a pain in him that made my chest ache, but before I could ask what he meant, he typed the security code into the box and pushed inside, then turned to me.

His tie was already in a loose knot, which he slipped off now. My pulse scrambled. That damn tie.

"Come here," he said.

I did as he asked, and when we were close, he took my wrists and wrapped one side of the tie around my hand, firmly enough that it wouldn't slip. He did the same with the other end, leaving a foot of space between them.

"Pull it tight," he said.

I gripped the soft fabric, and when I drew it tight it made a soft *snap*.

Then he grabbed the slack, and led me to the corner of the room, where the punching bag still hung. Confused, I watched as he lifted the heavy sack until it unhooked from the chain. He set it on the floor, out of the way, while the chain swung from the exposed ceiling beam.

"Anything I want," he said, almost like a question, but not.

"Yes."

He lifted the slack in the tie and hooked it over the S curve on the last link of the chain. It wasn't high enough that I had to stand on my tiptoes; my fists hung just above my forehead. Still, the power dynamic was clear. He was in control. I was his to do with as he pleased.

I shivered.

"You can let go whenever you need to," he said.

I understood why he was telling me this. The one and only time he'd bound me hadn't started off so great.

When I nodded, he reached behind my neck, and slowly

untied the back of my halter top. When the straps were loose, he pulled them forward, revealing my flushed breasts one inch at a time. The soft fabric scraped over my nipples, making me painfully aware of how they tightened, and tingled, and longed for his wet tongue.

When my chest was completely exposed, he stepped back.

"Beautiful," he muttered.

He didn't touch.

My toes curled as he moved behind me, and soon I felt his fingers in my hair. I'd used a large clawed clip to hold it back, and he released it now, allowing the wavy strands to cascade down my back. His fingers slid into it, untwisting the pieces, massaging my scalp. These acts were somehow more intimate than anything he'd done so far.

I shuddered as I felt him move to the back zipper. Slowly, he eased it down. The cool air brushed my spine, making me stand straighter.

"You're blushing," he said, drawing attention to the heat rising up my neck. His breath warmed my skin as he moved my hair and kissed the top of my shoulder.

My head fell to the side to give him more room. My eyelids drifted closed. A moan slipped from my mouth.

The zipper finally reached its stopping place at the bottom of my waist. Delicately, he peeled the fabric away, until it slid down my legs to the floor.

Apart from my heeled strappy sandals, I was completely naked.

"Nervous?" he asked, still behind me.

Gripping the silk tie, I took a slow, measured breath.

"A little."

"Why?" he asked. "You know I'm going to make you feel good."

"Because . . ." I gasped as his fingers slid down my sides to my hips, and then lower, to draw slow, tantalizing circles on my outer thighs. "Because I think you might torture me on the way there."

His fingers spread as his hips pressed against my lower back.

There was no hiding his arousal as I tried pitifully to grind against him.

"So impatient." Heat jolted through my veins as his palms pressed against my lower belly. "I'd be lying if I said I didn't like you that way."

I smirked.

"Close your eyes," he said.

He stepped away again, and in response, my body drew back into the space where he'd been. The chain rattled and my arms stretched as I reached the limit of my tether.

He crossed in front of me, far too dressed in his slacks and button-up shirt. The fact that he was so covered made me even more aware of my own bareness. My breasts heaved with each waiting breath. I scooted my heels together to conceal the apex of my thighs, but it was no use. Even as I closed my eyes, I could feel his gaze drawing the heat to my skin.

"Why are you hiding from me?" he asked.

A rustle of fabric reached my ears, and then he touched my ankle. I jumped a little at the contact. With my eyes closed, my body felt wildly sensitive.

"I'm not," I lied.

He eased my legs open. Not far, but enough for his other hand to slide between my calves. A bolt of pleasure raced up my thighs, and I clamped them shut.

He kissed my knee, licked the outside, then deliberately began to ease my legs apart again.

"Why?" he repeated.

I didn't want to talk. I wanted to feel. I couldn't do anything *but* feel. His fingertips were climbing higher, spanning the surface of my inner thigh. His tongue was making a curved line toward my center. My muscles flexed uncontrollably. Overhead the chain rattled.

"Because," I sputtered when he stopped. "Because I don't want it to end either."

Any of it. His touch. The feel of his mouth on my body. The way he held me in his sleep. The look on his face when I kissed him in front of my family.

The way my heart felt, right now, when it beat for him alone.

It should have scared me. I should have laughed and said something to take the pressure off. In the past I would have already been planning my escape, trying to envision a new apartment, new job.

I couldn't leave this room. Not even in my head. And I didn't want to.

His hand flinched, the only sign that my words had affected him.

"Show me," he said, so softly I barely heard him.

It was a different kind of bravery that had me pulling my heels apart, nothing like the courage it took to run from Bobby or face Trevor Marshall. This strength went soul deep, and was laced with a trust so fierce, I could have taken on the whole damn world if he'd asked.

Opening myself before him, I looked down, eyes wide and heart pounding, and said, "I want to watch."

His mouth warped into a grin, and his eyes gleamed with a devious kind of pride.

He kissed his way up my thigh, and then he positioned me a little, wider, reaching around to my buttocks to tilt my hips toward him.

Then he began.

It was different than when he'd gone down on me in the car. In the dark it had been impossible to see what he'd been doing—not that I'd been able to watch anyway. I'd thrown my head back and closed my eyes and let the feelings swallow me whole. But now I wanted to see. And as his tongue flattened against my swollen center, I couldn't possibly imagine anything as erotic in the entire history of the universe.

He warmed me up with slow, broad licks, starting deep and

working his way to the top of my slit. Then the tip of his tongue penetrated me, pushing into the folds. I cried out and nearly lost balance at the new riot of sensations, but my grip on the tie, and his arms around my hips, held me upright.

"That's it," he said, as if I was the one doing something right. "That's good. Right there."

He moved one hand to the front and spread me wide then, and began to lick consistently. A low moan rumbled from my chest, and my eyes lost focus as he tugged on my wet, tender lips with his own.

He moved higher.

"*That,*" I cried. "Oh, oh, oh."

He worked my clit, circling it, giving it light flicks and gentle sucks, and I shattered. The heat raced through me, so harsh it burned. Then there was nothing but that exquisite feeling, ravaging my entire body. I swung back, arms stretched taut by the chain, spine bowed, as he continued to support me with one arm.

Even then I felt beautiful.

He brought me back down slowly, with gentle kisses on my mound, my thighs, the bottom of my belly. A sheen of sweat covered my skin. His eyes were closed in bliss. He groaned against me.

And then he began again. This time his fingers entered me. Two of them, pressing upward to that place that felt like the most desperate kind of itch. Rubbing, rubbing, rubbing, while he licked me slowly, then faster, and faster.

I called his name. I begged him to stop. And then not to stop. And then never, ever, *ever* to stop.

Fireworks exploded behind my closed eyes. I came hard, so hard I nearly hurt my shoulders when my weight dropped against the bindings. My fingers were numb from squeezing the tie, but I didn't let go. I couldn't. Not when it felt like this.

He rose, kissing his way up my belly.

"Hurry," I demanded, half-crazed. "I need you. I need . . ."

He kissed my mouth, and I could taste myself on his lips and tongue. Salty, and dark, like him but more intoxicating because it was my desire that coated his body.

Taste what I did to you, he seemed to say. *This pleasure belongs to me.*

He undid his pants and hastily shoved them down his thighs along with his underwear. And then he dipped, and I jerked hard as his stiff cock grazed over my still pulsing clit.

"*Now,*" I cried.

He hiked my thigh up his hip and slowly thrust into me. I arched back, the chain pulling tight, the ceiling beam creaking under my frenzied movements. He filled me completely, until I could barely breathe. Until that sweet, burning stretch stole what remained of my concentration.

And then he lifted the other leg. The brunt of my weight was on my arms now, pulling the fabric taut, but I held strong. He didn't let me wrap my legs around him. He gripped beneath my thighs, and with a savage hunger in his gaze, withdrew, and watched gravity carry me right back over him.

"So fucking wet," he said. "Your thighs are slick with it."

His arms shifted beneath my thighs to bear most of my weight, and they flexed with each subtle movement. He bounced me off him hard this time, and when I rocked back he swore, and did it again. I rode him like I was on some kind of sex swing, and he pounded into me with a hard, deep passion that I could do nothing but take.

"Listen to us," he said roughly. "You feel so fucking good."

I took him deep. Again and again. He guided my body, but I claimed his.

The next orgasm ripped through me, and I stiffened, my blood on fire. He caught me before I fell, and when I regained my bearings, he was holding me, still with his cock deep in me. My damp breasts pressed against his shirt. My arms were free, though still bound by the tie, and I looped it behind his neck, trembling as I held on.

In a few quick steps he was at the couch, and sat with me straddling him. Weak and pliant, I used the tie around the back of his neck to pull him closer, and the fervent dedication in his kiss shook me down to my bones.

"Your shirt," I whimpered as his mouth worked down the cords of my neck. I would have done it myself if my hands weren't still tangled in silk.

He made quick work of it, and I sighed as my breasts smashed against his chest. My fingertips wove through his hair.

"You sweet, beautiful girl," he murmured.

Stronger again, I lifted on my knees and settled back down gently.

"Not that sweet," I said.

"Sweet," he argued, biting my lower lip. "Sweet and wicked."

I would show him wicked.

I slipped off his lap, and caught a flash of teeth as his cock sprang free, deep red and hard as iron. I rubbed myself against it, just one teasing slide before I lifted my heavy arms and lowered the tie down his chest.

He watched as I wound the slack in the tie around the base of his cock. Not tight enough to hurt him, but enough that his fingers dug into my hips.

"Mine," I whispered, and with my bound hands now on his stomach, I rose, and took him all the way to the base, until I could feel that soft, wet silk against my entrance.

"Jesus Christ," he muttered. My fists tightened on the tie.

I rocked my hips and squeezed him, and his face tightened into a grimace.

"Mine," I said again.

Moving faster, I tilted forward, and bit him in the shoulder.

"Fuck, *fuck*, that's good," he ground out.

He joined me, fucking me while I fucked him, holding me still so he could go deeper. Again, I felt the tension build, seemingly impossible after all the pleasure I'd already experienced. It spread across my pelvis, warming, blushing, and then burning as it rippled up my spine and out my limbs.

With a guttural groan, his head tilted back, and he forced me to be still. My last coherent thought was to release the tie, and it unraveled from my hand like a rubber band, releasing the pressure on his cock.

He came and came. His orgasm kept mine going. I could feel the burst of liquid inside me. Feel him swell and shudder. His forehead fell forward, onto my shoulder, and he gave one final, jerky thrust, and then fell back against the couch cushions.

We stayed like that a long time, too tired to move even if we'd wanted to.

"You're going to have to carry me to the kitchen," I said.

His response was hard to make out, but it sounded like he was accusing me of trying to kill him. I smiled. But when I tried to push back, my arms felt like lead.

"In a minute," he mumbled. And then he looked up at me with a lopsided smile. "Hungry?"

"I just did the equivalent of one hundred and seventy-five pull-ups, so yes."

"We have dessert."

"We do?" I rolled off the side in the most ungraceful manner possible. He chuckled.

When I was able, I put on his button-up shirt and went to clean up. I returned to the kitchen to find him standing at the counter with a giant chocolate cake. A candle stuck out of the center of it, and its soft glow flickered off the dimly lit walls.

"Happy birthday, Anna," he said.

I gave him a puzzled look. "It's not my birthday." He knew this. My birthday was in May, the day he'd gotten out of jail.

"I'm a little late," he said with a shrug. How someone could be a sex god one minute and absolutely adorable the next completely baffled me.

"How'd you even get this in here?" I asked.

"I brought it up when you were talking to your dad." He scratched one hand over his head, then sat on one of the stools.

I laughed. "Why?"

"I've messed up a lot of things. Everything, actually."

The playful energy between us grew heavy.

"No more apologies," I said, taking a step closer.

"No." He shook his head. "Just . . . thank you."

That sadness slipped over him again, just for a moment before he smiled it away. I didn't want him to hurt anymore. I moved between his knees and kissed him on the nose.

"You're going to sing, right?"

"Sing?"

"Yeah," I said. "It's my birthday."

He cleared his throat. "You asked for it."

Alec turned out to be a terrible singer, which was delightful to me since he was so damn good at everything else. We passed on plates and dug into the cake with forks, and after the sugar buzz set it, we smeared frosting over each other's bodies and then licked it off.

Some time later we found ourselves in the shower. We used every drop of hot water, and then tumbled out in a wet tangle, laughing uncontrollably.

Before we fell asleep, we made love one final time. Right before he came he told me he loved me, and for one gripping moment before my thoughts scattered, I wondered if he'd actually meant good-bye.

Twenty-eight

woke to a gray morning, with just enough sunlight in the room to tempt me into falling back to sleep. My fingers stretched over the rumpled sheets while my legs extended, leading me to give a satisfied little groan. But any hopes I'd had of curling up against a hard, warm body dissipated as I reached the end of the mattress.

My eyes opened, confirming my suspicions. Alec wasn't in the room, and as I listened, I couldn't hear him in the kitchen either. I snatched a blanket off the floor and threw it over my shoulders. He'd told me he would be here when I woke up. He wasn't needed in court at all today.

The kitchen was clean; no evidence of our chocolate frosting wars. Something pulled me toward the veranda, and when I looked outside the sliding glass doors, my heart settled. He was standing on the beach below the restaurant's deck, feet in the surf, slinging rocks out into the waves.

I watched him as the minutes ticked by, unable to look away. His back rounded with each throw. His hair was tossed around in the breeze. There was something about him that was utterly hypnotizing, and by the time I realized what I was doing, I was too late to curb my thoughts.

I wanted to watch him for the rest of my life.

It wasn't as uncomfortable as I'd thought it would be. Living with Alec wouldn't be easy, but neither of us would probably know what to do if it was. He was stubborn, I was flighty, and we loved each other, simple as that.

"Damn," I muttered, smiling to myself.

Just when I was starting to get a handle on things, he pulled the rug out again. Only this time, he probably didn't even know he had. Stupid man was messing with me without even trying now.

Searching for a little summer dress and flip-flops, I went down the stairs to meet him. Each step closer made me feel lighter. Just being near him made me happy.

He turned when he saw me approach, and when his gaze lowered to my legs, I did a quick spin to give him a better look.

"Hey," I said, and lifted on my tiptoes to give him a kiss.

He didn't kiss me back.

He turned back to the water, and threw another rock, this time with enough force to rip a hole through the ozone.

A weight descended on my shoulders.

"Um . . . is everything all right?"

"You're a bed hog," he said. "You're four feet tall and you take up three-quarters of a queen-sized bed."

Four feet? Try five-four. I crossed my arms over my chest as he picked up another handful of rocks and began to toss them.

"And you have an enormous amount of girl *stuff* crowding the bathroom counter."

Just a few products. And a blow-dryer. And okay, maybe some makeup and brushes. But in my defense it was a tiny bathroom. I thought it better not to mention that this was only about a third of the *stuff* I regularly used. The rest of it was still at my apartment.

"And?" Clearly I'd done something to annoy him. He might as well let it all spill now.

He threw another rock. A bead of sweat dripped down his temple, and he wiped it away on his shoulder.

"*And,*" he said, really heaving the next one, "the thought of not seeing you every day is breaking my fucking heart."

He'd run out of rocks.

I put my hand on his shoulder, feeling it rise and fall with each breath.

"What's going on?" I asked.

He stared out over the water. "I'm not going to testify against Max."

My hand fell.

The water splashed over my toes, and as the wave retreated I could feel the suction of the sand on my feet.

"What are you talking about?"

He wouldn't look at me.

"You have to testify," I said. "If you don't, you'll go to jail." That was the deal. He'd struck a bargain with the district attorney. If he testified, all charges against him would be dropped. He'd serve three months in the penitentiary, and play ball with the FBI, and this mess would eventually go away.

The thought of not seeing you every day is breaking my heart.

His moodiness over the past couple of days began to make sense.

"Dinner last night, and you and me after . . ." The way he'd held me too tight, and gotten me a birthday cake, and made love to me like it was the last time. He'd known our time was ticking. "Was that just some elaborate good-bye?"

"I love you, Anna."

I pulled my shoulders back to make more room to breathe.

"No," I said. "You're giving your testimony. You're sending Maxim Stein to prison, otherwise none of what we've been through matters."

"He'll keep using you against me."

"Not if you send him away!" I pulled my feet from the sand and positioned myself in front of him. "If we win this trial, he'll have nothing. No company, no money, no collateral. He won't be able to pay people to hurt us. It'll be over."

He met my eyes, the pain in them so deep I felt like someone had punched me in the gut.

"I can't take that risk," he said.

"You already have," I said, gritting my teeth. "And we've shown him that we can survive anything he throws at us."

"He'll release the pictures. They'll be all over the news."

"I don't care!" I planted my hands on his chest and pushed, but his feet were stuck in the sand, too, and he nearly stumbled before he caught himself. "They're just pictures."

I did care, of course, but if it meant keeping Alec, I'd submit them to the papers myself.

"Pictures he hurt you to get," he said. "Next time it'll be worse, Anna. This was the last warning."

His voice was so calm, so even. Like he'd already made up his mind.

"You don't get to make this decision without me," I said, feeling a twinge of desperation.

"It's done."

I swallowed the sob. He lifted his hand, as if to touch my face, but I backed up.

"I told my lawyer two days ago. Chances were slim I could put him away anyway. None of the names I gave corroborated my story—he's already paid them all off. Jessica Rowe is gone, who knows what he did to her. And there's nothing besides that car in Miami, and Janelle told me yesterday she can't pull a number off the plate. There's no reason to keep putting you in danger."

I was crying now. The wind whipped my hair in front of my face, and it stuck to my damp cheeks. I shoved it back.

"That's why Matt hasn't come back."

He nodded grimly. "The FBI doesn't have to protect me

anymore. Your pal Marcos has agreed to keep an eye out. Even after I'm gone."

This wasn't happening. This *couldn't* happen. Not after I'd only tasted our future. But the look on his face was set.

"You did this for me," I said. "You went to the FBI for me. If you hadn't . . ."

I was the reason he was going to jail. Because he'd wanted to do the right thing to be worthy of me.

"I'm doing this for you, too," he said gently. "I'm sorry I didn't do it sooner. I thought we could win."

I covered my eyes with the heels of my hands. All those things I'd seen, those things I'd finally let myself want, were slipping away.

"You can't give up," I said. "I won't let you give up."

He reached for me then, hands cupping my elbows. He kissed my forehead.

"I have to turn myself in tomorrow. You should go home to Cincinnati with your dad until all this clears. I talked to him an hour ago. He's already arranged for a protective detail."

It felt like the ground beneath my feet was giving way.

"Cincinnati isn't my home," I said. "Where you are—*that's* my home."

His head fell forward, his hair falling over his eyes.

"Anna, I had you longer than I was meant to."

I stepped back.

"Then you're a coward."

She said I was a coward if I didn't figure out a way to make it work. My father's voice rang through my head.

His eyes darkened.

"Do you love me or not?" I asked.

"You know I do."

"Then fight for me."

His gaze narrowed. "I am."

"Fight to *be* with me," I said. "Fight to *stay* with me."

Another wave hit the back of my calves. The tide was rising, the water stronger than before.

"Are you hearing me?" I asked. "Maybe I'm a bed hog, but you steal the covers. And you're a terrible singer. And you are hands down the most stubborn man I've ever known, but I love you and I'm *going* to love you the rest of my life. And you can't just do that to a person and then cut them loose."

"You think this is cutting you loose?" he snapped, his cool composure finally breaking. "I don't know how many times I have to tell you, you're it for me."

"Then don't let me go."

All the pieces that had scattered suddenly aligned with surprising clarity. I saw it again, as I'd seen it last night. A table surrounded by our friends. Alec's hand in mine. The way his hair would gray around the temples, like his father. Year after year of conversations, and arguments, and *kids* we would love together.

"I'm going away," he said, uncertainty thinning his voice. "And not just for three months. *Years*, Anna."

I felt like I was standing at the edge of a precipice. Alec facing prison scared the hell out of me, not just because I'd be alone, but because of the danger he faced when he walked through those gates.

"I know what we're facing." *Goliath*. And we barely had a slingshot. Maxim Stein's lawyers were the best money could buy, and all we had were Alec's truths.

He tilted his head.

"You'd wait for me." It wasn't a question; it was a baffled accusation, at best.

I snorted. And then I giggled. And then I grinned so wide my cheeks hurt.

"You'd *marry* me." He looked like I'd just told him I was part mermaid.

"That depends if you're asking."

Again, I felt that shift between us. Something was changing.

Something important, that would forever alter the course of our lives.

And for once, I welcomed it.

"I've literally got nothing to offer you. Even if we win and I get the company, it won't be worth anything."

I laughed. Was this the Middle Ages? I didn't need a dowry and three goats.

"I'll have you," I said. "That's all I want."

It took him a while to process this.

"That's all I want," he said finally.

"Well?"

He scratched his head. "Look, if you're fucking with me . . ."

I jumped into his arms. "Yes. Yes, yes, *yes*." I kissed his cheek. "I mean, no, I'm not fucking with you. Yes to the other thing."

He laughed, still confused. And then he lifted me higher and squeezed me so tightly I coughed because he was crushing my lungs.

"Yes?" he asked.

"On one condition."

"Anything you want."

"You testify. And we see how this plays out."

He froze, then set me down.

"Anna."

"That's my condition."

He shook his head, then bit his upper lip.

"You know I can't say no to you."

"Especially now." I smiled.

He gave a dry laugh. "I'm screwed, aren't I?"

"You're *so* screwed."

He kissed me then, and there wasn't even a hint of sadness within him. There was only pure, unfiltered joy, and when I wrapped my arms around his neck, he picked me up, and I thought, *This moment right now. This is the best of all of them, and I will remember it for the rest of my life.*

And then we were laughing, and spinning, and he was chasing me as I ran back toward the stairs that led to the apartment above the restaurant. He caught me before we reached the top and kissed me until the world tilted sideways. I barely escaped before he took me right there under the cloudy sky.

We almost didn't make it inside. As soon as he kicked the door shut, my hands were yanking on his belt and his were pulling the sundress over my head. It caught halfway over my shoulder, and he tripped on his pants, and we crashed to the floor, drunk on each other, and our doomed future, and the love we would risk our lives for.

He pushed into me slowly, and when he settled between my legs I smiled, and kissed him with the same tenderness he showed my body.

"Ask me," I whispered, as he found that pace I loved.

He looked into my eyes. "Marry me, Anna."

"Yes," I said. And as he moved deeper I said it again, and again, and again.

Twenty-nine

"Your phone is ringing," I said, eyelids heavy. Whoever it was had called twice in the last five minutes. If they'd called before that, I hadn't heard the ring over my own cries of pleasure.

"I'll call them later." His head rested on my stomach, and I combed back his hair with my fingers. The brush of his eyelashes on my skin tickled, and when I squirmed, he wrapped one arm beneath my lower back.

My dress was crumpled beneath my head as a pillow, but his pants still hung on one leg. I was still flushed, not just from what he'd done to me, but what we'd both promised.

We were getting married.

Maybe not today. Maybe not for a while. But we would have our happily ever after, even if we had to take on Maxim Stein's army of lawyers to get it.

"Mrs. Flynn," I said when the phone stopped. "That'll take some getting used to."

He kissed my belly button, drawing a new wave of heat to the surface.

"Not for me," he said.

I rolled onto my side, and he continued kissing my waist, my ribs. Slowly and leisurely, as if he had all the time in the world.

If he didn't, I refused to be sad about it now. Soon, the course of our future would be revealed, but until then he was right here in my arms.

"How long have you been thinking about this?" I asked.

He chuckled. "A while."

He kissed the side of my bare breast, and though my vision went a little fuzzy, I forced myself to keep talking.

"How long's 'a while'?"

"Since you first spent the night."

"That's not *that* long," I said. "I've been here, what? A week?"

"At my apartment downtown," he added.

"Oh. *Oh.*" That was months ago, before Alec had even gone to prison. Before Charlotte MacAfee had died, or her brother, Trevor Marshall aka William MacAfee, had tried to avenge her. I remembered it now, waking up from a nightmare. The way he'd held me and eventually, after I was settled, made love to me.

He rose on his elbow and kissed around my side to the back of my ribs.

"I already knew I was in deep." He kissed the top of my shoulder, "But that night I knew there was no going back. I even told Mike the next day."

I turned, so that he was forced to look at me. "What did you tell him?"

He kissed the top of my breast, making my breath hitch.

"I told him I met a girl. *The* girl."

I smiled. "And what did he say?"

Slowly, he drew my nipple into his mouth, swirling his tongue around the hard point. I arched into him, and his hands fanned out beneath my back, holding him to me.

"He said it's about goddamn time."

The laughter bubbled out. "Amy's got it bad for him. They kissed, you know."

"I heard. It was so good she ran into a closet."

I winced. "He makes her nervous."

Alec grinned, nuzzling his face into my hair. "He likes making her nervous."

"He told you that?"

I gasped as a warm, wet tongue tasted the soft skin beneath my ear.

"He might have mentioned it."

"What else did he mention?"

I was talking faster. It was just a matter of time before I lost the power of speech.

"I can't remember." His hard length pressed against my thigh, and I surrendered. My legs parted for him. My fingers slid down his broad shoulders. I could touch him forever.

And I would.

The phone rang.

Alec stilled, then groaned and muttered something about adding homicide to his rap sheet.

"Maybe it's Janelle," I said. My heart leapt at the possibility that she'd learned more about the car that had taken me. If she could find a plate number, she could find out who rented it, and maybe we could tie them to Stein.

"Don't move," Alec said, giving me a stern look. He pushed up, kicked his pants off the one ankle where they still clung, and snagged his phone off the kitchen counter. I stayed on my back on the floor, not a stitch of clothing to cover me, arms behind my head like I was sunning at the beach.

He looked at me as if I was purposefully punishing him. Which I sort of was. I bent my knees, and then opened them just slightly to give him a peek.

His gaze narrowed. He looked down at his phone, and scowled.

"Ben, hey." He cleared his throat. "Hang on a second."

My *dad*? Ew. My knees snapped shut. I sat up, shook out the summer dress, and then slipped it over my head. Apparently Alec felt better talking to my father with clothes on, too, because he grabbed his jeans off the floor and pulled them up over his perfect, bare ass. Even now I was sorry to see it go.

He took a deep breath.

I grinned. "You're going to tell him, aren't you? Go get 'em, tiger."

He exhaled in a huff.

"It didn't go so well the first time."

"The first . . ."

"Sorry about that," Alec answered, effectively cutting me off. I was standing now, staring at him incredulously. He'd already told my father he wanted to marry me? Surely I'd misunderstood. But he did say he'd been thinking about it for months . . .

"Listen," he said. "There's something I'd like to talk to you . . . Sure." Alec hesitated. His scowl deepened.

Uh-oh. I could almost hear my father cocking his shotgun.

"Where is she?"

She? Hang on.

"Jesus," he raked a hand through his hair. "Yeah. I'm coming." He looked up at me. "We're both coming. Whatever you do, don't let her take off."

Alec clicked off his phone, but continued to stare down at it. I came to him immediately, placing my hands on his biceps.

"What is it?" I asked.

"Jessica Rowe," he said. "Your dad found her."

Five minutes later we were hurrying down the stairs to the SUV.

"What about Janelle?" I asked. "Will she be sending more agents?"

I pictured an entire SWAT team showing up to take Jessica Rowe into custody, which was more than a little concerning. If she'd been purposefully evading the authorities, subtlety seemed the best course of action. We would have to play this very carefully.

"I'll call her when we find Jessica," said Alec, in a way that made me wonder if he and Janelle were on the best of terms. She probably wasn't thrilled that he'd retracted his statements about Maxim Stein, a case she'd been working on for months.

I jumped into the passenger side of the SUV. The engine was thrumming before I even shut the door.

"How far is it to St. Augustine?" I'd heard of it only in passing. It was on the east coast of Florida. Some kind of historical site, a vacation destination. Not exactly the place you ran when your billionaire boss and the FBI were looking for you.

"Three and a half hours," he said. "We'll get there faster."

I buckled up.

"What's she doing there?" I asked.

"No idea. He hasn't made contact with her yet. He's waiting for me."

Alec ripped out of the parking lot, and the car jostled as he drove onto the connector road that would take us to the highway. Unopened mail from the side compartment on the door spilled out over my feet. He must have forgotten it was here. I reached for the various envelopes, sorting them into a pile on my lap. While we climbed the on-ramp, I flattened the crinkled and bent edges, trying to distract myself from the anxiety spiking in my chest.

Jessica Rowe could change everything. She could vouch for Alec, verify his story. Two witnesses testifying that they had firsthand knowledge of Maxim Stein participating in white-collar crimes would put him away for certain.

"She's the missing woman my dad was looking for in the Keys, isn't she?"

Alec nodded grimly. "He had a pretty solid lead on her. I guess she tried to take a ship to the Caribbean but got caught with a fake passport. She disappeared after that."

It didn't surprise me that my dad could find someone the FBI couldn't. They had bureaucracy to deal with, the red tape. He didn't need anyone's permission to follow a lead, and as I'd heard numerous times from his colleagues growing up, he was a bloodhound when it came to solving a case.

I snorted. "Nice of you both to fill me in."

"You had enough on your mind."

"Nice of you both to make that executive decision."

"You're pissed." He smirked. "You know what that does to me."

I glanced down as he adjusted himself.

"You're impossible, you know that?"

He chuckled, gaze never straying from the road.

"What did you mean back there?" I asked, shifting gears. "You've talked to him about me, haven't you?"

"You're all we ever talk about."

"You know what I mean. About *you* and me."

Alec slouched into the seat. "About my intentions with his daughter?"

That sounded suspiciously like a quote from my dad.

"I told him I wanted to marry you when we flew to Cincinnati," he said. "He'd already shown me his gun collection. I figured lying about things wasn't going to help the situation. In hindsight, it probably wasn't the best introduction."

I stared at him. Blinked.

"You just said it. *I'm going to marry Anna.* Just like that."

He scoffed. "Give me a little credit. I asked his permission." He changed lanes. "And then in so many words he told me where I could shove my question."

I smirked. I couldn't help it.

"That sounds like him."

"I'm not who he had in mind for you."

It moved me that he cared. He knew my father's blessing was important to me, and so it became important for him, too.

I know good men can make mistakes, my dad had said. *What matters is how they fix them.*

"I think you might be just what he hoped for," I said.

A tense silence descended over us. The wheels whirred on the road. We passed a few cars on the bridge over the Bay, but nothing that made him take his foot off the gas. Soon we passed downtown, and I could make out the high-rise of his apartment where we'd lived both together and alone. Those months there without him had been painfully lonely and I hated the prospect of facing them again.

But I would do it. For him.

Needing something to busy my hands, I began looking through the envelopes. They were all for him, dating from as far back as a month ago. Junk mostly, but there was one letter with a return address for a hospital in Orlando.

The hospital where I'd been taken after I'd been missing.

Glancing over at him, I ripped open the top, and pulled out a bill for nearly thirty thousand dollars. Cue mass hysteria. My name was listed under "Patient," but Alec Flynn was the "Responsible Party."

"Holy shit," I said.

He glanced at the letter, then back to the road.

"That's better than I thought," he said.

Thank God for insurance, I thought. I double-checked to make sure they hadn't been billed yet.

"Alec, why is this addressed to you?"

He took the letter, folded it, and stuck it in the center console.

"Let me take care of you, Anna," he said, in a way that made my annoyance melt just a little.

"You don't have to do that." He didn't even have an income right now.

He patted my knee.

"I want to," he said. "And you're going to let me."

"Bossy," I muttered, trying not to smile. A few days ago I would have thought it was guilt that had moved him to pay for my care, but now I knew better. He loved me. I doubt he'd even thought twice before directing the bills into his name. Had our positions been reversed, I wouldn't have done any differently. We'd handle it together, just like everything else.

The next letter was from the department of corrections. Probably something regarding his completed parole.

"Maybe you should open your mail more often." I flashed him the letter, and when he nodded, I ripped it open.

The first page was a letter. Short and sweet, it informed "Mr. Alec Flynn" that the State of Pennsylvania, where Alec had been imprisoned, had a duty to warn him of the release of a convict who had at one time made a threat against him. Someone named Jeremiah Barlow, who was now out on parole.

I remembered the death threats Amy had told me about. Was this someone who had tried to come after Alec? The State of Pennsylvania could keep him if that was the case.

Chewing on my bottom lip, I turned to the second page, a printout, not unlike the documents I'd seen my father bring home when he was working on a case. There was a picture at the top. A man in his twenties, a little younger than me, though the hard look in his eyes aged him. He stared down the camera, lips in a thin straight line.

On his neck was a tattoo.

A black star.

I saw my nightmare, even with my eyes open. A white sky with black stars. A man's pale neck, marked by a black tattoo as he carried me in his arms. If there had been any air left in my lungs, I would have screamed.

Thirty

Alec swerved off the road onto the edge of the highway and slammed the car into park. Outside, cars whooshed past, but though I heard them, I couldn't take my eyes away from the letter from the department of corrections, now on the floor mat below my seat. I'd brought my knees to my chest, and was hugging them tightly, as if that letter was a rabid dog that might bite me.

"What is it?" Alec's hand closed on my biceps, then rose up into my hair. He turned my face to look at him. "Anna. Talk to me."

"*I'll carry her. She keeps falling.*"

"*How much of that stuff did you give her? She's not going to die, is she?*"

Maxim's voice. Maxim talking to the man with the tattoo. The man from the bar, who lifted me in his arms and carried me down the hallway with the silver snake candleholders. My legs hit the doorway as he tried to edge us through.

"*What are you doing?*" My voice, slurred, strange sounding, even in my own memory.

"*Just relax,*" Maxim said. "*It's nothing personal.*"

I blinked. The bar. I could hear the music, piped in. A band was setting up onstage. I was overdressed, people were looking at me. Men were looking. *Good, let them look. That's why I'm here, isn't it?*

One of them sat beside me. He bought me a drink. He touched my leg.

It felt wrong. I was a failure. I couldn't save myself even when I was drowning.

I still had some dignity left.

"*I need to go,*" I said.

"*My bad. Sometimes I can come on too strong.*"

I was too drunk. I needed a cab. He said he'd take me home. I missed Alec. I missed him so much. I couldn't even remember why we weren't together.

I was too drunk to disagree when he set me in the backseat of his car. Too drunk to notice we were going the wrong way until it was too late. I just wanted to sleep. I just wanted to forget.

"Come on, Anna," Alec begged, pulling me home with the sound of his voice. "Come back. Talk to me."

I blinked. And the memories dimmed in the background, into their rightful places rather than the shadows where they'd formerly been hiding.

"Alec?"

He looked horrified. How much time had passed? I glanced at the clock. Not even a minute. It had felt closer to a week.

He exhaled sharply, and then pulled my face to his. He kissed me hard on the mouth, and the sudden burden that had fallen over me lightened, as if he'd physically taken it on himself.

I grasped his hands on my cheeks.

"It's him," I said. "That's him. Why do you have his picture?"

Keeping one hand on my shoulder, Alec reached down to the floor and grabbed the letter I'd dropped. A muscle beneath his eye twitched as he looked over it.

"You know him?" he asked.

"He's the one from the bar. He took me. I remember the tat-too. A black star."

Alec's hand jerked as he looked back up at me. "Jeremiah Barlow."

"I guess." I couldn't recall him giving a name. "How do you know him?"

"He's the one who stabbed me in prison." Alec looked at the front page, and then muttered something I couldn't make out. "Looks like he's out. When the *accident* happened, Janelle made them put a notification of parole alert in his file. I didn't know he'd be out so soon."

He checked the postmark on the envelope. "This letter came four days ago. He's been out a month."

"Nice heads-up," I said weakly.

They were connected. Maxim Stein and Jeremiah Barlow. They'd worked together before I'd been taken, maybe just to hurt Alec. Maybe to hurt others.

"Maxim never hired him before that you know of?"

Alec shook his head. "Prison was the first time I saw him, but . . ." He hesitated. "There were a lot of Maxim's more private affairs that Jessica handled. Things he purposefully kept Bobby and I out of. I never knew why. For a while I thought they had a thing going, but if they did, it never amounted to anything."

The urgency to find Maxim Stein's secretary increased tenfold.

Alec faced me again. "What can I do? What do you need?"

I took a deep breath, and then another. If I'd transferred my fear to Alec, he'd transferred his anger to me. I could feel it now, biting at my nerves, fisting my hands.

"I need someone to arrest this asshole," I said.

It took some convincing, but Alec finally agreed to keep driving. While he did, I called Marcos, and filled him in on what I'd dis-covered.

"You're sure it's him?" Marcos asked, and I could hear the anger lacing through his voice.

"Positive. He stabbed Alec in prison, and it went down as an accident. He came after me in a bar. This guy *knows* us, Marcos."

It was one thing that he'd come after me, but the fact that he'd gotten to both of us felt like an even bigger violation.

"All right," Marcos said. "I'll talk to Detective Benitez and get a BOLO put out." He paused, and I could hear him typing in the background. "Good news for us, he already skipped parole in Pennsylvania."

A cold validation snaked down my neck. Jeremiah Barlow was already in trouble, we just needed to catch him.

"Why did he do time?"

"Check fraud," answered Marcos. "But that's just what they wrung him up for. He's got a dozen violations before that he's somehow slipped out of. Must have had a nice lawyer."

Like maybe one of Maxim Stein's lawyers. I didn't say this to Marcos—he still didn't know that Maxim had been behind my abduction, or anything about the pictures.

"Huh," said Marcos. "Looks like he used to be a pilot."

Maybe he'd flown one of Maxim's planes. That could have been how they met.

"I want to know everything you find out about this guy," I said.

"Yes, ma'am."

"We have to find him, Marcos."

Beside me, Alec flinched.

"Believe me," said my friend. "We're going to find him."

For the rest of the trip, Alec kept one hand on me—either on my thigh, or holding tight to my hand. He didn't let go, and I was grateful for that. I needed the steady reassurance that he was there, and he needed the same thing.

I told him what I remembered, though it wasn't much more than fragments. He told me the FBI had looked a little into Jeremiah Barlow's past after he'd been attacked in prison. There wasn't much. He'd been raised by an aunt in Pennsylvania, sent to boarding school in the seventh grade. Apart from a smattering of arrests, he hadn't ever done time before he was caught for check fraud six months ago. His pilot's license had been revoked after that.

"His aunt probably knew he was a psychopath. That's why she sent him to boarding school," I said.

Alec squeezed my hand.

"Schools like that are expensive. Maybe she's the one who taught him to forge checks."

He was right. Boarding schools weren't cheap. He must have been unbearable.

"We'll find him," Alec said. But though his words were calm, there was a danger brewing just under the surface. I loosened my seat belt and leaned closer, resting my head on his shoulder and wrapping my arms around his.

"I know," I said.

We stayed that way until we reached St. Augustine.

The beachside town on the eastern coast was different than most of the vacation places I'd seen in Florida. Grounded in history, whole areas had been preserved or re-created from the Spanish settlements that had been raised in the fifteen hundreds. Clashing alongside it were hotels, bed-and-breakfasts, and souvenir shops boasting guided tours. It was enough stimulation to immediately brew a headache at the base of my skull.

Alec called my father, and we met at a Denny's connected to a cheap motel near an old jailhouse. He wasn't inside, he was out in his car in the back of the parking lot, AC blasting, vents turned toward the enormous Great Dane spread over the reclined passenger seat. When my father saw us, he stepped outside, and we gathered in the shadow of a sprawling oak tree blanketed by hanging moss.

"She's been in there about twenty minutes," said my dad, after giving me a kiss. "Must have been going stir-crazy. She's barely left the motel room since I got here."

Alec brushed his hands on his thighs. "I'll go."

"I've been thinking that might not be such a good idea," said my dad. "Her statement won't be much good if she says you two talked it out beforehand."

Alec's jaw flexed. "It won't be much good if she disappears again either."

"Can't we just arrest her?" I asked. "The FBI has a search out on her for God's sake."

"We could call it in," my dad offered. "But that's not going to build much trust. I'll make contact. Convince her to talk to the feds. I can keep her from running."

I glanced to Alec, and the look on his face told me he was thinking the same thing. If Jessica Rowe hadn't wanted to talk to the police yet, she wasn't going to start now. My dad may not have technically been on the force anymore, but he was a cop through and through.

"I'll do it," I said. "Let me talk to her. I'm not part of the trial. I'm not a threat."

Both men looked down on me, worry in their eyes.

"I've got this," I said.

My dad crossed his arms. "You're just getting your feet back under you."

He was still worried I was going to crack, which, based on the way things had gone on the car ride here, wasn't totally off the mark.

"I'm all right," I assured him. "She's not scared of me. I'll start slow, and if I need backup, I'll wave through the window."

Alec looked at me for several long seconds, as if trying to see the truth behind my eyes. I squeezed his hand.

"I've got this," I said again, determination making me strong.

"All right," he said. "I guess we'll just . . . wait out here."

I gave him a devious smile that reflected none of my apprehension. "I'm sure you can think of *something* to talk about."

With that I walked toward the Denny's, and the woman who held the key to keeping Alec in my arms.

Thirty-one

Jessica Rowe, once secretary to one of the most famous men in the country, looked like hell. The jeans she wore didn't match her normally flawless business attire, and her peach sleeveless button-up hung loosely on her shoulders. Even her hair, usually shaped into a perfect bob, was stuffed back in a ragged ponytail.

She was sitting in a booth in the corner, the only spot in the restaurant that had a full view of the entire seating area. Despite this position, she didn't look up as I crossed the floor to her. Her eyes were downcast, staring at the fork she turned over and over in her fingers.

"Mind if I sit here?" I didn't wait for her to respond. I plopped down on one side of the booth, keeping close enough to the edge that I could stand if she tried to scoot out the other side.

Her eyes shot up to mine, and her face went even paler. Without makeup she looked a little older than I remembered. Maybe in her midforties.

"Long time, no see," I said.

"What are you doing here?" She glanced around the restaurant, as if expecting a full battalion to come marching through the doors. It was a good thing I'd left the guys outside.

"I'm looking for you." There was no point lying. She'd know the truth soon enough.

She started to move to the other side of the booth, snatching the small leather satchel sitting beside her.

"Please stay," I said. "I just want to talk to you."

"I'm sure." She reached a hand into her bag, and I caught a glimpse of the telltale yellow and black handle. It belonged to a weapon my father had trained me on when I was fourteen.

"Seriously?" I asked. "You're going to Tase me in the middle of a Denny's?"

Her shoulder jerked. "If I have to."

"You don't have to be afraid," I said. "I'm here with Alec Flynn. The FBI doesn't know, neither do the police."

She slowly withdrew her hand from her purse and leaned forward over the table. "What do you want?"

I thought of the first time I'd met Jacob, how I'd had to coax him with tacos to trust me, and even then it was hard earned.

"I want to help you."

"No offense, Ms. Rossi, but you live off tips. I don't exactly think you're in position to help me."

"We need to put Maxim Stein away for good."

She scoffed.

"I know you're afraid," I said quickly, realizing I was going to lose her if I didn't move fast. "That's why you're running. I'm scared, too. He came after me—he had his nephew Bobby kidnap me. He wanted me gone, just like he wanted Charlotte MacAfee gone."

She leaned back, brows flat.

"You knew about that," I realized, trying to harness my sudden fury. No wonder she was running. She knew a lot of things she shouldn't have.

"He had Alec stabbed in prison," I said.

Panic brightened her hard eyes.

"Quiet," she said. "Stop talking. You need to leave."

A waitress approached the table with a smile as big as a watermelon.

"Eggs over medium," she said. "Rye toast. What can I get you, honey?"

I lifted my hand. Smiled. "Nothing for me, thanks."

Jessica didn't touch her food. The waitress walked away, hips swishing from side to side.

"When Alec agreed to testify, the FBI protected him," I said. "They can protect you, too. That's why they're looking for you."

She laughed now. She laughed so loudly the people at the next table turned around and stared at us. It was a cold, cynical sound that chilled me right to the bone.

"Are you *that* dense?" she asked. "The FBI can't protect me. If Max wants me, not even God himself can help me."

I clasped my hands in my lap, losing the resolve I'd had when I walked through the door.

"If you put him away, he can't hurt you," I said. It hadn't been that long ago I'd told this very same thing to Alec. Maxim had seriously screwed these people up.

"Oh, he can," she said, almost to herself. She looked up at me. "He'll find a way. He has money. Money buys men who will do all kinds of unspeakable things. Money *makes* good men do unspeakable things." She trailed off, staring at the fork still in her hands.

"Men like Jeremiah Barlow?" I focused on the tremble in her lip, trying to block the black star tattoo from invading my vision.

"You know him, don't you?" I pressed. Again, a bolt of rage slashed through me. Maybe she was just another victim, manipulated by Maxim Stein, but the fact that she'd known Barlow, possibly before he'd come after both Alec and me, made me want to throw down with her right in the middle of this Denny's.

Her face grew pale.

"I know his name," she said, and immediately looked away.

"What else do you know about him?"

"Nothing." She shook her head. "Just that he's asked Mr. Stein for money over the years. For what, I don't know, but I always get the cash for him."

Stein had done a lot of deals in cash, from the sounds of it. Alec had said he'd paid Jessica cash bonuses on top of her salary.

"Where do you send it?" I asked.

"I don't. Mr. Stein delivers it personally."

Why would Stein be paying off Jeremiah Barlow? Was he another hit man, like Jack Reznik? Someone to do Stein's dirty work when Alec wouldn't? I wanted to press her for more, but I could feel her disengaging again. Her eyes kept darting toward the door.

"You know more than that," I said, my voice growing hard. This man had drugged me. Disrespected my body. Used me like a rag doll.

"I . . ."

"Tell me," I said. "Or I swear to God, I'll call the police right now and tell them you knew Bobby was going to try to kill me and did nothing."

It might have been Florida, but the air inside that restaurant turned bitterly cold.

"He's Max's son," she said.

I narrowed my eyes.

"Max doesn't have a son." That's why he'd named his nephew, Robert Calloway, to take over his company. Alec had told me this before. It was possible, of course, that there were children— Maxim certainly had been promiscuous. But it seemed unlikely that Alec wouldn't have known about it.

"He was married at the time. His wife didn't know."

I pictured the man with the black star on his neck next to Maxim Stein. It was like holding a rock next to a diamond. But the more I thought about it, the more I could see the similarities. Their faces were alike—prominent chins, thick brows, a challenging stare. They were both short, and from the brief bits I remembered of Jeremiah, overconfident.

"Are they still in contact?" If we could find Jeremiah, maybe we could nail Maxim for my abduction.

"I don't know," she said. "If you recall, it's been months since I've been in Mr. Stein's employ."

I watched her squirm, and wondered what Alec would make of this new information. I was anxious to get back outside and tell him.

"Mr. Stein will hurt you for turning against him," I said. "Like you said, he has the funds to do whatever he wants. But take away his money, and you take away his power. Without that, he's nothing."

She bit her thumbnail. "Even if I'm safe from him, they'll still send me to jail."

I felt her fear then, and how it had seeped over any hope for the future. There was no winning for her. Maxim Stein would make her disappear, and even if the feds kept her safe, she'd probably still serve time.

I thought of how she'd known that her boss wanted me dead. How many other lives had he ruined while she'd sat by in silence? She deserved to be punished, just not by Maxim Stein.

I wanted to grab her and shake her. This wasn't just about her. She was holding Alec's life in her hands, and mine, too.

"The FBI reduced Alec's sentence in exchange for his testimony," I said. "I'm sure they can work something out for you."

The seconds ticked by.

Please, I begged her in my head. *Please see reason.*

"I have nowhere else to go," she murmured.

"Yes, you do," I said. "You can come with me."

Janelle and Matt made it to St. Augustine before sundown. They took Jessica to a different hotel, and got us a room down the hall.

My dad left soon after we'd settled in. Alec may not have had a chance to discuss our relationship with him, but he had told him about Jeremiah Barlow, and my father was keen to get back to his contacts at the Tampa PD and see what had come of the search.

Alec and Jessica were kept separate, and while he reviewed some safety procedures with Matt, I went to get some ice for our room. It was just down the hall, but the creaking of a door stopped me before I got there.

Janelle stepped out into the hall. She was dressed in a business suit, hair back in a painfully neat ponytail. Looking at her, I was reminded of the first time I'd seen her in the hospital with Alec, when I'd gotten a strong dominatrix vibe.

"You shouldn't leave the room," she said. Inside, I caught a glimpse of Jessica pacing.

It was a little difficult to look at Janelle straight on, but I did it anyway. The last time we'd seen each other I'd been half-crazy, and before then I hadn't always been on my best behavior. She knew about the pictures as well, since Alec had asked for her help. She had become that person who only saw me during my worst times.

"I'm just getting ice." I held up the bucket. Our room was cool, but the flat of water Matt had brought was warm, and I wanted a cold glass after a crazy day.

"Go ahead," she nodded, making it clear she had every intention of watching me take the last ten steps.

I started forward, but then stopped.

"Listen, when I saw you at that motel in Lakeland I wasn't really all together."

She smirked. "You don't say."

I turned and took another step.

"It was my fault," she said, closing the door quietly behind her. "I shouldn't have met him then, like *that*." Her cheeks darkened. "I missed my husband."

"I get it," I said.

She gave a small nod, and though it didn't erase anything that had happened, for the first time it felt like we understood each other.

"Thanks for getting him back in the game," she said, nodding toward the room I was sharing with Alec.

I gave her a one-shouldered shrug.

"Thanks for trying to protect me."

She gave a dry laugh. "As if I had a choice."

I lowered my voice. "Do we really have a shot of winning this?"

She smiled then, and it honestly gave me chills.

"We're going to bury that bastard."

A surge of power shook through me. Maxim was going down. It was just a matter of time before Jeremiah was caught. Our struggles were soon going to be behind us, I could feel it. I went to get the ice, and when I passed again she gave me a knowing look.

"Try to keep it down tonight, huh?"

I batted my eyelashes innocently and pushed inside.

Alec was standing beside Matt at the dark cherry desk, staring at an open laptop with a deep-set scowl. When I closed the door, Matt shut the screen, and pulled it under his arm.

"I'll let you know what I find." He shook Alec's hand, a friendly gesture that made me realize they must have become friends over the past few months.

He smiled and squeezed my arm on the way out.

"He's looking into Jeremiah Barlow," Alec said when the door shut. "He's going to run some credit cards and bank statements, see if he can get a feel of where he's been hiding the last few weeks. Even if he's paying with cash like Jessica told you, he'll pop up somewhere."

"Okay." I didn't want to talk about Jeremiah Barlow right now.

Alec leaned back against the desk, arms crossed and brows furrowed.

"Max's *son*." He shook his head. "He never even mentioned a kid. I never even thought to look."

"Alec."

He snorted. "Son of a bitch can't be far. If he's on the payroll, Max will keep him close. Especially once he learns I'm back in court."

"Alec."

"He's going to do something stupid again once he sees me take the stand. I want you with someone at all times, all right?"

I kicked off my shoes.

"I'll add minutes to the cell I gave you. You've got to keep it on you. No more leaving it in the apartment."

I popped a piece of ice in my mouth.

"We're going to get him, Anna. Both of them."

I pulled the dress over my head. Before we'd left, I'd made sure to put on a bra and panties—a black lacy number that hugged my ribs like a cutoff tank, and a matching black thong were the first things I could grab.

He blinked. His lips parted.

"Now that I've got your attention . . ." I said, moving the melting ice into my cheek.

"Have you been wearing that"—he pointed to me—"under that"—he pointed to the dress, now in a puddle on the floor—"all day?"

"I have."

He pushed off the desk, desire drawing his muscles tight. Heat raced through me, even as my mouth stayed cold.

He took a step toward me. I took a step away.

His mouth quirked.

Another step, and I slipped to the side.

"Think you're faster than me?" he asked.

He lunged, and I bolted around the bed. When the mattress was between us, I slipped my thumbs into the waistband of my panties and slipped them an inch down my hips. He grimaced as I moved them lower, and groaned as I pulled them back up.

"Not faster," I said. "Just smarter."

"That was never a question."

I lifted my foot and set in on the bed. His gaze fell between my legs, to the narrow strip of fabric that was growing wetter by the second. I twisted the strap of my bra around one finger.

He muttered a curse.

I loved teasing him. And now that things were finally going right, I wanted to celebrate. Alec was mine, and I had him before me, wanting me, needing what only I could give him. I'd missed this for too long, and even as I stood now, drinking him in, I knew I would never get enough.

He tried to come around the side of the bed, but I sidestepped toward the headboard, cornering myself against the wall. He laughed, a dark, smooth sound that made my body ache. I switched the small sliver of ice to the other cheek.

"Looks like you're in trouble," he said, pulling his shirt off over his head. Each section of his abdominals flexed as he lifted his arms, making my fingers itch to touch.

"I don't think so." I crawled up onto the bed, toward where he stood on the end. My long hair fell over my shoulders, soft against my cheeks. The comforter sank beneath my hands and knees.

"I've got you right where I want you," I said.

I rose on my knees as I got closer, and slowly unbuckled his belt. The last of the ice melted on my tongue as I tugged his pants down, but before my tongue warmed again, I rolled onto my back and scooted to the edge of the bed. The room turned upside down as my head fell back and my hair stretched to the floor. His defiant cock stretched out over my face, already wet at the tip, and as the hunger rose in me, I reached for him with both hands. Before he could say a word, I had him in my mouth.

With a grunt he jerked forward, pushing himself against my freezing tongue.

"*Cold,*" he said. "Ah, Christ, that's cold."

I couldn't take him deep, but I could lick his smooth, salty head, and cup his balls in my hand. He jerked above me again as I slipped one finger behind them, rubbing that sensitive place beneath his sack that drove him crazy.

His feet adjusted, lowering his body so I could take more of him.

"Dirty girl," he said. "Suck my dick. Like that. *Fuck.* Just like that."

I groaned at the harsh rasp in his tone, and the vibrations made him tense. That familiar power dripped through my veins, and the desire to please him turned from a rush to an unquenchable thirst. I kissed him and stroked him with an urgency that had me digging my own heels into the mattress. Feeling him wring every bit of pleasure from my mouth had me hot as fire, and before I knew it, my own hips were churning.

He didn't even need to touch me. I was getting off on sucking his cock.

This deep, carnal knowledge set loose a deeper, more primitive need in me. I wasn't ashamed; there were no limits with us. Nothing was wrong when we were together. He'd told me that once before, but I didn't truly understand it until now.

I loved who I had become with him.

He touched me then. I arched into his fingers, spreading over my ribs, pulling down the cups of my bra to expose my breasts. He wasn't gentle with them. His big hands weighed them, and kneaded them, and then shoved them together with a light slap. The hardened peaks were aching, sending electric currents straight between my legs. Maybe he knew how much I needed his hard caress, because he pinched them both at the same time, and pulled them up toward him, and when I cried out around his cock, he let them fall with a hard bounce.

My teeth scraped down his shaft.

With a tight groan, he fell over me, catching himself before his chest smashed into mine.

"You want to play?" he ground out. "Let's play."

His change of positions had dislodged his cock from my mouth. I licked the base, and then sucked one of his balls into my mouth. He shuddered.

His hands slid heavily down my hamstrings to my bottom, where he massaged deeply enough to spark the nerves between my legs. Then he reached for the straps of my panties, and slid them over my thighs, stopping just above my knees.

I thought he'd touch me with his fingers. Enter me. Rub my clit. Instead he grabbed my ass, and hoisted my hips up to his waiting mouth.

He devoured me, licking my pussy like he was starved for the taste. He swirled his tongue around my entrance, forged through my lips with his nose, nipped at my inner thighs. I came before he even touched my clit.

My back bowed straight off the bed, pushing me deeper into his mouth, and I sobbed with the impact of that relief as the heat shot through my body. He kept eating at me, his teeth scraping my raw nerves, and when he sucked that small bundle of nerves into his mouth I lost all sense of gravity.

"Enough," he barked. *"Enough."*

He pulled back from my devious mouth, and my last sight was of his red, veined erection, shining from what I had done to him.

"No." I reached for him again. I wanted to scald him the way he had scalded me. So that his body could never forget.

"I have to fuck you," he said, voice tense and desperate. He turned me fast, so that my feet hung off the end of the mattress. My head was spinning from being upside down too long; the room behind kept moving. He grabbed my hips and pulled me to the edge of the bed. My legs were lifted, my ankles placed roughly over his shoulders.

"I have to be inside you," he said. With one hand on the base, he guided the tip of his cock into my body. I was so sensitive I bit the back of my hand to keep from crying out. He worked his way in, wetting himself on my desire, then pulling out. Another inch in, another inch out. Deeper with each measured stroke, until I was blind with lust.

"I love fucking you," he said, when he was buried to the hilt. "When I'm not fucking you, I'm thinking about fucking you. I'm dreaming about fucking you. I need you so damn much."

His filthy words were my undoing. I clenched around him, every sensation ricocheting out from that center, spinning me out of control.

"Look at me," he ordered. I couldn't even see.

"Look at me," he snapped again. And when I opened my eyes, he withdrew, and thrust back hard into my body. I gasped for breath, but there was none. Soon he was pounding into me, fast and deep, so deep that my breasts shook and I was forced to grip the comforter just to hold on to something.

He came over me and shoved me up the bed so that his knees were on the mattress.

"Show me," he said. And I didn't know what he meant until he changed the angle of his hips. When he thrust again, I could feel him in my whole body, straight to my fingertips, straight to my toes. My eyes went wide, my mouth open in a silent cry.

"There it is," he muttered as I bucked against him.

I clung to his shoulders, nails digging deep as he lost his rhythm, and wrapped his arms around my back for his last frenzied thrusts.

"I love you," he said, jerking into me once more, then holding on tight as he came.

He collapsed, his head on my shoulder, his chest on mine. I could feel his heart pounding and his warm breath on my ear.

"Baby," I whispered.

"Mmm?"

"We're going to win."

I smiled at the ceiling, hair clinging to my sweaty brow, and felt his lips curve up against my neck.

Thirty-two

Two days later, Jessica Rowe took the stand.

I sat in the second row of the courtroom, behind the prosecutor's bench, next to a thin man with beach-blond hair and a sunburned nose. Alec's lawyer was younger than anyone on Maxim Stein's team—somewhere in his midtwenties, and fresh out of law school. He was accompanied by his petite assistant, a pretty Latina woman with full hips who also happened to be his wife.

He was the third lawyer Alec had hired. The other two had dropped his case when they realized who he was up against.

His name was Jim Rolling, and he looked as awestruck as a twelve-year-old at his first pro baseball game. I tried not to let that fact bother me; a federal prosecutor was the one running the show today anyway. I assessed the man who would be interviewing Jessica as he stood beside the heavy oak table, reviewing a file of information. Silver hair. Rimless glasses. Hungry eyes, like a shark. According to Jim, he'd been with Stein's secretary for two straight days reviewing her statement.

Seated on my other side, Agent Janelle Jamison the dominatrix chewed on a toothpick, carefully assessing Stein's crew. Three men and one woman were gathered around the defense's table, all wearing suits that easily could have cost six months of my income at the salon. Stein had yet to arrive.

"So that's what renting out your private jet will buy," I said, remembering how Max still managed to afford his high-profile attorneys.

"Don't worry," said Janelle. "They're still sucking him dry."

A smirk curved my lips.

I checked the clock at the back of the courtroom. Quarter to nine. Jessica would take the stand in fifteen minutes.

Alec wasn't allowed to be here for this—his testimony needed to be untainted by that of the other witnesses, so he and Jessica had been kept separate. He was nearby in another room waiting for his lawyer. Though he'd tried to convince me to stay back with him, I'd had to come. I needed to hear Jessica lock in Alec's victory.

I needed to face Maxim Stein.

My stomach was in knots. I'd barely managed to eat dinner last night, and had opted for coffee only this morning. For the first time, Alec didn't push me into eating. He'd barely touched his own food.

I reminded myself we would have time later to celebrate.

"There's still a chance to duck out," said Janelle, without looking over.

"I'm fine." We both knew it wasn't true. I was going to sweat straight through the white blouse I'd worn if we didn't get this party started soon.

The door to the left of the witness stand opened, and two men in suits appeared, flanked by a woman with a U.S. Marshal badge. The first had shoe-polish black hair and a matching navy suit and tie.

The other was Maxim Stein.

From first glance he didn't look that different than he had

months ago when I'd laid my oil-slicked hands on his naked back. His silver hair was neat and trimmed, his clothing impeccable. He wasn't particularly tall—no more than a few inches taller than me. But he walked like he owned the whole goddamn world.

I stared at him, feeling the ice-cold claws of dread sink into my back. Images of my head on his shoulder, of my body strewn across his invaded my vision, and I forced myself to blink them away. I hated him. He disgusted me. I wanted nothing more than for him to rot in some cold jail cell, without ever knowing the soft, kind touch of another human being ever again.

As if he could feel my stare, Stein turned. His eyes found mine immediately, as if he'd known I would be sitting here. It was then that I saw the extra wrinkles on his face, and the way his chest didn't quite fill out the front of his pricey suit jacket. He was pale, as if he hadn't been out of the house in months.

We both knew that wasn't true.

I glared at him, and his brows lifted, a subtle surprise. And then he smiled.

"Son of a bitch," I muttered.

"Smile back," said Janelle, so quietly I barely heard.

It took some effort, but I grinned at him. It was the look I was going to give him when they slapped handcuffs around his wrists and carted him away. And at the sight of it, his own smile warped into a cringe, and he turned to face his lawyer.

I sat straighter. Prouder. I hadn't crumbled when he'd walked into the room. I'd stayed strong, even if that strength was fueled by anger. It felt like a victory. The first, in a very long line.

The judge came in shortly thereafter. She was a serious woman, humbling in her black robes and with her stark white hair. Her eyebrows remained flat as she took her raised seat behind the bald eagle seal of the federal district court, as if nothing could surprise her.

It took twenty minutes of proceedings before the prosecutor

called Jessica into the courtroom, and by that time I'd chewed my nails down to the quick.

Maxim Stein's secretary entered from the back of the room, escorted by another marshal. She wore a black pencil skirt and a soft blue blouse, but walked with her head down and her shoulders bowed. Once I'd thought of her as an ice queen, now she looked like a poor, beaten animal. Her eyes and nose were already red, as if she'd been crying.

The lingering fear that she might not be strong enough to do what needed to be done wormed its way back into the forefront of my brain. A lot was riding on this. Part of me wished I could give her a pep talk. Take her for a manicure. Do *something*. But from here on out, this was all out of my hands.

She was sworn in. She agreed to tell the truth, and nothing but the truth, so help her God.

She swore it.

Janelle glared at me when my heels tapped audibly against the tile floor.

The prosecutor rose. He asked her easy opening questions; if she knew the man seated with the defense attorneys, how long she had worked for Maxim Stein, the kinds of basic secretarial things her job entailed.

He asked her if, in her long twenty-four years of employment, Maxim Stein had ever made her feel unsafe.

There was an objection from the defense.

He asked if Maxim Stein had ever asked her to do anything illegal.

Another objection.

He asked if she had ever witnessed Maxim Stein engage in activities she knew to be wrong.

She began to cry.

"I was wrong to run," she said.

The defense didn't even have time to object.

"Take your time," said the prosecutor.

She pulled a worn Kleenex from her sleeve as the court stenographer tapped on her keyboard.

"This is a mess," she said finally, staring at the floor in front of the witness stand. "Mr. Stein's a good man. He's sometimes overly aggressive and single-minded when it comes to his business ventures, but he's not a criminal."

"Ms. Rowe . . ." The prosecutor hesitated. "You understand that you're under oath?"

"I understand," said Jessica.

"This isn't what we discussed."

"I tried to tell you."

The prosecutor returned to the bench to flip through his notes. His cheeks were stained red, and that cutthroat look in his eye had faded to something much less confident.

I shifted in my chair.

The prosecutor read from his notes.

"Yesterday, under oath, you told me that the defendant, Maxim Stein, told you that he was going to steal the Green Fusion engine design from Charlotte MacAfee. Do you remember saying this?"

"Yes, but . . ."

"But what?" interrupted the prosecutor.

"But I was afraid!" cried Jessica. She dabbed her eyes with her tissue. "I agreed with you because I thought I'd be in even more trouble if I didn't."

Maxim's attorneys whispered to each other. I couldn't still my heels from bouncing on the floor.

The prosecutor turned to the judge.

"Your Honor, this wasn't the same story I heard yesterday."

Her silver brows arched.

"It wasn't him," Jessica said, and looked Maxim right in the eye. "I'm sorry, Mr. Stein. I was afraid. I should have been here for you."

Voices began to rise, from around me, from the jury. The judge hit her gavel against her desk to call order.

"What the holy hell is happening?" I muttered to Janelle.

Janelle's mouth was open. Her eyes wide.

"Ms. Rowe, did you not say—" The prosecutor was silenced as his witness talked over him, gaining speed, like her words were water rushing from a broken pipe.

"Mr. Stein employed a young man many years ago to work for him. He was troubled, into drugs and who knows what else. A poor home life, I think."

"Keep to the questions, Ms. Rowe," warned the judge.

If I'd had a red flag, I would have been waving it now. I had a bad feeling about where this was going.

"Ms. Rowe, your testimony—"

"Alec Flynn was like a son to Mr. Stein. And Alec betrayed him."

Red flag. Red flag. Wave, wave, wave.

"*Jessica.*" The prosecutor rushed toward her, hands raised as if trying to calm her down. "Your Honor, the witness is contradicting everything she said yesterday under oath."

"No," Jessica said stridently. "It's the truth. He blackmailed Mr. Stein in order to get control of Force. I ran because I was afraid of what he could do, what Alec Flynn was capable of."

"Stick to the questions, Ms. Rowe, or I'll have you removed," said the judge sternly.

"Your Honor," said the prosecutor. "We need a recess to reassess the situation, as you can see . . ."

It felt as if someone had just pulled the rug out from beneath me. Everyone seemed to be speaking at once, but all I heard was Jessica Rowe's voice.

"He convinced a young woman, Ms. Anna Rossi, to help him. Anna was employed as Mr. Stein's masseuse and had access to his home office. I think she meant to steal the blueprints he'd been trying to procure from the Green Fusion company. I'm sorry, Mr. Stein. I'm so sorry."

My ears started buzzing. My fingers felt numb. This wasn't happening.

The prosecutor had been trying to talk over her, but finally gave up.

"Your Honor, Ms. Rossi . . . she's present in the courtroom. If she's to be called as a witness, she'll need to be excused."

Janelle stood, her hand squeezing my shoulder like a vice.

"You need to leave," she said, her voice flat.

"Get this witness out of here," said the judge. The gavel hit the desk with a sharp clap. "This court is in recess until eight a.m. tomorrow morning. Counsel, I'll see you in my chambers. *Now.*"

I was still in shock as Janelle led me from the courtroom down the wide hallway to a private room. My heels clicked too loudly against the marble floors. Neither of us said a word.

When she opened the door, Alec was already standing. Pacing, from the looks of it. His tie hung in a loose knot around his open collar, and his suit jacket had been laid across the back of one of the chairs that lined the far wall. His hair was a sexy mess. Had I not been reeling, I would have smiled, and remembered the last time he'd rolled out of bed that way, but instead it hit me like a blow to the gut.

Jessica Rowe's testimony was threatening to take Alec away from me.

"What happened." His words were barely a question. He could see the apprehension on my face.

Without answering, I turned to Janelle.

"It's bullshit," I said. "Maxim Stein got to her. I thought you were watching her!"

"We were," snapped Janelle, shutting the door behind her. The three of us faced off, corners of a triangle, each an arm's length away. "Stein never came within a hundred feet of her, I promise you."

"Then he must have called her. *Something.*"

Janelle gave me a withering look. "We monitored her phone. She never called anyone. I need to meet with my team. Stay here."

"Wait." I reached for her as she turned toward the door. "What happens now? What does this mean?"

"What *happened*?" Alec asked again.

I didn't want to tell him. If there was a way not to, I would have.

"It means my case is royally screwed," said Janelle, shaking free of my hand on her shoulder.

Immediately I remembered why I didn't like her.

"Your *case*?" My voice was rising. "This is his *life* we're talking about."

She left the room, the door slamming behind her.

Alec grabbed my wrist and spun me toward him.

"Talk. Now."

Facing him, held in that familiar, heated glare, I nearly buckled. I felt like I'd been the one to fail him.

"She lied," I said.

Voice trembling, I told him everything that had happened, right from the moment Maxim Stein had walked into the courtroom. When his face fell, and his hair swung in front of his eyes, I wrapped my arms around him and held him as tightly as I could.

I wasn't ready to let him go. I would *never* be ready.

Hope wasn't lost. Surely the prosecutor would find a way to poke holes in Jessica's testimony, make the jury see how clouded her judgment had become in the face of fear. He had the FBI behind him for God's sake.

Alec's lawyer walked in not long after, accompanied by his wife, who gave me a sympathetic pat on the arm. His face was still flushed, though he didn't look nearly as confused as he had in the courtroom.

"I assume Anna filled you in," he said. We'd met a couple of times over the last two days in preparation for Alec's testimony. I hadn't been included of course, but Alec had been reluctant to let me leave his sight.

"What's next, Jim?" asked Alec. I could feel the invisible walls he was drawing around himself. I remembered them all too well from the first time I'd met him, when he'd been hiding the truth.

I reached for his hand, and squeezed it tightly.

"The secretary takes the stand again tomorrow morning. The prosecutor will have another shot at her, then the defense gets their questions. I've got to tell you, what happened in there wasn't what I expected."

"What any of us did," said his wife.

Jim inhaled slowly. "Anna needs to take the stand."

"No," said Alec flatly.

His lawyer rested his hands on his narrow hips. "I know you wanted her out of it, Alec . . ."

"No," he said again.

"W-why?" I stammered. "Because Jessica Rowe lied about me?"

"Yes," said Jim. "There are other ways to clear your name . . ."

"Then do them," said Alec.

"There are other ways," continued Jim, with a sigh, "but they won't be nearly as effective, and I'll be honest, this isn't the time to attempt to be stealthy. The prosecution has a solid case. We need to clear this up and move on."

"*Without* Anna."

"These are serious accusations," said Jim. "We may not have a choice in the matter."

"Alec," I said. "Just hear him out."

"No," said Alec sharply. He turned me toward him. "I never would have done this—any of it—if I'd thought you'd be dragged into it. I'm sure as hell not changing course now."

I touched his face. This sweet, stubborn man would risk everything just to protect me.

"Will it help keep Alec out of jail?" I asked Jim, without turning away from Alec.

"It might," replied Jim.

"Then tell me what I need to do."

Thirty-three

Once I'd agreed to testify, Alec and I had been separated. He'd fought hard to keep me out of it; as I forced myself to walk away I heard him threatening to withdraw his testimony again.

I looked back at him one time, and reminded him of his promise.

A day passed. Then another. I was brought to a different hotel. Agent Tenner kept watch outside my door this time, but there was no trace of the man who'd begged me to make dinner in the safe house, and whined about how loud Alec and I had been in the bedroom. He was all business. He barely even acknowledged me apart from a stiff nod.

I wasn't permitted to talk to my father, or Amy, or even Marcos, and it was killing me not to hear if he'd had any leads on Jeremiah Barlow. I was stuck in that room, alone, with a television that seemed to only show updates of the trial, and room service I hated ordering because I had no one to share it with.

But I was helping Alec. And I was saving myself, too, because according to the prosecutor, no one else could prove that Jessica Rowe had been lying about me. If I refused to take the stand, I looked guilty, and the defense would use that to shift the blame off of the real criminal, Maxim Stein.

I didn't have a choice.

The morning I was brought into court, I wore a navy blue dress with silver buttons and swept my hair back into a neat knot at the base of my neck. I held my head high as I was led through the door by security, and as I was sworn in I thought of Jessica Rowe, and the jail time she would face when they found out she'd lied under oath.

It wasn't my first appearance in court. I'd been called as a witness before I'd become a masseuse, when I'd been assigned to children who'd been abused. It wasn't often, but occasionally a custody hearing would include the testimony given by the social worker on the case. Those experiences, and this one, were night and day. Before I'd been convinced I was doing what was right. Now I was just trying not to do something wrong.

Even so, I stared straight at Maxim Stein as I climbed the steps into the witness box, despite the fact that I'd been instructed not to look at him. I wanted him to know I wasn't afraid, even if I was, and that he might have stepped on everyone else in this world, but he couldn't crush Alec, and he sure as hell couldn't crush me.

The prosecutor rose first, and gave me a small reassuring wink.

"Can you state your name for the court, please?" he asked

All eyes were on me. The jury and judge, the attorneys, the stenographer with her ready-to-type fingers, and even the Bane of my Existence, Maxim Stein. I looked out over the audience in the back of the room and had to reign in the wave of emotion when I saw my father sitting near the aisle.

He'd always done what was right. He'd taught me to do the same.

There was no turning back now.

"Anna Rossi," I said, irritated by the tremor in my voice. I leaned closer to the microphone and repeated my name more confidently.

I was prepared for every question he'd asked me thanks to Janelle. I'd even rehearsed my answers in the hotel room. The truth was easy to tell—Yes, I did know Maxim Stein and Jessica Rowe, his secretary. Yes, Alec had told me that Stein was planning on stealing the Green Fusion design without a patent. No, I had no intention of taking the patent for myself.

I told my story, but there was no relief when the prosecutor sat down. Now was where things got tricky.

The defense attorney looked slick with his unnaturally black hair and cuff links that cost more than my life. He gave me a polite, obligatory smile as he approached the stand, and though I'd been prepped for what he might say, I couldn't help but feel small.

I sat straight, and pictured Alec.

"Ms. Rossi, you met Maxim Stein in February, correct?" The attorney's face was hard to read. I reminded myself that his presentation was a crucial part of his arsenal of skills.

"Yes."

"And you knew Charlotte MacAfee from Green Fusion, right?"

I pulled at the end of my skirt nervously.

"I did."

"Would you say you met her between three and five times?"

Before I could stop myself, I pictured her the first way I'd seen her. Naked, with Maxim Stein plowing into her from behind.

I cleared my throat. These numbers must have come from the proceedings yesterday with Jessica.

"Something like that." My magnified voice cut through the uncomfortable silence.

"Yes or no will be fine," he said.

My jaw tightened. "Yes."

He turned suddenly, as if remembering something, and walked back to the desk where Maxim Stein sat. I focused on Alec's old boss again, feeling the anger clear away some of the nerves while Stein's attorney rifled through some papers.

"You've lived in several places prior to landing in Florida, correct?"

Jim had told me to expect him to delve into my past, though how deep he would have been able to dig, I was unsure.

"Yes."

"How many jobs would you say you've started and then quit?"

"I . . ." I glanced at Jim, seated behind the prosecutor, feeling my face warm. "Seven or eight. Maybe more."

"So it's safe to say you needed money."

"Objection." The prosecutor stood. "Relevance, your honor."

"Overruled," said the judge. "Determining if there is motivation to lie is certainly relevant." She smoothed back her white hair, leaning back as if relaxed in her black chair.

"No," I answered, knowing he was alluding to the idea that I was some kind of gold digger. "I've never been hard up on money." If things were tight, I'd always been able to find work.

The defense attorney considered this.

"You're a masseuse, is that right?"

"That's right."

"So you see people who accumulate a lot of stress, who need a chance to decompress."

"Yes."

"I've had a massage or two in my day," he said, smiling now. "Dim lights, soft music, not a lot of clothing."

"I wear a professional amount of clothing, I assure you," I said.

He laughed. The jury seemed to wait for his permission, and they chuckled, too.

"Would it be safe to say you see people when they're vulnerable?"

The judge shifted in her seat. "Where is this going, Counselor?"

"How much do you charge an hour?" he asked, throwing me off balance.

"Seventy dollars is the salon rate," I said. "For my home-based clients I have a sliding scale."

"You charge a woman named June Esposito thirty dollars an hour."

I flinched, drawing to mind my sweet, elderly client with lupus. Sometimes she didn't even pay thirty dollars. Sometimes she bartered homemade tamales, because that was all she could afford with her medical bills.

The fact that she'd been pulled into this pissed me off.

"Like I said, I use a sliding scale," I told him.

"Is that why you charged Maxim Stein three hundred dollars for his session?"

I felt the weight of the jury's judgment on my shoulders.

"That was a price that was offered," I said. "I . . . didn't argue over it."

He had me suddenly wondering if I should have.

Stein's attorney went on to ask me how many hours I worked a week. He estimated how much I made a year, and then speculated that it must have been hard walking into the home of a man who wanted for nothing.

The prosecutor objected to that, too, but it didn't matter what the judge said, because the point had already been made. I was poor. Maxim Stein was rich. Why wouldn't I have wanted what he had?

The defense attorney kept driving the point home, though. He showed me the nondisclosure agreement I had signed when I began employment with Stein, and asked if I was aware that at the time of our first appointment, Maxim was worth over three and a half billion dollars.

I'd sworn not to lie. I said yes.

Any insecurity I'd had was overcome by frustration. He was attacking me with his curious tone and his silver tongue, and even though the answers I gave were technically correct, they left out so much of the truth. Within twenty minutes, I was fumbling, rethinking my previous actions, positive that I looked like the most suspicious person in the world.

Alec had endured this scrutiny nonstop since he'd first gone to the FBI. For the first time I really understood why he'd wanted to shelter me from this. In his position, I would have protected him, too.

When the attorney seemed satisfied that everyone and their mother understood that I was a shady character, he changed course.

"Was it your plan when you started working for Mr. Stein to steal the Green Fusion blueprints and sell them to a competitor?"

"Objection," called Jim. "Argumentative, your honor."

"No!" I said, shaking my head.

"Overruled," said the judge. I knew she wasn't on my side—she wasn't supposed to be on anyone's side—but I couldn't help wishing she'd help me out.

"No, it wasn't your plan initially?" he asked. "Or no it wasn't your plan?"

I felt like he'd kicked out one of the legs on the witness stand, and left me scrambling to stay upright.

"I never stole the Green Fusion blueprints," I said. "I never intended to, I never would have, I never wanted to. I would *never* steal something like that."

"But you *would* steal other things?" His expression stayed absolutely blank.

"Objection!" called the prosecutor.

"*No,*" I said again, feeling the sweat bead on my forehead. The air-conditioning in this room made it frigidly cold, but the overhead lights were bright, and the stares of those around me were accusing.

"My father's a cop," I said, reaching for the only thing that came to mind. "He taught me not to be a thief."

"Your adopted father," clarified Stein's attorney.

"My *father.*" I could hear the anger in my tone, and tried to rein it in. I glanced over to the faces of the men and women in the jury. He'd completely tainted their opinions of me. I could already see they'd dismissed any kind of honor I might have.

The attorney took a deep breath.

"You initiated an intimate physical relationship with Mr. Stein's head of security immediately after you first visited Mr. Stein's home, is that correct?"

I hesitated, feeling the panic welling up inside me.

"Y-yes."

The prosecutor objected, but it was overruled.

"Can you state that person's name for the court?"

I wanted to tell him it was none of his business, but I answered, because I had to.

"Alec Flynn."

"Before Alec Flynn went to the FBI and served time for his crimes, would you say you two were close?"

I wanted to tell him it was none of his business.

"Yes," I said.

"Did he love you?"

I swallowed. "Yes."

"Are you aware Alec Flynn is also a witness in this case?"

"Yes."

"And that he is the person who originally accused Mr. Stein of inappropriate business conduct, and that's why he's here today?"

"I know that," I said.

"Are you aware that Mr. Flynn himself is facing charges of felony murder, conspiracy, corporate espionage, and racketeering?"

My mouth went dry.

"He didn't kill anyone."

"Alec Flynn was just as much a part of this organization as my client. If he claims Mr. Stein committed these crimes, then he is equally as responsible in the eyes of the law."

I could say nothing. Not one word.

"He's looking at a minimum of thirty years," continued Stein's attorney. "If this goes south, he'll be an old man when he gets out of prison."

Alec could go away for thirty years.

Thirty years.

We would never marry. Never have a family. He would be in his sixties when he could hold me again.

"Watch yourself, counselor," warned the judge.

"Do you understand what that means if *you* took part in this?" asked the attorney.

I was shaking.

"Yes," I murmured. I would go down, too. For something I didn't even do.

"Last warning," said the judge. "Get back on track or you're done."

Stein's attorney gave a small nod. His stare returned to me. I tried to look back, but it felt like the wooden walls of this witness stand were closing in, making my space smaller and smaller.

"How long after you began your employment did your romantic relationship with Maxim Stein begin?"

"*What?*" I asked, too loudly.

No. *No, no, no.* It was like watching a train crash in slow motion. I knew where this was heading, but felt powerless to stop it.

"Your affair with Maxim Stein. When did it begin?"

"It didn't," I said. "I never had an affair with Maxim Stein."

"But you did have a sexual relationship with him?"

"No."

And then my nightmare came true. He returned to the desk, where another lawyer handed him a gray folder. From it, he drew several eight-by-ten color photographs. I didn't even have to see them to know what they were, and maybe it would have helped if I'd acted surprised, but as it was all I could do was focus on keeping what little composure I had left.

He carried them up to the judge.

"I'd like to admit these photographs into evidence."

"No," I said. "I know what those are. They're not what you think."

"Ms. Rossi," cautioned the prosecutor. He had risen, and was striding toward the bench, brows drawn in concern. We should have told him about these, but even with as ugly as Maxim could get, I was still surprised he had brought the pictures out here, in front of a whole courtroom of people who he needed to believe he was a good man.

The judge admitted the photos.

The prosecutor looked at them briefly. He objected on the grounds of relevance and was overruled. Then again based on the fact that he hadn't seen them before. He was overruled. Muttering something under his breath, he retreated to his bench.

"You said these aren't what I think," said the defense attorney. "Can you explain what they are?" He handed me the photos.

My black dress. My head on Maxim's shoulder.

My naked body.

"You don't understand," I said.

"Who is in the photo?" he asked.

"Please," I begged. "It's not . . ."

"I'm going to advise Ms. Rossi not to answer that," said the prosecutor.

"Overruled," said the judge.

Silence. I looked out, and saw my father, who looked as white as a ghost.

"It's Maxim Stein and me," I whispered. The sickness was rolling through me now, threatening to climb up my throat. I remembered waking up, disoriented, on the ground outside the restaurant. I remembered Alec sitting in the chair beside my bed at the hospital. The medical test—*you got lucky, Ms. Rossi.*

"And when were they taken?" asked the attorney.

I straightened. "Just a few days ago."

"How could they have been taken recently?" he asked, with a condescending laugh. "Mr. Stein is on house arrest. Are you suggesting that he somehow removed his ankle bracelet, traveled to the location of this hotel to meet you, and then took these pictures?"

I stared at Maxim Stein.

"That's exactly what I'm suggesting," I said, and even though I knew it was already too late, that the jury and judge would never believe me, I kept on. "I'm saying that last weekend I was drugged at a bar by a man I'd never seen before, taken to a hotel in Miami, and posed in pictures without my consent."

"Another man? What other man is that, Ms. Rossi?"

"Jeremiah Barlow," I said. "Maxim Stein's son."

I felt a ball of ice form right in the center of my chest the second I said it.

"Maxim Stein doesn't have a son," said the defense attorney. "He doesn't have any children. If he did, wouldn't his heir be entitled to a piece of the company? Child support? Something?"

"Ms. Stein paid him in cash."

"You know this for a fact?" asked the defense attorney. Behind him, Maxim stared daggers at me. I wished everyone would turn around and see the guilt on his face, rather than the insecurity on mine.

"I . . ."

"You have evidence that Maxim Stein has a child. A birth certificate maybe?"

"N-no."

The prosecutor was shouting something. Jim was on his feet. Maxim's attorney was saying something back to him. I didn't hear any of it as I continued on.

"I do have evidence that I was taken. I was found outside Orlando and brought to a hospital where they found Rohypnol in my system. I can deliver my medical records, and I can direct you to the hotel in Miami where he brought me for those pictures."

"Order!" called the judge, for the first time today sitting straight in her chair. "Order! Counselor, get ahold of your witness."

"This all happened this past weekend?" The defense attorney's voice rose above the others. "According to Jessica Rowe's testimony, you were in Miami with Mr. Stein months ago, in February, when he was there for business."

Alec had suggested this might happen after the pictures had first surfaced. Maxim would try to say that we'd had an affair before, and that jealousy had driven Alec to go to the FBI. He'd thought *Maxim* would accuse me of it. Not his secretary.

"No, that's not right," I said. "She's lying. I don't know what Mr. Stein said to scare her, but she's lying."

"She was under oath," said Stein's attorney. "As are you right now, Ms. Rossi."

"I'm telling you the truth," I said, slapping my flat hand on the table so hard the microphone rattled.

"Was Alec Flynn telling the truth when he accused my client of stealing the Green Fusion design?" pressed the attorney, standing close now, just beyond the witness box. "Or was he angry because you'd betrayed him by sleeping with his boss? I can tell you right now, I'd be furious if my girlfriend went behind my back like that."

"Counselor!" ordered the judge.

"I'd do anything to see the guy who touched her suffer. *Anything.*"

"Alec didn't do this out of spite," I said.

"So he wasn't upset? Ouch. Maybe you didn't mean as much to him as you thought."

This was falling apart. I closed my mouth. I had to. Everything I was saying was coming out wrong, and this fucking snake was leading me right into his den.

The judge pointed her finger at the prosecutor, who was still trying to put the brakes to this inevitable crash.

"That's it," she snapped. "We're taking a recess."

"I just have one final question," said the defense attorney.

The courtroom stilled.

"Ms. Rossi," he asked. "Do you often go home with strange men you meet at bars?"

I lowered my eyes, and succumbed to the nightmare.

I was going to lose everything.

Thirty-four

Alec's testimony was the next day. I waited by the window of the hotel room, staring out into the busy streets of downtown Tampa, hoping that someone would bring me word as soon as he had been dismissed.

My appearance yesterday in court had been a disaster. The prosecutor had done what he could to patch things up regarding Jessica's accusation that I had been a part of the plan to steal the Green Fusion blueprints. There was nothing to do about the pictures—they were out for my father, the news, *everyone* to know about—but he'd managed to prove that I had not, in fact, been in Miami with Maxim Stein during the time Jessica had accused me of. I'd been working. Derrick had no doubt scrambled to get copies of my old work schedules.

The minutes turned to hours. Numbness had taken away much of the sting, but I still felt the passing of time. How long before they took Alec away? Would they do it today? Tomorrow? Would I even be able to see him before they did?

They'd told me I couldn't make any phone calls.

I was sort of tired of being told what to do. It wasn't like I had a lot to lose now anyway.

Amy answered on the first ring.

"Hey," I said.

"Oh God," she said. "You sound bad. It's bad, isn't it?"

"It's bad," I said. And started to cry.

For the next ten minutes, we barely spoke, but she was there on the end of the line, and that's what mattered.

At five thirty, there came a knock on the door. I didn't get up. It was Tenner; it had to be. He'd taken to bringing food inside and setting it on the hotel room desk when it became apparent that I wasn't ordering room service.

When I didn't answer, the door opened.

I didn't turn around. I stayed planted on the windowsill, and closed my eyes to shut out the people rushing by on the street below. It occurred to me he had news of the trial, but now that the time had come, I didn't even want to hear it. The dread that had wormed its way into my stomach told me it wouldn't be good.

"The first time I saw you, you were sitting in your car, AC blasting, eyes closed. I kept wondering what you were waiting for, parked on the street like that."

I had turned sharply at the sound of Alec's voice, but wasn't able to move when I faced him. He had his hands in his pockets, and his shoulders hunched a little from the great burdens he carried. Despite this, he smiled, and the warmth that had been missing in his absence shimmered through me.

"The neighborhood watch," I murmured. "You busted me for illegal parking."

"It wasn't illegal," he confessed with a small shrug. "I didn't like the idea of you waiting for anyone but me."

He'd made up a reason to talk to me. Even now, I was glad he had. I would never regret his presence in my life.

"And here I am, waiting for you again."

He glanced at the ground, where he rotated the heel of his shoe over the carpet.

"Seems only fair since I've waited for you my whole life."

I rose then, and went to him, sliding my arms within his suit jacket and resting my cheek on his chest. He curved around me, so that we were like two puzzle pieces fitting together.

"How long do I have you for?" It felt like I was always wondering the answer to this question.

"We'll know tomorrow morning," he said. "I'm all yours until then."

I could hear it in his tone. He didn't expect this to end well. He'd already accepted he was going away. If the jury suspected that he had lied to the federal prosecutor about his role in Maxim's affairs, his former plea deal would be off. He'd be taken to jail to await his own trial, with a bail set so high there'd be no way I could bring him home, and a chance of getting off would be close to impossible thanks to the case Stein's lawyers would throw against him.

"Just until then?" I asked.

He held me tighter.

"For as long as you'll take me."

I blinked rapidly and forced a steady breath. If we had limited time, I wouldn't spend it crying. I wouldn't let his last memories of me be with a broken heart and runny mascara.

"If the hold's off, I need to call Marcos," I said. "I haven't talked to him in days. He's been watching Maxim's house, trying to see if Jeremiah Barlow's tried to make contact . . ."

"He hasn't."

"Well, maybe my dad . . ."

"Anna."

The way he said my name made me halt. As much as I wanted

to chase leads, find something to keep him in my arms, he needed me here, now.

"What do you want to do?" I asked.

He pulled back to look at me. His knuckles skimmed my cheeks, and then burrowed into my hair, combing it down the center of my back.

"I want to take you out," he said. "And then I want to take you to bed."

"All right," I said.

He took my hand in his, and kissed my knuckles, and then he led me right out of that room to the elevators. As I passed Agent Tenner and Janelle, standing in the hallway, my worst suspicions were confirmed. They hardly glanced up at me, and when Alec passed, they didn't even say good-bye.

We got takeout tacos for dinner, and took them to a park by the Bay. It was a quiet place, and the press didn't follow us. Alec held my hand as we walked out to the pier, and sat on a bench overlooking the water. I felt his gaze on me constantly, though when I met his eyes, he looked away.

"Tell me something I don't know about you," I said when I'd finished my second taco. I thought he'd been keeping up with me, but now that I looked I saw that he'd barely touched his first.

"Like what?"

"Like your favorite color," I said. "I don't care."

I wanted to know everything. I wanted to keep every piece of him I could if we were separated.

"Red," he said. "When it's lace and on your body. Black. When it's lace and on your body." He reached behind my back to wrap a piece of hair around his fingers. "Pink." His hand lowered to my thigh and began to slide up beneath my skirt. "Definitely pink."

It took me too long to slap away his hand. There were people around. But I could still feel his touch on my bare skin.

"How'd you lose your virginity?" I said.

He snorted. "The way all fifteen-year-old boys do. With an older girl in a dressing room at the mall."

I barked out a laugh.

"I don't think that's how most fifteen-year-old boys lose their virginity." I smacked his chest when he grinned like he had something to be proud of. "How much older was she?"

He sighed wistfully. "Old enough to buy me beer."

"I'm fairly sure that's illegal."

"I guess you haven't heard," he said, "I have a very questionable past."

His words were light. His tone was not.

"You're such a bad boy. Kind of makes me want to go to the mall and find a dressing room." I scooted closer. "If you're good to me, I might even buy you a beer afterward."

His brow quirked.

"As tempting as that sounds, I'd rather have you on a bed," he told me. "Where I can see all of you."

Again, I felt my throat tighten. I didn't want this to be the last time he touched me, but if it was, I wished I'd had the ability to make it more memorable.

"I don't even have anything sexy to wear," I said, swiping my hair back.

"It doesn't matter what you wear." He gathered the half-eaten food off our laps. "Come on. Let's go."

I could barely look at him on the car ride back to Mac's restaurant. Every time I did, my eyes stung and my throat tied in knots. I held his hand so tightly my knuckles turned white, but he didn't say a word about it. Every few minutes he brought my hand to his lips, or rested our joined hands on his chest.

Every time I glanced at the clock, a small wave of panic took hold of me. The minutes were going by too fast. Morning, and the fate of our love, would be here too soon.

We walked in silence up to the stairs to the safe haven we'd made a home these past few days. So much had changed since I'd first come here. I'd been so afraid, on the verge of losing my mind, and Alec had brought me back one touch at a time. He'd saved me, just like he always did.

I wouldn't die without him. But I couldn't really live, either.

With the key in the lock, he paused.

"Would it be easier for you if we didn't go inside?" he asked. "We could drive around. Do something else."

I put my hand on his, aware of each jagged, broken piece of my heart.

"Would it be easier for you?"

"Yes," he said quietly.

We didn't leave.

I helped him turn the key in the lock, dismantle the security code, and push inside.

Without turning on the lights, I took him by the hand and led him to the bedroom. The air was cool and stale, this place having been left empty these last few days, but soon that would change. It would be warm, and the darkness would embrace us, and every inch of him would belong to me.

He kissed me. Softly at first, but as the seconds passed, the things he'd been holding back began to break, though. I could feel it in the pressure of his lips, and the desperate caress of his tongue, and the way his hands trembled as they cupped my cheeks.

I slipped his jacket off his shoulders, pulled his tie free, and unbuttoned his shirt, my own hands shaking. There was no stopping my tears now. They ran freely, and he kissed them, too, holding me close even as he pulled my dress over my head.

"Say this isn't the last time," he said. "I don't care if it's a lie. Just say it."

I slowed. My fingers loosened their grip on his shoulders, and I smoothed them up his neck to his face.

"Alec."

He moved me back toward the bed. I felt the mattress behind my thighs, but didn't sit.

"Baby, wait," I said.

His chest was rising with husky breaths. I held his face in his hands and forced him to look down at me.

"I love you," I said. "I'll love you the rest of my life." I kissed his chin, and his lips, and his flexing jaw. "This isn't the last time, I promise."

I believed that now. Even if they tried to take him tomorrow, I was going to dedicate every second he was gone to getting him back. And if I had to wait, I would wait. I would do whatever I needed to do in order to hold him again.

He murmured my name.

"Make love to me," I said.

He laid me gently on the bed and then took his place at my side. We touched each other slowly, hands and lips memorizing every curve, every muscle, every single place on the other's body that led to a gasp, or a sigh, or a groan. We loved each other until time became meaningless, until our hands and lips moved with a greater urgency, and only when the tension became unbearable, did he move between my thighs, and fill me.

He said he loved me, and that I was beautiful, and that he was afraid. And I soaked up all of it, taking all his fear and passion the same way I took his cock. With a desperate, aching need to make us both whole.

There came a point, at the very end, where we were.

Thirty-five

I listened to Alec's heavy heartbeat, my cheek against his chest, my arm wrapped so far around him that my fingers rested between his back and the mattress. He held me, too, one hand on the small of my back, the other tangled in my hair. My head was pleasantly fuzzy from what he'd done to me, but that didn't stop the doubt from squeezing in.

Morning was coming, and that judge, and the twelve men and women of the jury, had the power to take away the man I loved more than anything in this world. They had the power to condemn me, too, though the last time I'd talked to the prosecutor, it had sounded like I was in the clear.

Hooray. That made me feel so much better.

I thought back over the utter train wreck that was my testimony, wondering if I could have said something different to clear Alec's name. Stein's attorney had run me straight into the ground, first by alluding that I was a money-grubbing whore, and then with Jessica Rowe's accusation that I'd had an affair with her boss. It didn't make sense how she would have known I'd been in Miami any time, much less February.

It didn't make any sense at all actually.

I sat up.

"Who knew that I was taken to Miami?" I asked Alec.

He lifted himself onto his elbows, and even in the dark room I could see the scowl on his face. "What do you mean?"

"Who knew?" I asked. "You and me. Maxim, obviously, and Jeremiah Barlow. Janelle, and maybe her team. Who else?"

"No one else that I know of," he said.

"Did Janelle tell anyone else about the pictures?"

"No," he said. "She was clear they'd stay between us until she had enough evidence to bring down Max and Barlow."

"She never told the prosecutor they were taken in Miami?"

"No. Where's this . . ."

"Did *you* tell anyone else they were taken in Miami?"

"You know I wouldn't."

He was sitting fully upright now, and placed a hand on my knee.

"What's going on?" he asked, concerned. "Did you remember something?"

My head wasn't foggy anymore. It was crystal clear. I sprang from the bed.

"Maxim Stein never came within a hundred feet of Jessica Rowe, that's what Janelle said. The FBI would have intercepted any calls she made or received."

Alec swung his long legs off the side of the mattress while I began to pace.

"She knew I was in Miami, Alec. Stein's attorney told me she testified that I was there with him in February. Why would she say that?"

He rose. "To add fuel to the theory that you had a relationship with Max."

"But why Miami? Why not pick New York? Or London? Or goddamn Pakistan?"

He tilted his head.

"She knew I was there, she just lied about *when*."

Alec turned, and snagged a pair of jeans from the dresser drawer.

"Your dad tailed her down to the Keys," he said. "That's only miles from the hotel where you were taken."

My hands started to shake.

"She could have been there when I was."

I'd thought Maxim had gotten to her, scared her, and that's why she'd testified the way she had. But now it seemed entirely possible that she'd planned on protecting him the entire time.

He jerked on his jeans, and flipped on the light. His phone was on the dresser, and he reached for it now, scanning through a list of numbers before he pressed Send.

"Who are you calling?" I asked.

"The hotel in Miami."

"I thought you said it was closed for renovations." I found my dress on the floor, and hurriedly pulled it on.

"The other hotel, across the street."

Where the pictures could have been taken.

"Mark, hi, it's Alec Flynn, we talked last week about . . . Yes, that's right. Listen, I have another favor to ask of you."

I listened as he gave the details of Jessica's appearance and was put on hold. While he waited, I raced to the kitchen, where the prepaid phone had been placed back in the drawer beside Alec's gun.

I reached for them both now.

Quickly, I dialed my father's number, placing the weapon on the counter. It went straight to voice mail. Thinking he was just on the other line, I called again, but again, there was no answer.

"Dad, it's me, call me at this number as soon as you get this." I nearly hung up, and then stopped myself. "Just look in your missed calls folder and press SEND. Yeah, yeah, I know, you're a detective, of course you could have figured that out."

I hung up and dialed the next number.

"This is Marcos."

"Hey, it's me. Have you found anything on Jeremiah Barlow yet?"

He sighed. "No. But look, he's not in the wind, yet. We'll catch him."

"I want you to check on Jessica Rowe, Maxim Stein's secretary."

"Yeah, I know who she is. Why?"

"I need to see her."

"Pretty sure the FBI's not going to go for that."

"I think she's a part of this," I said. "I think she helped Jeremiah Barlow somehow."

He sighed.

I waited.

"How sure are you?" he asked.

"Do you want to know an honest percentage?" I asked. "Or can I get away with just saying I've got a really strong feeling about it?"

He sighed again. "I'm near the hotel where she's being held. I'll go do a wellness check. Say someone called in that she was trying to jump out her window or something."

"I love you, Marcos."

"Yeah, yeah." He hung up.

When I turned around, Alec was fully dressed, standing in the threshold of the bedroom door.

"A woman matching Jessica Rowe's description checked in at the hotel next door the night you were taken," he said. "She stayed one night, and paid in cash. The manager had been prioritizing guests to views that faced the ocean or the strip on account of the construction, but she specifically requested a room on that side."

My knees weakened, and I sat on a nearby stool.

"She took the pictures," I said. "Or someone did from her room."

Alec came to me, and knelt, taking my hands in his.

"What happens now?" I asked.

"We call the FBI and tell them what we know. Mark, the hotel manager, says he'll do whatever he can to help."

I could hardly believe this was happening. It seemed too good to be true.

Alec smiled, and then he laughed, and kissed me hard on the mouth.

Jessica wouldn't be able to talk herself out of this. She was still the key to this trial, only not in the way I'd thought. Her part in my abduction would lead to the unraveling of Maxim Stein's whole defense. It would start with his parole violation when he'd gone to Miami, a desperate attempt to create a false reason for Alec to bring a case against him, and fall apart from there.

The prepaid phone I'd set on the counter rang. It was so loud, I jumped.

"Marcos," I said when I recognized the number. Alec nodded.

"Hey," I said. "That was fast . . ."

"She's not there," he said. "FBI had a guard on her, but he thinks she might have ducked out when he checked the floor."

"Maybe she really jumped," I offered morbidly.

"Someone would have seen that," said Marcos. "She's running. Only question is, where to?"

I set the phone down.

"She's gone," I told Alec.

"Janelle's contacting the local PD about roadblocks in and out of the city," Alec said as he hung up the phone. "She's going to the port authority, too, just in case Jessica tries to get on a cargo or cruise ship."

We were in the SUV, driving over the waterway toward the police department where we were supposed to meet the FBI. Alec drove fast, but not fast enough to keep up with my flying pulse. We had hours left until the jury shared their findings, and already I could feel the dark sky beginning to gray with the impending dawn.

"She knew she was going down," I said. "Lying under oath was just the start of it. She's making one last attempt to get out before they cart her off to jail."

And cart you off, too.

I shivered.

"Where would she go?" Alec muttered. "She wouldn't go back to anyplace she'd been, that would be stupid. She knows your dad tracked her across Florida."

"If I was her, I'd leave the country," I said. "Somewhere that the United States couldn't haul me back."

"She can't get on a plane without an ID," he said. "Not even a jet."

"Not even if it's one of her boss's jets?"

"They're all grounded . . ." he trailed off.

I stared at him, Mike's voice in my head.

"*He's been chartering one of his private jets out to old oil company clients for money.*" It was how Maxim Stein had continued to fund his legal defense.

"Alec," I said. "Jeremiah Barlow's a pilot."

"Shit," he said. "Hold on."

With a screech of tires, he cut across three lanes of traffic to catch the exit that would take us toward the airport.

Thirty-six

A lec drove straight to the back entrance of the airport where the private jets were housed in their enormous domed hangars. It had been a long time since I'd been here—the last time Alec had taken me on my first private jet flight. It was when I'd learned he was scared to death of flying. It wasn't until later I'd found out that he'd gone to the FBI while I'd been walking around Central Park, completely oblivious to the nature of his "meeting."

When we got to the security gate, Alec muttered something about letting him do the talking, but I wasn't given the chance. The booth beside the gate was empty, despite the fact that the light was on.

"The guard must be on a break," said Alec, but I wasn't so sure. TSA initiatives had made airports some of the most secure places in the country, and an unmanned entrance that gave access to private planes seemed highly suspicious.

Wanted felons, like Jeremiah Barlow, might even be able to slip through.

Alec put the car in park and stepped outside. I shivered as he pulled his shirt over the gun, tucked into the back of his waist-band. After looking around, he climbed into the security booth and lifted a clipboard. I watched him tear a paper off the top, and shove it into his pocket. Then, he pressed a code into the se-curity box, and the electronic gate rolled open.

The clock on the dash flashed 1:47 a.m. as Alec reentered the car and sped down the road beside the runways.

"This is crazy," I said. "Jessica's probably just going to confession or something." That was probably the best place for her now.

Alec reached for my hand.

"And even if she did come here, she could be anywhere. She could have gotten on any of these planes."

He squeezed.

"And even if she *did* come for Stein's plane, who's to say it's even here? It could be halfway over the Atlantic right now."

Alec released my hand to reach in his pocket. He removed a crumpled paper, which I smoothed out over my lap—a computer printout with a list of times and corresponding numbers.

"What is this?"

"Flight manifest," he said. "The fourth on the list is Stein's plane. Check the time."

"Oh-two hundred," I said, checking the clock again. "Two a.m. That's ten minutes from now."

The engine roared as he switched gears. In the distance, a large commercial plane descended. It looked as if it was heading straight toward us.

Alec made a small, audible moan. I touched his cheek, al-ready finding it clammy. He leaned into my hand.

"There," he said, pointing ahead. Only the car's headlights and the red blinking lights that lined the runway lit our path, but up ahead were a dozen hangars. Half of them were open. Most of them were dark. All except the one on the end.

"Is that Force?" I asked, trying to remember where Stein's planes were housed.

"Yes."

It could have been perfectly innocent. Just some wealthy clients getting ready to board their flight to somewhere in Oil-land. But the needling in my gut told me differently. I leaned forward in the seat as Alec slowed, and parked in the shadowed alley between two hangars.

"Stay in the car. I'm going to take a look." He withdrew his phone from the cupholder where he'd tossed it, and placed it in my hand.

He stepped outside. With the door open I could already hear the loud whir of the plane's engine, even through the metal wall of the hangar

"*Stay in the car,*" I repeated. Not likely. If backstabbing Jessica Rowe was here, I wanted to see her for myself. And if Jeremiah Barlow was here, I sure as hell wasn't going to get caught alone with him.

Closing my door softly, I crept toward the enormous open garage, my sandals making soft crunching noises over the gravel. Alec saw me and motioned back to the car, but I ignored him. I squeezed the phone tightly in my hand, getting closer to the building's gaping mouth where we'd be able to look inside. Voices could be heard now, muffled over the noises of the plane.

Heart pounding, I followed as Alec grabbed my wrist and held me close behind him. When we reached the edge of the hangar, he looked first, and I could tell from the stone hard grip on my arm that we'd found what we were looking for.

I smashed myself between the metal wall and his body, taking a quick glance around the corner. Thirty feet away in the large, brightly lit room, a white sedan parked beside a private luxury jet.

Not just any white car. *The* white car. The one that had stopped behind me at the park, and had nearly hit me when I'd run into the bar. The same car that had been photographed in the security tapes leaving the renovated hotel in Miami. Now that I'd seen it I felt confident that Jeremiah had been following me for some time.

Hunched over, reaching into the backseat, was a woman in a black wrap dress. She stood suddenly and slammed the door, gripping her mousy brown hair in both hands. After a second, she released it, and spun toward the plane.

Even from the distance I could see the difference in her appearance. She wasn't ragged and beaten anymore. This was the ice queen, complete with her designer dress and spike heels.

The anger spiked in my chest. I backed up a step, and dialed Marcos's number.

"Yeah," he answered.

"It's me," I whispered. "We're at the airport. The private hangars. You better get over here quick. Jessica Rowe's here, and it looks like she's about to get on a plane."

I glanced around the corner again, Alec keeping a firm grip on my shoulder.

"On my way." Over the line, I heard the rising scream of his patrol car's siren. "Anna, you gotta get out of there, okay? Cops show up, there's going to have a lot of questions as to what you're doing . . ."

I didn't hear what else he said.

A man was jogging down the steps that led into the cabin. A young pilot, in navy slacks and a white collared shirt. He didn't have to turn to the side for me to see the large black star tattoo on his neck.

The walls holding back the memories were shaking, or maybe that was Alec's hand, still on my arm. I could hear his teeth grinding near my ear, feel the anger rise up in him like a cobra ready to strike.

Jeremiah Barlow strode past Jessica Rowe, opened the back door of the sedan, and dragged another man out. The second man wavered on his feet, shoulders thrown back awkwardly but head bowed. It took a moment to realize his arms must have been bound behind his back; they were hidden beneath his brown leather flight jacket. Though he wasn't facing us, I could tell it wasn't Maxim Stein. This man was too tall, and his hair was light, not the full platinum wave that Stein sported.

"Anna, get in the car," Alec said.

The man struggled as Jeremiah pulled him toward the plane.

"Anna, go." Alec jerked me back, but it was too late. I'd seen the man's face, bruised, and bearing a hard grimace.

I dropped the phone.

There was no thinking, just a pure rush of adrenaline as I shook free of Alec's grasp. I felt his grip burn my skin as I fell to the ground, and scrambled back to my feet. My vision had compressed, closing in on all sides. I could only see my father. My *dad*. The man who couldn't be hurt. Captured by a man I knew to be even more dangerous than Maxim Stein.

I didn't make it five steps into the hangar before they saw me.

"Let him go!" Alec yelled from behind me.

Jeremiah moved fast. He grabbed my father, and had a gun pointed to his temple before I could skid to a stop. I stared at them, hate and fear merging into a powerful, lethal drug that scored through my system.

"Get on the plane!" Jessica shouted, leading the way.

Jeremiah followed her order, pulling my father backward to the steps. My dad didn't make it easy. He dropped down, forcing the younger man to carry him. Still, Jeremiah was strong, and with his forearm pressed against my father's throat, he succeeded in getting him up the steps.

Alec passed me, gun braced before him in his strong, steady hands.

"Anna, back up," Alec said, voice cold. "Go. I've got this."

"Get her out of here!" my dad yelled, just as he disappeared into the cabin.

"No!" I ran toward the plane again, unarmed, but strong enough to tear that jet apart piece by piece.

As we passed the car, a gunshot ricocheted through the air. Instinctively, both Alec and I ducked, and before I could raise my eyes again, I was shoved hard to the side, behind the back tires of the white sedan.

"Stay down." Alec's eyes were wild, though not half as crazed as I felt. Beneath the car I could see the stairs that led into the cabin of the plane lift, revealing the landing gear behind it. I'd fallen onto my side, but rose into a crouch to see over the trunk of the car.

The door was closing. The jet's engines made a loud churning sound as it lurched forward.

"Dad!"

If that plane took off, my father was gone. I'd never see him again. I knew this as clearly as I knew my own name.

Alec's fist tangled in my hair. He pulled my face to his, and smashed his mouth against mine for one hard kiss.

"I love you," he said.

And then he ran for the closing door.

The plane turned hard toward the exit behind me, and I watched, horrified, as Alec ducked beneath the tip of the wing. The blast of wind from the engine caught his clothes, and they rippled across his body as he leaned against their pull.

Gun still in one hand, he made it to the door of the plane. His hands reached into the side, but couldn't pull it down while still holding the gun. The plane rolled past me, the wing hanging halfway over the roof of the car.

In Alec's efforts to open the door, he dropped the gun. He glanced after it as it clattered to the ground, and even in that split second I could see the decision in his eyes. Get on the plane, or go for the weapon. Leaving it where it fell, he jerked the door open, and forced down the steps, arms flexing. Before I saw if Jeremiah or Jessica was waiting in the threshold, I was on my feet, unwilling to leave Alec undefended to face two dangerous criminals.

Alec crawled into the plane, disappearing into the shadowed interior.

A second later I heard his shout of pain.

I swept the gun off the ground, and raced toward the still open door. The plane was rolling, but not fast enough that I couldn't hop aboard the bottom step. Still, I scraped my knees on the skid-proof pad, and had to cling to the base of the steel railing so I didn't topple off. When I regained my balance, I clutched the heavy gun against my chest and crawled up into the cabin.

A shadowed figure stood above me, and even as I lifted the gun, I knew I was too late.

"Anna," said Maxim Stein. "So nice of you to join us."

Thirty-seven

Maxim leaned against the back of a seat, dressed more casually than I'd ever seen him in jeans and a thin black sweater. He assessed me as he always had when I'd come to his home to give him massages. Like I was nothing more than a servant, despite the fact that I was armed.

He had his own weapon though, which he pointed directly at my father, sitting in one of the plush leather seats beside a window, draped with lacy white curtains. Dad's posture was rigidly straight on account of his bound arms, and his nose and mouth were stained with dry blood.

Swallowing a sob, I readjusted my hands on the gun, and aimed it clearly at Maxim's chest. We were moving faster now; I could feel the pull from the wind outside and braced myself against the corner beside the door.

From this position, I had a clear view of the center aisle, where Alec lay across the floor, facedown. Jessica Rowe crouched beside him, what looked to be a gun in her hand.

My heart stopped.

My hands wavered.

Not a gun, a Taser.

"Alec?" My voice was barely a whisper. *"Alec,"* I said again, this time a little louder.

He didn't move.

I stared at Maxim.

"Alec, get up!" I called.

Jessica stood, gripping a seat for support. "Help me throw him out."

"Don't you touch him," I growled.

"We can't *throw him out*," snapped Maxim, revealing just a hint of the stress hiding beneath his cool exterior. "It's too late for that. If he survives the fall, he'll tell the FBI I did it."

"Then kill him first."

My eyes shifted to her, shocked at her frigid tone, even now when I knew the harm she could do.

"And be extradited for murder? Not just for one, but three?" Maxim gave an annoyed groan. "My dear, you think too much like a woman. These problems don't just disappear when you sweep them under the rug. They fester, and stink. Better to take them with us, and dump them somewhere they'll never be found."

Jessica frowned. "They'll think Alec and his girlfriend skipped town because he was going to jail."

"That's right," said Maxim.

My jaw was clamped so tightly closed, my teeth ached.

"Anna," said my dad quietly. "There's still time." He glanced behind me toward the open door. We were outside now, and had slowed to turn. The line of red lights outside the cabin window told me we had reached the runway.

From the pilot's cabin came the muffled voice of air control, alerting the pilot that we were clear for takeoff.

"Let us off," I told Maxim, as he leisurely made his way across the cabin to sit beside my father. My dad winced as Maxim's weapon pressed into his ribs.

"Anna, jump," said my dad.

"All three of us," I continued to Maxim. "Let all three of us go. You'll be halfway over the Gulf before the police find us."

"Who says we're going over the Gulf?" asked Maxim.

My mind shot through the alternatives. He wouldn't go stateside; there was nothing for him there. He'd have to go over the Atlantic. Europe maybe? Alec had told me Force did business with big oil companies in the Middle East. Maybe that's where he was heading.

"I don't care where you're going," I said. "Just let us leave."

Maxim gave a smug smile. "You seem quite concerned about the welfare of your private investigator."

"Close that door!" called Jeremiah from the front of the plane.

Stein sighed. "Anna, would you be so kind as to shut the door. It's the button right there to your left."

His persistent calm was pissing me off.

"Move that gun and I'll do whatever you like."

Maxim snorted. "I'm hours away from losing my company— my entire *empire*. What makes you think I'm in the mood to negotiate?"

It was a diversion. The last I'd heard, he was winning. After what had happened with Jessica's testimony, and my humongous failure, I'd doubted anything Alec had said would even be considered by the jury. Bringing down Maxim Stein had turned into the biggest white-collar cluster fuck since the creation of Wall Street.

My dad seemed to have had enough. He turned fast, throwing his shoulder into Maxim Stein. Jessica screamed.

"Go!" Dad shouted, just as the sound of gunfire cracked through the small space.

For a moment, time was suspended. No one moved. I couldn't breathe. I couldn't even hear above the rushing in my own ears. And then my father went still.

"Dad!" I rushed toward them, forgetting that Maxim still held a gun. Forgetting that I did, too. Only seeing my father, the first person who'd ever been straight with me, who'd really loved me, crumpling to the floor.

I rolled him onto his back, hands flying over his chest as the plane rocked to a sudden halt.

"Dad?" He was bleeding from the shoulder. Dark, red blood stained his already dirty shirt. The jacket had fallen off in the scuffle, and I grabbed it now and pressed down on the wound. His green eyes, still open, focused on mine with a hard, angry intensity.

"That was your break," he muttered.

"I'm not leaving you." I swiped at the tears dripping down my nose with the back of my hand. "How bad is it?"

He groaned as I tied the arms of the jacket around his shoulder.

"Just clipped me. Where's the gun?"

I searched our immediate area, and zeroed in on the weapon still in Maxim's hand. He pointed it in my direction now, and as I stared down the barrel, a dark despair twisted in the pit of my stomach.

"Dad," Maxim said, still breathing hard as he picked himself up off the floor. "The things we do for kin . . ." His perfect wave of hair was mussed, and his cheeks had gone ashy white.

"What have you done?" Jessica shouted at her boss.

"What have *I* done?" Maxim countered. "We wouldn't even be here if you'd stayed in Miami like I told you."

"I couldn't. You know that," Jessica snapped. "He'd followed me all the way down the coast!"

It occurred to me she was referring to my father.

"And had you told Jeremiah he could have handled it then," shot Maxim. "But because you didn't, Anna's *father* is now bleeding all over my floor."

"What the hell is going on back here?" At the sound of Jeremiah's voice I twitched, and turned to see him on the wooden aisle beside Alec. "You can't fire a gun in here. Surely you of all people know that."

In his hand was the weapon I'd dropped in my hurry to get to my father. It must have slid down the wooden aisle. Fear gripped me as I contemplated what he'd already shown himself to be capable of. This was not a man I wanted to be holding a firearm.

He assessed me with a chilly smirk.

"Last time I saw you, you had considerably less clothes on." Jeremiah tucked the gun into the back of his belt and strode quickly toward the open exit. There, he pressed a button to raise the door. As it suctioned close, I felt our last chances of survival slip away.

We had nothing to lose now.

Jeremiah returned to the aisle to kneel beside Jessica. She'd been trying to fasten Alec's wrists behind his back with a curtain she'd pulled off the window.

"And last time I saw *you*, you had a shiv in your back," he said to still unmoving Alec.

"There's a special place for people like you," I growled at him.

He looked up at me, and for a split second a memory overlapped with the present. I could see him as he'd been in the bar, just after he'd bought me a drink. Eyes bright and grin dangerous.

"You believe in karma?" he asked. "Think I'm going to get what's coming?" He stepped on Alec's back while Jessica hurriedly tied the knot. Now that he had a gun he seemed to find this whole thing amusing.

"I know you will," I said.

"What does that mean for you?" he asked. "You must have done something really bad to end up passed out in the back of my car." His voice lowered. "Do you even remember taking off your dress? Oh that's right, I did it for you."

A spike of fury had me rising to my feet, but I held tight as Maxim's weapon pressed against my side.

"Get your kid under control, Stein," my dad said through his teeth. "Or I'll do it for you."

For a flash I wondered if my dad had found proof that Maxim

was Jeremiah's father, or if he was still relying on the information Jessica had told me in St. Augustine. Either way, my father may have been flat on his back, but Maxim wavered when he saw the resolve in his eyes.

"Get this plane up in the air!" Maxim barked.

Jeremiah retreated to the cockpit.

Come on, Alec. Wake up.

The engine switched to a higher gear, roaring outside the closed door. We lurched forward.

Jessica stood, and inhaled through her nostrils. She marched over toward us. "Who did he tell?"

"It doesn't matter who he told," said Maxim. "By the time we hit Swiss airspace we'll have new passports waiting for us."

Confused, I glanced to my father, who forced a smile.

"Ms. Jessica Barlow," he said to the secretary. "Looks like your apple didn't fall far from the tree."

Her eyes hardened.

"Barlow?" I said, blinking at the woman before me.

Max mentioned she had a kid once, years ago, but there's nothing on paper. Alec had told me that when I'd first come to stay at the apartment above the restaurant.

"You're Jeremiah's *mother*?" I asked.

I thought of the night I'd met him at the bar, and the pictures, and how Jessica Rowe had taken them from her room at the neighboring hotel. She'd done this for her son. Her son had done this for his father. The rage grew sharp inside of me as I stared at her.

The plane picked up speed.

"The paperwork was buried pretty deep," my father said. "But I found the name change documentation. And the birth certificate. No father listed, that must make you feel bad, doesn't it Stein?"

Maxim snorted, and then laughed coldly.

"Should it?" he asked. "Little bastard got more than enough of my money."

My mind turned to the high salary and cash bonuses Alec

had told me Jessica received. Before she'd testified, she'd even told me that Maxim Stein had given Jeremiah money himself.

This family gave *dysfunctional* a whole new definition.

Behind Jessica, Alec's head turned slowly to the side. It took everything I had not to call out to him.

"Sit down!" shouted Jeremiah through the open door.

The force of the jet's sudden acceleration pushed me back, and I had to release my father to keep from rolling down the center aisle.

"Stop the plane," I said to Maxim. "I've called the cops. They're probably already here. If you stop now, they won't come down as hard on you."

"It's too late for that," said Maxim.

The nose of the plane tilted up. I clung to the seat, one hand on my dad's chest. He bent his knees, trying to keep himself from sliding down the aisle, but it put more of a strain on his shoulders. With his arms bound he could barely move.

"If you're not going to get rid of her, tie her up and put her in the luggage compartment," said Jessica. She took a seat and fastened her seat belt. Behind her, Alec's foot twitched.

I stared up at her as the wheels left the ground.

"You had me back in St. Augustine," I said. "I honestly thought you were scared."

Her brow arched. "We all do what we have to in order to survive."

I forced myself to look at her, even while Alec's knee bent.

"Does that include sending your own child away to be raised by his aunt?" I asked. "Did Maxim make you do it? Or was that your choice?"

She glared at me, her Taser pointing at Alec's back. "That's not your business."

"Must really piss you off that Maxim didn't choose him as heir to the Force fortune."

"He's taken good care of us."

"He's paid you off, you mean," I said. "So he could keep whatever number wife he was on happily ignorant."

"Ease up, Anna," warned my dad quietly.

"He kept Jeremy out of it," she snapped. "I didn't want my son falling into this life."

"And yet here he is," I said, "Driving your getaway plane."

While I'd been talking, Stein had watched me closely. He gave a small nod now, as if impressed.

Alec rolled fast, taking Jessica off guard. He'd ripped his hands free from the bindings she'd secured, and slapped the Taser out of her grip before she could fire again. I dove for it, and as my hand closed around the handle I jammed the metal clamps against her calf—the closest part of anyone I could reach—and pressed the button. It shook as the charge ran up her leg, and she let out a short scream before arching back in her seat. Alec was already charging Stein, but stopped suddenly, as if he'd hit an invisible wall. A moment later I released the trigger of the Taser, frozen by the gun pressed to the back of my skull. Jessica slouched, every muscle slack, eyes closed.

"What's going on?" shouted Jeremiah from the pilot's seat. "What was that?"

"Nice of you to wake up, Alec," said Stein.

"Max," he said warily. "I'm not an expert, but I think you've exceeded the tether on your fancy ankle bracelet."

Stein snorted. "House arrest didn't really suit me. Fortunately, my probation officer felt the same way."

"How much did you pay him?" I asked. Stein twisted my hair around his wrist and yanked my head back, pressing the gun to my temple. I siphoned in a tight breath.

"You don't want to do that," Alec said, in a voice that even now gave me chills. My dad was trying to push himself into an upright position, using a seat as leverage.

"Believe me," said Alec's old boss. "I don't want to do any of this. But you've put me in a position where I don't have much choice."

I was hauled onto my feet, and automatically gripped a small stationary table as the plane continued to ascend. Stein forced the Taser from my hand and from the sounds of it, shoved it into his pocket.

"Put the gun down," said Alec, balancing against the back of a seat. "You can't fire it in here anyway. You'll risk blowing out a window, destabilizing the cabin pressure."

"And then we'll all lose consciousness and the plane will crash," finished Stein, and at the mention of crashing, Alec's jaw clenched. "I taught you that, remember? I taught you everything you know. I paid for your goddamn college degree, Alec. I made you a king in this company."

"There was only one king," said Alec harshly, never taking his eyes off Maxim's. "Everyone else was a pawn."

Behind me, Stein scoffed. "You didn't seem to mind until she came into the picture." I bit my tongue as Stein bumped the barrel of the gun against my head. "Don't be noble and try to tell me she had nothing to do with it. I know you, Alec. I've known you a long time."

"No, you're right," said Alec. "She had everything to do with it."

He took a step closer, and there was a fire in his eyes I'd only seen traces of before. There was no way Maxim couldn't feel the power coming off of him. It terrified me, and Alec was on my side.

"If she wasn't around," Alec said in a low voice, "I wouldn't care what you did. I wouldn't care what *I* did. But she makes me decent, Max, and that was something you never tried to do."

He moved closer.

I could hear Max's clothing rustle as he shifted, feel his movement in the gun pressed to the back of my head. I kept my eyes on Alec's, not allowing myself to wonder what would happen if he decided we'd done enough talking and pulled the trigger.

The plane hit a patch of turbulence, and Alec's jaw clenched. My dad tilted again to the floor, and grunted in pain as he fell on his wounded shoulder.

"I tried," said Maxim, voice raised. "But I failed. You betrayed me, Alec, and you won." He laughed dryly. "My lawyer called just after you finished testifying. You know what he told me? *Get your affairs in order.* The jury will finish deliberating tomorrow, but they will find me guilty, and when they do, I'll be ruined. Done. Because of you."

"You ruined yourself," said Alec, now only six feet away. I wanted him closer, so that I could touch him, run my hands over his chest. Feel him, if only for the last time.

Another bump in the plane. And this time Alec gripped the leather seatback with both hands. Sweat dripped down his jaw as he forced a shaky breath.

Maxim leaned forward, so that his chest came flush with my back.

"And now I'll ruin you," he said quietly, slipping the barrel of the gun down to the back of my neck. I shivered as I felt a puff of breath against my neck. "Anna knows it's nothing personal. We've had this conversation before. Her skin really is quite soft, Alec."

His eyes narrowed, but his rage felt like nothing compared to mine. It took over my body in a flash, and before I could think it through, I threw my weight backward and swung my elbow into his ribs.

The next moments happened so fast, they barely had a chance to lodge into my memory.

Maxim fell, though not because of me, but my father. He'd kicked Maxim hard in the back of the leg, and as he tumbled forward onto his knees, I was thrown to the ground.

"Move, Anna!" shouted my dad.

Alec charged just as I rolled to the side. He crashed into Max head-on.

"Mom?"

I looked back, just in time to see Jeremiah shaking his mother's still form. When she remained limp, he dropped her, and stared at her in shock for one blank second. Then he turned, rage in his eyes, and clambered toward the other men. I saw him reach for the gun in his waistband, despite the fact that he'd been the one to yell at his father for firing earlier.

"No!" I screamed, and pulled myself up to my feet.

Jeremiah swung the gun in my direction, but it was knocked out of his hands by Alec, who'd turned when he heard my voice. Alec shoved me hard to the side, and I landed in a seat just as the plane hit another bump that threw everyone to the right.

In horror, I glanced up at the open, swinging door of the empty cockpit.

Before I could rise, or speak, or even join the scuffle, there came another shot. I clapped my hands over my ears, hearing nothing but ringing as the plane lurched through another bout of rough air.

Jeremiah fell to the ground, bleeding from a wound on the left side of his rib cage. He threw back his head, gasping, revealing the full outline of the black star on his pale, white neck.

Our pilot had been shot.

Thirty-eight

"Jeremiah?" Maxim's voice was the first sound that broke through the rush in my eardrums. He still held a gun, and it took a moment to realize he'd been the one to fire, not Alec. My gaze tore around the cabin, searching for a hole in a window, trying to assess what the destabilization of cabin pressure would feel like.

There was no sign we were going down. Not yet anyway.

Maxim dropped the weapon as though it were burning hot. It skittered across the floor in my direction, and I scooped it up fast. Before Stein could rise, Alec grabbed him around the throat and slammed him back against the side of a seat.

"Stop!" I shouted. "Alec, the plane. No one's flying the plane!" I searched for the other weapon, and found it behind my father on the floor.

Alec didn't release Maxim Stein.

"Anna, my hands," said my father. "Untie them. Hurry."

I rushed around Jeremiah to my father, finding his wrists rubbed raw from the rope that bound them. It took my fumbling fingers too long, but finally I freed him. He flexed his hands, shook them quickly to regain the circulation, and then took the gun.

It took some prompting for Alec to loosen his hold, but when he finally did, I tied Maxim's wrists together as firmly as I could, and took the Taser for myself.

"Jeremy?" A weak female voice came from a seat down the aisle.

Alec's expression was torn as he looked over Jeremiah Barlow, now shaking and curled into a ball on the floor. This man had stabbed him in prison, taken the woman he loved—I was sure there was nothing he would have liked to do better than let him die.

But he knelt, and reached beneath the man's shoulders to pull him up. Jeremiah groaned in pain.

"What happened?" Jessica was closer now.

"Get up, you son of a bitch," muttered Alec. "You've got a plane to fly."

"He's not flying anything," said Maxim grimly. He sank into a seat, paying no attention to my father, or the gun now trained at his chest.

"What did you do?" demanded Jessica. "Alec? What did you do?" Her voice hitched.

"I didn't do anything," Alec muttered. "Ask your boss."

"Max?" She was standing now, and walked toward us on wobbling legs, gripping seats on either side of the aisle. She fell to her knees beside Jeremiah, hands out to the sides, as if she wasn't sure what to do with them.

"He can't fly," I said quietly, watching as a cough wracked through Jeremiah's body. The blood on his chest made the bile crawl up my throat, or maybe it was the knowledge that we were thousands of feet above the ground without a pilot.

I didn't want to die.

Alec rose quickly. He glanced at me, just long enough for me to see the terror in his eyes before he spoke to my father.

"You've got this, Ben?"

"I got it," Dad answered. "What's the plan?"

Alec siphoned in a breath, as if preparing to jump into cold water.

"Sit down, all of you."

I didn't listen. I followed Alec right to the front of the plane. He didn't look surprised when I took the small foldout seat behind the pilot's chair. The dashboard blinked with lights—red, green, white. There were dials and buttons, all of which I had no idea what to make of. A wide window wrapped around the front of the cockpit, the night beyond our view black as coal, the land thousands of feet below us twinkling with city lights.

It was almost beautiful, but for the knowledge that we might be very soon crashing headfirst into it.

The autopilot light was glowing from the center of something that looked similar to a steering wheel.

"I don't know what I'm doing," Alec confessed.

"You took pilot's lessons," I said.

"I never got out of the simulator."

I swallowed. "You probably could have not mentioned that."

"Anna . . ."

"Land the plane, Alec. You can do this."

I wished I felt as confident as I sounded. I reached around the back of his seat, squeezing his shoulder. He touched my hand briefly, then took a deep breath and picked up the radio.

"Mayday, Mayday," he said. "This is . . ." he clicked the button. "Where's the number?" He must have found it somewhere, because he pushed the Talk button on the radio again. "This is N-two-nine-four-six. Our pilot's been injured."

A few seconds later someone responded.

"N-two-nine-four-six, this is air traffic control. Identify yourself."

"Alec Flynn," he said. "I'm . . ."

"We know," interrupted the operator. "What's the status of your crew?"

"Two shot," said Alec. "One restrained."

A woman came on the line.

"Alec, it's Janelle," she said, and I'll be damned if I wasn't happy to hear her voice. "Local PD alerted us that you'd reached the airfield."

Marcos. He must have arrived shortly after we'd taken off.

"Is Stein with you?" she asked.

"Stein, Barlow, and Rowe," answered Alec.

The radio turned to static for a few seconds before she returned to the line.

"One big happy family. A private investigator called me earlier with information linking them all together."

My father. I nearly smiled.

"I'm turning back to Tampa," said Alec.

She put someone else on the line. An experienced pilot, who assured us he'd given enough flying lessons to get us down safely. He guided Alec through a series of tasks I didn't understand. First, to locate the airspeed indicator, and make sure we didn't fall below one hundred and forty knots. When Alec took the jet off autopilot, I bit the inside of my cheek hard and squeezed his biceps.

"So far so good," I whispered to him.

"I fucking hate flying," he responded.

Alec redirected our course and turned the plane back to Tampa. I dug my heels in as the force pulled me against the safety harness. It wasn't the smoothest transition, but we had yet to make a nosedive.

"How's it going up there?" my father called.

"We're still in the air, aren't we?" I shouted back.

As we closed in on the Tampa airport, the bright lights of the city gave way to the black waters of the Bay. Even from this high up we could see the long string of red markers lining the runway.

The operator on the line had gone quiet, waiting for us to make our descent.

"Talk to me," Alec said quietly.

I didn't know what to say. I wished there was something encouraging I could tell him, or something that reflected the intensity of what I was feeling as I looked down on the hard ground below.

Instead I said the first thing that came to my mind.

"I want to get married on the beach. That beach you took me to when we first got together. I'm going to wear the prettiest dress you've ever seen, and underneath, I'll have on blue panties."

"Blue?" I could hear the smile in his voice.

"For my something blue," I said. I knew practically nothing about weddings, but I knew that much. "Paisley will be a flower girl. And after, I want to spend a week in bed with you."

"That can be arranged," he said.

"And I want a house," I said, my words growing stronger. "It doesn't have to be big, but I want a nice kitchen where I can cook. And I want our families to come over for barbecues. And if I ever run away I want you to chase me. That's what I want."

"I love you, Anna," he said.

He might as well have said *I'm sorry*.

"Hey," I said, squeezing his shoulder. "We're here because of Maxim Stein. He's here because he lost the trial. He *lost*, baby. That means we won. That means we're done with him, and you own one of the biggest private aviation companies in the world."

"That's worth approximately six dollars."

"Well," I said with a watery laugh. "Then you can sell it and buy a Big Mac."

The stars above twinkled, just like the lights of the city below. They were hypnotizing, I couldn't look away.

Alec shifted in his seat.

"We're going to bring it back," he said.

There was a familiar confidence in his voice.

"You and me," he said. "We're going to rework the whole company. Start from the ground up. Take it in the direction Max should have years ago."

"I'm in," I said.

"I love you," he said, and this time I heard the voice of the man who could have moved mountains if someone gave him a shovel.

"Land this plane and marry me, Alec Flynn."

"Yes, ma'am," he said.

The pilot returned to the line then, and walked Alec through the landing procedures. Alec lined the plane up with the red flashing lights, and began our descent, pulling back on the throttle to reduce the power. It felt like we were free-falling at one point, and I had to bite back the scream. But Alec held fast, knuckles white on the stick. He extended the flaps and lowered the landing gear as the ground came closer and closer, and the engine roared louder, and in the last seconds before our wheels touched the runway, I loosened my belt and reached around the seat, holding on to his shoulders for dear life.

We bounced, and then bounced again. And then the plane slowed.

And then the plane stopped.

From outside I could hear the sirens. Flashing red and blue lights barreled in our direction.

"We're alive?" I couldn't let Alec go. I doubted he could breathe with how hard I was squeezing him.

"Why does that sound like a question?" He gave a shaky laugh. I released the seat belt and jumped into his lap, kissing him all over the face. He still gripped the throttle with one hand.

"I don't think I can get up," he said.

"You don't have to," I told him. And then I kissed him some more.

The police were the first to board the plane, followed closely by the FBI. They took Maxim and his secretary into custody, and Jessica bawled while they were read their rights. Before the end, she was already ratting him out, trying to make a deal with the FBI to get her sentence reduced.

I really hoped that wasn't an option.

The paramedics came and took Jeremiah. My father went as well, though in a different ambulance. He made certain to shake Alec's hand before they loaded him into the truck. We told him we'd be right behind him.

Before we could follow, Janelle took our statements, and told us that they'd found the airport security guard passed out in the trunk of the white sedan. She was looking for the prosecution to add assault of a federal employee to Maxim's long list of charges.

"I treated you like a son, Alec." Maxim's voice cut through the sirens, through the other voices, through all of it. The sound had been permanently ingrained into my mind, like nails on a chalkboard.

I turned before Alec. He'd heard it, but seemed to be debating whether or not to give the man who'd nearly killed him the time of day. Marcos had cuffed him and was loading him into the back of the police car. I had no doubt the arrest of an escaping Maxim Stein was going to boost his stock around the department ten times over, and I was glad for that.

"You tried," said Alec.

He glanced back toward the ambulance, where the gurney holding Jeremiah Barlow was currently being loaded. Maxim followed his gaze, hunching in his seat. All traces of the billionaire business tycoon were gone, and left in its place was a desperate, shriveled old man.

Alec placed his hand in mine, and led me away from the planes and the flashing lights. Away from Maxim Stein. Away from all of it.

Toward something better. The unknown.

Epilogue

Things were good with Alec. Perfect, even in their imperfection. As the dust settled, we found our rhythm, one with laughter, and good food, and long nights that led to heavily caffeinated mornings. But I was still me, despite how he'd changed my life, and the time came when that old urge returned, and quickly became impossible to ignore.

He'd known it would. He'd even put it in his vows.

If you need to run, I'm coming with you.

I smiled as I thought of that now, and attached the white thigh-high to the new garter strap I'd picked up a week before the wedding. It matched the little baby-doll nightie Amy had given me for my bachelorette party.

I straightened it in the mirror, listening as Alec finished his phone call on the other side of the door.

"No, we're switching everything that direction. That's right. Green Fusion. *Yes*, I promise you the patent was approved."

I smiled at the passion in his voice. We'd talked this through after Alec had taken over Force Enterprises. The company had been worth almost nothing by the time Maxim Stein was put away, but we didn't need a whole load of money. We needed each other, and with Alec's passion and good business sense, we were going to build something great.

Force Enterprises was switching to green technologies.

I considered giving him a moment to finish the call, but decided against it. I was his wife now. Mrs. Anna Flynn. I could distract him anytime I wanted. And since we only had a few days off before I had to finish the class I was taking to renew my social work license, I was going to make the most of my distractibility rights.

I pushed the door open, and stood in the threshold, hands on my hips.

He was pacing in front of the sliding glass doors wearing jeans and a plain black T-shirt, the sun setting on the long stretch of ocean beyond. We'd reach St. Thomas tomorrow, our current runaway destination. But for tonight, the honeymoon deck of this cruise ship belonged to us.

He'd been in the middle of a sentence, but stopped short when he saw me, mouth gaping.

I smiled. Then did a slow turn to give him a better look.

"Right . . . What?" he said to the person he'd been speaking to. "Look, something just came up. I've got to call you back."

He hung up the phone. Tossed it on the small nightstand. Then gave me a long, smoldering look that started at my patent leather pumps and stopped just below my shoulders. As always, my pulse fluttered under his gaze, and the need tightened inside by belly.

I twisted the strap of the tiny nightgown around one finger and sauntered toward him.

"My new favorite color is white," he said. "Definitely white."

"Yesterday it was pink." As in, the pink teddy I'd worn on the first night of our trip.

"That was yesterday," he said, eyes now glued on my backside as I crawled onto the bed and stretched out like a cat. "I'm a complicated man, Anna."

"I can see that."

I rolled onto my back, crossing my knees just so he would have to uncross them. His fingers slid up the inside of my ankle.

"Everything go all right with the call?"

His thumb rubbed up the back of my calf as he gently eased open my thighs.

"It did," he said. "There's still a chance to back out if you don't feel good about it, though."

"I'm about to feel *real* good about it," I said, dragging him over me. When he was close, I kissed the tip of his nose. I didn't want him second-guessing this deal he'd worked so hard for.

"It's perfect," I said. "Force goes green, and the patent proceeds to go CASA. What's not to like?" Alec had made certain that a portion of Trevor Marshall's payment for the Green Fusion patent went straight to a payee, who would later delegate it toward his mental health care. The rest of the funds would be donated to someone who hadn't attempted to kill me.

Alec's mouth found my neck, and nipped a line down to my shoulder. I gasped.

"Good," Alec repeated as he settled his weight between my legs. His hand rode up the underside of my thigh, stopping just short of my center. "Then on to my next order of business. Punishing you for interrupting my very important meeting."

"On *my* honeymoon."

His mouth lowered over my breast, and teased my nipple through the sheer fabric.

"Let me make it up to you," he said.

And he did. Three times over.